# THE THREE FIRES

## NACUSTI CHRONICLES VOLUME III

J. R. DOUGLAS

*For Alfredo, my brightest light.*
*Te amo.*

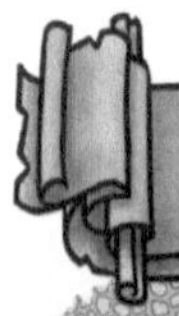
TOR'ALAN
LION DISTRICT
WASP DISTRICT
THE CENTER
FARM DISTRICT
MARKET DISTRICT
CROCK DISCTRICT
1
2
3
4
5
6
7
8
1 - ENTRANCE PORTAL
2 - THE ARCHIVES
3 - THE CENTER CASTLE
4 - TEMPLE OF LIGHT
5 - TRAINING COURTS
6 - THE DORMITORY
7 - DEN OF DARKNESS
8 - SOLDIER BARRACKS

WASTELANDS
PYWELL MOUNTAINS
MERINTHIA'S PASS
DARLANGSON
ANGUIS RIVER
NALAWIN
REPUBLIC OF EVARTIA
JANLAKA
MASDAAN
KARANADEE RIVER
REGADENSIA
WESLINTON
TOR'ALAN
GORT'HAAL
LINDOMER
VALECIUM
SOUTHERN ISLES
BERNADOOTH
DENSBA

# CONTENTS

# CHAPTER 1

# THE TOWER

At the last moment, Zakolor parried a broadsword that would have cleanly separated his head from his body. Another slice curved toward him. But he held tight to his staff, vibrations rattling through his arms, and gave it a sharp jerk upward. The ground beneath his foe jumped, catapulting the man back down the hill.

Into the vicious battle unfolding in the valley below.

Zak gripped the staff and searched for signs of his magus Sorwin, or his other teachers, Shira and Kaleb. He wanted to fight alongside them, defeat the combined forces of the Consortium and the Disciples, but he had been ordered to stay on the hill and protect the League of Kingdom's leadership.

Pain—sharp and hot—lanced his arm. Zak looked down at the bandage covering his wound, the one Zandorn gave him weeks ago.

It still hadn't healed after their confrontation in the Eyewood, where Zak had lost the black caladrius. Not even Bazil or Archlumen Sashina could get it to close completely, though neither of them found any lingering effects, so he kept it wrapped up. He scratched at the bandages but forced himself to stop. It'd only make it worse.

High King Marius and a smattering of council members, generals, and senior mages, all arguing above a hastily constructed war table behind Zak. Marius gripped the wooden edge with white knuckles, appearing more haggard than he should as a noble in his late twenties. He hadn't been the same since Limba Dar's betrayal in Masdaan, when his advisor had sold the League out to the Consortium and the Disciples.

Most days, Marius floated through meetings with glassy eyes, nodding along to questions and suggestions with no clear opinion. The old Marius only reemerged whenever Limba Dar was mentioned, as if the name alone riled him to sentience.

And that morning, Limba Dar had been mentioned plenty.

It had all happened so fast, Zak didn't know exactly where they were—somewhere in the southwest of Regadensia. The Firepost detailing Limba Dar's whereabouts had arrived mere hours ago, and Marius immediately forced General Lupa to mobilize all of Tor'alan.

Zak shouldn't have been surprised.

*Behind you!* Jolsu snarled.

Zak whipped around at the dragon's warning and thrust out a hand. An emerald shield of pure magic appeared, blocking three fireballs that would have hit him square in the chest.

"Thanks," Zak breathed.

*Never mind that. Take care of the mage.*

Partway down the slope, the attacker readied another

spell. But a wave of water tumbled them down the muddied hill before Zak could do anything.

"Stay focused," Olivia said, a few paces down the ridge. Her tone was curt, but with her auburn curls tied back, Zak saw the corner of her lips twitch.

"Right." His cheeks reddened, and it wasn't due to the effort of battle.

Another body broke from the mass below and darted toward the hill.

Zak pulled his arm back, green flames alighting his palm, ready to strike.

"Wait." Olivia grabbed his wrist, her hand cold against his skin. "She's one of ours."

The soldier trotted up the steep incline, tripping twice in her haste. Zak relaxed as she caught her breath, straightened, nodded to him and Olivia, and approached General Lupa. He leaned down, expression hardening as he listened to the message.

General Lupa's booming voice carried far enough for Zak to hear. "Our scouts have located Limba Dar, Your Majesty. He's holed up in the tower across the valley."

"Take me there," Marius ordered.

The generals and council members around the table shared confused looks.

"But, Your Majesty," the soldier who brought the news spoke up. "Disciple mages have barriers covering every inch of the tower, and reports say that Queen Ymona is leading the Consortium forces. It is too dangerous for you to approach—"

"I don't care!" Marius flung his arms as he yelled, untucking his tunic and mussing his already unkempt hair. "*Former Queen Ymona lost Evartia to rebels. She is no threat.*" He turned on Lupa, raising a finger high to reach the general's face. "Take me to Limba Dar. He *will pay* for his crimes!"

"Your Majesty." Tansil's calm voice rang out. With his sleek brown hair and pressed saffron robes, he appeared the opposite of the wild-eyed high king. "Allow me to detain Limba Dar and bring him to you."

"Oh no, not again, *elf*," Marius spat. "You were there in Masdaan when he escaped. You cannot be trusted."

Zak grimaced on Tansil's behalf. The Archmagus had suffered the brunt of Marius's mood swings over the prior months.

Tansil's jaw hardened. "Perhaps in your wisdom, High King Marius, if I am unworthy, you could choose a more appropriate representative?"

Marius scrunched up his nose as he evaluated the soldiers and mages around him. "General Lupa, you and the closest regiment will join me. And you!" His outstretched finger pointed directly at Zak. "I'll take the *Nacusti*!"

Zak lurched and could have sworn his stomach fell into a bottomless ravine.

"Which one, Your Majesty?" Euphemius asked. From where Zak stood, most of the tiny merchant was obscured behind the war table, except for his top hat and bushy eyebrows.

"Both of them!" Marius snatched a sheathed sword leaning against a weapon rack and marched toward Zak and Olivia.

Euphemius followed, protesting.

Zak no longer worked for Euphemius. Sorwin made sure the contract was voided once Olivia had recovered from her *vitaligo*. But the merchant still had Olivia in his grasp, and he showed no signs of wanting to risk his *investment* on Marius's desperate hunt.

Other nearby council members also voiced concerns about putting the *Nacusti* in danger, but Marius didn't seem to hear them. He closed the distance to Zak and grabbed the collar of his red uniform.

"You want revenge too, don't you, *Nacusti*?" Zak winced. Marius smelled rancid and sour, like rotten fruit. "He played us all." Spittle flew as he turned back to the war table. "He made us dance to his lies. But now it's our turn. Soon we'll make him dance upon the gallows!"

Tansil appeared between Zak and Olivia while Marius was distracted with his monologue. He guided them by the shoulders into a quick conference.

"Zakolor, send for Sorwin. I'll shadow your progress, but my presence will only agitate Marius further."

"Of course, Archmagus."

*I'm ready*, Jolsu said.

Zak reached for his and Jolsu's magics, pulling a sliver of each. "*Customateria*." A ball of green light appeared in Zak's palm and morphed into a tiny Jolsu. Emerald scales glistened in the midday light as leathery wings unfolded and surged, sending the sparrow-sized dragon speeding down the hill toward the battle.

"Olivia, most of the Disciples are from Masdaan. Their

mages specialize in advanced fire magic. Your mastery of water and earth will prove invaluable."

"Yes, Archmagus." Olivia nodded once, looking otherwise undeterred by the unexpected assignment.

"Thank you both." Tansil frowned. "This isn't—he's gone too far. When this is all over, I promise I will personally prepare for his removal. The entire League is in danger with his unsteady hand at the helm. We should have done something long ago."

Marius swept over them then, pulling Zak and Olivia in his wake. General Lupa collected soldiers as they vaulted down the hill and circumvented the thickest parts of the fray.

A tight triangle formed around Marius. Spears and swords clanged against shields as the soldiers on the outer flanks rebuffed attacks.

Zak stayed alert, running directly behind Marius and deflecting fire and demons with well-placed barriers. "Save your energy," he said to Olivia, jogging to his right. "We'll need you at the tower."

She didn't argue but nodded grimly.

The formation stopped once when a wicked serrated blade ran through the burly soldier at the front. A scuffle broke out, and the packed group began to separate, drawn into the chaos of battle.

Marius squeezed the leather-wrapped hilt of his sword, but his step faltered. He stopped, remaining fixed to the dirt beneath his boots.

"Three Fires," Zak cursed and lunged forward, intercepting an attack meant for the high king's throat. He parried two more blows from the Disciple's spear, then blasted his gut with a stream of fire. The man screeched and fell motionless to the ground.

*Any word on Sorwin?* Zak asked Jolsu.

*Still looking. But other help is on the way.*

*Other help?*

The dragon didn't respond, and Zak wouldn't have heard if he did because four more Disciples charged the rear of the scattered formation.

Olivia bisected the squad with a slicing wave of water and took the two on the left.

Zak glanced behind him. Marius was still frozen. Whatever fervor imbued him earlier had dissolved, at least temporarily.

"*Tegoperignis.*" A fiery shield erupted around the high king.

Charging forward, Zak silently thanked Kaleb for the endless hours of weapons training. He saw the subtle shift of weight in his opponent's legs and read the swinging attack from the right. He swatted it aside and, with a quick series of jabs to the torso, dispatched the first attacker.

The other one dropped back, and Zak felt the surge of foreign magic.

*A mage!*

Deep red blades of fire appeared in the mage's palms. She held them low as she thrust forward.

Zak's staff arced down to meet the fiery weapons, but the wooden shaft cut clean in two. He twisted out of reach, but the swirling shield around Marius was right behind him.

Retreat wasn't an option. He had to protect the high king.

The mage leered and darted forward, fiery blades angled at Zak's chest.

He caught them with scale-covered hands. Obsidian talons curled around the red flames and squeezed, snuffing the magic.

The mage paled before Zak decked her with a hardened fist and snarled.

Dragons loved battle.

Approval rumbled through the bond with Jolsu.

"Reform!" General Lupa called. "To me! Make haste!"

Olivia's opponents were splayed on the ground, and she strode toward Zak without a scratch upon her skin or a fold of fabric out of place.

*Typical.* The thought nudged a smile to his lips.

He released the shield around Marius as the group mustered around the king.

"Well," Bazil said, emerging from the fray. His jet-black braids were tied low with a leather strap. "Jolsu told me to come help, but it seems you have everything in hand."

"There's plenty more to do." Zak clapped the priest on the shoulder as he fell into a trot next to him and Olivia.

The small regiment crossed the valley and closed the remaining distance to Limba Dar's hideout without incident. The stone tower shimmered in reds, oranges, golds, and browns, the layers of barriers coalescing upon one another. Zak thought it looked beautiful before remembering they had to break through the complex magic. Plus, it protected the most duplicitous, treacherous person he had ever met—and that tarnished even the most beautiful of magics.

"Now, *Nacusti*," the high king said. "Get us inside."

None of the Consortium or Disciples were stationed outside the tower, giving their small group a chance to evaluate its defenses.

Olivia stretched her palms out and stepped carefully around the foundation's circumference.

Zak followed. "Can you bring the barriers down?"

Her brow pinched. "The door is the most fortified point. We'll need to make our own entryway." A low hum sounded from her throat as she inspected the barriers. "Here!" She pointed to a section of the tower thick with mortar and stone.

"As you say, *Nacusti*." Zak smirked, and Olivia rolled her eyes. She abhorred the title as much as Zak did.

"Tansil was right, the barriers are fire. I'll use water to create an opening, then you burrow a door in the stone for us. Think you can handle that, *Nacusti*?" She drawled the last word out with no shortage of spite.

Zak laughed and nodded. Despite their chaotic surroundings, this moment felt important. Their training was being put to the test. It was time to show that both of them, together, could bring down the Consortium.

As soon as Olivia shot a spout of water at the barrier, it hissed and steamed. The heat forced them both back a step, and small fireballs broke off from the swirling mass of magic and pelted toward them.

Zak couldn't get the words out for a spell in time.

A turquoise shield flashed around him and Olivia, catching the flames.

"Always be ready for the counterattack," Bazil instructed.

"Thanks, Professor," Zak said. He'd tried out a few nicknames for Bazil over the last few weeks when he started filling in for Sorwin during his and Olivia's training sessions more often.

"Still not fond of that, but it's better than any other name you've come up with so far." He gave a playful wink to Zak. "I'll defend, you both focus on getting us into the tower. Marius is losing patience already."

The high king paced back and forth behind them. General Lupa stood at the left end of his route and the rest of the soldiers formed a ring around Marius.

Olivia resumed her watery attack. The liquid pummeled the fiery barrier harder than any battering ram.

Zak could tell it wouldn't be much longer. He reached for his magic and the familiar steadiness of earth, asking it to heed his call, his will.

"There will be at least a handful of mages inside." Olivia raised her voice above the torrent of water and spitting fire. "Probably soldiers, too."

"We'll be ready," Zak said, more for his sake than hers. Between Olivia's magical prowess and Bazil's speed and strength, he still felt like the weak link whenever they sparred.

*There's no room for doubt in combat, Parignis.*

Zak sent a pulse of acknowledgment through the bond. Jolsu was right.

The barriers crackled and relented, peeling back from the stone of the tower where Olivia had attacked. "Now, Zak!"

she yelled.

He ran forward and pulled on his magic, pushing against the stone with his palms. "*Terramotus!*"

A section of the stone tower burst inward, spraying debris into the room. Zak heard shouts and yelps as the stones struck several bodies. He charged through the dust cloud with an emerald shield raised in front, Olivia and Bazil at his back.

Three Disciples were down already, and Bazil quickly dispatched two swordsmen by the stairs on the right. No one else was on the first floor, but Zak heard rapid footsteps pounding from above.

General Lupa ducked through Zak's makeshift doorway, closely followed by Marius and a handful of soldiers.

"He isn't down here." Marius's eyes darted around the room. "Up! We go up!" He lunged toward the stairs, and Lupa stumbled after him with a stricken expression.

"Three Fires," Zak cursed. "He's going to get himself killed."

"Or us," Olivia muttered.

"Either way, we need to move," Bazil said.

They bounded up the stairs into a fierce melee. The next floor of the narrow tower was the same as the first, a single room with little space for swinging swords or slinging spells.

Zak stayed close to Bazil and Olivia, catching weapons and fire with emerald shields while his friends counterattacked. Flashes of fists and slices of water cut through a number of Disciples before they charged to the third floor behind Marius.

Limba Dar stood alone on the far side of the room, staring out one of the rough-cut windows. There was no glass. Wind whistled through the slivered opening between solid stone blocks just wide enough to view the tower's surroundings.

"I knew you'd make it here," Limba Dar said without turning. Zak had almost forgotten how the man's voice grated against his ears. "Once I saw the *Nacusti* with you, it was only a matter of time."

Marius shook with rage but didn't step toward his former advisor. "You," he said. "You did all of this." He waved his sword in the air, gesturing to the tower, the battle, the war. "Your betrayal led us all here. I asked myself countless times, 'Why? Why would Limba Dar betray me? What did he seek that hadn't been readily provided by *my* generous hands?'"

*He's been looking forward to this*, Zak realized. He watched the high king's hands clench around the sword hilt, sweat dripping down his neck.

Limba Dar faced Marius then. "You remain so naive, *High King*." His gaunt face twisted as he spat the title. "You provided nothing but embellished chains and a front-row seat to the occupation of my country."

"That's what this is about?" Marius looked taken aback, like he expected a different response. "The Woolbins have been in Weslinton for ages—"

"Aghoomi! It is named *Aghoomi*!" Limba Dar stamped his foot, and the soldiers around Marius tensed, raising their weapons.

General Lupa stepped in as the high king faltered.

"There's no escape for you, Limba Dar. Surrender, and we will take you in peacefully."

Limba Dar laughed. "And what choice do I have? I am no soldier, I have no magic. My only weapons are words, and those have lost their potency with this company." He glared directly at Marius and held out his wrists. "I am your prisoner once again, Your Majesty."

The room hushed as Marius seethed. "Take him," he finally ordered.

General Lupa signalled, and a soldier rushed forward, binding Limba Dar's hands with rope.

As the group descended the spiral staircase with their prisoner, Zak watched the high king. The encounter didn't go as Marius had anticipated—that much was obvious. But Zak didn't know what he had wanted from Limba Dar. Remorse? Regret?

*Unlikely he'd find either.* Limba Dar was many things—cold, obnoxious, cloying, and ambitious. But he was also calculating. Intelligent. He wouldn't have betrayed Marius and the League without believing in the real possibility of success.

Zak shuddered, wondering what he had been promised and by whom.

They exited the tower through Zak's crudely made door to a crowd of League soldiers and mages. A perimeter had hastily assembled around the tower.

Zak surveyed the battlefield and noted the tide had swung significantly in their favor. The semblance of a line of League uniforms connected the tower to the war table across the valley, pushing Disciple and Consortium forces further south.

Jolsu's tiny form flitted through the throng of soldiers, making a few of them gasp and duck out of the dragon's path. He landed in Zak's palm and disappeared.

"I'm too late, though you have things well in hand." Sorwin emerged, out of breath, and patted Zak, Olivia, and Bazil in turn, congratulating them on the successful—and involuntary—mission.

"As do you," Zak said, glancing at nearby mages raising earthen ramparts and conjuring heaps of sand and stone.

Sorwin scratched the back of his head, ruffling his shaggy golden-brown hair. "Yes, well, Tansil and I did what we could." His gaze drifted to Marius and Limba Dar and darkened. "We'll have much more to deal with soon."

Whoops and hollers rose from the surrounding soldiers, which quickly gained scattered applause, and by the time whistles and cheers joined in, Zak craned his neck to see Marius and Limba Dar at the center of a thunderous celebration.

The high king smiled broadly, raising his arms—sword still clutched in one—and walked the perimeter of the gathering. He seemed alive again for the first time in months.

"My loyal subjects," Marius said. "My soldiers and mages, my siblings in arms. Today is a good day. Today, we took the first step to right a wrong, to heal a deep wound caused by this *creature*." He leveled the sword at Limba Dar. "Today—"

A terrible squelch sounded as Marius's severed head flew through the air.

Zak couldn't comprehend it. No one moved or spoke or made a sound, all frozen by shock.

But when the head halted in midair, blood dripping from the stump of its neck, screams and shouts erupted, and the crowd collectively stepped back.

That was when Zak saw her.

Renna.

"Today *is* a good day," she said. She stalked forward, a predatory smile baring her teeth as she looked up at Marius's floating head. "Today, we relieve humans of the notion they are fit to govern themselves. Today, a reminder is given that the gods are your true rulers. Soon, false kings and queens will fall, and all will bow to the divine."

"Burn the Contract!" a voice called from the distance.

Zak barely heard it. He separated from the crowd, stepping into the ring along with Sorwin, Olivia, and Bazil.

Renna's smile widened. "Ah, *Nacusti.*"

He tried not to look at Marius's terrifying expression. "*Ignitelum!*" Spears of green fire shot from his hands and arced toward Renna.

A crimson barrier appeared around her, deflecting the attack.

"*Sylvaligo.*" Olivia crouched to the ground, thrusting her hands into the dirt. Thick roots erupted around Renna and snaked toward her legs.

With a stomp, Renna burned through the roots with a flash of fire.

"Resist all you like, the outcome will not change," Renna said.

Everything about her—her vicious smile, her words, her cruelty, her smugness—stoked Zak's anger, boiling his insides.

The crowd scattered as Zak flung more fire. Renna didn't seem bothered in the least. Bazil mumbled at his side, re-opening his gates of power. Sorwin constructed a hurricane of water and wind to drive the dangerous woman back from the retreating League forces.

For a brief instant, Renna's cocky expression broke, but she danced beyond the storm's reach.

"You need time to accept your fate," she called. "That is understandable. Make peace with it, and rest assured that the Consortium will usher in the second Era of Divinity."

She walked backward, never breaking eye contact with Zak, and disappeared into a shimmering blue portal.

As soon as Renna was gone, Marius's head fell to the ground with a horrendous *thud*.

Zak turned away and clenched his fists. He couldn't look, but that didn't change anything.

The high king was dead.

Queen Ymona watched Renna play with the League, much like a cat with injured mice. She batted them around, laughing as they scurried and squeaked.

Ymona almost felt bad for them. For how little they understood, for how weak they were in comparison to Zandorn and Renna. The League may sense the end is near, but they had no idea that they'd already lost.

*I know that feeling.*

Unbidden memories of the rebellion in Evartia swarmed her mind, of how she and her brother Yuri had underestimated their enemies. He had lost his body—nearly his life—and she had barely escaped. Ymona clutched the diamond hanging from a fine gold chain around her neck. *Zandorn will make good on his promise to restore you, brother.*

A weak pulse emanated from the stone.

"Your Majesty," a voice behind her called.

She didn't turn. "Speak."

"The Disciples are nearly routed. Our own forces, along with the Consortium's, are reforming away from the League's new front. What are your orders?"

Ymona gazed across the valley. Renna had disappeared after her performance. The League was in disarray, scrambling with the loss of their high king. But that wouldn't last. Not with Tansil and Sorwin and Lupa nearby. She had spent years on the League's council and knew its inner workings too well. Bureaucracy lay in a thick fog around the council's daily operations, but in the heat of battle, its leaders were adept and made fast, calculated decisions.

There was no advantage to press, and Renna's message had been delivered.

"Order a retreat. Establish portals at the rear. We return to Pywell."

# CHAPTER 2

# HEADHUNTING

Zak ripped off his blood-and-dirt-stained uniform and shoved the red fabric into a wicker basket. Once full, it immediately rose into the air, pushed through his bedroom door, and sped down the Dormitory hallway.

The charmed basket—Inguma Foucher's latest effort to get Zak to adhere to a regular laundry schedule—would return tomorrow with the uniform clean and pressed.

*Rather genius bit of magic,* Zak had thought when she gave it to him. Then again, he'd expect nothing less from Inguma, the caretaker of the Dormitory and widely regarded as the third most powerful mage in the Elemental House—just behind Tansil and Sorwin.

Marius intruded upon Zak's thoughts. His final moments, a strange juncture of anger and triumph, forced Zak to pity the high king. Would Marius have recovered from his madness over Limba Dar? Would he have started living and leading again, rather than surrendering to the hurt of betrayal? There was no way to know—and there would never be a chance to find out.

He eyed his mended staff leaning in the corner while pulling on a clean linen tunic. Sorwin had fused the broken pieces, but Zak questioned—not for the first time—whether he should keep a weapon that fractured so easily. He could still feel the heat of the mage's fiery blades, how they sliced through the wood with ease.

*You don't need a twig when you have dragon claws,* Jolsu scoffed.

"You may be right." His scales and claws had saved him. Zak could have also conjured his soul weapon, a sleek, dark-stained staff with an emerald tip. It was made of pure magic and willpower, which could have deflected the mage's attack, but it required attention to sustain.

Sorwin had relentlessly drilled into his training that magic is fallible, that it may not always be available when he needed it, or a solution to a problem he faced. Especially in the chaos of battle. Did the same hold true for his dragon claws?

Elpida paced excitedly on his quilted bed, distracting him from worrying about weapons. Her bronze scales glittered, mirroring the gilded dusk light shining through the window.

*Tell me more of the battle!* she demanded. Jolsu had recounted the major events to the tiny dragon, but she turned her attention to Zak now. *What did it taste like?* Her talons flexed, poking holes in the patchwork quilt.

"Take it easy!" Zak picked her up. "You'll ruin the bed, and we both have to sleep there."

Elpida snarled. She despised it when Zak carried her, and now that she was the size of a large cat, it was getting more difficult by the day.

He put her down on the desk, where she resumed her pacing.

"Battles don't have a taste," he said. Though that wasn't entirely true. The scent of burning flesh and the tang of blood brewed into a revolting concoction he *could* almost taste. Zak twitched, nearly gagging, and pushed the memory away.

*They do, you're just being overprotective like* him, Elpida complained.

A rumble of annoyance—with a thread of sadness—passed through the bond with Jolsu.

*You must remain a secret, my hatchling,* Jolsu said with a patience he barely clung to. *While the Consortium does not know you exist, you remain safe.*

*I cannot remain secret and small forever.* Her scaly tail lashed, knocking over a stack of spellbooks.

"She has a point there," Zak said. He bent to collect the tomes into a new pile on the floor. "How long can you delay her growth, anyway?"

*As long as I need,* Jolsu insisted.

Elpida hissed.

Zak sighed. He hadn't learned much about rearing the baby dragon. Jolsu had only shared information when needed for Elpida's survival. She ate meat—*any* meat—and drank water. Meals weren't difficult to acquire. Tansil had informed the kitchens to supply Zak with whatever he requested. Everyone in the Center knew Elpida was in his care, but only a select few knew she was a dragon. Most still thought her a strange lizard that had belonged to the Druid Terasi.

And while her growth was consistent, it wasn't faster

than any other animal Zak was aware of. Cats, dogs, horses—even the wyvern hatchlings Zak saw in the stables grew
at a similar steady pace.

Except, of course, when Zak had brushed Elpida's nose
in Tansil's office for the first time. She had doubled in size in
an instant.

"Terasi seemed to think Elpida could help with the war,"
Zak said. He and Jolsu had had this conversation before. They
both knew one another's lines like a well-rehearsed play. "If
she were bigger, had wings and breathed fire—"

*Just because a hatchling's growth can be hastened with a
parent's magic doesn't mean it should be,* Jolsu repeated for
the hundredth time. *Dragons are migratory. Hastened growth
was necessary in the wilds for hatchlings to fly their first season.
Elpida is trapped in this tiny room. There is no need for her to
grow.*

Besides an occasional midnight walk around the Center or smuggling Elpida to the training session courts, Elpida rarely left Zak's room. And any time Zak made physical
contact with her, Jolsu withdrew his magic, shutting it tight
behind thick stone walls, buried in a deep, deep cavern.

Elpida had leaped up to the windowsill during the debate. She stared out the latticed glass, watching a world she
could not be part of. Her tail no longer thrashed, and her
claws had retracted. She sat still as a statue.

Zak felt Jolsu's protectiveness, the love that motivated
him to keep his only living family secret and safe and small.
It was a natural reaction for one who had sacrificed so much.

But Zak's heart ached for the little bronze dragon as he

silently slipped from the room, leaving her alone again.

"The High King's body is being prepared for the funeral ceremony and cremation. Both will be held in Turrimare on Foursday." Hildewyn's hunched form rocked side-to-side as her short arms shuffled through a stack of parchment. Deep wrinkles creased her cheeks and forehead beneath strands of wispy silver hair carefully tucked into a low bun.

Zak had never met Regadensia's steward before she swept into the council meeting and began reading official documents, preparing everyone for what would happen following Marius's death. Though Hildewyn appeared ancient, her mind seemed more intact than the former high king's had been in his final months. Which, Zak had to admit, was not a high standard to surpass.

Her voice warbled as she orated the next document. "As High King Marius Fern, third of his name, was unmarried, without an heir—legitimate or otherwise—and having no blood ties close enough to lay claim to his titles and lands, Regandensia must form an accession council to determine inheritance and name the next monarch."

Gasps and murmurs echoed in the council hall.

"What does that mean?" Zak whispered to Tansil and Sorwin, both seated to his right.

"It means a new king or queen of Regadensia will be chosen," Tansil replied.

"That isn't true." King Gyrnavo's deep baritone quelled

the room. "My cousin, Lord Gideon Woolbin, is also cousin to High King Marius. He qualifies as a close blood tie able to inherit the throne."

Zak blanched. Not long ago, he had bumbled his way into insulting Lord Gideon, the Baron of Masdaan, in his own household. It wouldn't bode well for him if the baron became the new King of Regadensia, and therefore the new High King of the League of Kingdoms.

Hildewyn's sharp brown eyes narrowed on Gyrnavo. "Lord Gideon Woolbin is ineligible because he is *your* vassal in Weslinton, Your Majesty. Regadensian succession law clearly states that no one outside the country's borders may inherit any titles, lands, or significant deeds or contracts."

"Then I shall relieve the baron of his current titles. I should think he'd be happy to ascend to a higher station," Gyrnavo retorted.

"And what, you'll assume Masdaan in Gideon's stead?" Minister Qor asked, with no small amount of venom. "Just because you lost Haramil to the Disciples doesn't give you the right to take from your vassals—your own blood, no less."

Gyrnavo sneered at Minister Qor. "It wouldn't be done without his consent. And Evartia has no business in succession now that you're democratic."

Qor and Gyrnavo lobbed arguments back and forth. Zak almost pitied Gyrnavo. He had lost his home—even if it was stolen from Aghoomi generations ago—to the Disciples a few weeks prior. The siege had been swift and brutal. Reports had detailed how spies infiltrated Haramil's walls and disabled most of the defensive barriers and charms overnight with terrifying precision. By the morning, King Gyrnavo and those loyal to him had fled the capital city and sought refuge in Tor'alan.

Then again, Haramil never stood a chance when Fanum Ket, the most powerful mage in Weslinton, revealed himself as the leader of the Disciples. Zak had felt his power and magnetism firsthand in Masdaan. The Eelikuh sent letters to the League and leaders across Valecium, declaring Haramil the capital of Aghoomi once again.

Other cities and settlements in Weslinton were quickly routed or bent the knee to Fanum Ket. He hadn't named himself king, but it was clear he wouldn't relent until all of Aghoomi was free from the Woolbins.

Masdaan was one of the last remaining strongholds.

Finally Hildewyn, sensing Qor and Gyrnavo would continue their spat endlessly, came as close to shouting as her wavering voice could manage. "It doesn't matter if Lord Gideon is no longer a baron. He has held titles outside of Regadensia, and his loyalties would always be questioned. No accession council would ever select him."

*Marius has been gone mere hours and the scavengers are already circling*, Zak thought.

*The little king leaves behind a ripe carcass*, Jolsu said.

*Ew, Jolsu—did you have to say it like that?* Zak couldn't stop imagining Marius's headless body lying in a field, being picked over by wild dogs and birds.

The dragon's amusement fluttered through their bond.

Hildewyn's warble brought his attention back to the meeting. "Due to Regadensia's predicament over its monarch, the country—represented by leaders of sound mind—is forced to withdraw its entitlement to the position of High King or Queen of the League of Kingdoms. While it will remain a member of the organization, the authority will pass to one of the other member countries, decided upon together by all council representatives."

The hall fell so silent that Zak could have heard a mouse squeak beneath the floorboards if it dared.

Regadensia had been the main force behind forming the League of Kingdoms decades ago. Aided by Tansil, Marius's grandfather rallied the other countries to stand against Zandorn and the Consortium, then served as the first High King.

But now, the title was suddenly available to Darlangson, Evartia, or Weslinton, within each of their grasps.

*Three Fires.* This would erode deliberations even further.

He shot a glance at Olivia across the table, sitting beside Euphemius. As a *Nacusti*, she had the honor of attending council meetings now. He could read her abhorrence for the session as she rolled her eyes, and he fought to hold a snicker back.

"I am not sure who is most *appropriate* for the elevated position," Euphemius said, peering around the room. "But, Steward Hildewyn, I happily offer my services on the accession council. As a Regadensian and the largest private benefactor of the League, I believe I could be of some use."

"Your petition is noted, Mr. Van Ilia," Hildewyn replied.

*What is Euphemius up to now?* He never made a move without thinking several steps ahead. Zak shifted uneasily in his seat, all too familiar with the tiny merchant's scheming nature.

"Well, who's it going to be?" General Lupa barked. "Minister Qor, King Gyrnavo, or Prince Sorwin? You're the three options. I don't care who it is, but I need the new leader instated immediately. The Consortium and Disciples are on the move again, and I can't mobilize League forces without their authority."

Zak sat up straighter. *Sorwin could be named High King?* He hadn't considered it. With Sorwin's casual demeanor and deference to Tansil, Zak often forgot about his noble blood, about what his role on the council meant. Even though he sat in the small chair next to Tansil, Sorwin represented Darlangson.

"Though it pains me, I am unable to commit to High King at this time," Gyrnavo muttered. "Weslinton requires my full attention."

Minister Qor snorted, which she took as her cue to speak. "I am an elected official of Evartia. It wouldn't be *appropriate* for me to assume the title." She stared at Euphemius as she stressed the word.

Euphemius stared back blankly.

"That leaves you, Sorwin," Archlumen Sashina said. The bright, rose-colored silk of her dress floated behind her movements as she peered at him.

Sorwin recoiled from the octagonal wooden table. "Oh no, I don't think—"

Minister Qor interrupted. "What if this is an opportunity for something different? What if the League has run its course? Perhaps it is time we considered disbanding the organization."

The entire room erupted in quarrels. Zak thought he saw the lavish tapestries and framed paintings adorning the walls shake, threatening to topple with the uproar.

"Perhaps it isn't disbanded entirely," Archalium Rinka said. "But what if we learn from Evartia's example and pursue a democratic leadership for the League? We can vote for a council leader."

"Regularly changing leadership is a quick way to instability in the middle of a war," Lupa growled.

"It wouldn't be every *month*, General. Terms could last years if we make it so." Rinka gripped the opal hanging from a silver chain around her neck, running a finger across the shiny surface.

"You've been unusually silent, Tansil." Euphemius's gaze narrowed on the elf. "Would you not endorse your protege?"

Tansil's chin rose a fraction. "Sorwin is more than capable of holding the position, I assure you. But as Archmagus and an elf, I do not find it my place to weigh in on this leader's appointment."

Zak grimaced. *Ever the neutral party. Sometimes to a fault.* If Tansil withheld his opinions, Sashina seemed to be Sorwin's only supporter.

He looked at his magus. Sorwin's hands twisted in his lap beneath the table.

*Is he nervous?* Perhaps he *really* doesn't want to be High King, or maybe Tansil's words stung deeply.

"We're getting nowhere," Zak said, hoping to break the tension between Tansil and Sorwin.

Thankfully, Sorwin stopped fidgeting and a ghost of a smile painted his face. "It's clear we need help."

"Who can help?" Zak's frustration snuck into his words. "We have all the leaders of Valecium here trying to solve the problem. Maybe that *is* the problem." The council had never been agreeable or well-functioning before, but now it was in shambles.

"Not all of Valecium's leaders are present," Tansil said. He shared a knowing look with Sorwin. "Are you sure?"

"I think we must, we're out of options." Sorwin tapped his knees with nervous hands before standing and calling the room to attention. "There is one more person we haven't mentioned who could lead the League."

The council members hushed, from curiosity or pure exhaustion from the deliberations, Zak couldn't be sure.

"Queen Alessa of Darlangson. By rights, she should sit on this council, but my sister granted me the honor of representing our country."

Unease rippled through the room. Minister Qor spoke first. "I've had no dealings with Queen Alessa beyond formal letters. Do you think her up to the task of leading the League?"

An emotion Zak couldn't place washed over Sorwin. "I *know* she's stronger, more resolute, than anyone in this room. She may be the only person in all Valecium that *can* lead the League."

As he spoke, Sorwin mostly stared down at the intricate carvings covering the tabletop. He radiated anxiety, his movements stilted and unsure.

"What's wrong?" Zak whispered to Tansil. "Wouldn't his sister leading the League be a good thing?"

If she were even the smallest bit like Sorwin, maybe she could corral the council into a functional body. Maybe they would encounter less internal resistance and be able to focus more fully on stopping Zandorn.

The elf sighed quietly. "Queen Alessa is an exemplary noble, and Darlangson thrives under her reign." Tansil hesitated but pushed ahead anyway. "Her relationship with Sorwin is complicated."

"Why?"

"Their brother and parents died when they were quite young. Alessa and Sorwin never dealt with the tragedy."

Zak looked at Sorwin, and this time he saw the too-bright shine in his eyes, tears pooling and reflecting the glow of the magelights drifting above.

*I had no idea.* He watched as the council mumbled an agreement to ask Queen Alessa to lead the League.

"I will write a Firepost to Queen Alessa today informing her of events and sharing the nomination," Hildewyn said.

"No." Sorwin still leaned on the table for support, eyes downcast. "I'll do it. I'll speak with her."

Something heavy dragged at Sorwin's shoulders. His relaxed, curious nature disappeared, replaced by a vacant shadow of himself. It was like an old wound had reopened and struck him stone-still.

*What happened to his family?* Zak wondered.

# CHAPTER 3
# BYGONES

The hum of the portal's energy tickled Sorwin's skin as he left Tor'alan behind and stepped onto the grounds of his childhood home. His proficiency with portals had continued to improve—most of the time they didn't even hurt anymore.

A light frost coated the apple orchard. Sorwin drifted through the ranks of trees, his hand grazed a barren branch, and tiny shards of ice glinted in the morning glow. He pulled his blue cloak a little tighter. Kaleb had draped it across his shoulders before he left the townhouse. Sorwin could tell that a hundred questions had danced behind his dark eyes—about his sister and the tragic loss of their family—but he thankfully withheld them and simply wished him luck.

*I will tell him someday*, Sorwin thought. *Just not today.*

Brenstel stretched beneath the balcony on his right. How long had it been since he glimpsed the city? Years, somehow too many and not enough. The capital city had always seemed so far away when he was a child, peering at it from the elevated palace grounds. He had spent hours staring at its warren of streets, dreaming of adventure.

"You always loved this view," Alessa said.

Sorwin didn't turn as his sister approached, halting an arm's length away. "It promised mystery, opportunity," he said softly.

"Two of your favorite things, a puzzle and a chance."

"Fitting, then, that I am here to present both to you."

He looked at her perfectly braided brown-and-gold hair beneath a twining crown of silver vines and roses studded with orange opals and sapphires. A cream silk gown with gold embroidery fluttered in the soft breeze passing over the balcony. She didn't appear a day older than the last time he laid eyes on her.

"*Benevita*, Alessa." He bowed, one arm bent at his waist.

"At least you remembered your manners." Her brown eyes found his. She—like Sorwin—never enjoyed the formality of titles. She probably would have stormed off if he ever addressed her as Queen. "What brings you home after all this time?"

That solicited a single laugh from Sorwin. "As if you don't already know. Haven't your spies informed you?" Alessa's network was equal parts impressive and terrifying. In the letters they exchanged over the years, Sorwin swore she was more informed about the inner workings of the League than him. A remarkable feat for someone who never once visited Tor'alan.

The corner of her mouth twitched. "I'd like to hear it from you."

"Perhaps in a more hospitable setting?" A flurry of

snowflakes drifted between them. Winter always arrived early at the palace, nestled along the ridges of the Darlangson Mountains.

Alessa led him inside, and each room they passed through assaulted Sorwin with forgotten memories.

The clear glass panes in the conservatory let in so much light that it had been one of his favorite places to read.

In the main hall, he and his siblings spent hours sliding down the grand banisters. He could almost hear the echoing ghost of laughter.

He hesitated by a door that led to the royal family's private quarters, where his bedroom had been. Alessa had strode past it, and he frowned before catching up to her.

It struck Sorwin as odd that the palace appeared empty. A veritable army of servants, cooks, and footmen walked the halls in his youth, keeping the family and a constant rotation of guests and dignitaries fed and cared for. But he hadn't encountered a single person in the cold corridors while following Alessa.

She turned and led them to the monarch suite. Three sets of doors were sealed tight, and Sorwin wondered if they were still the same well-appointed banquet, meeting, and trophy rooms from his father's reign.

He followed Alessa through the fourth set of doors into the study. A fire crackled in the hearth and leeched some of the chill from his bones.

"Tea will be ready in a moment," Alessa said. She moved toward a tiered service cart to the right of a solid Janlakan hardwood desk.

Sorwin drifted about the room, the familiar scents of old tomes and firewood washing over him. Near the far wall, he crouched to inspect a tiny scene ensconced behind a glass panel. Miniature wildflowers sprouted from a layer of soil while clouds that could fit in his palm drifted about the display, occasionally dousing the flowers with rain. An orange ball of fire hovered above it all, providing heat and light to the little world.

"You kept this?" Sorwin asked.

Alessa glanced at him while she poured tea from a gilded kettle. "Of course I did. That was your first real thesis on your campaign for magical education."

Sorwin soundlessly crossed the carpeted room. "Yes, don't remind me of the failed attempts."

"You mean the endless water wheel that is probably still rolling itself across the ocean? Or how about the enchanted scarves with a frightening penchant for strangulation?"

"I said *don't* remind me." Still, he chuckled at the energetic—if not poorly executed—experiments of his youth. "All I really wanted was for Father to acknowledge there was much more to magic than warfare."

"Yes, well, he got there eventually with your persistent presentations." Alessa set a finely decorated teacup before each of them, then perched in a high-backed armchair. "I think he finally hired theory tutors out of fear you'd destroy the entire palace if left to your own devices."

Sorwin's smile faltered. "A lot of good that did him. Or Mother. Or Henry."

"Sorwin, I didn't mean—"

"I know." He had expected the past—their family—to come up. It was inevitable, which was why he had dreaded coming, why he had stayed away for so long.

Alessa sipped at her tea, set the cup down, and elegantly folded her hands in her lap. "Why don't you tell me why you're here, Sorwin?"

He almost forgot how abrupt she could be. "As I'm sure you're aware, High King Marius Fern was killed in combat by Renna of the Consortium."

"Beheaded, apparently," Alessa said. "A wretched end."

Sorwin nodded. *Of course she already knows the details.* "His untimely departure has left Regadensia without an heir, and the League of Kingdoms without a leader. The council met yesterday to discuss a change—"

"Are you sure about this, Sorwin?"

"What?"

"Are you sure about this?" she repeated.

He hesitated, but continued. "Weslinton and Aghoomi are at war, Evartia is a new democracy, and Regadensia is choosing a new royal family. The League doesn't have another option. It has to be you."

"I'm not asking about the League, I'm asking about you." Alessa's expression was stoic, unmoving, but Sorwin saw the slightest twitch in her pinky finger, and the way her eyes darted to his untouched cup of tea.

Sorwin let out a frustrated sigh. "This isn't about us. This is about fighting the Consortium, about the future of all Valecium."

"Once committed, this cannot be undone."

"I know that! Don't you think I know that?" Sorwin surged to his feet and paced the length of the study. "That's why I'm here. I had to be the one to ask you, to make this happen. I knew you wouldn't agree without speaking to me."

"Of course I wouldn't. It's been almost twenty years since I've seen your face. All I have are decades worth of weekly Fireposts with updates on the League. You have been a dutiful representative on the council, but that wasn't what I wanted at all."

Sorwin halted his pacing and stared into her round eyes. "What did you want?"

Alessa closed the gap between them. The top of her head barely crested his shoulder, and she had to stretch to cup his cheek in her tiny hand. "I wanted *you*, brother. You're the only family I have left, and I feel like I lost you that day, too."

"I suppose you did, in many ways." He had never considered their distance like that before. "I thought you would be grateful for the space."

She shook her head. "I don't blame you for what happened, Sorwin."

"You should," he said with a dark certainty.

"You didn't kill Mother and Father. You didn't kill Henry."

"I didn't save them either." His voice was quiet, small.

"Fah!" Alessa grunted and flung her arms in the air. It was her turn to pace. "You were a boy participating in an outdated magical tournament against your will. Do you remember? Henry pushed you to be his dueling partner. And why wouldn't he? You were always a genius with magic, even in battle, even when you preferred to have your nose in a book. And Mother and Father, well, they should have listened to the reports coming in from the south. The Rot had crept further north, and they did little to assuage the damage. They should have heard the discontented rumblings before the assassins came."

"But—they had reports?" Sorwin hadn't heard that before.

Alessa pounced on his uncertainty. "Yes, Sorwin! They did, many of them. I read them all after my coronation, and some before. I loved Mother and Father with all my heart, but they were negligent in this regard. They did not deserve to die, but the assassin's motivation wasn't unfounded."

"I never knew...I thought the mage worked for the Consortium." It had been too painful to pry too deeply into why his parents and brother had died. When the investigation discovered the Consortium had been involved with the mage that killed them, that was all the information Sorwin needed. His parents and brother were gone, and the details didn't seem to matter. It only mattered that he wouldn't see them again, wouldn't hear their laughs or feel their hugs.

"He did work for the Consortium, but only just before the tournament. They were his means, not his reason."

"I'm sorry for leaving you alone," Sorwin said. "Does that have any bearing on why the palace is empty?"

Alessa's neutral exterior settled back over her like a veil. It was a skill she had honed in their youth, and Sorwin found it fascinating and unsettling. She could bottle up the most intense emotions in the blink of an eye, leaving not a trace of a grimace nor a single strand of hair out of place. She resumed her poised position in the armchair.

"I prefer a leaner staff than our parents enjoyed."

*I may have moved far away, but you have always been the distant one.* He didn't share these thoughts, but instead asked a question. "I half expected to find you with a husband and children when I darkened your doorstep."

"There hasn't been time." She picked at the embroidery on her gown, adjusting the folds of the fine skirts.

"I haven't the right to press, but Alessa, seeing what Regadensia is going through without an heir—"

"I accept."

Sorwin sighed. "Alessa."

"I accept the position of High Queen of the League of Kingdoms, and all burdens and responsibilities that accompany the title. I understand this would relieve you of your seat on the council. However, I'd very much appreciate it if you remained, at least until I am settled and acquainted with the current situation."

"We both know you're more than acquainted." A narrow grin tilted his face. "I'm at your service."

"Splendid." Alessa assumed a queenly, decorous air. "This is a new beginning for the League and for us, Sorwin, and as such, I'll expect a dinner invitation within the week to meet Kaleb."

Sorwin couldn't breathe as all the blood in his body rushed to his cheeks. He sputtered, and Alessa dropped her dignified guise and snickered like the mischievous girl he once knew.

"I swear I'll hunt down every last informant you have, Alessa," Sorwin vowed.

"You can try, dear brother, but genius or not, you will fail."

Sorwin scowled and his cheeks burned as she laughed harder.

# CHAPTER 4

# MESSAGES

Zak's shield held firm against the flood Olivia had conjured. The green fire hissed and spat as water battered against it, filling court seven with a murky haze.

"That won't work," he called over the clash of magic.

The spout of water stopped. Zak couldn't see through the mist, but he kept still, listening for Olivia's next move.

A root sprouted between his feet and coiled around his right leg. Another came from behind, gripping his waist. A third twined up, reaching toward his extended arm to pull it down, and his shield along with it.

"*Dracomanus!*" Green scales rushed up Zak's arms. The fire shield dissolved as he shredded the roots with his claws, ripping like parchment before the strength of a dragon.

*Jolsu!* Zak called.

*I'm ready*, the dragon responded.

Zak's vision blurred for a moment as Jolsu's magic trickled into his eyes. He searched the training court through the golden tint. He twisted—there—behind him, the glow of Olivia's magic shone through the mist.

"*Pennilma.*" Two strong, leathery wings unfolded from his shoulders. He leaped into the air and flew near the top of the court dome, using the steam to obscure his movements. "*Customateria.*"

Jolsu appeared in the air next to him, the size of a hunting dog. He dropped straight back to the ground and made a raucous, spitting flames and roaring, trying to draw Olivia's attention.

Using the distraction, Zak pinned his wings close to his body and dove toward the glow of Olivia's magic. He stretched his arms out and grinned, ready to catch her unawares.

He crashed into a solid figure and grunted. Immediately, his mistake became apparent when tiny thorns snapped and embedded into his scales as he tumbled. When the momentum finally subsided, he sat up. The figure next to him looked like a scarecrow made from twisted branches covered in rose thorns.

A decoy.

Cold metal pressed against Zak's throat. He leaned away, but Olivia caught his neck.

"I win again," she whispered, breath warm against his ear.

He almost wasn't upset for a moment. Feeling her touch, her closeness. The scent of flowers—of blooms in Springrise—overwhelmed him. But then he pushed the dagger away from his throat and scowled. "How did you hide? I used Jolsu's magic sight."

She shrugged and sheathed the dagger. "I knew you would the moment the steam filled the court. All I needed was to give you a target." She jabbed a thumb at the discarded scarecrow. "I funneled some magic into Twiggy so he'd light up like a birthday bonfire in your eyes."

"Twiggy?" Zak laughed and, for a second time, found himself almost not caring that Olivia bested him. Again.

"What?" She shrugged. "It's accurate."

"Can't fault you there."

A strong and exacting wind swirled the mist into one specific spot. Bazil stood at the end of the funnel, holding a blue jar aloft as the last of the fog raced inside. He corked it and set the jar down before walking over to Zak and Olivia.

"It was a clever idea," Bazil said to Zak. "But you moved too fast. You didn't check your target before striking."

"I thought I did," Zak grumbled. He accepted Bazil's outstretched hand and stood, brushing grass and damp soil from his training garb.

"That was the point," Olivia said with a smirk.

"And you," Bazil rounded on her, his dark braids swaying with the movement, "should know better than to try to break through Zak's shields. Even Sorwin struggles against them now."

Olivia crossed her arms. "Fair point."

Zak stuck his tongue out at her.

Bazil nodded once. "He left me in charge of your magical training while he negotiates with Queen Alessa. I won't have him disappointed upon his return."

"And I daresay he won't be." Kaleb's deep voice carried from the edge of the court where he stood at attention near the stone block wall. "I'll make sure he knows about your commendable efforts—all three of you."

"I'm sure you will, *personally*, Major." Zak wiggled his eyebrows.

Olivia elbowed him in the ribs.

"Catch your breath, then we shall move on to weapons," Kaleb said, ignoring the jest, but Zak thought his upper lip twitched a fraction, which was an enormous reaction for the very stoic soldier.

Wincing and gingerly massaging his side, Zak padded to the wall and drank deeply from the waterskin. Olivia stood next to him, doing the same.

"How is Vess?" he asked.

"She's settling in."

"That's good. And your connection?"

"Getting stronger. Each day I feel her emotions a little deeper, hear her voice more clearly."

Zak nodded. "It's only been a few weeks since you became a *Nacusti*, but your progress is already much faster than mine and Jolsu's at the start."

Olivia reddened at the praise. "It probably helps that Vess doesn't hold a multigenerational grudge against me."

"It does indeed," Zak said in an overly serious tone, wistfully shaking his head.

*The grudge was justified, Parignis,* Jolsu said. He projected the thought so Olivia could hear too, and she laughed.

"Ah—you said 'was' which implies you've moved past it." Zak smirked as the dragon grumbled vague annoyance across their connection.

"Anyway," Olivia interrupted their banter, "I still can't

use Vess's magic. It's a wonder she resurrected me with one of her phoenix feathers." A shadow crossed her face, and she bit the corner of her lip as the past—her death from the *vitaligo*—filled the silence between them.

Zak fought a grimace. The idea of Kal, his childhood best friend, having anything to do with Olivia's death, angered him. How could two people he held so dear have been at such odds? If he had been there to stop them fighting...but he'd been too late.

Olivia had a faraway look on her face.

"Hey." He gripped Olivia's cold hand. Their eyes met. He wanted to bring her back to now, to the present, where she grew stronger by the day.

And for a moment, they existed in a different time and place together. Not in the middle of a war for the fate of all Valecium, not as the last two *Nacusti*, but just as a boy and a girl holding hands.

*If that were true*, Zak thought, *maybe our first kiss wouldn't have been after her resurrection. Maybe it would have been in a moment like this.*

The memory of her lips sent a strange jolt through his chest.

As quickly as they slipped into the moment, it shattered as Zak and Olivia both seemed to realize in the same breath that they were, in fact, holding hands in the middle of a training session in court seven.

Olivia took a step back and ran a hand through her auburn curls, stammering something about a new short-sword maneuver.

"Yeah, let's try that. Kaleb is waiting." With the heat radiating from his cheeks, Zak could have sworn they were on fire.

Jolsu snickered.

*Not. Helpful.* Zak said to the dragon.

Zak spent the next hour sparring with Olivia, taking feedback from Kaleb, and following demonstrations led by him and Bazil. The priest healed any minor bumps and bruises they accumulated. At the end of the session, he left covered in sweat and once again very aware of his need for more tunics and trousers.

When he left, the door of court seven thundered as it opened, alerting him that the sealing charm had been temporarily broken. Zak closed the door behind him, and the purple sheen covered it once again.

Tansil stood at the edge of the path, arms folded rigidly at his waist.

"Archmagus," Zak said with a nod.

"Ah, Zakolor." The elf blinked out of a daze. "How were your lessons today?"

*I still can't best Olivia, which means I have no hope against Zandorn, so the League and all of Valecium are most likely doomed. Also, we held hands, which was nice, but awkward.*

"Fine," he said instead.

"That's good." Tansil didn't seem to notice Zak's strife. "I was hoping you'd join me to examine Karazul's *senligo.*

"Of course, Archmagus."

Zak walked beside Tansil across the manicured lawns of the Center, the elf's long brown hair glowed in the sunlight almost as bright as his green eyes.

Every few days, Zak joined Tansil to check on Karazul's binding and discuss developments in the war against the Consortium. Luckily, the assassin had remained trapped in a spell, rendering him unconscious for weeks. Though how long he'd stay that way was anyone's guess.

Since their time in the forest with Temaway, Tansil had slowly adopted a new radical transparency in his leadership of the Elemental House—at least with Sorwin and Zak—in direct opposition to his previous secretive style.

Today was no different.

"Your dream," Tansil said. "Is it the same?"

"Yes. Still a sapling surrounded by darkness."

"Hmm. Keep working with Shira—I've no doubt the two of you will uncover its meaning."

Zak didn't respond. His latest vision had proved an even greater conundrum than the one of the black caladrius. Night after night, a small tree no higher than his knee entered his dreams, called to him, whispered words that he could never quite hear. A nearly-talking tree. It was a message, but Zak didn't know who it was from or what it meant.

A disturbance on the path ahead drew Zak's attention.

"Adept Rauffe," Tansil said, coming to a stop.

Rauffe Werbeggen, one of Zak's least favorite mages, was—well, Zak had difficulty understanding exactly *what* he was doing. His muscled back rested against the bright white-and-purple castle wall, and he sidestepped along its smooth edge like a crab on the beach. He showed no sign of hearing Tansil's address.

"Is he...okay?" Zak asked.

"I'm quite unsure." Tansil strode forward. "Rauffe?" He snapped his fingers once.

The loud *crack* caught Rauffe's attention, and he froze with one foot midair. He flushed deeper than a ripe pemberry and quickly righted himself, tugging at his red and bronze tunic. "Archmagus," he said with a stiff bow.

"I seem to have caught you rather...focused?"

Zak stifled a laugh with a cough.

"Y-yes, Archmagus."

Tansil waited, but Rauffe didn't seem eager to elaborate. The elf frowned. "Focused with what, Adept?"

Rauffe blinked several times. "Exercise, Archmagus."

"Exercise?"

"Correct, Archmagus. For combat training."

"It seems an unorthodox maneuver."

Rauffe eyed Zak for a brief moment, looking almost panicked. "It's for my legs." He patted his thighs for emphasis. "Makes them stronger."

Zak almost interjected a comment about how Rauffe would need much more than strong legs to improve in combat, but he didn't get a chance.

"Ah—I see. Well, as you were, Adept." Tansil nodded once before continuing down the crushed gravel path toward the castle vestibule.

Zak lingered for a moment longer, exchanging a look with Rauffe. As funny as it had been to catch Rauffe in such a strange predicament, something felt wrong. Rauffe was a bully, and he should have been embarrassed by Zak catching him. Yet he ignored Zak entirely, and his customary swagger had been absent when he spoke with Tansil.

"What are you really doing?" Zak asked.

"What business is it of yours, *Nacusti*?" Rauffe sneered.

*Well, there it is*, Zak thought, shaking his head.

"Wasn't that odd?" Zak asked Tansil after catching up to him.

"Hm?"

"Rauffe's—erm—exercise."

"Oh, quite. Though no more strange than what summoners are asked to do before contracting their first demon. That includes extensive choreography, an embarrassing memory, and eating a handful of charcoal."

"What?"

"Yes...I wasn't fond of the taste myself."

Before Zak could ask any questions about the peculiar ritual—or the fact that Tansil apparently had at least one demon—the elf drifted off the path just outside the tall doors of the castle.

"Um, Archmagus?" Zak called.

Tansil's ochre winter robes fanned in a semicircle as he squatted to inspect something.

*Are all elves this prone to distraction?* he wondered.

*Temaway certainly was in his youth*, Jolsu said.

Zak smirked. *I would have liked to see that.*

He peered over Tansil's shoulder. A thin-stemmed plant with four pointed leaves had thrust itself through the dry Winter grass.

"What could possibly be in season now?" he asked.

"This is no regular growth," Tansil said.

"What is it?"

"A message, a summons."

"It looks like a sprout to me."

Tansil sighed. "It's a star leaf, a type of tree only the elves can grow. Each point represents one of their tenets of leading a balanced life: body, heart, mind, and spirit." He gently tapped each leaf as he dictated.

"'The elves'? But you're an elf too, Tansil."

"Sometimes I wonder if that's true anymore."

After a moment, Zak pieced together Tansil's words. "Wait—the elves are *summoning* you? To Nalawin? But aren't you...didn't they..." He didn't have the heart to say *banished* out loud.

"Yes, and yes," Tansil confirmed.

Something round bulged the stem, then pulsed up between the folds of the leaves. It glowed a bright green—much like Tansil's eyes. The elf delicately lifted the object and held it in his palm for Zak to observe.

"The seed."

"Why did they send it to you?"

"It's complicated." A muscle in Tansil's jaw jumped. "I have a feeling this is to do with our recent trespass in the Eyewood."

"That was over a month ago! Why now? And how did they even know?" As far as Zak was aware, the League and Consortium had entered the wood in search of the black caladrius, had a minor skirmish, and exited before the elves had any notion of their presence.

"Not much escapes their Sight. As for 'why now,' elves aren't known for punctuality. A month is a moment." Tansil's brown lips moved as he mumbled something, and an ice blue orb formed around the seed before it disappeared from his hand. "It will be safe for now, until I decide what to do."

"What would happen if you went to Nalawin?" Zak couldn't keep the worry from cracking his voice.

Tansil forced a smile and patted his shoulder. "You know, in my eyes, humans grow so rapidly. Did you notice I have to look up at you now, ever so slightly? And you're more than simply taller, Zakolor. Your magic and wisdom have grown in equal measure." He adjusted the long sleeves of his robes. "Come, Karazul awaits us—though he may be unawares."

"Yes, Archmagus," Zak said, with no small amount of concern.

Karazul couldn't remember his brother's face.

They held hands, and he pulled Karazul along a forest trail that opened into a scenic valley with a pond. From the overlook, he could see a small village being built below—the first of its kind. His brother skipped and hopped, overcome with excitement.

"What are they doing with those trees?" Karazul asked. He peered down at the people scurrying about with stone tools. They hacked at the bark and stacked the fallen wood into a pile.

"Building! Isn't it wondrous?" his brother said.

"Hmmph. Seems too busy, too much effort."

His brother laughed, a beautiful sound that lifted Karazul's heart. He was the only one who could make him almost smile. "Of course it seems that way to *you*, Niltris."

And when his brother turned around, the dream became a nightmare. His face—it was a blur, a nothingness that should have been something, some*one*.

Karazul wanted to look away, but he forced himself to stare, to confront the strange absence.

"What's wrong?" his brother asked.

"I can't remember you."

"Niltris, why hurt me this way?"

"I—no, brother. I can't see you, I can't recall your name." What was this pain, this torment that stabbed at his chest?

A deep cackling rumbled as the light of day was snuffed out. A dark shroud settled over them, and even though the words came from his brother's lips, Karazul knew it was no longer he who spoke. A distorted voice took over. "You don't remember me? How could you forget what you did? You left me, you chose this. How could you do this to me?"

Karazul fought to release his hand, but his brother's grip tightened.

*Wake up!* He urged, but nothing happened. He was trapped in this nightmare, stumbling from one vision to the next in an endless procession. How long had it been?

His brother threw him with unnatural strength. He should have crashed into a tree, but the forest around them disappeared, and he slid along a rough, dark surface.

"I will find my way out of this prison and kill that

flea-ridden elf," Karazul swore. He stood and readied himself for the next vision, the next torture.

# CHAPTER 5

# LADIES AND LORDS

"Again," Renna said.

Kalbick groaned, but stomped across the room back to his starting position.

Renna smiled. *Good boy.*

They were in a forge on one of the middle levels of Pywell's old dwarven fortress. The room had been cleared of all tools, tables, and metal—anything having to do with smithing. His father was a blacksmith, and Renna didn't want any reminders of Kal's former life, but the space was large and built to resist the intensity of dwarven craftsmanship. It was a perfect location for her pet's training.

With a wave of her hand, scattered stone fragments reassembled themselves into figures with swords, spears, and magic. Renna watched as Kal flowed in a near-effortless dance among them, destroying one after the other.

The entire route would take him at least half an hour

as more figures appeared from the floor and walls, launching ambushes. His dark blue magic glittered as it flashed around the circular room.

"Like poetry." Renna sighed. It was good to have him back, but he had much work to do to be rid of the tainted magics he had acquired during his captivity. She let a snarl twitch across her face at the thought of the League with their grubby hands on her prized *sorgeus*.

She held out her empty glass, and Gunther—her giant assistant—lumbered over from his station against the wall. He poured pemberry wine into the vessel and retreated once again.

"We'll rid him of this infection, just as we did the League of their precious king," she said to no one in particular. Renna sipped at the red liquid, reveling in the reminder of Marius's severed head flying through the air, catapulted with such grace and finesse.

When Kal finished the latest drill—his fourth consecutively—she beckoned him over and grabbed his chin. Her Influence thrummed like a steady heartbeat in his core.

"You were always mine, weren't you?" It wasn't a question.

"Yes, my lady," Kal said.

Renna released him to the baths under Gunther's care. He was well within her grasp, but still—precautions had to be taken. She wouldn't underestimate the *Nacusti* or his mentors again. No, they would find it impossible to leverage any advantage against her, especially now when her plans were so *close* to fruition.

Back in her chambers, Renna breathed the fresh air circulating from the oasis below. She approached the opening and smiled at the greenery, a constant reminder that her will need only be voiced to be obeyed.

Across the room, on a raised dais behind a Janlakan hardwood desk, she poured a pitcher of water into a round porcelain bowl. Pricking the tip of her finger with a dagger, three drops of blood fell into the bowl, swirling like red clouds.

"*Nuntiumsanguis.*"

Shadows darkened the room, stretching further than they should have up the walls, reaching from behind the objects that cast them. The water rippled as a raspy voice gurgled from its depths. "What news?"

Renna stared at the bowl and clutched her hands at her waist to keep them still. "My lord, Zandorn progresses each day in his research with the black caladrius. I have no doubt he will find a way to unravel the Contract soon."

"He could strike it down now. Why does he delay?"

"Zandorn is cautious. He wants to preserve the caladrius's magic for further use, if possible."

"He pursues a loophole in the bird's sacrifice?"

Renna smiled. "Exactly. Imagine if we could channel its power rather than extinguish it with one spell?" She shifted her weight, trying to contain her excitement.

"Hmm. And the rest of the preparations?" the voice asked.

"Besides the black caladrius and the Contract, we also have the *cordeus*." She pulled the stone from her pocket—it never left her side—and even though the voice could not see it, she knew he felt the echo of its magic. "I also recovered my dear Kalbick."

"I care not about your toy mage," the voice spat.

"You may in time, my lord, when you see what a powerful *sorgeus* he has become."

"Tell me of the Druid," he demanded.

"Terasi's body has been disposed of as you instructed, buried in a grave of runic death stones surrounded by the Rot. We believe he was on his last life anyway, but reincarnation should be impossible now."

"Good." The edge of the voice softened. "And Zandorn discovered some of the secrets of reincarnation?"

"He did. He still believes it will prevent his wife from ever leaving him again, after her resurrection." She shook her head at the thought. *What a sad man Zandorn is.*

"Continue to play your role, child, and soon we will be rewarded for our efforts." With a final ripple, the surface of the water stilled, and the shadows in the room retreated.

"Soon," Renna said with a twisted smile. "Very soon."

# Chapter 6

# THE UNKNOWN

The spiky grass of court seven poked at Zak's back, arms, legs, and scalp. His chest heaved. To his right, Olivia looked to be in the same breathless state.

"We lost again," he said.

"Salted Magerus," Olivia cursed.

Sorwin stood before them, a little worse for wear with a singed sleeve and mussed hair, but certainly not appearing as if he had just defeated two *Nacusti*. "What went wrong that time?" His remorseful expression made it apparent he didn't want to ask.

Zak sat up and picked at blades of grass between his feet. "We didn't coordinate our attacks or cover for each other's weaknesses."

"At least you're aware." Sorwin sighed and pinched the bridge of his nose. "If you can't defeat me—"

"We have no hope against Zandorn. Yes, we're *very* aware," Olivia said. She flicked her wrist and a waterskin soared through the air. Catching it, she drank deep before handing it to Zak.

He held it and stared at the stitching that bound the leather together. "How did they do it?"

"Hm?" Sorwin prodded.

"The original *Nacusti*, how did they defeat the gods? Shouldn't two of us be more powerful than one mortal?" He unintentionally squeezed the waterskin, soaking his hands as liquid squirted out. *Fantastic.*

Sorwin smiled—his tired but supportive one—and looked Zak and Olivia over before speaking. "I think we've accomplished all we can by sparring today. When you told me about your time with Temaway, I recall some excellent advice he shared with you. Do you remember?"

"Let Jolsu guide me," Zak said. A comforting rumble pulsed across his bond with the dragon.

"Exactly. I think he—and Vess—are the only ones that can provide insight into the previous *Nacusti's* abilities." Sorwin conjured two tufted cushions with a snap of his fingers, then collected a few books from the bench near the wall. He paused at the door. "I'll tell Kaleb you need to meditate today instead of weapons practice. Do use the time well." Thunder pierced court seven as the door opened and closed, and Sorwin was gone.

"Subtle as ever, isn't he?" Zak joked.

Olivia rolled her eyes. "Ever since I met him." She stretched and settled on one of the cushions, the teal fabric clashing with her red uniform. "Shall we?"

Zak sat on the other cushion—a maroon paisley—and shrugged off a tingle beneath his collar as he took Olivia's hands.

He closed his eyes, inhaled and exhaled deeply, and found his center. When he opened them again, he still sat across from Olivia, but everything appeared covered in a blanket of grey. And, the most significant difference from a moment before was that a phoenix and a dragon had joined them.

"It took you long enough to come seeking answers," Jolsu growled.

Zak smiled. There was no anger in the dragon. "We've been a bit busy."

"We're aware."

Zak glanced at Vess. The phoenix preened beneath a wing, her feathers a dazzling array of sunset hues—even in the muted light of the *inriloc*.

"Let's focus," Olivia said. "We don't have the skill to sustain the *inriloc* for long." She shifted on the cushion so she could look at Jolsu and Vess. "What can you tell us about the previous *Nacusti* and their magic? How were they able to defeat the gods?"

"Valecium was different back then," Vess said in her high-pitched voice. "It was the Era of Dominion, when the gods limited free will and magical studies. To become a powerful mage, one was either favored by the gods or was cunning enough to learn in secret."

"Temaway was devoted to Cerevita," Zak said. "What about my ancestor, Adrastus?"

"He was cunning," Jolsu said, with more than a little pride. "A leader, a rebel. He organized an underground academy and saw the opportunity to end the gods' dominion even before the *Nacusti* were created."

"So Temaway and Adrastus were accomplished mages before they became *Nacusti*." Olivia's eyebrows raised. "And I'm assuming the other four were as well?"

Vess chirped. "Indeed. The other two elves also excelled in nature magic, like Temaway and Adrastus. One of the humans was a priest, the other a summoner."

"Olivia, you were powerful before you merged with Vess," Zak said. "I suspect you only need time to develop your bond. But I've only been studying magic for a few months. I can't change my past to start earlier."

Olivia squeezed his hand. "Don't minimize your progress, Zak. You've come further than anyone could have predicted in such a short time." She looked at the Guardians again. "There must have been more than power behind their victory. Did the *Nacusti* have any weapons or help?"

"Of course, plenty of both." Jolsu's claws flexed into the soil. "They were strategic. They used the gods' hubris against them and baited them to fight on *their* terms. And not all the gods were on the same side. Cerevita, as you know, supported the *Nacusti* as much as she was able. She couldn't directly fight Azubelux and Baltenebris, but she did what she could."

"Other gods fought in the war? Who?"

"Most of the earthly gods followed Cerevita's lead, either abstaining or supporting." Vess hummed for a moment, thinking. "Pluvius and the other water gods took up arms. There were others...I—I can't recall their names." Her beak snapped twice in frustration.

"Jolsu?" Zak asked. "I know it was a long time ago, but you must remember allies from such an important war."

Jolsu bristled. "Naturally. There was Pluvius, as Vess said. Dionne led their elementals. The Virtues and Vices mostly fought for Azubelux and Baltenebris."

"Virtues and Vices?" Zak parroted.

"There is a hierarchy within the Divine realm. Azubelux is the Father of Light and leads the Virtues—gods of health, love, and empathy. Baltenebris is the Father of Shadows. He created demons, and the Vices—war, vanity, greed—fall under his purview."

"I see." Zak scratched his head. "Then there must have been other gods following Cerevita that helped?"

Wisps of smoke curled from Jolsu's snout. "Yes, there was a whole mess of minor gods involved, but there was someone else very powerful leading the charge. I—I can't remember who." Jolsu blinked, head twitching, just like Vess's had.

Zak's eyes narrowed. "Something is wrong."

"What do you mean?" Vess asked.

"Neither of you can remember the names of gods—who you would have known for hundreds of years at the time—that fought beside you in a war where you made the ultimate sacrifice? Doesn't that strike you as odd?"

"Zak's right," Olivia said. "Both of your memories failing isn't a coincidence. Someone or something tampered with them, and that means there's only one other who can give us answers."

"Cerevita," Zak said.

Zak and Olivia tracked down Tansil in his spire-top office. The elf fiddled with a tiny green orb, which Zak recognized as the star leaf seed. Apparently Tansil was taking his time deliberating over the elves' message.

And perhaps that was in their favor, because he didn't put up much resistance when Zak and Olivia asked to speak with Cerevita. He inquired about their purpose and seemed equally troubled by the gaps in the Guardians' memories.

"Should we get Sorwin?" Olivia asked.

"No, we'll fill him in after," Zak said. With any luck, Sorwin and Kaleb were enjoying a rare relaxing afternoon. Zak wasn't in a hurry to spoil that for his magus.

Together, the trio took the many steps down from Tansil's office to the vestibule of the castle, then descended further into its depths as the Archmagus bypassed the protective charms shielding the throne room. The Contract was no longer there to be protected, but after Archalium Vermig was killed and Baltenebris's *cordeus* was stolen, Tansil and Sashina kept their gods' *cordeus* locked away in the throne room. Plus, extra defenses had been added with Karazul sleeping in his cell just down the hall.

Footsteps echoed in the cavernous chamber as they crossed to the three colossal thrones—one of sharp-cornered white stone, one of serrated obsidian, and one woven of green branches.

A seat for each of the Three.

Tansil retrieved Cerevita's *cordeus* from a hidden compartment along the side wall and approached the green throne. Branches from its base stretched toward the stone, lifted it from Tansil's palms, and cradled it like a delicate flower.

Zak knew what would happen next. The bright flash of light still burned against his eyelids, and when he blinked them open, Cerevita perched upon the living throne. Her green skin reminded him of fresh sprouts in a pasture. An earthy scent flooded the room, like soil after a day of rain.

"*Benevita,*" her voice—steeped in power—spoke through Zak, Olivia, and Tansil.

"*Benevita*, Mother." Tansil bowed his head.

Cerevita's eyes alighted on Olivia. "*Much has happened since last we spoke. Temaway bequeathed a generous gift upon you.*"

Olivia—never one to shy from anything since Zak had known her—blushed a deep red. "He saved my life."

The goddess smirked, a dazzling thing, and her long brown hair almost floated as she spoke. "*He did, and you gave him well-earned rest.*"

She nodded and looked down, finding something interesting to stare at between her boots.

Tansil cleared his throat. "We are grateful for Temaway's sacrifice, and do not take Vess's presence lightly." He nodded at Zak and Olivia in turn before looking up at Cerevita again. "We come bearing questions, in hopes you have the answers."

"*Speak, child, and I will help if able.*"

The elf held a hand out toward Zak, gesturing him forward.

Though it was Zak's third time in Cerevita's presence, his insides still fluttered and twisted.

"*B-benevita*, Cerevita." He swallowed past the dryness in his throat. "While meditating with Jolsu and Vess, Olivia and I discovered something troubling."

The longer he spoke, the easier it became. He recounted the entire conversation while the goddess listened attentively, barely moving in the green-tinted light that filled the throne room.

"And with the gaps in both Guardians' memories, we hoped you would recall more details about who helped the *Nacusti* and how they defeated your brothers. Perhaps there is a strategy or something we can use to best Zandorn."

Cerevita folded her slender fingers together. "*Everything Jolsu and Vess shared was accurate. The minor gods fought according to their hierarchy, which meant we were almost evenly matched.*"

Zak frowned. "If Azubelux and Baltenebris were both against you, wouldn't you have been outnumbered?"

A line appeared in her flawless brow. "*I didn't stand alone—there were other gods.*"

"Can you name them?" Zak pressed.

"*Of course. Pluvius and the water gods—*"

"No," Zak said, heart leaping at his boldness in interrupting the goddess. "We know your minor gods followed you. What other gods allied themselves with the Guardians to win the war?"

"*I—*" And then something terrifying happened. Cerevita

shook her head, just as Vess and Jolsu had before. When she focused her attention on Zak once again, she said, "*What did you ask, child?*"

Zak looked to his companions for help, but both appeared speechless—Tansil's mouth slightly agape, and Olivia blanched whiter than the stone of the castle.

"Jolsu?" he asked aloud. "What is happening?"

*I don't know*, the dragon said, projecting his response. *Something is blocking our memories.*

"What could be powerful enough to interfere with the memory of the Goddess of Life and Mother of Magic?" The thought alone was dizzying.

"*I wasn't...*" Cerevita hesitated. "*I wasn't always the Mother of Magic. There was another before me.*" She grimaced—almost appearing in pain—before she reclined in her throne. "*I can remember no more.*"

"Another goddess of magic?" Olivia asked. "How is that possible?"

"And why can't anyone remember them?" Tansil asked.

"*My children.*" Cerevita's golden irises focused on each of them in turn. "*This mystery is troubling, and I would charge you to explore it. Unraveling its secrets may prove useful in your efforts against Zandorn. Perhaps answers or allies await.*"

Cerevita faded from view, like sunlight behind a cloud. The room felt too big in her absence, and the warmth she had brought seeped away into the cold walls and floors.

Zak immediately began pacing, barely resisting the urge to tear his hair out. "That's it? No answers, just more questions? Where would we even *begin* to investigate a centuries-old memory curse strong enough to affect Guardians and a god?"

"Tansil." Olivia somehow maintained her composure, and Zak was too frazzled to understand how. "Weren't you alive during the Guardian War? Do you remember anything?"

"Yes, but as a young elf only a few decades old at the time, I was kept to the glade."

"What does that mean?"

"It means that I had no contact with the outside world, and no knowledge of the Guardian War until after the fact."

"Knowledge." Zak halted. He had been half listening through his exasperation. "There's someone who may have knowledge of the Guardian War. They were alive during the conflict, anyway."

"Who?" Olivia asked.

"Malu."

# CHAPTER 7

# TRACKING

Fireposts streaked red across Tor'alan's cloudy sky, ricocheting off the giant iron post in the Center. Within an hour of speaking with Cerevita, Tansil had summoned Zak's closest friends and allies.

Sorwin, Kaleb, Shira, and Bazil met Tansil, Zak, and Olivia in the Archmagus's office and were briefed on the conversation with the goddess. Zak delivered most of the story, as Tansil still seemed preoccupied with something.

"Three Fires," Bazil cursed, which was entirely unlike him. "What creature could be powerful enough to hide memories from gods and Guardians?"

"I shudder to think," Sorwin said, arms crossed over his chest. "And the idea to track down Malu—why do we think he won't be equally as hampered?"

"Because," Zak said, "everyone who signed the Contract—Cerevita, and the Guardians through their *Nacusti*—can't remember the finer details of how they won the Guardian War. According to Jolsu and Vess, Malu didn't fight in the war and didn't sign the Contract. There's a chance his memory is intact."

"It's worth a try." Shira shrugged and looked pointedly at Zak. "Maybe we could track him down the same way we did the black caladrius?"

Zak shook his head. "I don't think so. I haven't had any visions of Malu, just the tree in the dark." *What I wouldn't give for a teaspoon of Shira's Sight skill*, he thought.

"We should go to Masdaan," Olivia said. "I doubt we'll stumble on him again—looking back, Malu planned our first meeting. But maybe he'll be in the Kapana, or we might pick up his trail there."

"It's the only lead we have." Zak leaned against the long table that used to be Elpida's terrarium, waiting for Sorwin to digest everything they had told him, hoping he would see something they hadn't.

For his part, Sorwin tapped his stubbled chin with a thumb. When it seemed he may never break from thought, Kaleb nudged his elbow, and Zak snorted at Sorwin's glassy-eyed surprise.

"Forgive me," Sorwin said with an embarrassed smile. "Olivia is right—Masdaan appears to be the only path available. But there is someone we must see first, in the off chance they are of assistance."

"Who?" Bazil asked.

"Limba Dar."

The air in the room solidified, and Zak found it difficult to breathe. Somehow, in the midst of the chaos following Marius's death, he had forgotten they had captured the traitor. "Why?" Zak asked, failing to keep the venom from his tone.

Sorwin didn't miss it—he rarely missed anything when it came to Zak. "I share your feelings, Zak, but remove them from the situation for a moment of objectivity. Limba Dar is from Masdaan, and he was working with the Disciples. If anyone knows of a rogue god hiding in Aghoomi, it would be him."

"Hasn't he been interrogated already?" Shira directed the question to Kaleb.

He nodded. "Aye, but General Lupa didn't recover anything useful. The conversation was...hardly fluid. Limba Dar is not as we remember him—something in him broke after Marius's death." Kaleb's lips formed a thin line, serious even for the stoic soldier. "I think he feels guilty."

"He should," Zak spat. "He's done almost as much to hurt us as Zandorn." He scratched at the bandage on his arm as the wound underneath burned.

"Be that as it may," Sorwin said, "we have an obligation to do everything within our power to win this war. Right now, that means questioning Limba Dar—or what remains of him—in hopes he can lead us to Malu."

Sorwin approached Tansil, who had sat silently behind his desk during the entire meeting, and had a private word with the elf before turning back to the group.

"Well, let's be off. Kaleb, Shira, and Bazil, with me to Limba Dar's cell. Zak and Olivia, go pack what you need for a journey and meet in the vestibule in one hour."

Zak angrily stuffed an extra adept uniform with bronze details at the cuffs and collar into a leather satchel. He stomped toward the narrow desk under the single round window in his bedroom, snatched a book titled *Serious Sight: Peering into Far-Flung Futures* from his desk and tossed it onto his bed.

He had protested his exclusion from Limba Dar's interrogation, arguing that he had every right to face the traitor head-on. But Sorwin would hear none of it, saying he was too emotional to remain focused on the task at hand.

*He's not wrong, Parignis,* Jolsu's deep voice rumbled. *Limba Dar hurt you, and that is difficult to forget.*

"He hurt all of us!" Zak shouted. "Why am *I* singled out?"

*You and Olivia were both excused, by your telling,* Elpida said. Her bronze tail flicked soundlessly on the quilt. *Perhaps to give you time to prepare for the hunt?*

"So Sorwin says." Despite clinging to his anger, it began to soften and slip away. He didn't have the strength to hold much of anything against Sorwin—he'd been correct so many times in his decisions concerning Zak over the almost year they'd spent together. There was no reason to believe he misstepped now.

Still, Zak harbored doubts about their ability to track Malu. A trickster god that eluded signing the Contract would be no easy quarry.

Arranging the last few belongings in his satchel into a

little nest, he held the bag open and Elpida—begrudging-ly—crawled in. Zak closed the top and fastened the ties while she hissed and scratched.

"Hey! Don't rip anything!"

*How long must I be captive in this cage?*

Zak scoffed. "At least you get to come with us. A little gratitude would be welcome."

She poked her head between the folds of oiled leather. *Thank you for nearly killing me with the stench of your human drapings.*

"They're called clothes," he sighed.

*I told you this was a bad idea,* Jolsu said.

"Don't you start. I need one reasonable dragon between the two of you."

It had been difficult convincing Jolsu that Elpida should accompany them to search for Malu. His instinct to protect his hatchling made sense, and Zak had used that to his advantage.

"She'll be safer with us," Zak had said earlier. "A Magerus, two *Nacusti*, a priest, a summoner, and an expert swordsman. Besides, everyone who knows who she really is will be on this search. Except for Tansil. But he doesn't seem to be in a caregiving mood."

*You're putting her directly in the Disciple's path, and potentially the Consortium's!* Jolsu had countered.

"Elpida is there already. First with Terasi, now with us. Sheltering her from danger won't save her, it will only leave her ill-prepared, like it did me."

Seventeen years. That was how long he had lived without

knowing about Jolsu, about his heritage, about the true dangers Zandorn wielded. He wondered—over and over—how different the war would be if he had never been hidden. If he had been trained from a young age. If he had more time before Zandorn had stolen the Contract.

If, if, if.

He wouldn't let the same fate befall the bronze dragon. Not while she was in his care.

*Fine,* Jolsu had relented. *But she will remain at our side to observe only.*

"She may need to grow and protect herself—"

*Observe. Only.*

A chill had needled Zak's neck, like a cold draft passed through their bond.

"Cerevita's grace," Zak had groaned.

He left his room and descended the spiral staircase at the end of the hall, exited the Dormitory, and hastened toward the castle vestibule.

Sorwin ran a hand through his unkempt hair and tugged at the ends of his rumpled periwinkle tunic. As Kaleb watched his nervous movements, a small dimple appeared on the man's right cheek.

"Oh, Baltenebris blast you," Sorwin cursed. He paced the other way, toward the vestibule entrance.

Somehow, Kaleb enjoyed his anxious tics. "They're endearing," he had said a few days prior. "And I like that I can observe exactly what you're feeling."

"That makes one of us." Sorwin was no stranger to withholding emotions. He had literal lessons on the art of stoicism as a young royal, as keeping a reaction within an appropriate and previously established framework during a state dinner could be the difference between peace and war. Or so his parents, ambassadors, and tutors had informed him.

But they were all gone, and when Sorwin was with Kaleb, something changed. At first he thought he was being disarmed, stripped of his control in the face of the soldier's overwhelming charm. Yet the more time they had spent together, the more Sorwin realized it was the opposite. Kaleb empowered him to be his true self. His unequivocal acceptance of all Sorwin's characteristics—the admirable, the faulty, the anxious—let him be more himself than he'd ever been.

"Perfect and terrifying," Sorwin mumbled.

"Pardon?" Shira asked with a smug grin.

"Nothing." His eyes narrowed. "What did you See?"

She laid a hand on his elbow and guided him a step to the left. A moment later, a pigeon swooped into the vestibule and left droppings where he had stood a moment before.

"Thank you," Sorwin said. He blasted the white substance with a stream of water, diluting it into the stone entryway. Once the grey and blue floor shone in the glow cast from magelight sconces hanging from the walls, Zak and Olivia arrived.

"What happened with Limba Dar? What did you learn?" Zak asked immediately.

Sorwin smirked. Zak's eagerness—while challenging—was one of his best qualities.

"Unfortunately, not much." His smile faded, sombered into disappointment. "As Kaleb told us, Limba Dar isn't coherent. In fact, he only uttered one name over and over during the entire interview."

"What name?" Olivia asked.

"Fanum Ket."

Zak's head tilted. "The Eelikuh? Why him?"

"He's leading the rebellion against the Woolbins," Kaleb said, resting a hand on the pommel of the sword strapped to his belt. "He announced himself as the head of the Disciples. There's no question now that Limba Dar had worked for Fanum Ket."

"And there's something magical about Limba Dar's condition." Bazil tied his thick braids back with a leather strap. "I couldn't identify the source, but it is a powerful binding—not unlike the one that holds Karazul."

"A *senligo*? Couldn't we undo it and have a proper conversation with him?" Olivia asked.

Bazil shook his head. "Doubtful. Archlumen Sashina examined him herself. She even opened the fifth gate—the Gate of Throne—to attempt extracting information from Limba Dar's mind, but the *senligo* threatened to overtake her too."

A heavy air settled over the group, and Sorwin couldn't afford to let it linger. "It isn't ideal. We all hoped to garner a deeper understanding of the Disciples and Malu from Limba Dar, but we must press on with what we have in hand. Finding Malu is still our best option. If we fail, a second path may be through Fanum Ket."

"He's technically our enemy right now, isn't he?" Zak adjusted the satchel on his back, and a flash of bronze glinted between the thick pieces of leather.

"Indeed. Which is why we're not starting with him." Sorwin didn't like the idea of approaching the Eelikuh at all. He led Aghoomi's mages for a reason, and Sorwin didn't want to test their collective might against him if possible.

Kaleb stepped through the wide vestibule entryway and squinted at the sky. "We should get moving. There aren't many hours of daylight left."

Sorwin led the hastily formed squad out of the Center and toward the entrance portal. He silently thanked Queen Alessa—his sister (why was it so difficult to think of her as such?)—for handling the council. He had explained the plan in a slapdash Firepost and didn't wait for a response, though an apple appeared in his study not ten minutes later. He ran a thumb over the shiny red skin, nostalgia washing over him. As children, each of them had used one of the symbols from the Darlangson family seal to exchange secret messages.

Henry—as the future king—had been the rose. He had always loved fiercely.

Alessa, by far the wisest of the three, assumed the apple.

And Sorwin, whose magic let him soar, became the hawk.

Croi had squawked from her perch in the corner, buried her beak in her side, and reemerged clutching a single feather.

Without a word, Sorwin had taken the feather from his familiar and bowed to her. Orange light covered the feather, and in a flash it disappeared. He had hoped it would bring a smile to Alessa.

Nearing the entrance portal, Sorwin let the memories fade and addressed the group. "You've all been briefed on Masdaan's tense climate. It's the last hold loyal to the Woolbins, and while battle hasn't broken out yet, there have been several reported skirmishes at the edges of the city. We're searching for Malu, and Aghoomi's civil war will make it all the more difficult. Stay alert. Don't overreact to any threats. We do not want to be the ones to light the fire."

Taking nods and murmurs from everyone as signs of comprehension, Sorwin turned to the entrance portal. It was the one place in Tor'alan that the Archs and council agreed to allow portals to be opened after Kalbick stole the Contract and escaped through one. Hand-selected mages and soldiers constantly guarded the raised dais, too. They parted when Sorwin and the others approached.

With a gesture—and no small amount of magic—a tall blue door appeared. It shimmered and rotated slowly, like a very calm whirlpool had been strung in the air. One by one, each of them went through the portal. Kaleb first, followed by Shira and Bazil. Then Olivia, and finally Zak.

"No rest for the brilliant." Sorwin plunged in after them.

Exiting the portal, Zak stumbled into a narrow alleyway and bumped into Olivia.

"Sorry!" He instinctively caught her shoulders to prevent them both from toppling over. She turned and their momentum carried them into a wall. One of Zak's hands shot out to stop himself from crushing Olivia, and their faces hovered an inch apart. The cold clay wall pressing against his palm drew a sharp contrast to the heat coursing through his body as their eyes met and held each other's gaze.

Olivia froze beneath him for a moment. But then she blinked and shoved him in the chest. "Watch it," she said quietly, absent her usual conviction.

"Yes, *Nacusti*," he said with a wry smile.

Olivia rolled her eyes, then glanced at his arm. "Is the wound still bothering you?"

Zak reached for the bandage on his arm without thinking. "It doesn't hurt most of the time. Just itches." Besides refusing to close, there hadn't been any other negative effects with the wound, which seemed minimal considering Zandorn had given it to Zak.

Olivia nodded and adjusted the collar of her uniform.

"Is it different with Euphemius? Now that you're, you know…"

"A *Nacusti*?" She shook her head. "It's better and worse. He makes me follow him more often, showing me off like a prized pet every chance he gets. He detests me being away from Tor'alan without him, but when Sorwin requests my help for assignments like this, Euphemius can't say no. It wouldn't bode well for his reputation if he withheld a *Nacusti* from serving the League of Kingdoms."

"Then let's make the most of your reprieve," Zak said with a smirk. He had the sense that a deeper sadness clung to Olivia about her forced employment, but he didn't want to pry. Besides, he had his own guilt to stomach about leaving her alone with Euphemius.

"You all know what to do." Sorwin's voice brought Zak's attention back to the task at hand as the rest of the group gathered.

Croi appeared on Sorwin's outstretched arm and vaulted into the air with the beat of silent wings. Further down the shadowy alley, Shira summoned Ubba. The ratlike imp with leathery wings and a bulbous nose sneezed seven times before dropping to the ground and sniffing wildly.

"Your turn," Zak said to Jolsu.

The dragon's magic covered his eyes. All of Zak's friends—except for Kaleb—blazed a bright gold in his vision, alight with magic. He turned away from them and headed toward the narrow mouth of the alley, which opened onto a quiet street.

Except, it shouldn't have been quiet. It was the main road leading from the city gates to the Kapana. When Zak visited Masdaan before with Euphemius and Olivia, it had been so crowded with people that he had barely been able to see any of the buildings around him.

Now it was empty.

Peering around the corner, he spotted the upper half of the Kapana. A golden glow covered the rotating glass panes of the pyramid. The magic blazed so bright that Zak could barely look at it.

"*Pennilma.*" Wings with green scales appeared on his back. With a leap, he flew to a nearby rooftop and huddled close to the tiled ridge, scanning the city.

"There isn't much concentration of magic outside the

Kapana." He kept searching, hoping to see more flecks of gold, but none appeared.

*Then we know where we must go*, Jolsu said.

Zak floated back to the ground, wings fading. Croi and Ubba hadn't had luck in the search either, and Sorwin agreed with Jolsu's assessment. Carefully, the group moved through the mosaic streets toward the Kapana.

The market was subdued. An older woman with a woven basket shuffled away down one of the many disorganized avenues, and two children playing were hushed and scooted under a canvas tent. None of the bustle and excitement Zak remembered was present—barely a handful of stalls were open at all.

But there were plenty of guards, all dressed in Masdaan's beige uniforms and posted at every entrance and intersection. Their shoulders stiffened and fists twisted around saber pommels as Zak's group passed by.

Something didn't feel right. Besides the obvious tension of a city on the brink of battle, the guards' attention never wavered from Zak and his friends. A few even left their stations, drifting closer, stalking like predators with hungry eyes.

Three guards moved to block the path ahead through the market.

Sorwin halted and held up a hand. The rest of the group stopped as well. "Can we help you with something?"

One of the guards laughed, a mocking sound. "It's the other way 'round. You can help *us* with something."

"Of course, we're all on the same side here."

"Well see, that's the rub, isn't it?" The man paced around

them, and as Zak followed his circular path, more beige uniforms appeared from the market. "I'm not sure we are."

Zak glanced to the side, then behind. They were surrounded.

"Masdaan is still very much a part of the League, last I checked." Sorwin's arms fanned out low.

Zak recognized the defensive position—one they had practiced many times in his daily lessons. He subtly mirrored Sorwin and turned slowly in the opposite direction.

"The city belongs to the League for now," the guard conceded. Metal scraped as he drew his blade from its scabbard. "But *we* do not." A low murmur of chortles from the guards briefly livened the quiet market. It was not a happy sound.

"We'll give you one chance to surrender," the guard continued. "The Eelikuh would like to speak with you," he pointed the tip of his blade at Sorwin, "and the *Nacusti*. Both of them."

"They're well-informed," Shira quipped, drawing her iron staff across the front of her body.

Kaleb drew his shortsword and addressed the guard. "You won't separate us."

"We can take them," Olivia said.

"Avoiding that would be preferable," Sorwin reminded her.

The guards—all of them—took a step closer, shrinking the circle around them. "One chance. What'll it be?"

*Sharp and metallic,* Elpida said. *This is what it smells like, isn't it?*

*Yes, Little One. Battle is upon us. Remain hidden,* Jolsu

said.

"Looks like we're beyond avoiding, High Magus." Bazil's turquoise magic glowed around his fists.

"Zakolor?" Sorwin asked.

"I'm ready." Despite the tightness in his gut, he couldn't keep a smirk from his lips.

"Now!" Sorwin commanded.

"*Tegoperignis!*" Zak's emerald fire erupted around their group, covering them in a shield even Sorwin would struggle to break. It immediately caught several fireballs and two arrows that the guards had shot.

"Well done, you!" Shira shouted. Colorful streaks appeared at her fingertips as demons rushed from her *lapidaemas*.

Zak accepted the praise and held firm. His job was to protect his friends, and he took it seriously. The fire shield shimmered as it deflected weapons and magic. Sorwin and Olivia launched counterattacks of fire and water, careful not to damage the surrounding market. Kaleb and Bazil had darted outside the shield, each taking on a handful of guards.

He had witnessed Bazil's inhuman speed and strength in battle before—both had saved him in the struggle for the black caladrius. But Kaleb...Zak had only seen him fight against Karazul, and at that time, none of them had been a match for the assassin. Even in their countless hours of training, Kaleb always focused on Zak's needs and never demonstrated what he was truly capable of.

But now, Kaleb's blade sang as it arced through the air, ringing as it parried an axe before jutting the pommel into a guard's jaw. Then he ducked under another attack and spun on his knees before standing and defeating the next in a series of strikes.

Even Zak could tell Kaleb still held back, that he didn't draw blood with his sword and only rendered the guards unconscious. Despite that, Zak had never seen a more graceful fighter. The metal of his blade acted as another limb, completely synchronized with the rest of his body.

*I see why he's touted as the best swordsman in the League.*

*Parignis!* Jolsu roared.

Zak jumped and nearly dropped the shield. "What?!" He searched for a threat, but saw nothing.

*At your feet.*

Zak looked down.

Elpida stood there, hissing and scratching at the air, as if she would charge into the fray at any moment.

"You're not quite ready for that, Little One," Zak said. He picked her up with one hand and set her on his shoulder.

*I could be, if* he *would help me grow*, she spat.

"And *you* need to keep calm in the middle of a fight!" It felt odd scolding Jolsu, but it made Zak stand a little straighter.

*We'll see who is calm someday if you're lucky enough to have children, then unlucky enough to watch them be defenseless.*

"*Customateria.*" Zak conjured Jolsu, roughly the size of a cat. He was pleased with how solid and real the dragon's visage seemed. "There, now stop whining and let me focus."

Jolsu grumbled but said nothing, and a tiny pulse of

gratitude crossed their bond as he hovered near Elpida.

As it turned out, Zak's attention was no longer needed. The scuffle had been quickly resolved. Several guards sprawled unconscious or incapacitated. The ones that retained their wits either ran or tried to grab a comrade to hobble away with.

Zak lowered his arm and the fire shield disappeared. He stepped forward, approaching Kaleb as he held a blade at the lead guard's throat.

"P-please, I don't know anything!" he stammered.

Sorwin stood before him, arms crossed. "It seems you've found the rose's thorns."

A beat passed in silence. The guard looked confused, and Zak empathized.

"What?" the guard asked.

"Yes, what?" Bazil chimed in.

"You've found the rose's thorns," Sorwin repeated. He looked around at the group and was met with more confused expressions. Zak scratched the back of his head.

"Saying it again doesn't make it more clear." Shira wore a wicked grin.

"It's a common phrase!" Sorwin blushed, frantically searching his companions for support or recognition.

"I don't think it is." Kaleb spoke softly, still holding a sword at the guard's throat.

"Three Fires." Sorwin pinched the bridge of his nose.

"Whoa, language!" Bazil joked.

Zak couldn't help but laugh.

"What I *meant*," Sorwin glared at Bazil and Zak in turn

before turning back to the guard, "was that we wanted to resolve this peacefully, and you provoked us. So now we are due compensation."

"I don't have anything, just a few Bronze Marks on my belt. You can have them!" the guard said.

"No, that's not—"

"You're a prince, Sorwin, surely you don't need to extort this poor guard," Shira said.

"Quiet, you!" Sorwin pointed at her. "We're getting distracted again." He sighed, a heavy thing, and ran a hand through his hair. "Just tell us where the Eelikuh is. Despite your welcome, I fear we need to speak with him."

"He's in Haramil," the guard said shakily.

"Aghoomi's capital?"

"Yes. After Woolbin lost the siege and fled, the Eelikuh took up residence. But you won't get to him there. I heard his ancestors built that palace and he knows its secrets better than any false king."

"We'll see. Let him go." Sorwin nodded to Kaleb.

The guard rubbed a hand across his neck when Kaleb lowered his blade, but there wasn't a scratch on him. He wasted no time collecting his saber from the dirt and scurrying off into the warren of the Kapana.

"Was that wise? Won't he tell the Eelikuh we're coming?" Zak asked.

"He already knows." Sorwin stood still for a moment before collecting himself. "Right. I think the trail has gone cold here. Luckily, I've been to Haramil. Who's ready for their second portal of the day?"

Zak groaned, as did Bazil.

Olivia punched them both in the arms.

## CHAPTER 8

# HARAMIL

The portal opened into a sitting room on the second floor of Darlangson's embassy in Haramil. Olivia and Shira checked the halls of the stately townhouse, then peered through the windows overlooking the street. Kaleb and Bazil helped Sorwin to a tufted bench—whose sallow complexion worried Zak.

"I'm fine," Sorwin said, waving them all off. "Portals are...tiring. I just need a moment."

"We'll find answers here." Zak puffed his chest, hoping he sounded more confident than he felt. "Then you'll only need to open one more to take us home."

A weak smile accompanied Sorwin's nod. "There shouldn't be any guards in the embassy. Alessa withdrew them when the rebellion began."

"Not much movement on the streets." Olivia's nose pressed against a thick glass pane.

Zak undid the clasp on his satchel and checked on Elpida. The portal didn't seem to bother the little dragon in the slightest, but confinement did.

"Stop scratching at the leather," Zak pleaded. "You'll tear a hole in the side and everything will fall out—including you!"

*That's my intention.* Her tail flicked back and forth, knocking against a book and a spare tunic.

Well, at least she was honest.

While Sorwin recovered his strength, Shira sent Ubba to scout nearby. It turned out the embassy was only a few blocks from the palace. The imp led them from street to street, avoiding the few Disciples patrolling the city.

The palace loomed ahead. Curved plaster walls and domed turrets sparkled with mosaic tiles and inlaid ruby borders. Across a wide avenue, the group huddled beneath an awning at what appeared to be a cafe. Except there were boards nailed across the windows. In fact, now that Zak thought about it, hardly anyone walked the streets. Just like in Masdaan.

"Where is everyone?" he asked.

"Hiding." Kaleb's dark eyes flitted up and down the road, searching for threats. "Haramil hasn't been under Fanum Ket's control for long. The city is holding its breath until the rebellion is squashed or victorious."

"And for now, that's to our advantage," Sorwin said. He looked to Shira. "How should we get inside?"

Shira paused while her Sight sifted through a multitude of futures. "There's a weakness in one of the wards." She pointed to the right of the main gates. "A small pocket that can be ruptured."

Sorwin grasped Zak's shoulder. "Your talent with shields is needed again. If I isolate the imperfection in the ward, can you put up a shield to exploit it?"

"Of course, Magus."

It was happening. Zak had felt the change over the last few weeks, the shift from burdensome apprentice to capable *Nacusti*. He had more work to do—both him and Olivia—but Sorwin wouldn't ask for help unless he was sure Zak could handle it.

And handle it he would.

He followed Sorwin to the mud brick wall surrounding the palace. A small section of the brownish surface crumbled beneath Sorwin's hand, creating a ridged cavity. Stepping inside, an orange magelight appeared, and Zak saw a gleaming section of the barrier. It was difficult to focus on, like it preferred dancing right outside his periphery—just like the barrier protecting Tor'alan.

"Now comes the fun part." Sorwin smiled.

Zak smiled too, happy to see Sorwin's restored enthusiasm. But even in the orange glow he appeared too pale.

"Barriers are similar to shields, as you know. But whereas a shield relies on constant support from a mage, a barrier only needs occasional maintenance once affixed to a proper anchor."

"Magus, I'm not sure we have time for a lesson while infiltrating a palace holding a leader of a civil war."

"Quite right—I'll catch you up later, if everything goes well." His hands—glowing orange—floated over the barrier, never touching it. "On my word, make a shield—a small one, only big enough for us to walk through—inside the punctured barrier."

"You're sure this will work?" Zak trusted Sorwin implicitly, but with advanced magic, any number of things could go wrong.

"Oh yes. If we *did* have time for a lesson, you'd understand why barrier maintenance is so important." Sorwin's brow furrowed. "Ah! There it is. Ready?"

Green fire rolled across Zak's fingers. "Ready."

Lightning crackled, arcing from Sorwin's hand to a point on the barrier. It swirled into a circle no bigger than a fingernail, and Zak immediately cast his spell. "*Tegoperignis.*"

Green fire sprang toward the lightning and expanded until the hole in the barrier was nearly the size of a door.

"Well done, Zak. Hold it there." Sorwin crept to the opening of the cavity and beckoned the rest of the group in. One at a time, they sidled by as Zak diligently held the barrier back with his shield. It wavered only once when Olivia inched by and the faint scent of wildflowers permeated the air.

She glared at him.

"Sorry," he whispered. He hoped the darkness of the tunnel hid his reddened cheeks.

When everyone had passed through, Zak did as well, and the green fire and lightning faded as the barrier melded back into its original shape.

Inside, the makeshift tunnel opened into a courtyard which didn't look anything like the rest of Haramil. The city, wedged between riverbanks and a desert, had sparse vegetation. But the courtyard had sculpted topiaries, bursts of vibrant flowers, and carved fountains gurgling with water. It reminded Zak more of Regadensia than Aghoomi, and perhaps that was the point. The Woolbins had lived here for centuries—they must have spared no expense transforming the palace into an oasis.

Croi circled overhead, powerful wings tilting to catch currents to keep aloft.

Sorwin squinted up at his familiar. "There's one patrol covering the entire inner wall. Croi puts them on the opposite side of the palace from us. Another stroke of luck." He didn't sound happy about it though.

"Something wrong?" Bazil asked.

"It's too easy." Kaleb tightened the lace on one of his bracers. "We're a breath away from the leader of the Disciples and haven't had a single scuffle."

"You think it's a trap?" Shira held her *lapidaemas* in a white-knuckle grip.

"Potentially. With your Sight, you'd be the first to know." Sorwin scratched at his chin. "What would Fanum Ket gain from capturing us? Tor'alan and the League haven't interfered with Aghoomi's war. We've only fought one another when they've stood by the Consortium."

"Maybe that's enough for Ket to deem us enemies," Olivia said.

"Perhaps. But he's strategic. He would have heard about our run-in with the guards in Masdaan. If he wanted to keep us out, this place would be crawling with Disciples. It's more likely that he wants us to come to him, but going in without knowing why puts us at a disadvantage."

Zak adjusted the satchel strap on his shoulder and ignored Elpida's hissing. "Even if it is a trap, we can't turn back now. We don't have any other leads on Malu."

"Unfortunately, you're right." Sorwin sighed, a rough and rattled sound. "Let's get on with it, then. Bazil, do what you can to deflect light from us. Shira, bend the shadows to obscure. I think Caligo may serve you well in this moment."

"One step ahead of you," Shira said. A tiny white smoke cloud floated above her shoulder before she disappeared completely.

*That invisibility demon is terrifying*, Zak thought.

*Then be happy they're on our side*, Jolsu said.

Swift and nearly silent, the group scuttled through Haramil's palace. Shira, unseen, slunk a few steps ahead and whispered when each hall was clear. Bazil's magic created a strange warping in the air around them, which Zak understood would make it difficult to spot them from afar.

There weren't many guards inside the building, and the certainty that they crept right into a trap grew within his gut. But they didn't have a choice—Fanum Ket was the last lead they had in tracking Malu.

Ubba flitted down the hall toward them, sneezing wildly as he bobbed in the air. He landed on Sorwin's shoulder, presumably because he couldn't see Shira's invisible one.

"Ubba says there's a very strong essence in a chamber down the hall to the left." Shira cooed at the little imp, praising his scouting.

"That must be Fanum Ket." Sorwin quickly doled out instructions, planning for the probable ambush that awaited them. He conjured Zak's staff and passed it to him.

Zak squeezed it in his sweaty palms. He wanted to conjure Jolsu, to feel the protection of the dragon beside him. But Fanum Ket would undoubtedly see that as a threat and would all but ensure a fight.

*I'm right here with you, whether you see me or not.*

*Thank you, Jolsu.* It was enough. It had to be for now.

Ubba led them up a steep set of stairs. At the top, three decorative archways draped with sheer fabrics ushered them into a chamber which turned out to be a throne room. Sorwin and Kaleb walked slowly in front, followed closely by Zak and Olivia, with Bazil in the rear. Shira—still invisible—was somewhere in the room.

At first, Zak thought the room was empty, but a shift ahead caught his eye, and he couldn't mistake the man that stood before them.

Fanum Ket.

"Eelikuh." Sorwin bowed. Zak and the others awkwardly followed his example.

"High Magus." Fanum Ket was exactly as Zak remembered—tall and powerful—like a mountain. A feature of the landscape, protruding from the earth. Yet his movements were fluid and dangerous as a shark darting through open water.

"I have reason to believe you were expecting us."

One corner of Fanum Ket's lips ticked up. "Some of you. I didn't prepare for so many...guests."

"Yet you seem unbothered all the same." Sorwin stood perfectly still, and Zak admired his composure. "Why are we here?"

"Isn't it you that should tell me? You let yourselves into

my home, after all." Fanum Ket's boots echoed on the tile floor as he crossed in front of the ornate throne.

Zak studied the room, searching for any hint of hidden mages or traps. From their first meeting, Sorwin had impressed upon him the importance of remaining alert, to observe his surroundings. But he didn't see anything obvious and sensed no other magic. Fanum Ket seemed well and truly alone.

That made Zak's stomach twist into a tighter knot.

"Limba Dar is in our care, and he had little to say besides your name," Sorwin said.

Fanum Ket clasped hands behind his back. "A necessary safeguard. I had a feeling Limba Dar didn't have the constitution for revolution, despite his blood. A pity."

"His blood?" Zak gulped. Sorwin had asked them all to let him lead the discussion, but the question slipped out unbidden.

"Ah, *Nacusti*. We meet again." Fanum Ket's narrowed gaze made Zak want to squirm, but he fought the urge. "I'm surprised you seem unaware of Limba Dar's noble lineage."

That drew a gasp from Zak. "Limba Dar is a *noble*?"

"A descendant of Aghoomian nobility. That's why his name holds the divine sequence."

"What?"

Sorwin explained. "Aghoomi was always a spiritual nation, worship of the gods woven deep into their culture and government. Each noble family took two names that followed the divine sequence: one with five letters, and one with three."

"Why five and three?"

"Five represents the divine, and three for the Three Fires."

"Why is five significant for the gods?"

"Well—I—because—" Sorwin blinked, and for the first time since entering the chamber, he seemed unsettled. "I can't remember."

Even Bazil, the most devout of their group, appeared puzzled. He shrugged when Zak appealed to him silently.

Zak looked at Fanum Ket, whose wolfish grin prickled the back of his neck. "Then you're a noble too. Your name has the same sequence."

"Descended from kings—though we didn't call them that. My ancestors ruled Aghoomi, and much has been forgotten over the centuries. That is why I am reclaiming Aghoomi, to restore what has been lost."

Sorwin found his voice again. "We're not here to interfere in your revolution. Our war is with Zandorn. All we seek is information."

Fanum Ket did something that Zak never imagined the serious man would.

He laughed.

"Oh, Sorwin—I applaud your boldness. You sneak into *my* palace, which I liberated from Woolbin, who is *your* ally in the League, and you tell me you're here simply to *talk*? Why in the name of the gods should I believe you aren't here to capture or kill me?"

"Because while I can't condone bloodshed, what you're doing isn't fundamentally wrong. The Woolbins invaded Aghoomi and took your home. That never should have been allowed to stand. We're here because you may be the only person who can help us find Malu."

Confusion painted Fanum Ket's face. "You seek a trickster god? Have you forgotten about the Contract?"

"I think you know well enough that it didn't expel every god from Valecium."

"You believe those unsubstantiated whispers perpetuated by my Disciples?" Fanum Ket considered each of them individually. "You're even more desperate to stop Zandorn than I realized."

"They're not rumors. We met him." Olivia stepped forward as she spoke. "Zak and I both did."

"Ah, the new *Nacusti*. You're rather interesting. I was surprised to hear Temaway was still alive."

"You say that like you knew him," Sorwin observed.

A deafening silence sucked the air from the throne room. Fanum Ket blinked several times, then did another thing Zak thought impossible for the Eelikuh.

He rolled his eyes.

"This game grows tiresome," Fanum Ket said. With a gesture, his figure blurred behind a wall of mist. When it cleared, it was no longer Fanum Ket that stood before them.

It was Malu.

Zak and his friends all jumped backward.

"Surprised?" Malu cackled and paced before the throne. "I can't *believe* I gave it away with such a silly little thing. Blasted Temaway—Cerevita's pet—always was a bur in the wine."

"You—" Zak's eyes widened, his pulse pounded in his

chest and ears. "It was you, you were the Eelikuh the whole time?"

"Oh no, that would be ridiculous. I've only been the Eelikuh for a few weeks. I took over when his *revolution* wasn't quite revolting enough."

Malu waved a hand, and the real Fanum Ket appeared in the throne, hands bound and mouth gagged. He looked unharmed, but immediately shook and squirmed and tried to yell, but all Zak could hear were muffled groans.

"None of that now." With another gesture from Malu, Fanum Ket disappeared. "Don't worry about the dear Eelikuh. He'll be happy as a pipit once the war is over and Aghoomi is his. Quite the compensation for a few weeks of captivity, wouldn't you agree?"

Zak didn't know what to think—it was difficult enough keeping up with the revelations let alone process them. Luckily Sorwin's brilliant mind was already at work.

"You didn't bring us here to reveal your identity, did you?" Sorwin stated more than asked.

Malu grinned. It looked hungrier than when he wore Fanum Ket's face. "Correct, High Magus. You really are a sharp mortal. Ah, the fun we'd have, if only we had the time." He sighed and draped an arm against the back of the throne.

"Why are we here?" Sorwin repeated his question from the beginning of the conversation.

"Why indeed? Well, I can answer much more clearly now. I was one of Aghoomi's patron deities. Never as powerful as Azubelux or Baltenebris or Cerevita, but I had a place here. A home. I want it back." His tone sharpened, and Zak witnessed the double-sided nature of the trickster. He was so different from when they met in Zindost, his pet and familiar shop. There, he had been playing a role—even when he revealed to be much more than a humble shopkeeper. This fiery, terrifying creature who went from laughing to threatening in a moment was the real Malu.

"So you're conquering Aghoomi, but you said you would give it to Fanum Ket. What do you get out of it?"

"What all gods want: to be worshipped. It makes us stronger, more...permanent." Malu's fingers danced along folds of fabric hanging from archways as he carefully walked about the room. "Once Aghoomi is under Fanum Ket's leadership, the Disciples will have a home, and this country will reclaim its status as the most devout in all Valecium. And who will they have to thank? Why, me! And shouldn't they *give* thanks, say, in the form of prayer?"

"That doesn't explain what you want with us." Zak gripped his staff, keenly aware of the futility of the wooden weapon against a god.

"Ah, but it does! The *Nacusti* were created to be a bridge between the divine and mortals. Your predecessors were strong enough to defeat the most powerful gods. I'd rather take a diplomatic approach. What will you do, *Nacusti*, if I restore Aghoomi and reveal my presence to Valecium? Will you allow me a happy existence, or threaten to subject me to the Contract?"

Zak and Olivia shared a look, and he was relieved to see his untethered confusion mirrored in her wild eyes. At least he wasn't alone in feeling out of his depth.

"We couldn't say now," Zak offered. "W-we'd have to talk about it, ask the leaders of the other nations—"

"Oh, how disappointing." Malu frowned, an exaggerated curl to his lips. He had circled part of the room, standing off to the left near a door. Quick as lightning, his hand grasped at the air. Shira appeared, Malu gripping tight around her throat.

Kaleb's sword was drawn before Zak could even move.

"Careful, little soldier." Malu lifted Shira off the ground, and she gasped and scratched at the god's arm.

A moment later, green fire swirled around Shira. Zak focused with all his might on protecting his friend, his Sight mentor. The flames surrounded her in a perfect sphere, and Malu snarled and dropped her, clutching his burnt arm.

Bazil ran to Shira's side, passing through the shield unscathed.

"Crafty little *Nacusti*," Malu spat.

"You won't harm any of us," Zak said. Fire danced around his fists.

"This is why I wanted to take the diplomatic route. I find violence so *boring*. There's no nuance, no tact. It's just brute strength and flexing power. That didn't save my fellow gods from the Contract, did it? No, only trickery—intellect—spared me their fate."

"That's why we're here, Malu." Sorwin held his palms up, showing he posed no threat. "We spoke with Cerevita and Jolsu and Vess—none of them can remember the details of how they won the Guardian War, and who exactly helped. You're the only living being in Valecium that was involved in the war and didn't sign the Contract. We were hoping you could fill in the gaps for us."

Malu shook his arm, and the burns from Zak's fire faded. "I may be crafty, but you underestimate Baltenebris's cleverness."

"What do you mean?"

"You can't outrun a shadow." The god slouched into the throne, one leg over an arm. He conjured a bowl of sandberries and popped a handful into his mouth. "Baltenebris and Azubelux were rivals for eons. Such is the nature of shadow and light. But they were on the same side in the war—both fought for forced devotion.

"But the *Nacusti* were powerful and had recruited gods to their side too. When the tide in the war turned and Azubelux's conviction wavered, Baltenebris knew he would lose. That was why he wrote the Contract."

"Baltenebris wrote the contract? Why?" It didn't make sense to Zak that a god bent on dominating all mortals would ban himself from Valecium. He'd always been taught that the *Nacusti* had forced the gods to sign the document.

"He didn't have a choice. He was out of moves to make, and conceding to a treaty ensured he got *something* out of the war. And believe me—he did. Baltenebris had very strict requirements during negotiations."

"What were they?" Sorwin asked.

Malu shrugged. "Couldn't tell you."

"Weren't you there?"

"Of course, but I don't remember."

*Not again*, Zak thought. "How can you not remember

something so pivotal to your own fate?"

Malu chewed on another sandberry. "Not fate—existence. Why don't you read the Contract? It's all written down."

Sorwin grimaced. "We don't have it, Zandorn stole it."

"Well, that's a pity."

"A pity?" Zak's anger roiled. "We might be at the beginning of another war with the gods, and all you have to say is 'that's a pity'? Don't you care at all?"

Malu smirked, and Zak wanted to punch him. "I care about many things, just not the same things as you."

"You care about Aghoomi, and your creatures—if that shop wasn't a total lie."

"Correct, and it wasn't. I *did* point you toward the black caladrius, if you recall."

Zak didn't want to give him any credit for that just now. "If Zandorn destroys the Contract, Baltenebris and the other gods will return and start another war. What will happen to your precious creatures and Aghoomi then?"

"We're at war *now*, little *Nacusti*. We will carry on as we always have."

"Agh!" Zak threw his hands in the air and turned to Sorwin. "We're getting nowhere. Even if he didn't sign the Contract, Malu doesn't know anything. Let's leave while we can and come up with a new plan."

Sorwin agreed. "We've run this trail cold. Let's return to Tor'alan and reconvene."

"If you're out of clues, perhaps I could help." Malu's leg swung off the throne's armrest.

"In exchange for what?" Sorwin rested a hand on Zak's shoulder and pulled him closer.

Malu scoffed. "Oh nothing so dramatic. Only your...discretion. I plan to reveal my identity when the time comes, but not yet. If you keep my secret, I will share something to help your cause."

"Give us a moment." Sorwin gathered the group—Bazil had healed Shira, though the skin on her throat was bruised. Kaleb and Olivia both twitched with battle energy. Zak moved between them and squeezed both of their shoulders.

"What do we think?" Sorwin asked.

Kaleb shook his head. "I don't like it."

"Have we a choice?" Bazil wondered aloud. "We don't have any other options for finding out what happened in the Guardian War."

"Making a deal with a trickster isn't a choice I'd like to make again." Olivia crossed her arms.

Zak sighed. "Last time, his help *did* lead us to the black caladrius, or at least figuring out the bird was in my dreams. The cost seems clear this time: we keep his identity secret. The only question is if the information is valuable or not."

The group fidgeted, clearly uncomfortable with trusting Malu. Shira didn't speak, but nodded when Sorwin asked for her opinion.

"Fine." Sorwin stood before Malu, who still reclined in the throne. "We'll keep your secret *if* this information guides us to what we seek."

"Hmm. Such a clever little mage. I hope you survive this war—I'd like to play with you again." Malu eyed Sorwin up and down before smiling and leaning forward. "We have a deal." The god extended a hand, and Sorwin took it in a firm handshake.

"Now," Malu said, "if you haven't figured it out yet, there were powerful memory charms embedded into the Contract. It affected even those that didn't sign the document. A rather brilliant and annoying idea Baltenebris had. However, memories can be hidden and obscured, but never truly erased. You simply need to go where they were made to *revisit* the past."

"Speak plainly, trickster," Sorwin barked.

"The altars." Malu grinned and looked directly at Zak and Olivia. "Have you tried visiting your Guardian altars?"

Zak frowned. "Isn't that where the Guardians lived? Why would we need to?"

"Oh, a great many things happened there. Ask your dragon."

*He's right,* Jolsu said. Zak felt his words project to everyone nearby. *We became Guardians at the altars, and mortals sought our help there.*

"Where is your altar, Vess?" Olivia asked.

The phoenix's lilting voice carried into Zak's thoughts. *In Nalawin, northeast of the Eyewood.*

"Breaching the elven border a second time would not be wise," Kaleb said.

"Indeed. What about Jolsu's altar?" Sorwin asked.

Zak blushed, embarrassed he didn't already know the location of his dragon's altar.

*Do not fret Parignis, you've already been to my altar,* he said privately to Zak before addressing the group. *It is west of*

*Densba, in the Southern Isles.*

Zak gasped.

Sorwin's hands rested on his hips. "Well, that's an easy decision. Once we exit the palace barrier I can portal us right to Densba. And I should think your parents will be happy to see you, Zakolor."

Home.

Zak was going home.

# CHAPTER 9

# THE PAST

Karazul wandered down an old road. The wheel-worn path was overgrown with thick grass. He leaped over a hedgeline and barely made a sound on the leaf-covered forest floor. Ducking between two trees that curled together, he found a modest camp with a firepit, canvas tent, bedroll, and axe.

*My camp.* He almost remembered it, the smell of the dry wood burning, the nearby warren of rabbits he hunted, the cluster of pemberry bushes he harvested. He had spent time there, though how much he couldn't recall. Only, something was there that shouldn't have been.

A mage stood at the corner of the tent, hands clasped at his waist, waiting.

"Who are you?" Karazul asked. Even as he did, he felt odd. He knew the man, didn't he?

"I am Zandorn," he said. "A mage with an offer."

"An offer of what?" Karazul kept his distance, circling to stand near the axe which leaned against an old pine tree.

"You seek someone—your brother." Zandorn held up

a hand when Karazul tensed. "Be still, I do not have him. However, I may be able to help you find him."

"What will it cost?" Nothing was ever free.

Zandorn smiled, but it wasn't a natural thing. It was forced and jagged. "You have a unique set of skills that would help my cause. If you enter my employ for a time, I'll share what information I collect on your brother."

A parchment appeared on a stump at Karazul's feet. He picked it up, but the inked text blurred when he tried to read it.

*What is this memory?*

"This is a contract," Karazul heard himself say.

"A precaution. I would be remiss not to protect myself."

*This isn't right.* Karazul had met Zandorn in a tavern for the first time. Somewhere in Evartia after assassinating a merchant guild leader. That had been well before the revolution, before Ymona and her brother were deposed. Unless...

Karazul turned, and the forest camp melted away.

*Where am I now?*

Lindomer. He knew the port city well. The salted breeze, the strong fish odor wafting from the docks. He hastened down an alley between lopsided buildings, up a creaking stairwell, and shut the door on a decrepit room. Everything was there that he needed: a bed, a single chair next to a small table with enough room for maps and a journal with scribbled notes.

Karazul crossed the room and picked up the journal, but again he couldn't read it. The text swirled as his eyes darted across the lines.

*What is this magic?*

Zandorn stepped from the shadows. Karazul felt him before he saw him.

"Who are you?" Karazul asked.

*I know him!* he screamed, but he couldn't hear himself.

"I am Zandorn," he said. "A mage with an offer."

Tansil stood over Karazul's bed. The assassin twitched and grimaced like he was having a bad dream.

"The *senligo* still holds, but is weakening," he said.

"I still cannot fortify the binding." Sashina stood behind the elf, dressed in pale pink robes.

"Better to let it expire so we may question him directly." Rinka ran a finger over the opal hanging from her neck, grey hair pulled into a taut bun. "I have a few demons that make excellent interrogators."

"Would they have any effect? With his anti-magic—"

Rinka waved off Sashina's hesitation. "He will wake eventually, and we cannot let him go. It's not as if he'll stay willingly."

"I need you both to watch over him while I am away." Tansil turned from the assassin to focus on his fellow mages.

Sashina frowned, something Tansil rarely saw on the Archlumen's face. "Away? To where?"

"I've been summoned home to Nalawin."

"Is leaving now wise? Especially to go there?" Even Rinka's iron facade broke into concern.

Tansil felt the pull now, how it had grown each day since receiving the seed. He couldn't resist much longer. Nalawin was a tree, and he but a branch. If the trunk swayed, he must follow.

"I do not have a choice, though you are right to be uncertain. I must admit, I do not know what will happen or how long I will be away. There haven't been many cases of banishment and summoning." None, in fact. But it wouldn't do any good to worry his fellow Archs any more than they already were.

Rinka and Sashina shared an uneasy look. They must have sensed the time for debate had passed, because they left the room and proceeded upstairs to the castle vestibule.

Tansil went with them. It was almost time for the council meeting, and several members loitered outside the room. He spotted Queen Alessa conferring with Euphemius and approached.

"Archmagus," Queen Alessa said with a nod.

Euphemius barely spared Tansil a glance as he continued a verbal flood directed toward the queen. "—and you know the trickiest part of the accession process is finding a Regadensian noble with the proper pedigree not only to govern, but to establish a respectable lineage that will endure for centuries. We don't want another Fern situation on our hands within a generation or two. What would it all have been for, in that case?"

"Am I interrupting?" Tansil asked.

"Yes," Euphemius spat.

A polite curve tilted the queen's lips, though Tansil

didn't quite consider it a smile. "Mr. Van Ilia was regaling me with the tribulations of Regadensia's succession."

Euphemius twisted one end of his bushy mustache. "It's actually *accession*, Your Majesty. And there are so many titles to distribute. The Fern's duchy is one of the largest, of course, and managed mostly by stewards. But we can't simply elevate a person into nobility because they happened to be in the right place at the right time. No, that wouldn't do at all!"

"I haven't seen you this excited in a number of years, Euphemius." Tansil stared intently at the short merchant.

"Why, it's quite a thrill to serve Regadensia and its people during such a trying time. Do you know there are three counties within Fern's duchy, and former High King Marius—may he rest in peace—held all of them? That means we need *three* new counts. And I haven't even begun on all the cities that need barons."

"I harbor no doubts you'll choose someone *appropriate* for each noble seat." Tansil was admittedly pleased with himself for throwing Euphemius's favorite word back at him, and for the minor gasp and look of disdain it elicited. In all the years he'd known the foul little man, he never once verbally crossed him. Sorwin usually had that well in-hand.

But Tansil wasn't the same elf he had been. Not since spending time with Temaway. The ancient *Nacusti* was the first elf he had seen in centuries, and witnessing his isolation in his grove, and then his death, changed Tansil. It loosened something, began new growth on a branch he thought well and truly matured.

In truth, Tansil didn't mock Euphemius for petty reasons. He simply needed the merchant to shut up.

"Your Majesty, if I may have a moment of your time, there's something we need to discuss," he said to Queen Alessa.

"By all means." She led Tansil down the hall to her chambers at a brisk pace, apparently eager to leave the stunned Euphemius behind before he recovered. Two guards stood at attention at the office door, donning the Brenstel red and gold livery. Once inside, Queen Alessa gestured to the only armchair not burdened with towering stacks of parchment and ledgers.

Tansil took the seat, not wanting to offend by refusing. Though he didn't know Queen Alessa well, she didn't seem that sort. Still, he needed something from her. Better to placate.

"Please excuse the mess, Archmagus. This new position comes with history I am woefully unaware of, as I was fortunate enough to have Sorwin manage Darlangson's relationship with the League." She stood by the hearth, warming her hands by the crackling fire.

"I will pay it no mind, Your Majesty. In fact, it's a happy sign that you have assumed the responsibilities with such ardor. The League needs strong leadership now more than ever."

Queen Alessa nodded, her ruby tiara glinting in the warm light. "Council meetings thus far have been...revealing."

"And not half as caustic as usual. Your mere presence is a balm."

Quiet held between them, thick as stone. "You're not

how Sorwin described you in his Fireposts."

Curiosity got the better of Tansil. "Where do I deviate from your expectations?"

The queen smoothed nonexistent wrinkles from her dress—a pale taupe with curling golden vines. "Aloof was a word often used, perhaps distracted. Brilliant, always," she rushed to say, "but I always had the sense that Sorwin struggled to connect with you." Her eyes landed directly on his as she finished.

*How cunning.* It was obvious she wanted to see how he reacted to a subtle jab, but Tansil had a feeling it had less to do with him and more to do with her brother. "I cannot speak for Sorwin, though I cautioned him at the beginning of his tutelage that my kind do not relate in the same way humans do."

"Yet here you are, quite engaged and outspoken. Direct, one would say, from the exchange you had moments ago with Euphemius."

"I've changed recently."

Fire danced in the queen's eyes. "And what sparked that change for an elf nearing a millenia in age?"

Tansil paused, wondering how the conversation had turned so drastically away from his original intentions. He sighed and looked at the queen. "I may not be what you expected, but you're every bit as Sorwin described."

"Dare I ask what words he used?"

"Clever. Regal. Tenacious. All admirable in a more than capable monarch."

A genuine smirk graced the queen's lips before fading.

"I'm happy we met after all these years, Archmagus. Thank you for your candor, and for all you have done for my brother."

"I did little but provide opportunity. Sorwin seized his apprenticeship with an enthusiasm I've yet to see rivaled."

"Now *that* sounds exactly like him." She laughed, a delicate sound like windchimes. "But you haven't answered my question, Archmagus. What stirred you?"

*Clever indeed.* "An amalgamation of things, but most recently, this." He pulled the star leaf seed from his pocket. The bright green glow pulsed as Queen Alessa stepped closer, inspecting the object as Tansil explained what it meant.

"You wish to go to Nalawin now? Yet you mentioned how important strong leadership is to the League." Queen Alessa stood unmoving before him.

"I don't have a choice. This seed needs to be planted, and it will only flourish in Nalawin. The pull—it isn't just emotional, it is magical. The star leaf is tied to my people's longevity, and it is a summons I cannot refuse." Tansil didn't care if he pleaded. His words were honest—he had to go to Nalawin, even if he didn't want to.

The queen circled the room exactly once before stopping by the hearth again. "Very well. I will not stand between you and your people. We—humans—owe you more than we can repay, and maybe this will be a small contribution toward that debt."

"Thank you, Your Majesty." Tansil stood and bowed. "I have every confidence that Sorwin will manage in my stead. He's every bit as capable—and twice as curious."

A flicker of pride tipped the queen's chin up. "Go in peace, Archmagus. We look forward to your swift return."

On the way to his office, Tansil chanced upon Inguma wrangling two young acolytes—each by an ear. He pitied them, but then again, the white castle wall had clearly been defaced with a crude representation of a group of people dancing naked upon a table.

"Is that supposed to be me?" Tansil inspected a lean figure near the center with long brown hair. He shrugged. "Not terrible work, but the eyes are all wrong."

Inguma gaped right along with the acolytes at Tansil's assessment, her tall lavender hair making the expression appear even more wild. She recovered in a flash, whereas the young mages did not. "I believe it is supposed to be the council, Archmagus. I'll have it removed immediately after dealing with these two." She twisted the ears in her hands and the acolytes yelped.

"Thank you, Inguma. And while I have you, I'd ask one more thing."

When he spoke to Queen Alessa about Sorwin's capability, he had been completely honest. Perhaps even underestimating his former apprentice. Sorwin was every bit his equal in magic, and far surpassed him as a leader. Tansil had long considered stepping down as Archmagus to pass the title on, but Sorwin had vehemently refused any conversation on the subject.

"As you know, I am departing for a time. Sorwin will handle day-to-day functions of the Archmagus while I am away, but he recently recused himself from council meetings.

I would ask you to be the Elemental House representative in the meetings and report to Sorwin—as a kindness to both of us."

Inguma didn't hesitate for a second. "Of course, Archmagus. I am honored to help however I may."

With that handled, there was really only one more thing to take care of before departing.

Tansil ascended to his spire-top office and settled at his wide desk with a parchment and quill. He stared at the blank page for untold minutes. But, finding a sprig of courage, the words flowed once ink met parchment.

He wrote to Sorwin, explaining as much as he could of the situation. He apologized for his behavior leading up to today—the summons from the elves had pushed him into a deep state of contemplation at the most inopportune time. He thanked Sorwin for leading when he could not, for protecting Zak and Olivia when all Tansil could do was wander aimlessly about the Center. He was ashamed, and that made it much easier to accept the summons. In truth, it was difficult to distinguish if he ran toward the elves or away from the League.

When he finished the letter—confession—he sealed the parchment and muttered the charm to send it blazing off out the window. He didn't know where Sorwin and the others were in their hunt for Malu, but the Firepost would find him anywhere in the world.

Tansil puttered around the office then, adjusting piles of reports on his desk and organizing leftover dishes from meals past on the side table. It was all nonsense. Procrastination.

Nothing stood between him and Nalawin but fear now.

And so, with a deep inhale, he departed his office and went to Tor'alan's entrance, determined to open a portal to Nalawin before he lost his nerve.

# Chapter 10
# Home

Zak recognized where the portal left them in an instant. They were at the edge of the woods near his home, where Kal had saved him from Burvenin. He stared across the clearing, sunset lighting the sky in a warm burst of red, and could almost see the dark mage carrying off his friend once again.

"It should have been me."

A hand squeezed his shoulder, and without turning he knew it belonged to Sorwin.

"We cannot change what was, but we can determine what will be."

Zak dragged the back of a hand across his eyes and glanced around the group, thankful for the friends he had made since leaving Densba. Each of them had given more than he could ever repay, but he would try nonetheless. He would keep going, keep fighting Zandorn and Renna and the Rot, and as he looked at each of their weary faces, he was certain of one thing.

*I am not alone.*

Jolsu rumbled, fierce happiness that his lesson had finally sunk into Zak's thick skull.

"Would you like to see your parents first?" Sorwin asked.

Zak shook his head, as much as it pained him. "After we find the altar. Once Mother sees me we won't escape any time soon."

Sorwin smiled at the assessment, but Zak could see how even that small effort taxed him. After opening three portals, it was a wonder he still stood. He didn't without help—Kaleb slung one of Sorwin's arms over his shoulder, supporting him as they trudged toward the coast.

Zak led them all—Olivia, Shira, Kaleb, Sorwin, Bazil, and Elpida tucked in his satchel—down a very familiar path, the one he and Kal had skipped and ran along countless times as children. Because Jolsu had been right, Zak knew exactly where his Guardian's altar was hidden.

He had never wondered why he had been drawn to the seaside cave. It seemed natural, the urge to explore the lair full of wonders. Kal had seemed equally as excited in their youth.

Listening to the waves crash into the beach, sudden understanding washed over Zak.

"This was where we first met," he said to Jolsu.

The dragon passed agreement over their bond. *You didn't know it at the time, but you stumbled your way into our inriloc.*

Zak remembered. Right after he'd fought Burvenin, after Olivia had been stabbed by Karazul, he thought he'd passed out. But when he had opened his eyes, he saw Jolsu's emerald scales for the first time.

As they entered the mouth of the jagged cave, white

sand gave way to packed dirt and rocks. Through centuries of neglect, a semblance of a wide path—big enough for a dragon—still cut down the middle of the lair. It abruptly ended, cut off by a sheer rock wall.

"It seems smaller than I remember," Zak said.

"Time changes most things, especially perspective," Kaleb said.

"That was quite profound." Sorwin blinked at the man holding him upright.

"Don't sound so surprised," he said with a wink.

"Anyway." Olivia frowned at the pair of them before examining the cavern. "Where is the altar? This seems like an outer chamber."

"*Customateria.*" A likeness of Jolsu appeared at Zak's feet. Elpida climbed down from her perch in the satchel, pawing at the green form of her father. Jolsu hissed and backed away.

"Jolsu?" Zak asked, drawing the dragon's attention back to the matter at hand.

His miniature form flew in the air, and Elpida growled, unable to follow. *This is not a wall, but a door.*

Zak eyed the huge mass of stone. Sorwin was exhausted, and Zak was confident he couldn't move the door alone.

"Give me a hand?" he asked Olivia.

"Only if you pull your weight."

Together, their magics poured over the stone. Zak felt a gap to the left, and Olivia must have too. They shared a quick nod and both pushed with all their might. The slab slowly shifted, sliding into the crevice like a pocket door.

A thick cloud of dust swirled around. With a gesture, Sorwin sent a gust of wind to clear it away. What remained was breathtaking.

Rays of light filtered through holes in the stone—some small, some big enough for a horse and wagon to pass through. The cylindrical room swirled upward and looked like a hollowed-out bees nest.

"The entire cliffside is the altar?" Bazil almost tripped up the incline as he moved to the middle of a sweeping platform.

*Before Nelvowig and I became Guardians, this was our jyrnen's roost. Our home.*

"There must have been hundreds of dragons here." Shira's voice rasped, still recovering from Malu's strangling.

*Thousands,* Jolsu said. Zak didn't miss the sadness in his tone.

Zak moved slow and careful. Despite its simplicity—austerity, even—a thick reverence covered the room. This was a place of importance, of history, of power. Its weight pressed against his skin as tiny motes danced in the sunbeams sneaking through the perforated walls.

"Gather around, everyone. Sorwin has an idea." Kaleb assembled them all in a line at the end of the central platform, holding hands. Jolsu landed on Zak's shoulder, and Elpida curled around his ankle.

"We can use a spell to revisit memories of the past here," Sorwin explained. "But I'm sure there are many in a place as ancient as this. Jolsu, can you think of any that would aid our cause?"

*I am not sure.* The dragon's tail flicked through the air.

*Perhaps we start at the beginning, when Nelvowig and I became Guardians. There was a ceremony here, and many gods and mortals attended. It wasn't long before the war began. Maybe we'll learn something of use.*

"Sounds a good place to start," Bazil said.

"In my weakened state, I'm afraid I won't be able to sustain the spell for long. We can try, but we may need to return tomorrow after some rest." Sorwin's face scrunched in frustration.

Zak, standing on his left, squeezed his hand. "We'll figure this out, together."

That brought his familiar smile out. "Right you are. Okay everyone, hold fast to one another. If you break away from me, the illusion will falter." He rolled his shoulders, and Zak felt Sorwin collect the remaining dregs of his exhausted magic. "*Tempraes memoria.*"

The sunbeams disappeared. Well, not entirely—but everything was washed in an array of grey shadows. It reminded Zak of the astral plane, where Sorwin had taken him once to meet Kal. Everything existed in a subdued version of reality.

But the most striking difference was the hundreds of people and creatures surrounding them.

There were dozens of dragons. Their scales hinted at many different colors, even in the grey blanket of the spell. Humans crowded around the edges of the platform. Judging by their attire, representatives from across Valecium must have traveled to the remote cave for the event. Which made sense, given Jolsu's ceremony had taken place long before Densba had been settled.

"There you are!" Zak spotted Jolsu in the center of the room, powerful wings folded close, sitting on haunches rippling with muscle. Next to him was another dragon—Nelvowig, he assumed. She was nearly as large as Jolsu and her scales appeared darker.

*There she is.* Longing crossed their bond, followed by sorrow, pain, love. The concoction of grief-stricken emotions took Zak's breath away, and in that overwhelming moment he knew exactly what it felt like to lose the one he loved most in the world.

The miniature Jolsu flexed his claws into Zak's shoulder. *I miss you,* he said. But it was clear Nelvowig, nor anyone else in the memory, could see or hear him. They were only a glimmer of the past.

"What color were her scales?" Zak asked.

*A deep red. She appeared almost purple in the evening light.*

Zak passed love, support, sorrow through their bond. It wasn't enough, but it was all he could offer in the moment.

"What are we looking for?" Olivia asked.

Sorwin shrugged. "We're not entirely sure. Anything that hints at the *Nacusti* being made, or any alliances that exist. We need hints of the war to come and how it was fought."

Zak watched and listened. The murmur of the crowd filing in for the ceremony echoed around the cavern. He was disappointed that no dwarves attended—he'd hoped to see one of the mysterious beings. But there were a handful of elves across the room huddled together by a twisting stone pillar.

"Temaway!" Zak shouted in excitement. The elf looked

so young standing among his fellows. Straight back, hair smooth and silky like Tansil's. It still appeared light, but Zak guessed it was more of a golden color than the white he had known.

"Incredible," Sorwin spoke with awe. "To see one of the fabled *Nacusti*...before he was one, of course."

"You get to see two *Nacusti* every day," Olivia said. And—at Sorwin's stricken face—she added, "I'm joking, Sorwin. It's obviously different. Meeting Temaway was life changing."

"The *Nacusti* were his idea, right?" Kaleb asked.

Bazil answered. "His and Cerevita's, though now that we're aware of a memory charm affecting gods and Guardians, I wonder how accurate our records really are."

*They're correct on that account,* Jolsu explained. *The Guardians were a first step in granting mortals autonomy. It was Cerevita's wish, but Temaway was the strategist. Once we realized the Guardians could not fight against the gods, he came up with the idea of the* Nacusti.

Something drifted by. "Is that water...flying?" Zak couldn't comprehend the four blobs of water—somehow attached but not—floated through the air. He looked around, but no mage seemed to be controlling the substance.

*A water elemental,* Jolsu explained.

Sorwin gasped. "I've always wanted to see one! It's often overlooked, but many beings other than the gods departed after the Contract was signed. The divine hierarchy was vast, and swaths of them didn't want to risk staying without their deities. Unfortunate for us, as the world would be much more colorful with their presence."

The mood in the memory shifted. The crowd quieted and Jolsu and Nelvowig both sat at attention. Temaway strode forward, arms outstretched, as if welcoming someone.

And he was—because out of thin air five figures appeared, all far too large to be human or elf, each radiating power even in the distant memory.

Gods.

"Cerevita," Zak whispered. She stood in the middle with her long cascading hair and dress of living vines and leaves.

"Azubelux!" Bazil cried.

The God of Light, with bright, angular robes stood to the left of Cerevita, arms crossed. He had no hair and appeared as dark-skinned as his sister. He had a fierce presence, but there was a warmth there too, and Zak was happy that Bazil had the chance to see his chosen god.

"That's Baltenebris next to him," Shira said.

The God of Darkness appeared the opposite of Azubelux in every way. Light skin, wavy hair, and dark shadowy robes that never quite stopped shifting. Zak couldn't look at his eyes—black orbs with no white at all—without a shiver running through him.

"Who are the other two gods?" Olivia asked.

"Who would stand with The Three?" Kaleb echoed.

Zak peered at the next god in line. He was a little shorter than the rest of them, his face softer, kinder. He almost looked adolescent, but that was unlikely for an ageless being. Dark robes—Zak guessed they would be blue—glittered with bright spots, like he wore the night sky.

"Impossible," Sorwin breathed.

"What?"

"Look! The one on the end!"

Zak did. The man stood next to the young-looking god. He blended in perfectly with the grey tones of the memory spell, as if he was barely there in his high-collared grey tunic, simple breeches, and combed hair. But his clothing wasn't the surprising part.

It was that Zak recognized him.

"Karazul?"

*How?* Jolsu gasped.

He couldn't explain it, but somehow, Karazul—the anti-magic assassin that had dogged Zak's every step since leaving Densba—stood in a line of gods, and was clearly one of them.

"This doesn't make any sense." Olivia's voice cracked. Seeing Karazul stand there, she was probably reliving their duel, when he ran her through and she nearly died. Zak wanted to pull her into a tight hug, but he couldn't drop Sorwin's hand and break the spell. Not yet.

"How is there a god none of us recognize, and another that shouldn't be a god at all?" Bazil sounded frantic, distressed.

"This is it," Sorwin said in an even tone. Zak didn't know how he remained so calm. "This is the clue we were looking for. Remember what Cerevita, Jolsu, and Vess all said? There were others—other gods, other allies—that fought in the Guardian War. And then there was Temaway. Zak—you said that Temaway *recognized* Karazul, that he called him by a different name."

"Niltris," Zak said. The name had stuck with him. He didn't want to forget any detail about Karazul no matter how small in case it could help him defeat the assassin once and for all.

"If Karazul—Niltris—is a god, that would explain his inhuman abilities," Kaleb reasoned. The man twitched, and Zak remembered he had been cut down by the assassin as well.

"But..." Zak's mind whirled. "Why don't we remember Karazul, or the other god?"

Sorwin gasped. "Remember what Malu said? Baltenebris wrote the Contract and had strict conditions. If Karazul is a god that we don't remember, that means Baltenebris used the Contract to hide him from the world, which means—"

"Temaway was right," Olivia said. "Karazul is an ally."

"Three Fires," Zak cursed.

They didn't witness much more of the memory. Right as Jolsu and Nelvowig received an infusion of magic from the gods and became Guardians, Sorwin dropped to a knee and the spell released.

"You pushed yourself too far," Kaleb said. He crouched and wrapped an arm around his partner.

"I'll be fine." Sorwin panted like he had run a hundred laps around court seven. "After some rest—we can return tomorrow—to see more."

"I don't think we need to." Zak paced around the circular

platform, thinking aloud. He felt all of his friends' eyes upon him. "We know Karazul was a god at one point, even if he doesn't seem to be anymore. We should return to Tor'alan and remove the *senligo* to find out what he knows."

"That's assuming he knows something." Olivia crossed her arms. "Remember when Temaway confronted him? He seemed *confused* by his recognition."

"It's likely he's under the same memory charm as Jolsu, Vess, and Cerevita," Shira reasoned.

Zak watched Elpida scratch at a sigil carved into the stone floor. "Maybe, but he's the best lead we have right now."

Discussion of the memory and Karazul's identity continued for a few more minutes, which gave Sorwin the chance to rest before the hike back up the cliff to Densba. But, the conversation came to an abrupt halt when a bright golden hue sparkled around Elpida.

"Are dragons supposed to glow?" Bazil asked, taking a cautious step back.

*No! Stop her!* Jolsu cried.

But it was too late.

"Cover your eyes!" Zak buried his face in the crook of his elbow.

When the flash of light faded, Elpida had more than doubled in size. She trotted around the platform, and the top of her head reached Zak's ribs. The most prominent difference, though, were the two small wings between her shoulders. She craned her neck to observe them flapping as she hopped in excitement.

"What just happened?" Olivia jumped out of Elpida's

prancing path.

"Dragons can grow with magic, but *what* magic did Elpida use?" Zak asked Jolsu.

*This was our home for centuries—much dragon magic had seeped into it.* Jolsu sighed. *I didn't think enough would be left for growth…I should've been paying closer attention.*

Elpida—in her raucous celebration—stirred up a cloud of dust from the abandoned *jyrnen* cavern. She sneezed, and a tiny streak of fire shot from her maw.

The not-so-little bronze dragon froze.

*Fire!* she yelped. Inhaling deep, she expelled a long breath in which another ember crackled. *Finally!*

Until now, Elpida hadn't been able to produce more than a modest puff of smoke.

"Light me, that's something." Bazil whistled at the spectacle of the dragon breathing fire for the first, second, and third time.

"I understand your worry, Jolsu, but it might be time to embrace Elpida's training. I don't think anyone in Tor'alan will believe she's an overgrown lizard with those wings." Zak bit his lip to hold back a laugh.

*You may be right,* the dragon relented. His small green form still perched on Zak's shoulder. *But don't tell her yet—let her enjoy this moment unspoiled by the future.*

Something burned in the back of Zak's throat, and he couldn't utter a single word, but he sent proud, love, family along their bond.

Jolsu nudged Zak's cheek with his nose. *Let's go, Parignis. It's time to see your parents.*

# CHAPTER 11

# THE ELDRIMAI

Tansil's bare feet sank into the cool moss on the forest floor. While his recent trip to the Eyewood had been his first step into elven territory in centuries, it was nothing like his home.

Everything in Stjarunni was exactly as he remembered. The settlement—not an accurate description, but there really wasn't one for elven cities—grew in a ring around the Arheim, the home tree. Elves paused in the openings of their *tredoms* as he passed, watching his shameful procession from the hollowed tree dwellings. He had been banished. He wasn't supposed to be there.

Tansil found himself wishing they had doors to shut in his face, but no elf would ever fell a tree. Not when they could live in harmony together.

He walked slow on purpose. It would make things easier—even slightly—if he readopted the elven habits he had shed over centuries of living with humans. That was why his boots lay abandoned at the edge of the forest. He hadn't changed from his robe—a maize fabric with delicate red embroidery that took on a luster against the sea of green—into simpler garb because even his asceticism had limits.

The Arheim towered over the surrounding trees, singular in its magnificence. Long, powerful branches stretched up and out so far that Tansil walked beneath the immense boughs for minutes before reaching the base. At one of the bigger openings of the trunk he peered inside the partially-hollow tree, watching a handful of elves drift about their business. A tall elf trimmed one of the exposed roots, while another tended lilies growing in a pool. Magic curled around both of them, as natural as a breeze.

Tansil wandered to the center of the Arheim. The entire base was elevated, as if the tree stood on its ancient roots. There he sat, holding the star leaf seed in his palms, meditating and waiting.

Much of elven culture revolved around patience, and as the hours trickled by, an unexpected burst of empathy for Sorwin twinged in his chest.

*How many hours—days—did I make him wait for me?*

Too many, he was sure.

The cloud of his contemplation parted when Tansil sensed the *Eldrimai* approaching.

Their presence was unmistakable. They were the Arheim, the Arheim, them—the two were as indistinguishable as the curls of moss he sat upon. Tansil had forgotten how overwhelming the *Eldrimai* felt in his mind, how they pressed against his thoughts—even more so than Cerevita. Because they were family, Tansil but a blossom from the Arheim, and the *Eldrimai*—the Tender—the closest thing any elf would have to a parent.

"*Benevita.*" The *Eldrimai* approached, arms outstretched.

Tansil gently placed the seed on the ground, stood, and did the same. Their fingers entwined and foreheads pressed together, holding the position for a minute, breathing one another in and out. An unexplainable tranquility seeped into Tansil, pushing at his worries and responsibilities. The thrum of the *Eldrimai* and the Arheim a steady pulse in his consciousness.

When they finally parted, Tansil took in the older elf. They had always been short, but time had turned them ancient. Many wrinkles sagged below their eyes, their shoulders hunched, and pure white hair flowed down to their feet over brown and green robes.

"*Silvefni,*" Tansil whispered. He reached for the long sleeves of their robe, wanting desperately to feel the softness of the magical fabric, but hesitated at his own boldness.

The *Eldrimai* chuckled and held out an arm. "*Temp sin-is snerta?*"

"Yes, I had almost forgotten about it." Smoother than silk and stronger than iron, *silvefni* was woven from the mucus of worms that ate the insides of the trees surrounding the Arheim, which coincidentally also created the *tredoms* where the elves resided. That made it impossible for anyone to produce besides the elves. The folds swam in his palm. How many centuries had passed since Tansil had felt it? It would have been before his banishment...five hundred years? Six?

"After such time, your elvish slips too," the old elf said.

"I-I hadn't meant to—" He had replied in the common tongue as a matter of habit.

The *Eldrimai* wore a mischievous grin. "I know."

"Of course you do." He retrieved the star leaf seed and cradled it to keep from fidgeting.

"Let us walk." The *Eldrimai* offered Tansil their hand, and he supported them as they walked side-by-side through the wondrous gardens.

"In all my years traveling, I never found a comparable sight." Tansil admired the waterfalls that ran down curling stone crags, the round *skinaru* bushes with shining petals of white, yellow, orange. Thousands of tree worm cocoons dangled from the long branches of the Arheim, awaiting their transformation.

"Much like the elves, these creatures and plants depend on the Arheim, they are drawn to its magic and shelter."

Every elf they passed presented their palms and foreheads to the *Eldrimai*, and Tansil didn't miss the sharp glances cast his way. Most of them he recognized, they had either blossomed before he left, or were older than him. Yet even the younger ones knew his story—their icy demeanors said as much.

"Why did you beckon me here, *Eldrimai*? It is clear I am not wanted."

They stepped carefully over a gnarled root. "Nature is a path of growth and reaction, unpredictable to the great Seers of the Eyewood. Even our Green Lady has regrets."

"I wonder if that's true." In their many conversations, Tansil never once had the suspicion that Cerevita regretted anything. But if she did, it was well hidden.

The *Eldrimai* had led them up one of the hillocks with a perfect view of the Arheim and ring of *tredoms*. They sat on a smooth boulder with a flat edge, patting the surface next to them.

Tansil heeded the request and sat. "You haven't answered my question, *Eldrimai*. My presence antagonizes your people."

The short hike had tired the *Eldrimai*, but with stillness their breaths resumed a steady rhythm. "Many feelings present as anger when they are something else entirely. Can you think of any?"

"Fear," Tansil said immediately. He had felt that often enough in regards to Zandorn. "We fear what we cannot control, and lash out."

"Yes, fear is the root of much anger. It is meant for survival, but as we said before, nature can make mistakes too. It can be provoked when we aren't in danger, when a threat is fabricated."

Tansil looked down at the seed in his hands. "Your people wouldn't be wrong to think of me as a threat."

"Perhaps. Yet confusion can also lead to fear. That which we do not understand can be the most terrifying of all—for its danger may be limitless in our imagination."

"What is there to understand? My branch brought decay to the Arheim, and it had to be cut away. A trimmed branch cannot be reattached."

"No, they cannot. But sometimes, they can begin the cycle anew." With a delicate touch, the *Eldrimai* cupped

Tansil's hands and raised them so the star leaf seed hovered before him.

A long silence stretched between them before Tansil recovered from shock. "You can't mean—me? Become a Tender?"

"It is your time."

"But I was *banished*! By *you*! Cut off, cast out—and very recently I disrespected that fate by stepping into the Eyewood!" The idea that he would be welcomed back was ludicrous enough, but to be made an *Eldrimai*, responsible for an Arheim and elven life, was beyond irrational.

"Why were you banished?" the *Eldrimai* asked.

"You know why," Tansil growled.

"I do. Do you?"

*Infuriating.* Tansil had forgotten the games the *Eldrimai* played, disguised behind the thin veil of lessons. They did not fool him, but he had to play nonetheless.

"Because of a selfish act," he said.

"Perhaps. But there is more to it than that, isn't there?"

Tansil sighed. "The Arheim—you—told me to save that human." He did not wish to relive his past mistakes, the biting pain still remained after centuries.

"Ah, it was not me. You may feel me and the Arheim as one—and we are in many ways. Yet the Arheim is our lifeblood, and I but the Tender." A dangerous twinkle lit the *Eldrimai's* eyes. "Perhaps you will know this for yourself one day."

"Regardless, I saved a human life with a *flosfrae*." Saying it aloud, the sight of the beautiful flower bud he plucked from the Arheim rushed back to him. "There's no way of knowing if the flower would have blossomed into an elf, but—"

"But you took it without my permission," the *Eldrimai* finished for him.

"Yes."

"And it was not yours to take."

"No."

"So you put the needs of one above the wishes of the many."

"I did." And it didn't matter if the Arheim had asked him to. Neither the *Eldrimai* nor any other elves had known of his deed until it was done. It had been a betrayal of the highest order.

"And why did you go to the Eyewood?"

Tansil stood, pacing on the grassy overlook. "I had to, to fight for the Leauge. To try and stop Zandorn and the Rot. To help the *Nacusti*—Cerevita's last creation in Valecium—triumph."

"But you knew going to the Eyewood broke the conditions of your banishment."

"Yes."

"And you did it anyway—despite the potential consequences—to help your friends and all the people of Valecium."

"Yes."

"So you put the needs of the many above the wishes of one."

"I—" For once, Tansil was speechless. Decades in council meetings sparring with selfish merchants and misguided leaders hadn't prepared him to face such brutal honesty.

But looking at the *Eldrimai*, there was nothing brutal in their smile. "You have learned your lesson, Tansil. Better than we thought you would—and faster, too. But you are no stranger to our slow pace, how it differs to the rest of the world." The *Eldrimai* stared at the green leaves overhead. "The Arheim and I are dying, as all things must in time. You will be the next Tender, the next *Eldrimai*. You will grow our home and our people for millenia to come."

"Is this another punishment?"

The *Eldrimai* gaped, truly shocked.

Tansil pressed on. "You pushed me out, a severed branch alone in the world. And when I found my way after centuries of wandering, you rip me from my new home, and expect me to take root in your soil once again?"

"Tansil—"

"How *dare* you?!" The earth quaked beneath his feet and dark clouds gathered above in the blue sky.

The *Eldrimai* hunched forward. "Perhaps I rushed you here."

"No. No amount of time would prepare me for this, because I refuse. I will never tend to people that cast me aside." He thrust the star leaf seed at the *Eldrimai*, but they did not reach for it.

"The seed is yours, whether you accept its charge or not. It chose *you*, Tansil. I know you feel the pull of it already, the call within. But you should not answer if you are not ready."

"On that we agree, and I never will be." He stormed away, thunder rumbling through the sky.

# Chapter 12

# BRONZE AND SILVER

From the moment Zak walked into his parents' house, Clairise began crying. She threw her arms around him and sank to the floor. He sat with her for a good ten minutes before convincing her that he wouldn't disappear if she let go long enough to climb into a chair. But then—when she dried her eyes and saw all the guests accompanying Zak—she refused to sit still, insisting upon rushing about the small cottage, adding more ingredients to a pot bubbling over the fire and sending Ageric to pull jars of food from their Winter storage.

"I would *never* forgive myself if Sorwin or any of your friends went hungry on my doorstep. After everything that man has done for you—the shame!"

"What about a dragon?" Zak had asked as Elpida stalked into the room, bronze scales flickering in the firelight.

"Cerevita's grace!" Clairise's hands covered her mouth in an instant.

It took a while to explain everything—well, nearly everything—Zak left out the bits about mystery gods and tracking them down, but he included details about Jolsu and Elpida and the dragons' former home down the coast. It was only fair to share the information as his parents shared their home. And they seemed to follow most of the story, albeit wide-eyed and with some headscratching.

"Someone will have to run to see if Miss Nurin has any scraps," Clairise said.

"The butcher? I can go." Zak smiled and hugged his mother while she chopped more vegetables, resting his chin on top of her pinned curls. It was good to be home.

After the impromptu feast—in which Clairise somehow whipped up a batch of crushed citrus tarts, Zak's favorite—Elpida fell asleep by the hearth, Sorwin, Kaleb, Shira, and Olivia walked to the inn down the road, and Zak and Bazil climbed the ladder to the loft.

"Do you think Karazul has any idea who he is, or was?" Bazil asked when he had settled on a pile of blankets on the floor.

"I don't know...but if he does, he's one of the best liars in the world."

"That's true. I wonder if he'll remember anything if we figure out how this memory charm works. Maybe he could tell us about the other gods."

Zak heard Bazil tossing back and forth for most of the night. *He must be excited.* Speaking to a god was an incredible opportunity for a devoted such as Bazil. Even if Karazul wasn't his chosen god, he still respected the divine seats.

But for his part, Zak was all nerves. It was bad enough the dangerous assassin had divinity coursing through him, but the fifth mystery god worried Zak just as much. Who were they? Were they also wandering the world without memory, like Karazul?

After a mostly sleepless night—he had fallen unconscious long enough to dream of the lone tree in a wasteland again—he dressed early and climbed down the ladder. Winters in the Southern Isles were mild, and there was hardly a chill in the air compared to Tor'alan. Zak let his mother fawn over him in between breakfast preparations, wearing a wide smile he couldn't pry from his face if he wanted to.

*Home.*

After two plates of buttered bread and eggs, he followed the steady clang of metal to the forge and found his father striking a long bronze rod. Ageric waved him over with the hammer in his hand.

"Let's see if you can put that fancy magic to work," his father said with a wink.

Zak heated the bronze with controlled flame until it glowed, then Ageric hammered it out, stretching it further and further. They settled into a comfortable rhythm, sharing the satisfaction of silence and sweat as they worked.

*This was it,* he thought. *This was the life I had imagined.* For years, he had trained with his father—and Kalbick's—to take the forge over one day. He had wanted it, or at least had preferred to spend his time soot-covered instead of in Densba's schoolhouse. There had been daydreams, of course. Visions of adventure, of joining the League and making a difference. He now scoffed at his own naivety.

A soothing happiness crossed the bond with Jolsu. *I, for one, am happy you chased adventure. We may not have bonded otherwise.*

*Really? Would that have been possible?*

*Yes, Parignis. A few of your ancestors were afraid of our power and kept me buried.*

Sorrow needled at Zak. *That must have been awful—I'm sorry, Jolsu.*

A surge of fine-past-different-now came from the dragon, and Zak nodded to himself, happy that was true.

All while assisting his father, Zak didn't ask questions. Ageric seemed to know when he needed instructions and offered a few words then. He had always been a quiet man, but never timid. After seeing more of the world—and the people in it—Zak's respect for his father had grown.

Ageric had worked the bronze into a flat sheet and scored specific points. "We've been getting more orders from the League, even way down here," his father said. "There's a big battle approaching, isn't there?"

"There is." Zak often left out the more dangerous details from the Fireposts he sent home, but he couldn't lie right to his father's face.

Ageric nodded, as if long-held suspicions were confirmed. He opened a storage closet at the rear of the forge and pulled out something tall and thin wrapped in leather. Surprisingly, he handed it to Zak.

When Zak blinked and didn't move, Ageric explained. "Sorwin's kept us more or less updated with letters on your training. He mentioned your connection with a staff, and well—I don't know two licks about magic, but I can swing a hammer just fine."

Zak pulled at the twine and the leather wrappings fell away, revealing a sleek bronze staff. An etched grip divided it in half—the lower end had a blunted point, and the top twisted into a flame with a hollow spot at the center.

"I started it a while ago. Tougher than iron, that is, so it won't crack on yuh. The only thing missing is a proper stone for the tip. But I already spoke to Sorwin and he'll get it sorted once you're back in Tor'alan."

"Wha...how...?" Zak ran his hands along the cold, impossibly smooth metal. He held it aloft, marveled at the lightness as he swung it through the air. He channeled a sliver of magic into it, and the bronze staff accepted it willingly, almost eagerly, as a green flame appeared at the tip.

Zak didn't know what to say, so he hugged his father tight, hoping he understood how much the gesture meant, how much he loved him.

Ageric's strong arms squeezed him back.

A loud *snap* from the woods behind the forge interrupted the moment, and Zak winced as a sharp pain pierced his arm.

His wound—the one Zandorn gave him.

"Zak?" Ageric asked, concern pinching his brow.

Zak looked out the open doors of the forge and stopped breathing at the sight before him.

"Burvenin?" he gasped.

It should have been impossible—Sorwin had killed the

burly man months ago, right before Renna and Karazul took Terasi the Druid. But here he was, striding rigidly toward Zak and his father, glassy eyed and mouth agape.

Ageric grabbed a shovel leaning against the wall and took a defensive stance.

Burvenin swung an arm, launching a fireball toward them.

Zak lunged forward, the green fire of his shield burning through the attack. "Go get Sorwin!" he yelled to his father.

Ageric hesitated, eyes flashing with worry.

"Go!" Zak said again, and this time his father ran through the workshop into the house.

Another flurry of silver fire blasted into Zak's shield. "*Na...cu...sti.*" Burvenin still advanced, however slow, with pallid skin that had been carelessly stitched together.

"Jolsu? What is he?" Zak squashed his panic at the sight of the gruesome mage. He had to focus and keep his shield stable.

*Undead*, Jolsu snarled with distaste. *One of Zandorn's experiments, no doubt. You must burn him, Parignis. Leave nothing but ash.*

"Suppose it's as good a time as any to break this in." He planted the bronze staff into the ground and tipped it forward. "*Ignisaveru.*"

Dozens of embers appeared in the air and darted toward Burvenin like angry hornets. The undead mage groaned and swiped them away with an arm, a surge of silver fire rushing toward Zak.

It crashed against his shield, forcing him back a step.

*Stop playing and attack for real!* Jolsu said.

"I'm not playing, I'm getting the measure of him." Last time they fought, Zak had rushed in fueled by rage and fear—and Jolsu's influence, though he didn't know it at the time. He had learned too much since then to make the same mistakes.

Wave after wave of the fiery silver river slammed into his shield, forcing him to a knee. His shield protected much of the forge, but a few stray embers sprayed toward the thatch roof.

*Do you have the measure of him* now?

Zak gritted his teeth. He couldn't let the house burn, not again.

"*Terramotus!*" The earth under Burvenin rippled and lifted, sending the man careening back into the woods. Zak turned and whipped the bronze staff through the air, quenching the embers that had burrowed into the eaves.

Zak ran through the brush after Burvenin. The man struggled to his feet, moving slower in death than he had in life, but Zak didn't relent. Jolsu appeared at his side, the size of a large dog, and leaped into the air.

Burvenin's empty eyes tracked the soaring dragon, which was exactly what Zak had wanted.

Funneling his and Jolsu's magic through the bronze staff, he pointed the tip toward his enemy. "*Igniligo.*"

Strands of green fire swirled around Burvenin, wrapping in tight rings from head to toe. He stiffened and fell over, writhing against the fiery bonds.

"Lord of Light!" Bazil emerged from the kitchen's rear

door, no doubt summoned by the commotion. "Is that Bur-venin?"

"What's left of him." Some of the stitches holding the man together had burned, and his flesh peeled like old parchment. Zak grimaced from disgust.

Jolsu landed next to the mage and breathed a heavy stream of fire upon him.

"Jolsu! No!" Zak yelled.

But it was too late. When the dragon stopped, nothing was left of the undead mage but smoldering ash.

"Why did you do that? We could have learned something from him!" At the very least there could have been a chance to pull information about Zandorn's research from the man.

Jolsu shook his head. *There was nothing but base instinct in him. We would have gained only death by keeping his husk.*

"I think Jolsu is right," Bazil said, and Zak felt betrayed again. His expression must have said as much, since Bazil added, "I couldn't sense anything from him—no life, no presence. It was like someone animated his body and attached magic to him."

"Well, *now* we'll never know what we could have learned, will we?" He glared at Jolsu, but the dragon showed no remorse as he sat on his haunches, tail flicking.

When Sorwin and the others arrived, Zak explained what had happened.

"This was a message," Sorwin said. "Zandorn must be finalizing his necromantic preparations. He'll want everything perfect when it is time to resurrect his wife, and he wanted to remind you—us—that we're not slowing him down one bit."

"He's right on that count," Olivia mumbled.

"But," Sorwin continued, "we're not helpless. In fact, we have a god to interrogate." His customary smile had a dangerous curl to it, and Zak lightened at the sight of his rested magus and the sliver of hope they all clung to.

"Let's go," Zak said. "Back to Tor'alan."

# CHAPTER 13

# AWAKE

When Karazul woke, everything hurt.

His eyes wouldn't open, so he groaned and wiped the crust from his eyelids, every muscle more rigid than iron.

"How long?" he wheezed, throat drier than the Dunes of Ajax.

"Almost two months."

That voice. *So I've been captured.* He squinted against the abrasive light as blurry figures came into focus. A few of them crowded close together in the small chamber.

"*Nacusti.*" He coughed, and the young mage handed him a cup. Karazul downed the water and coughed some more. Someone refilled the cup and he drank three more times before handing it back.

"Where is that gods-cursed elf?" he growled.

"Do you mean Temaway? He passed away after your fight."

Karazul pushed himself to sitting and thought *he* might

pass away from the pain wracking his entire body. His legs and arms looked small. Two months unconscious would do that to a body.

"What did he do to me?"

The tall one—Sorwin was his name—spoke. "He put you under a powerful *senligo*, a binding of the mind. We kept you alive through energetic transfusions, though your anti-magic abilities made that an interesting process."

"The elf knew me." And now he was dead. Where would Karazul go for answers now? Back to Zandorn? Not if his dreams were true, if the visions were actually memories.

It was all ruined.

"He did, and now so do we," the *Nacusti* said.

Karazul rested his head against the wall, getting a proper look at the boy. He was seated at his bedside, and yet Karazul could tell he had grown. His neck looked thicker, and an excited vein jumped up and down, betraying his quickened pulse. The room was cold, yet tiny beads of sweat collected over his temples. These little details screamed at Karazul, he couldn't stop himself from noticing them. Not after decades of sizing up marks, determining who would run and who would fight while he played the dutiful assassin.

Yet one thing in particular about the *Nacusti* caught Karazul's attention. His eyes. They were not the eyes of a mark. No, theirs were shifty, constantly darting around rooms and looking over shoulders. Many of them had deserved death. They had been liars, cheaters, schemers, predators. He never took a job unless the employer had a clear motivation. It made things cleaner afterward because often, so many people would have wanted the mark dead that less questions were asked, and he could disappear with a heavier purse.

But the *Nacusti*—Zakolor—stared straight at Karazul. His gaze didn't waver once.

In all their encounters, he hadn't determined if bravery or stupidity drove the boy.

"What do you mean you know me now? You *have* known me. I've haunted your dreams for the better part of a year." He let a wolfish grin spread his lips and chuckled when the boy flinched.

"We saw your past, saw who you really were. Both you and your brother." He crossed his arms and leaned back, a smugness settling over him.

*Brave*. He had to give the boy that much. *And very, very stupid.*

Karazul had no weapons and wore nothing but loose trousers. Yet weakened as he was, a simple letter opener or shard of glass would be enough to slit the boy's throat.

His skull pounded and he winced against the pain. "How dare you mention my brother? I am in no mood for games, *Nacusti*. Speak plain or leave me in this prison."

"We saw you and your brother at Jolsu's Guardian ceremony. It was centuries ago, and you were both there. You were both gods."

The pain between his eyes sharpened like a blade. "That is a lie—"

"What is your brother's name?" a girl asked.

Karazul studied her—the pinch of her brow, the long red

curls, the taut posture. "Didn't I kill you?" he taunted.

"You tried," she answered, cool and quick.

*Brave, not stupid.*

He shook his head. "Why do you want to know my brother's name?"

"It's a simple enough question. Why not answer?" she prodded.

"Whatever, it doesn't matter. His name is—" A blankness emptied his mind. *Strange.* "My brother's name is—"

It happened again. Just as he was about to speak, the name disappeared, dancing off the edge of his tongue. Fire raged within him. "What have you done to me?" He raked a hand toward the boy, but there was no strength behind it. Zak caught his arm easily and guided him back onto the bed.

"That's what we're trying to tell you," the boy said. "You were a god, and now you're not. The same may be true for your brother. We need to understand why, because we think you may have been key to winning the Guardian War, and that you might be the same for defeating Zandorn."

Thin bedsheets twisted in Karazul's grip. "Zandorn lied to me." Repeatedly. For decades. In the cold light of consciousness, the blurry borders of his visions began to solidify. "I knew he would use me for his own ends, but I thought he would make good on his promises eventually."

Sorwin edged closer. "He promised you help, didn't he? With your brother?"

"Information." Karazul closed his eyes. He couldn't speak his brother's name, and he couldn't see his face in his mind's eye. How had he been duped for so long? And not just by Zandorn, but by his own doubts? "I cannot be a god."

"But you are, or were," Zak urged.

"Then I must be the god of nothing. Of failure." He blinked slowly. At least that would make the absurd idea palatable. Wouldn't he know if he was a god? His gifts were powerful. Anti-magic was rare—almost nonexistent—but godlike? That seemed farfetched.

Except...

The gaps in his memory. He had never picked at them for fear of discovering something too painful. But under the influence of the *senligo*, his past began to stitch itself together, a tapestry of trauma.

How long had he been searching, forgetting, and starting over? How many times had Zandorn trapped him in service over the last century of this godsforsaken war? At least a handful, from what he had witnessed in the dreams. And before that—the rush of past lives jumbled together. He couldn't name his brother or see his face, but he remembered the warmth of his hand, always pulling him forward, setting him in motion. Karazul remembered that without his brother, he truly had been nothing.

And Zandorn's lies had kept him trapped for years.

A familiar rage crawled beneath his skin as he stared directly into Zak's eyes. "I will help you with Zandorn under one condition. Let me go."

The boy's head quirked in confusion. "We cannot do that. You've hurt and killed so many—"

Karazul waved a dismissive hand. "I've attacked everyone in this room, yet here you are, asking for my help. I usually enjoy a delicate approach to negotiations, a bit of a dance. But after the torture of that elf's little spell I'm in no mood. There is something I must find out for myself before I can help you. In order to do that, I need you to let me go."

His request was met with shocked silence.

Finally, the brave girl spoke. "How are we supposed to believe you won't run right back to Zandorn?"

"I'll never listen to a word that snake speaks again," he spat through gritted teeth.

His captors shared glances amongst themselves, each packed with questions that Karazul didn't have the patience to answer. He rolled his eyes. "We're all mutually dependent on discovering the truth of my situation. Help me do so, and then I will help you, and then I can finally find my brother."

The *Nacusti* leaned forward, looking ready to agree, but the soldier near the door interrupted before he had a chance. "Outside, everyone."

Karazul leaned back and smiled, despite his frustration. "You cannot keep me here for long," he said. The boy hesitated before exiting, and that was the only sign Karazul needed.

The seed was planted. It wouldn't be long now.

"He's right," Zak said. He closed the door to Karazul's room as he shuffled into the murky hall. Sorwin, Kaleb, Shira, Bazil, and Olivia all waited for him. The group came straight to the assassin's quarters after returning from Densba, seeking answers. But they only found more questions. "Once he recovers his strength, I doubt we can keep him locked up."

"He'll be the least of our concerns if Zandorn destroys the Contract." Sorwin tapped his chin, thinking.

"Perhaps, but him escaping isn't the same as us letting him go." Kaleb's arms crossed over his military leathers. "He has too many crimes to account for to negotiate release."

"And there's still plenty he isn't saying." Shira's dark hair wisped about her face in the drafty hall. She startled and laid a hand on Zak's wrist. "Don't go back in there, nothing good comes from it."

Zak had thought about it, wondering if a conversation between just the two of them would merit anything. His blood boiled at the sight of the assassin, but he was willing to keep his anger restrained if it meant finding a way to defeat Zandorn. Instead, he nodded, trusting whatever glimpse of the future Shira had seen. "So we tell him we'll think it over. And in the meantime, there's something I want to try."

An hour later—after everyone had a chance to go home and bathe and eat—Zak sat cross-legged on the green lawn of court seven with Sorwin and Olivia. After explaining his idea, he was disappointed that neither of them seemed too thrilled.

"But what if you're caught? Spying on the Consortium with your spirit is too risky." Olivia's knee jostled his as she readjusted her position.

The fleeting touch distracted him for a moment. "It—uh, well, that's why I thought you and Sorwin could come?" His upward inflection made it a question rather than a suggestion.

Sorwin shook his head. "Unlikely. Projecting a spirit

without the aid of a spiritwalking brew is very difficult. Most mages can't do it. I suspect your ability is somehow linked to your Sight."

"Oh." Zak hadn't been expecting to go alone, but he remained undeterred. "Still, with Karazul here, it's a lot less likely I'll be noticed and expelled, right?" The assassin's anti-magic had been the primary reason Zak hadn't tried this sooner. "Terasi showed me how to enter Pywell Mountain. I can be there and back in no time."

"Technically yes." Sorwin scratched at his recently shaven jaw. "But what are you hoping to discover?"

"Anything. Maybe Zandorn's plan for the Contract or what they need to break it. The fact that they haven't destroyed it yet means either they haven't figured out how, or they're waiting for a specific moment."

"Knowing their plan would make it easier to disrupt," Olivia said.

"Exactly!" They were starting to see the opportunity he did. "Jolsu will be with me, I won't be alone."

"Fine," Sorwin relented. "But I want you retreating the *second* you encounter Renna or Zandorn or Kalbick. Understood?"

He flinched hearing Kal's name thrown in with the Consortium leaders, but he agreed. He didn't have a choice for now. Whatever magic Renna had used on Kal had penetrated deep into his mind, and no matter how badly he wanted to rescue his friend, it wouldn't be as simple as a conversation.

*Defeat the Consortium first, then save Kal,* he told himself.

*We'll get him back, Parignis,* Jolsu echoed.

Sorwin conjured wind chimes that were charmed to move without any actual wind. The three of them settled into their cushions, meditating.

Zak could feel Sorwin's and Olivia's magics pulsing—orange and amber, both warm and powerful. He wondered how they perceived the green of his and Jolsu's, if they felt distinct like the ocean and sky, the way it did to him, or if their magics bled together like a distant horizon.

He had never intentionally spiritwalked before. He had done it once on accident while asleep, and once when Terasi had called to him. Zak had thought it a dream at first, but he quickly realized the Druid had come to guide him, to give him a final message and request.

Guilt soured his gut over the Druid's death. He never would have been caught if Zak hadn't appeared in that field, dropped right at Terasi's feet by the *indagomius*. That infernal stone and Zak's eagerness to prove himself had forced the Druid to defend him.

*Three Fires.* He pushed the distractions away and refocused on his breathing. He'd never find answers to their questions by dwelling on the past.

Instead of focusing on his magic like he usually did while meditating, he imagined himself floating. He recalled the weightlessness of his spirit, how easily he moved through the air with a thought. The metallic chimes carried him up, up, up and out of his body until utter delight at seeing the back of his own head almost reeled him back in.

"I did it!" he shouted at his magus and friend. But Sorwin

and Olivia sat unmoved, undisturbed. They couldn't hear him, not now.

He floated a little higher, refamiliarizing himself with spiritwalking. He'd never had this much control before, and had never seen his own body from the outside. It felt unreal, and a sudden desire to get far away from himself overwhelmed him, but he didn't fight it. He used the energy to fly quickly to the west.

It didn't take long to find the Rot. The sea of darkness crept ever forward, draining the life and magic from the land. Soon there was nothing but the eerie grey beneath him, and it would have been easy to get turned around in the monotony, but it was a clear day and Pywell loomed far in the distance.

Time didn't seem to flow the same while he was a spirit. Or maybe it did, but he perceived it differently. Either way, within moments he floated through the thick stone walls of the mountain. The wards and barriers surrounding the fortress pricked at his glowing form, but none barred his entry.

He floated into a sprawling room with wide platforms. A few portals hung in the air, mages and soldiers coming and going between them. He fought the urge to hide from the bustle of activity below. It wouldn't matter—most people wouldn't be able to see his spirit, and only the most gifted would sense his presence.

He watched a pair of mages tug a line of shackled youths out of a portal and down a cavernous hall.

*This must be what happened to Kal.* Burvenin must have brought him to Pywell after abducting him from Densba.

*Focus, Parignis,* Jolsu reminded him.

The dragon was right—there would be time for Kal later. He drifted closer to the soldiers, eavesdropping on their conversations.

"Didn't sleep a wink," one man said.

"When's your next raid?" another asked.

Nothing useful. Zak moved to the next group.

"—it's better than being on the front, I can tell you that much." A muscular woman thumped a spear into the hard stone floor.

"What do you mean?" the thin man beside her asked.

The woman leaned in conspiratorially, and Zak floated closer to listen. "Pretty sure Renna sent Queen Ymona to die. Why else would she be holding a line near Gort'haal? There's nothing in the dwarven lands of worth."

"Careful," the man warned. "That's close to treason."

"Bah! There's no treason without honor, and we abandoned that the moment we joined the Consortium."

"I'm worried about Horace. He's supposed to deliver the message to Renna."

Zak perked up at this. If he could find Horace, maybe he could follow him to Renna. He had promised Sorwin he wouldn't get too close, but maybe someone with helpful information would be in her proximity.

The woman shrugged. "As I said, it's better to play messenger than stay on the front."

The man grunted but said nothing else. Zak watched him closely, and his gaze drifted across the open room. He lifted his chin in greeting to a man across the way who waved a piece of parchment in the air before departing into a tunnel.

*That has to be Horace!* Zak sped after the man, accidentally passing right through a group of soldiers. They shivered in his wake, and Zak scolded himself for being careless.

He caught up to Horace and floated just above and behind his clipped stride. His movements were tight, rigid, and Zak pitied the man. Delivering a message to someone as vile as Renna carried inherent risk.

*You must be cautious as well. She could easily sense and trap your spirit,* Jolsu warned.

*I will be.*

Within two more turns, Horace arrived at a chamber with thick stone doors that had been thrown open. He paused at the threshold to run a hand through his hair and tug at some of the wrinkles in his black and blue uniform. Apparently satisfied, he squared his shoulders and strode ahead.

Zak floated through the wall to the right of the door, keeping his distance from Horace. Inside, the round room was sparsely appointed, only a single tufted chair and smooth table were positioned on the left—neither empty. Plates of decadent food spread across the table, and Renna perched upon the chair.

Even though his body was clear across the continent, Zak swore he felt his heartbeat hammering in his chest.

Horace approached her, bowed, and held out the letter. "Message for you, my lady, from Queen Ymona."

Renna snatched the parchment from his hand. "And what does the *former* queen request today?"

Horace shifted his weight between his feet uneasily.

"M-more soldiers, my lady. And supplies for the front."

She read the letter and laughed exactly once before it caught fire in her hands. The crimson flame devoured it in seconds. "Tell Ymona I'll think about it."

Renna's attention refocused on something, and Zak followed her gaze across the room.

Kal.

Shirtless and covered in sweat, Kal swung a sword through the air in a complex pattern before striking at a training post.

"Faster," Renna instructed.

Kal reset, widening his stance before launching into the pattern again, even quicker than before.

Spirits were driven by pure will, and when Zak's thoughts focused on Kal, he unwittingly drifted closer to him.

*Parignis*, Jolsu warned.

*I know*, he said. *But he's so close, I can feel his magic, his rage.* It was palpable, and Zak didn't know if he could sense it because of his spirit form or if it was so overwhelming as to somehow invade the physical world.

"What should I tell Queen Ymona about a timeline for a response?" Horace asked.

His voice, and the ensuing silence, recaptured Zak's attention.

Renna stared daggers at the messenger, and Horace took an involuntary step back. "You can tell her anything you'd like, since none of it will matter come the Year Festival. In fact, tell her that—survive until the third day of the Year Festival, and all her wishes will be fulfilled."

*The third day? What could be happening then?* Zak wondered.

*Zakolor!* Jolsu yelled.

Zak whirled around. He had drifted to the center of the room, dangerously close to Kal. His friend seemed to stare right through him, and when his hand reached out, Zak knew he was in trouble. Immediately his magic began draining, funneling toward Kal.

*Gods-cursed sorgeus!* Zak pushed against Kal, willing his spirit to leave the room. It was like swimming against the tide as Kal kept pulling and pulling.

"What are you doing?" Renna asked.

Kal looked at her, and the momentary distraction was all Zak needed to fly away, passing through layers of chambers before breaking through Pywell's thick walls and soaring across the open skies back to Tor'alan.

"Nothing," Kal said to Renna.

Her eyes narrowed, but after a moment she waved a hand at him. "Start again. And fix your form—you're weak on the left side."

"Yes, Renna."

Kal hefted the sword, wiping sweat from the leather grip on his trousers before resuming his starting position.

The presence he had felt—it was Zak. He didn't know it when he started absorbing the magic, but then that distinct green energy flowed into him, along with a sense of sadness and desperation.

There was no mistake. It had been the exact same when he absorbed magic from Zak months ago during the battle over the Druid.

He slashed with blinding speed, slivers of the wooden post chipping away. It was almost heartwarming to know Zak still cared for him, still wanted him back after all this time. After everything he had done.

The training post toppled over, cut clean in half.

*Don't worry, Zak. I'm coming for you, too.*

Kal smiled.

# CHAPTER 14

# EXPERIMENTS

"Elpida, please stop moving!" Zak shouldered past the bronze dragon. She took up nearly all the floor space in his tiny room, and with even the slightest movement she'd knock him over as he sidled toward the desk under the window.

*There is nowhere to be! When can I leave this little hole? It isn't fit for a dragon.* She snorted, and dark smoke swirled from her nostrils.

Shira had cloaked Elpida with her invisibility demon when they returned from Densba and smuggled the dragon across Tor'alan unseen. But Zak couldn't ask her to do the same thing each time Elpida needed to stretch her legs—and now, wings. Zak and Jolsu didn't want to let Elpida out of their sight, but the current living situation was no longer viable.

"I'll figure something out, okay? Just, can you shift to your right a little?"

She stood and bumped against the rusted trunk at the foot of the bed, which startled her into whipping around and growling at it, but the quilt snagged on her tail. Then she started circling to try and pull the fabric from her scales and crashed into the wall.

All the while, Zak shouted and jumped on her to try and help. They both tumbled to the floor, arguing and snarling.

A knock sounded at the door.

They both froze mid-brawl.

"Zakolor? Everything okay in there?" Inguma's musical voice carried through the bedroom door.

"F-fine!" Zak grunted, trying to disentangle from the quilt and Elpida's limbs. "Just some—oof, stop it—rearranging!"

Elpida hissed when he accidentally stepped on a claw, and when Zak shushed her, he immediately regretted it. She bared her fangs and reared up to her full height.

Inguma continued from the hallway. "Each room has an optimized layout, there isn't much space for a different configuration. If you'd like some assistance—"

"No!" Zak yelled, both at Inguma and Elpida.

But neither listened.

Elpida beared down, pinning him to the floor, corded muscle taut in her legs, just as Inguma cracked the door open.

"Adept Zakolor, you must use a more respectful tone—"

Zak coughed, all the air driven from his lungs, and peered up at Inguma from his spot on the floor. She blinked at him and Elpida, and none of them moved for an impossible amount of time.

Inguma recovered—much quicker than Zak would have—and stepped into the too-full bedroom and closed the door. "I see your lizard has grown."

*I am a dragon.* Elpida sat on her haunches and fanned out her wings, which were still too small for her to fly, but big enough to knock a stack of books from the desk.

"Clearly." Inguma's lavender hair frizzed around her face and enhanced the wild look in her eyes. She sighed and adjusted the half-moon spectacles on her nose. "I suppose this is Tansil's doing, having you look after her?"

"Yes," Zak said sheepishly, jostling from beneath a large bronze paw.

"And I assume he isn't aware of your...challenges?" She gestured vaguely to him, Elpida, and the wrecked room.

"No, Magus. I haven't had a chance to update him since his return." In fact, the reverse was true as well. Tansil had been tight-lipped about his time with the elves, and Zak had more than a few questions.

"Well, whatever this is, it isn't working." Inguma pursed her lips, apparently weighing her options. Zak picked at his collar beneath her evaluating gaze, and even Elpida had the decency to dip her head in embarrassment.

Eventually, Inguma shook her head. "Give me a few hours, I'll sort something out."

"You're brilliant, Magus! Thank you!" Zak hugged her before he knew what he was doing, but pulled back the moment his awareness caught up to his excitement, the tips of his ears burning.

"You have somewhere to be?" she asked Zak. She fought to keep her lips in a firm line, which suggested to Zak she found some of this humorous, or perhaps questioned her own decision to help.

He nodded, thanked her again, and begged Elpida to behave as he left the cramped room.

It was difficult not to run across the Center, into the castle, and down to the protected bowels of the ancient structure. Enough eyes already watched him stride across the manicured lawns, and any haste would surely breed a new round of rumours about his latest misadventures. Already there was talk of where he had disappeared to for those two days. If only his peers could spend as much energy fighting the Consortium as they did speculating about his every move, the League may have won the war by now.

If only.

There was no small amount of debate over what to do with Karazul. After Zak's spirit walk, they knew they had some time now—roughly six weeks—until the third day of the Year Festival, before whatever Renna and Zandorn had planned would unfold. Zak didn't pretend to know any of the details of their mad genius, but he suspected that the destruction of the Contract would play a key role. Why else would they have stolen it?

That was why his main focus became stealing the Contract back. And even though he hated the idea of working with Karazul, if there was any shred of truth to the assassin's willingness to help, he presented their best chance of success.

"He's been inside Pywell. He knows the layout of the tunnels and was part of their inner circle. I don't think we can steal the Contract without Karazul's help," Zak argued.

Sorwin had the most misgivings. "It's too dangerous.

Karazul's demands offer too many variables. Why would he return to us if we set him free?"

Tansil was there for the debate—physically, if not mentally. He was more present than when he left for Nalawin, but when asked about what happened, he'd utter things like "ridiculous" and "contradictory" before changing the subject or staring blankly out the nearest window. What Zak found most odd, though, was that he hadn't worn boots since his return.

So it came as no surprise when the Archmagus took a neutral stance on the matter. "There's merit and risk to both options. We'll have to decide whether to trust him or not—there's little else we can do."

Zak put his hands on his hips, adopting the stance Sorwin had used in many council meetings. "Look, I'm not saying we can trust Karazul completely, but we can start small. He wants information about his brother, and we've already given him more than Zandorn ever has. Why don't we use that to our advantage?"

A line appeared in Sorwin's brow, the one that meant he was deeply intrigued. "What did you have in mind?"

Zak smiled. "A little test."

With Tansil and Sorwin's help, Zak had gathered everyone he trusted in an abandoned prayer room deep within the twisting corridors of the ancient temple beneath the Center castle. It was the safest place to conduct his experiment, plus

Tansil was able to slip Karazul through the defensive charms and guards with relative ease.

For his part, Sorwin arrived a few minutes later and set a large glass jar on the floor in the middle of the room. A single Rotter ricocheted around the magically sealed container, hissing and squelching its black amorphous figure. Luckily, the League had managed to trap a couple of the heinous creatures and kept them on hand for studying.

Zak stood next to the jar as everyone—Tansil, Sorwin, Kaleb, Bazil, Shira, Olivia, and Karazul—lined up against the wall. He steeled himself and adopted the air of orator, lifting his chin and holding his shoulders back, just as he had seen Sorwin do a thousand times.

"Thank you all for coming. Before we begin, it's important to mention that this...experiment...isn't sanctioned by the council. Will secrecy be a problem for anyone?" He looked specifically at Kaleb, though Sorwin or Tansil could have found this equally as difficult.

Kaleb paled a little. Breaking his oath was a big request for the duty-bound soldier. Yet he nodded, and the rest of Zak's friends did too, apparently unbothered.

"Good," Zak continued. "As you all know, there are some similarities between Karazul's abilities and the Rotters. Both drain magic from anything they touch. I thought it a coincidence, or maybe that Zandorn created the little beasts based on Karazul's anti-magic. But something about the similarities always troubled me."

He paced around the jar and the Rotter cowered, trying to flee, but it had nowhere to go.

"When we fought for Terasi, my shield stopped Karazul. At the time, I thought it was because I channeled so much magic into the spell that he couldn't keep up, but that wasn't it. He had swatted through every other spell that came his way, so why not mine? Then I remembered—that had been the first time I connected with Jolsu.

"Then in Masdaan, the same thing happened with the Rotters. They couldn't get through my shield when they attacked at the council meeting. And my fire was the only thing that stopped them when they attacked Tor'alan, and when they streamed from the portals in the battle for the black caladrius."

He took a breath, feeling the heavy weight of attention upon his shoulders. No one else made a sound as he strode down the line of people he loved until, at the end, he reached the one person he hated most.

Karazul.

"Then we found out *you* were a god, and that changed everything."

"What's your point?" Karazul snarled.

Zak didn't waver. "*Nacusti* were imbued with the magic of the gods, which means your divine abilities aren't as effective against me, and now Olivia. Which *also* means that your anti-magic isn't "anti" anything. It *is* magic. And so are these Rotters."

"Three Fires," Bazil cursed, and then immediately covered his mouth with a hand.

Surprised sounds and movements came from the others too. Sorwin addressed him first. "Are you proposing that these Rotters are somehow connected to Karazul?"

"Exactly." Zak walked back to the middle of the room and nudged the jar with a boot. "And if that is true, then there's a chance Karazul can control the Rotters, or dispel them, or maybe both."

All eyes turned on Karazul.

The assassin didn't move. A hard line crossed his brow and went down his jaw. "What is it you want from me, *Nacusti*?"

Zak smiled. "It's simple. We'll open the jar and see how the Rotter reacts to you."

Karazul laughed. "You said if I entertained your little experiment that you would trust me enough to meet my demands. But you never said it would be life or death. If you're wrong—which is *very* likely—then that Rotter could kill me with a touch."

"He has a point, Zakolor." Kaleb crossed his arms, clearly uncomfortable defending the man that had run him through.

Zak didn't relent. "No, he doesn't. Because he is a god, so he will not die, especially not from his own magic. And even if I am somehow wrong, it's more than fair for him to try. After all the lives he's taken, all the damage and chaos he created, a quick death would be a mercy."

He had thought about this confrontation so many times. Not in this exact setting, not even the part about giving Karazul a chance to live. But since Vermig's murder, he had imagined daily what he would say to the gods-cursed assassin if he ever had the chance.

Karazul stared, beady eyes studying every little piece of

Zak. He didn't know what the man saw, but something informed him of Zak's resolve. "Fine. But I personally witnessed Zandorn control these beasts. So when I die, I will return from the pyre to haunt you for the rest of your days."

The assassin stumbled forward on atrophied legs. The state of his body may have been the only reason Karazul hadn't escaped yet, and Zak was grateful for the side effect of the *senligo*.

Zak knelt and gripped the lid of the jar. "I'll put a shield around the opening to keep the Rotter inside. You'll be able to reach your hand through unscathed."

"Lucky me," he said in a monotone voice. Karazul crouched beside Zak, sending a shiver through him. "I'll see you after the funeral."

Zak scoffed and yanked the lid off the jar with one hand, using the other to form a flat disc of fire over the opening. The Rotter had swirled up the side toward the momentary gap, but it slunk down now, cowering at the bottom away from the green flames.

"Go on." Zak gestured to Karazul with the lid.

"I want you to know, if I had any strength in me right now, I'd get rid of your meager shield and let this Rotter drain us all to death."

The venom in his words told Zak he spoke the truth.

"Then it's a good thing you're at *our* mercy right now."

All of his friends took a step closer, and Kaleb's blade appeared at Karazul's throat.

The assassin sighed. "Ah well, can't blame me for one final threat, can you?" And then he flexed his hand three times before plunging it into the jar.

The Rotter flinched and retreated, maybe expecting an attack. But when none came, it leapt onto Karazul's hands, embracing its base instinct to consume.

Zak waited for any indication that Karazul resonated with the Rotter's magic, or for him to drop dead.

But surprisingly, nothing happened.

"I don't understand," Shira said. "He isn't dying, not now, nor in the next few minutes." She blinked rapidly, and Sorwin reached out a hand to steady her.

"What do you feel?" Zak asked the assassin.

Karazul manipulated his hand and fingers as the Rotter crawled over his flesh. "Nothing. It feels...light and dry, like it's barely there." He sounded just as perplexed as the rest of them.

Bazil approached the jar and held a hand near the glass. "It's definitely still a Rotter. I can feel its hunger from here."

Zak grew suspicious of Karazul for a moment, but he quickly discarded the idea of trickery. The assassin had been surprised at the experiment and its results. There was no way he could have prepared for it ahead of time.

"You can remove your hand," he instructed. Karazul did, and Zak dropped the lid back into place as his green flames faded.

Without hesitation, Kaleb grabbed Karazul in a firm grip and pressed a blade against his ribs, not giving the assassin a chance to even consider attacking or escaping.

"What do you think?" Zak asked Sorwin. If anyone could puzzle out the mystery of what just happened, it would be his magus.

"We're missing something." Sorwin paced along the far wall of the prayer room. "There is a connection between Karazul and the Rotters—there has to be, otherwise he'd certainly be dead. Perhaps it is broken, or disrupted. He doesn't have the full powers of a god, maybe that's part of it."

"But didn't we determine Zandorn manipulated the Rotters in Masdaan?" Olivia asked. "Tansil sensed his magic on them, right?"

"Both things can be true," Tansil said. "Karazul could have a connection to the Rotters and Zandorn could be exploiting it. He's an excellent liar...I succumbed to his charisma a century ago. That's why we're in this mess."

"Tansil—" Sorwin reached for the elf, but he waved off the gesture.

"I apologize, I need a moment." Tansil moved for the door, and as he turned the handle, a Firepost tore through the air and halted before him.

Tansil opened the ashy envelope and read the letter. "Cerevita's grace," he whispered.

"What is it?" Sorwin asked.

"It's Lindomer." He turned, dropping the letter to the stone floor. "Its walls have been breached by the Rot. They need the *Nacusti*."

Zak met Olivia's wide-eyed gaze. He pressed his lips into a thin line. "We'll take care of it," he said to Tansil, keeping his focus on his fellow *Nacusti*.

Quick as ever, Olivia covered her shock with a cold exterior. Zak knew her well enough to recognize it for a defense mechanism—a survival tactic she had learned to protect herself from harm.

*Good.* He needed her prepared. While he'd successfully faced Rotters before, it was time to test *Nacusti* magic against the Rot itself. And while he was at it, maybe there was a chance for another experiment.

"Are you ready for your first act of repentance?" Zak asked Karazul.

The assassin blinked, mouth agape. It was only the second time Zak had seen him off balance.

"You can't be serious." Karazul caught onto his idea.

"Oh, I am. Dead serious." Zak grinned.

# Chapter 15

# THE ROT

O livia stepped onto the edge of a sturdy road just north of Lindomer, the blue portal closing as the others arrived.

A scowling Bazil supported Karazul's weakened frame, who donned a hooded cloak. It had been surprisingly easy to smuggle him from the Center to Tor'alan's entrance portal. Then again, with Sorwin leading the charge and two *Nacusti* in his wake, no one had seemed eager to bar their path.

"Shira, keep Elpida hidden until we assess the situation," Sorwin instructed. "We don't need an adolescent dragon further traumatizing the locals."

"Too right," Shira agreed. She looked to her left. "Only I can see you, Little Dragon. Take care not to run into anyone."

*I am not little anymore.* Elpida sounded haughty, and Olivia imagined the dragon lifting her scaly snout into the air with the declaration.

The orange gems on Sorwin's sword hilt winked in the afternoon sun when he adjusted his belt. "Zak and Olivia, with me. Kaleb, Shira, and Elpida—follow at Bazil and

Karazul's pace." He turned and jogged to the east, Zak and Olivia both trotting after him.

Shouts and screams carried over the city walls as they ran along the outside. Olivia spared a worried glance at Zak, and his round eyes reflected her concern.

It wasn't until they turned the corner toward the south that they understood what had happened.

The Rot had crept toward Lindomer for years. Olivia remembered hearing about it long ago before she left her home in Parplanham. But it had always moved slow, creeping along a hair's breadth at a time. From the last report Olivia recalled hearing in a council meeting, the Rot wouldn't reach Lindomer's walls for another year at least.

Yet the middle of the western wall had crumbled to dust.

Olivia froze in disbelief. Dark grey and black streaks covered the ground, oozing through the gaping hole in the wall like a river of death.

"What do we do?" Zak asked, voice thin.

Sorwin's attention flicked around the scene of destruction before them, analyzing. "We need to stop the Rot's progression. See if your fire can cut off the flow into the city."

Zak stepped forward, but turned back to Olivia when she didn't move. "Coming?"

She rolled her shoulders. "Right behind you." Olivia silently scolded herself. She had worked too hard for too long to control her emotions—this was no time to let fear run rampant.

*I'm a* Nacusti *now. This is bigger than me.*

She stopped at the edge of the Rot, her calm demeanor

restored despite being a step from death. One touch of the substance would be enough to claim her life.

"Let's try basic flames to see what happens," she suggested.

Zak agreed, and they both reached for their magics.

Amber and emerald fire shot from their oustretched palms and crashed into the Rot. It hissed and squealed like wet logs in a hearth.

Vess was there, within her fire. Their bond had grown stronger each day, and now she saw the proof, because to Olivia's utter shock, the dark mass retreated from their fire—both Zak's *and* hers.

She truly was a *Nacusti*.

"It's working!" Zak shouted above the blaring flames.

"Carve a path!" Olivia yelled back.

She turned toward the ruined wall, standing back-to-back with Zak. Slow and controlled, they kept up a steady stream of fire, slicing through the Rot. Zak focused on the incoming stream while Olivia burned through the section that had made it into Lindomer proper.

His body heat seeped through her tunic and shoulders. Zak was always warm. At least whenever she was near him, which was usually during training.

*Stulmati.* She couldn't get distracted with ridiculous thoughts right now. She needed to focus on the Rot. If they severed it, found a way to shore up the defenses, maybe they could destroy the part that terrorized the city.

It took at least ten minutes, but eventually they had cleared a narrow path right through the Rot, and it didn't show any signs of reconnecting. They lingered in the middle of the broken river anyway, flames dancing across their fingertips, ready to strike at a moment's notice.

Bazil and Karazul and the others had hobbled over to Sorwin in the meantime and gathered near the Rot's edge.

"Now what?" Olivia shouted to Sorwin.

"Zakolor, put up a barrier. A wall!" he called.

She felt him slide down as his stance widened. "Watch my back, will you?" he said quietly. It was obnoxious how she could hear the smile in his tone.

"Fine." She wanted to say something more caustic, but her words failed and the corner of her mouth tugged upward.

*Salted earth.*

"*Parperignis!*"

A line of emerald fire blazed along the border of the Rot in both directions. When it reached the end, it roared and grew to a staggering height—higher even than the city walls had been.

With the barrier in place, Olivia and Zak stepped carefully through the narrow path toward the rest of the group.

"Well done, both of you." Sorwin clapped them each on the shoulder. It felt odd celebrating when so much destruction surrounded them, but Olivia wouldn't dismiss even the smallest of victories. She needed them—and so did everyone else.

"The main body of the Rot is slowed for now," Zak said. "We should focus on the section in the city next."

Smoke drifted over Lindomer's walls, with more screaming. Olivia's fists tightened, imagining the Rot tearing through buildings and families.

*But why now?* Why had the Rot suddenly become aggressive after a century of sluggish expansion?

She was about to voice her question when movement atop the southern rampart caught her eye. A person—dark robes, arms weaving. They were casting, but what magic did they work? Were they a mage raising a defense for Lindomer?

"Who is that?" Olivia pointed toward the mage.

"Three Fires," Zak breathed. "That's Zandorn."

"He spotted us." Karazul lifted his arm from around the priest's neck. His withered legs shook beneath him, but he was determined to stand on his own.

Zandorn sailed down from the wall on black feathered wings, landing a good distance away. He walked slowly toward them. Strands of Rot gathered at his back, forming a dark wave that sped toward Karazul and the others.

*Coward.* Did Zandorn not deem Karazul worthy of a discussion before he tried to end his life? Well, the man was smart—that much was true. He wouldn't give Karazul the thinnest of chances to fight.

An orange shield appeared in the Rot's path. Of course Sorwin was the first to react—he was too quick for his own good, and Karazul remembered too well being on the receiving end of his magic.

But the Rot didn't struggle one bit. It tore through the barrier and kept crashing toward them, a tidal wave of death.

It all happened so fast. The *Nacusti* were sluggish from carving up the Rot. They moved to erect their own barriers, but Karazul could tell they'd never make it in time.

The Rot wave thundered, closing in, everything turning to dust beneath it.

Karazul leaped in front of the wave and threw his arms out wide.

He didn't know why he did it. He didn't have a plan—which was strange. Karazul *always* had a plan, and a backup plan, and an emergency plan too.

But this time he acted purely on instinct, and he was more shocked than anyone that his instincts told him to sacrifice himself for the *Nacusti*.

"Run while you can!" he called over his shoulder. *Brats better be grateful.*

He closed his eyes, bracing for imminent death.

A boom roared across the desolate field with the impact. As the seconds trickled by and Karazul kept breathing and not dying, he opened his eyes.

Light—a grey glow—clung to him, emanating from his pale skin. He flexed his arms and legs. All his lost strength had returned, and then some. He felt more alive and more powerful than he had before succumbing to the *senligo*.

What happened? Where was the Rot?

"I knew it!" Zak exclaimed.

Karazul turned toward the *Nacusti* with a puzzled expression.

"You absorbed the Rot. I knew you were connected somehow!"

Looking down at his hands, it was difficult to dismiss the boy's conclusion. The Rot wave was gone, and he was stronger than ever. Did that mean...

"Am I a god?"

The visions. Everything he saw in the *senligo* had been real. They were memories—not illusions—muddled by whatever curse he was under, but real nonetheless. He had been there at the beginning of the universe, had witnessed the shaping of mountains and creation of demons. His brother—his face and name still eluded him, but he could almost feel the warmth of his hand, pulling him. Always pulling.

And of course, Karazul remembered all the times he met Zandorn.

He glared across the field, dust and ash swirled in the air between him and the mage that had tricked him.

"You lied!" he shouted.

Zandorn smiled, but it was a nervous thing. "I don't expect you to understand, but it was for your own good."

"It was for your benefit. You *used* me. For decades!" Karazul stepped forward, wishing he had his blades in hand. Then again, this was personal. He'd strangle the life out of Zandorn with his own two hands.

"I gave you stability, a purpose. Without me you'd still be wandering aimlessly, forgotten by the world every thirty years."

"What?" That halted Karazul in his tracks.

Zandorn had the audacity to laugh. "You see? You know nothing of your curse. But *I* do. I even know how to break it. And I can help you do so if you strike down those fools behind you."

Karazul was halfway between Zandorn and the others now. He turned, looking back at the *Nacusti*. The boy still appeared young, but there was no doubt he had grown. How had it been almost a year since he first attacked him in the Southern Isles?

Much had changed since then.

Karazul sprinted toward Zandorn faster than any mortal could and threw a right hook. The mage was fast too—a black barrier appeared. It stopped Karazul's swing, but it fractured under his immense strength.

Zandorn danced out of reach, readying for the next attack.

Karazul froze.

"There's no blood contract, is there?" If there had been, he would have died the moment he attacked Zandorn.

Again the mage smiled, and Karazul wanted to rip the lips from his face. "Ah, my dear assassin. I'm going to miss pulling your strings. But in a few years, your curse will wipe your existence and memory from the world, and you'll start anew. By then I'll have everything I want, but maybe I'll track you down and plant fake memories once again. Just for the fun of it."

Karazul yelled, all his rage funneled into his fist as he moved to strike again. But pain pierced through him, dropping him to a knee. He gasped, and the grey glow faded from his skin as the Rot seeped away into the ground.

"Well, isn't that interesting," Zandorn said. "I didn't know you could absorb the Rot—a rare miscalculation on my part. But it seems there is a limit to how long you can hold your magic without this."

From the folds of his pocket, Zandorn produced a stone. It looked more like glass filled with grey swirling water, an eerie nothingness hidden within its depths.

A weakness overcame Karazul. He stretched a hand toward the stone—he felt its pull, knew instantly it was his, part of him.

His *cordeus*.

Zandorn crouched just out of reach, brandishing the stone. "Yes, you'll never be a god without this."

The last thing Karazul saw was Zandorn squeezing his heart in a white-knuckled grip, then everything went black.

When Karazul sunk to the ground, Zak hurled a fiery lance at Zandorn. Black flames intercepted his emerald ones.

Without a word, Olivia leaped into action too. She conjured a pool of water behind Zandorn and directed its flow toward his ankles.

Zandorn brandished the grey stone in his hand, and the water disappeared.

"Why are you here? Why did you attack Lindomer?" Zak yelled.

"The answer is quite simple, *Nacusti*."

Zandorn reached into a deep pocket within his robes. At first, it looked as if he pulled out a long strip of fabric. But when he held it aloft, Zak saw a black velvet dress with ornate embroidery curling across its entirety.

"A bit of shopping, to prepare for my wife's arrival." Zandorn grinned, and Zak's stomach turned.

*All this death, all this destruction, for fun?*

Before Zak shook himself from the angry stupor, Zandorn spoke again. "I tire of this exercise, and so I must bid you all farewell for now. I think I'll even leave the assassin alive. It will be interesting to see what you make of him."

A blue portal appeared behind Zandorn, and his gaze never left Zak's as he cackled and stepped backward, disappearing through the swirling magic.

# CHAPTER 16

# GODS AND HEARTS

Zak knocked on the door. It swung open, revealing Sorwin with a pinched brow.

"Everyone else is here," he said softly, ushering him into the townhouse.

He followed Sorwin through his grand home to a dining room with a curved ceiling and a mural of a mage at a mountain pass. Her cloak billowed and arms reached skyward, as if moving the peaks themselves. Zak had only seen the mural a few times, but it always fascinated him, how the scene actually *moved*—slow and controlled—like the whole world was submerged in thick honey.

It was beautiful magic, something he had grown to appreciate more and more as the world darkened around him.

Zak and Sorwin each took a seat at the long table, the last of the party to do so. While Zak had taken Elpida back to his room—with Shira's help—everyone that had been in Lindomer congregated at Sorwin's house. Tansil had also joined as the only council member privy to the semi-secret operation.

Nobody spoke. The decadent buffet in the center of the table went untouched. Olivia's knee bounced under the table to Zak's right, Bazil sat stone-still on his left. Tansil had that faraway look, staring out the window. Shira was knitting near Sorwin at the end of the table. Kaleb fiddled with a knife and kept glancing at Karazul who sat beside him.

The assassin appeared the most distraught of them all. He was no longer frail—absorbing the Rot in Lindomer had restored his body somehow. His hands rested on the table, palms up, and he hungrily searched them, attention twitching from one to the other as if they could tell him something—anything—that would solve his problems.

And to Zak's surprise, the tiniest speck of pity rooted in his chest for the man. He had done terrible things, killed so many people, and that could not be overlooked. Yet Karazul had clearly suffered for years—centuries—and not even a god could withstand such cruel torture unscathed.

Plus, he had saved them all when he threw himself in front of the Rot. That counted for something.

Zak cleared his throat, and it sounded loud against the deafening silence. "I know it feels like we lost to Zandorn again, but we haven't."

He waited, but still no one said anything. Not even to rebuke his claim, and that worried him more.

They had lost the will to fight.

Sorwin gave him a half-hearted smile, one full of apology, absent any humor.

*Even Sorwin?* Zak's confidence wavered.

*Tell them,* Jolsu urged. *Tell them what you know. Show them how to believe again. The darkest nights need the brightest stars. Light the way, Parignis.*

Zak took a shaky breath. He had figured something out on his walk to Sorwin's townhouse, and he hoped Jolsu was right—that it would be enough.

"Before Terasi died," he swallowed hard, but kept going, "he gave me a message. He told me about Elpida, that she may be a help. And that was true—her fire had cleared some of the Rot surrounding Karazul earlier today. Now we have three weapons against that magic."

He spoke louder. "But Terasi also told me something else. He said that Zandorn's power was in Pywell. That we needed to get to the mountain to defeat him. I don't know why he couldn't be more direct, maybe he didn't know what it was, or maybe Zandorn prevented him from sharing too much. But now we know."

Sorwin and Bazil both turned their heads to look at Zak.

*It's working.*

*Keep going, Parignis.*

"At the battle with the black caladrius, Zandorn did something that Jolsu and I couldn't understand. We cast powerful magic at him—nothing that he couldn't handle, but overwhelming enough that it should have distracted him so I could escape with the bird. Except he swatted it all away like a gnat. I'd only seen one other person do such a thing."

Zak looked at Karazul, and the rest of the eyes in the room did too.

Karazul picked his head up, pulled from his reverie. "He has my *cordeus*. My heart."

"He does. And that's been the source of his power all this time, for nearly a century."

"What do you mean?" Sorwin asked.

Zak almost smiled at his magus's curiosity, but he couldn't get distracted. He had to keep going. "Think about it. Only Zandorn figured out how to survive in the Rot. Only Zandorn could extend his life—and a select few others' lives—unnaturally long. Only Zandorn could make the Rotters and trap Karazul into service, because he had his *cordeus*. All along we've been fighting Zandorn as a man, when really he's been channeling the power of the gods."

"I felt stronger." Karazul stared at his hands again. "When I absorbed the Rot, when I was near my heart. I felt stronger. I don't know if getting my heart back will lift my curse, but it will weaken Zandorn."

"How can we trust you?" A sharpness lit Kaleb's dark eyes. "After killing Vermig, the countless attacks on the League you've orchestrated. Why would we help you become a god?"

"Because it's the right thing to do." Bazil leaned back in his chair. "I don't say this as a devoted, but as a person. Karazul has been cursed. What does it say about us if we *don't* help?"

"It isn't that simple," Kaleb countered.

More voices joined the fray, and the momentum Zak had built quickly unraveled before him.

Olivia stood and slammed a fist on the table. "Listen!"

The arguments quieted. She pushed back the curls that dangled around her forehead.

"I am new to being a *Nacusti*—I won't claim otherwise. But the moment I became one, I felt the weight here." She put a hand to her chest. "It's crushing, like drowning, every day, over and over. Knowing that the council, the people of Tor'alan—gods, everyone in Valecium—is counting on me and Zak to stop Zandorn. That pressure is suffocating.

"And I've only experienced it for a handful of weeks. Zak has endured it for almost a year. Yet here he is, the only one among us to have a shred of hope. He never let the pressure defeat him. Now here you all are, competing to see who will give up the fastest. It's sickening. What Zak, Jolsu, Vess, and myself need now is for you to listen, stop arguing, and discuss how we will defeat Zandorn."

She abruptly sat again, gave Zak one curt nod, and found something very interesting on the far wall to inspect as her cheeks reddened.

Zak couldn't stop smiling. He'd rarely heard her speak so much all at once. Being a *Nacusti*, in his opinion, very much suited Olivia.

*Focus, Parignis.* Urgency laced Jolsu's request, but also a sliver of mirth.

"Right—thank you, Olivia." He followed her example and stood, blinking back the burning sensation in his eyes. "I agree with Kaleb that Karazul's crimes can't be forgotten, but for now, we have to trust him. He had a chance to betray us in Lindomer. Zandorn made him an offer, and Karazul refused. Still, I'll ask directly. Karazul, will you fight Zandorn and the

Consortium with us?"

"To my end, if need be," he said without hesitation.

"Good. And...do you prefer Karazul or Niltris?" Now that his true identity had been confirmed, Zak wasn't sure which the man favored.

"I—" Karazul's quick wit abandoned him. He cleared his throat. "I don't know if I will ever be Niltris again. For better or worse, I am Karazul, for he is all I remember. But, thank you. For asking."

The assassin couldn't meet Zak's eye, but Zak sensed it was more of a discomfort with vulnerability than anything else. Working with Zandorn, Renna, and Burvenin—when he was alive—surely hadn't been a safe environment. Open hostility and backstabbing was more likely the day-to-day.

Zak still harbored anger toward Karazul. That wouldn't disappear after a day of cooperation. But it became increasingly difficult to cling to it the more he learned about Karazul. In his own way, he was a victim of Zandorn's scheming too, and that only hardened Zak's resolve to defeat the mage before he destroyed Valecium.

Bazil leaned forward, resting his elbows on the table. "As touching as this moment is, we still have no plan, and Zandorn having a *cordeus* further complicates things."

"I disagree," Shira said, knitting needles clicking together. "Knowing how a spell works illuminates its strengths and weaknesses. We can't get to the Consortium with the Rot in the way. It's been their protection, their barrier, from the League. But now we know that Zandorn controls the Rot with Karazul's *cordeus*. Thus..." She trailed off, raising her eyebrows at Zak.

"We steal the *cordeus*," Zak finished.

Shira winked. Bazil whistled, and shifted in his chair.

"How, though?" Olivia asked. "If I were Zandorn, relying on the *cordeus* for protection and power and immortality, I'd never let it out of my sight."

"He has to," Tansil said. He blinked rapidly, turning away from the window and back toward the table. "No mortal can carry a *cordeus* for more than a few days at a time. The power is too overwhelming and would drive them to madness."

"Zandorn's already a bit mad, isn't he?" Zak said.

Olivia punched him in the shoulder.

"Debatable," Tansil continued, "but the madness the *cordeus* inspires is different. I saw it once, about forty years ago. The Archalium before Vermig carried Baltenebris's *cordeus* for a month, determined to use it to save his hometown from the Rot."

The elf shook his head, long brown hair shimmering in the glow cast from magelight sconces circling the dining room. "When I went to check on him, the entire town had evacuated, and I found him in an abandoned house, cradling the *cordeus* and whispering to himself and the stone. He wouldn't listen to any words, didn't respond to any healing magics. An hour later, he threw himself into the Rot under the belief he could destroy it."

"Gods..." Zak could scarcely imagine a worse fate.

"Tansil is right," Sorwin said. "As powerful and clever as Zandorn is, even he would need a break from the *cordeus*. Give me a moment."

Sorwin stood and left the room. When he returned, he rolled out a large map on his end of the table near the hearth and beckoned everyone closer.

Zak recognized the look his magus wore—partially narrowed eyes, careful nodding, finger tapping his chin. Sorwin was about to figure something out.

"If Zandorn can't carry the *cordeus* with him, he'd store it in a safe place." Sorwin pointed a finger to the middle of the Wastelands, in the western part of Valecium. "Pywell Mountain is the old dwarven stronghold that the Consortium has used for most of the last century. Terasi's message to Zak about needing to infiltrate the mountain means Zandorn must keep it there."

"It makes sense, we've never been able to get inside." Olivia crossed her arms and scrunched her nose in annoyance.

"Most of us haven't, except for Karazul, and Zak's spirit. We learned in Lindomer that *Nacusti* and dragon fire burn through the Rot, and so it would make logical sense to move Tor'alan close to the Darlangson mountains and carve a path to Pywell. That's why Zandorn would expect us to come from the east." Sorwin's hands darted around the map as he called out each location.

Zak frowned. "But that would take weeks. We'd never make it in time to stop Zandorn. And even if we did, me, Olivia, and Elpida would arrive at the Consortium's gates exhausted."

"Exactly, which is why we're going to do it anyway." Sorwin smiled.

"Come again?"

"A feint." Kaleb said.

"Yes! While we're creating a ruckus in the east, we can have the *Swift Star* positioned in the bay to the west. The mountain is much closer to the sea and it will be easier to cross the Rot from the water.

Sorwin pointed along the coast, and it was true—the land looked thinner there.

Olivia tilted her head, considering the plan. "Who will be on the *Swift Star*? If we're needed to create a distraction, that doesn't leave anyone to get through the Rot."

"Ah, but it does." Sorwin focused his attention on Karazul. "You wanted your heart back, yes?"

"If you get me inside, I'll handle the rest."

There was something chilling about the assassin's conviction, yet it almost inspired Zak's own belief.

"You won't be going alone. Tansil has the most experience with a *cordeus*, so he'll join—"

"No."

Sorwin nearly choked at the abrupt interruption. "Archmagus?"

Tansil stepped away from the group, clasping his hands together. "I won't be in Tor'alan for the assault, nor with Karazul. I'll be in Nalawin with the elves."

Zak couldn't believe what he was hearing.

"Why?" Bazil dared ask.

"My recent visit was...incomplete. And I have reason to believe they may assist us against Zandorn, especially if he means to destroy the Contract and return the gods to this plane."

"Do you think they'll reopen their borders now—and quickly—after being closed for centuries?" Kaleb asked.

"I won't know unless I try." Tansil's voice wavered, and there was a pleading in the intensity with which he stared at Sorwin.

Zak suspected that if Sorwin asked Tansil to stay, he would, no matter how badly he wanted to go. For that, at least, the elf had Zak's respect. Even if he planned to abandon the League when they needed him most.

Sorwin crossed the room to Tansil and gently gripped his hands. He towered over the elf, but somehow they seemed equals. "You've always encouraged my pursuits—no matter how absurd or nonsensical. I'd never stand in your way, Magus. Your presence will be missed here, but I know you'll be fighting for us still."

They shared a few more words, too quiet for Zak to hear, before Sorwin returned to the head of the table. "Well, we'll need someone else to accompany Karazul. I suppose that means—"

"Me." Shira stood and set her knitting aside.

Sorwin sighed. "Can no one let me finish a sentence?"

Shira laughed and patted him on the shoulder. "Listen, dear, we can have the discussion if you'd like, but I've already seen it, and you relent after I point out how versatile my demons are, making me the perfect mage for an impromptu infiltration."

"Are you sure?" Sorwin asked, genuine concern lining the question.

"As sure as a pemberry vines." She eyed the assassin.

"We'll get your heart, and I'll See any betrayal before you've even considered it."

"I have no plans to test your trust or your gifts, magus." Karazul sounded sincere, if a little caustic.

Sorwin snapped his fingers and ceramic cups with delicately painted roses appeared on the table, along with a large pot of tea that Shira pounced upon. "If that's decided, we still have much to plan. Settle in, everyone. It's going to be a long night."

*It will be*, Zak thought. This was it, he could feel it in his bones. One way or another, this war would be coming to an end soon.

The final battle approached.

# CHAPTER 17

# CHANGE

A harsh wind shook the tree's branches. It was more of a sapling, a young thing yet to develop rough bark and sturdy limbs.

It stood stalwart against the dark nonetheless, surrounded by corpses. Zak never recognized the faceless bodies—which wasn't as relieving as he'd hoped. They reminded him that death approached with abandon.

Each time he woke from the dream in a cold sweat he wished it was just that—a dream. But it wasn't. It was the future, a certainty.

But why the tree? Why the darkness? Why the corpses?

"Every image has a meaning," Shira said in their Sight lessons, which had become near daily occurrences. "Though they may not always be obvious."

"I hope this one isn't as literal as the other visions." Zak recalled the dreams with the black caladrius in the Yew Tree, and his first one—where he ran away from Burvenin through the forest surrounding Densba. Both had been exact in their predictions.

What if this one was too?

He shuddered and sipped at his tea, an earthy and fragrant flavor Shira deemed "perfectly appropriate for today," and she was right, as usual. The sitting room, which had been too warm only a few weeks ago, now warded the Winterfall cold from Shira's apartment.

Even after he left, the heat clung to him as he shuffled through the Market district, puzzling over the vision. He and Shira had tried the same partnered readings they did with the black caladrius, but it hadn't worked. Shira believed something interfered with their Sight, which made worry lines appear at the edges of her pensive expression.

Distracted by his thoughts, Zak almost ran into a stall and its keeper selling pemberry tarts. He apologized and bought one for two Bronze Marks, which satisfied the man's frustration.

Zak rounded the corner onto the main road in Tor'alan and leaned against a magelight post, biting into the slightly sour pastry.

With the cold and snow flurries, there weren't many people out, otherwise Zak may have missed spotting Rauffe down the street.

He stepped heel-to-toe toward the entrance portal, arms outstretched for balance.

"What the—" Zak had no inkling what Rauffe was doing, but something didn't sit right. He and Tansil had caught him acting equally as strange in the Center a few weeks prior.

Just as he pushed off the magelight post to confront Rauffe, a strong arm hooked his elbow and spun him around.

"There you are!" Olivia said. "You're late for *Nacusti* practice. I have a new idea for us to try."

"I—but—Rauffe—" Zak stammered and tried to look back, but Olivia's grip was like iron as she marched him toward court seven. After a few steps, he forgot all about Rauffe and focused entirely on the warmth from her hand on his bicep.

"Vess and I finally started piecing together some of Temaway's journal." Olivia waved the worn book in the air at Zak, who stood a few paces away on the training court lawn.

His eyes widened. "Really? What does it say?"

She turned over the pages, careful not to harm the ancient teachings. "Don't get too excited, there's still a lot we can't read, half-sentences and fragmented ideas. Temaway covered it in protective charms. He even shielded it so Vess couldn't remember its contents or read it alone. It requires her and a bonded *Nacusti* to decipher the pages."

*Temaway was always cautious and prepared*, Vess's high voice chirped. *That's why he survived so long.*

"Gods." Zak scratched his head, and Olivia fought a smile—he always looked young when he thought too hard. "So what did you find?"

"The Three Fires." Olivia found the correct pages and sat cross legged on the ground. Zak did too. "It's been the answer to fighting Zandorn the whole time, we just didn't realize it."

"What do you mean?"

"Remember Temaway's fight with Karazul? He used the Three Fires against him—a god, though we didn't know it at the time—and handily defeated him despite being on his deathbed."

*Breathe*, she reminded herself. Excitement bubbled easily when she finally felt like she was contributing to the cause, carrying her own portion of the *Nacusti* burden.

But she couldn't get distracted or let her emotions or magic run rampant. Not after the years she worked to control it, not after overcoming the *vitaligo*, not after dying and being reborn as a *Nacusti*.

She flattened the journal on the unseasonably green grass and spoke slower. "We need the Three Fires to defeat Zandorn, and Temaway left us instructions on how to master them."

"Three Fires." Zak meant it as a curse, and scoffed at himself for the timely phrase. He shook his head. "We have the Consuming Fire perfected, we saw as much against the Rot. But how will we learn the other two—which are supposedly much more difficult—in a matter of weeks?"

"I thought the same, and then I realized we can't, and we don't have to."

"O...kay. Can you tell me why?"

Olivia smirked. Zak was intuitive, had brilliant instincts for people and battle, but none of Sorwin's strategic mindset seemed to have rubbed off on his apprentice over the last year.

That was fine with Olivia. He clearly needed her help.

"Counting Elpida, there's three of us with fire that should work against Zandorn even if he uses Karazul's *cordeus.* You're right that we don't have time to learn the Curing and Creating Fires in the next few weeks, but we could each focus on one."

"We each take a fire." He sat up straighter, catching onto the idea.

"Yes. And since Elpida is new to fire magic, she'll continue developing the Consuming Fire. Then I'll take Curing and you'll take Creating."

Zak frowned. "Why?"

Olivia had thought about it relentlessly over the last few days, and her logic was sound. "Vess mastered the Curing Fire even before she became a Guardian, and she taught Temaway too. According to her, Adrastus and Jolsu used the Creating Fire to turn the tide of the entire Guardian War."

"Is that true?" Zak asked. He looked down and to the side, the same way he always did when speaking to Jolsu.

*It is.* Jolsu's deep voice rumbled. *I never learned the Curing Fire, but together Adrastus and I blazed bright with the Creating Fire.*"

"Why didn't you tell us sooner you can teach us this magic? We could have it mastered by now!" Zak exclaimed.

*It isn't that simple, Parignis.*

*We can guide you, but the Fire's secrets cannot be taught, only discovered,* Vess said.

Olivia nodded. "That's why it wouldn't have mattered if you started months ago. Time isn't a determining factor here—need and comprehension will be what win the day."

Zak stood and paced along the wall. Olivia gave him time to reckon with the information. It was a lot to take in—she was well aware—and if their roles had been reversed, she would have been much more resistant.

Sometimes she found his patience and persistence annoying, but today she couldn't be more grateful he possessed them.

He stopped after a few minutes. "I'm terrible at Thought casting. Isn't the Creating Fire the same idea?"

"Vess?" Olivia asked.

*In many ways, yes. Both rely on focused willpower to manifest magic. But Thought casting is nonverbal and non-physical. The Creating Fire can be used with Word and Guide casting.*

He didn't move except for the tapping of his fingers on his hip and the subtle movement of his jaw as he bit his lip. Olivia quickly diverted her attention away from his mouth to study the grain of the wooden door that sealed the training court.

Zak clapped his hands together once, the sound startling Olivia. "Fine, let's try it. What do we have to lose, anyway?" He grinned, knowing exactly what she'd say in return.

They'd developed a gallow's humor in their training sessions which intensified each day the Year Festival drew closer.

"Only everything," she replied.

Sorwin strode through the Center castle halls, thick boots echoing off the hard stone floor.

He had told Alessa everything—from the trip to Masdaan and Haramil, meeting Malu, jaunting over to Jolsu's altar, and finally the fiasco of uncovering Karazul's identity and confronting Zandorn.

It was fair to say she had been more than vexed.

But not surprised. She nodded along with his account, and though each detail deepened the crease between her brows, she never once appeared shocked or caught unawares. Almost as if she knew the broad strokes of his misadventures with the *Nacusti* and only needed the finer nuance filled in. Which was good, because that meant Sorwin hadn't technically betrayed his agreement to keeping Malu's identity secret.

He'd never understood how Alessa collected her information, what magic or spies she used, but whatever her methods, they were as sharp as ever. No secret could be kept from Alessa Darlangson.

And it was just as well, for Sorwin had been on the receiving end of too many secrets in his time with Tansil.

He turned right, down a long hall with latticed windows sealed tight against the Winterfall chill. Tansil stood in the hall, peering through the frost-covered glass at the modest courtyard beyond them. It was covered in snow now, but for most of the year the elf tended the garden with the love and attention of a doting parent.

"How did it go?" Tansil asked without turning.

Sorwin stopped a pace away. "Well enough. Alessa didn't condone our excursions, but she understands the position we're in with Zandorn. She'll convince the council of our plan."

"And what of Ms. Motchit?"

"Shira didn't volunteer lightly. She knows the risks as well as anyone—probably better, given her Sight."

"And you, Apprentice?" Tansil looked up at Sorwin, green eyes glowing bright against the grey stone hall. "How are you?"

Sorwin frowned. Tansil didn't spend time on conversation if it could be avoided. He never went through the motions when it was just the two of them. Never, not once in all the time they had been meeting in the quiet courtyard. Once a week, year after year, it had always been questions about the council or the Consortium or Zakolor, never about Sorwin himself.

Something was wrong.

"I would ask the same of you, Magus."

Tansil sighed. "There's a lot to be grateful for, living a life as long as mine. I've witnessed the reshaping of the world several times, the rise and fall of nations, learned so much about magic and the gods and Guardians. And yet, there is a steep cost with so much time. I have had near endless hours to become acutely aware of my shortcomings, my failures. I must apologize, Sorwin. I fear I failed you even more than I failed Zandorn."

After almost twenty years with Tansil, Sorwin had seen the elf in many moods, including weary and angry and inspired. And despite his short stature, the elf always had a commanding presence. Yet now, Tansil's sorrow shrunk him, making him appear small to Sorwin for the first time.

"Magus." He laid a hand on Tansil's thin shoulder. "You never failed me or Zandorn. It's true we had our differences—I'll never forget our first real debate over the merits of the astral plane."

"Why you continue to waste your energies on such a place is beyond me."

"I yield!" A fleeting smile crossed Sorwin's lips, seeing Tansil's fire return momentarily. "I never once begrudged those differences. I learned more than magic from you, Tansil. I learned about adversity, about taking the winding path, about determination, about the beauty in the simpler things. I learned a lot about myself because of you."

Tansil shook his head. "You overwhelm me with un-earned accolades."

"No, I'm telling you my truth. And I'll tell you Zandorn's as well: he made his own choice. I may not have been alive to see it for myself, but when his wife died, he had a choice. He could have grieved and moved on, but he chose to live in his sorrow. He's been stuck in the same place for a century, and that was never your fault."

"My head knows you're right, but my heart refuses to lay the guilt aside." Tansil clutched at his chest.

Suddenly, all of Tansil's strangeness made sense.

"You're not coming back, are you?" Sorwin should have seen it sooner, but when Tansil returned from his last trip to Nalawin, he thought things would be fine, that he had some sort of arrangement with the elves.

"You were always so bright, and far quicker than I'll ever understand." He reached into his pocket, pulled out a leather pouch, and placed it gently in Sorwin's palm.

"Not now," Sorwin said, "not when we need you most."

Tansil gently gripped his elbow. "That's what I'm telling

you, Sorwin. You haven't needed me for some time. In the last few months you've performed more of the Archmagus duties than I have. It should have been your title long ago, but I clung to it selfishly because it kept me here. But I cannot make the same mistake as Zandorn. It is time for me to move on."

His hand fell away and he walked past Sorwin down the hall, pausing after a few steps. Neither of them turned toward the other, but Sorwin heard his words clearly.

"I may no longer be here, but I am not quitting the fight. Zandorn is still my responsibility. Your plan is a good one, and I'll muster what aid I can."

Tansil's robes rustled as he left.

Sorwin stood alone and squeezed the leather pouch with Cerevita's *cordeus* as tears raced down his face.

# Chapter 18

# Belief

Zak hadn't slept—not even to dream about the tree surrounded by darkness and corpses. He had paced for an hour in his now-spacious room. The one next door had been vacant, and Inguma—the wonder that she was—removed the wall between them.

It had been just enough space for Elpida's hulking form. Jolsu had finally agreed to support her growth, and she now stood as tall as a horse.

There was no keeping her a secret any longer. Shira had left the city with Karazul, which meant her demon wasn't around to cloak the dragon every day, and there wasn't much point in hiding Elpida as the final battle approached. And though there would have been more adequate accommodations elsewhere in the Center, Jolsu didn't want to let her out of his sight. Neither did Zak, for that matter.

It was the first day of the week-long Year Festival, and Tor'alan had reached the Darlangson Mountains.

Fortunately, most of the city had been evacuated along the way, which meant Zak didn't have to explain why his roommate was a dragon to anyone besides the braver mages that dared ask.

The council had held daily public speeches by the entrance portal informing Tor'alan residents that the city's safety could not be guaranteed in the coming weeks. While no one would be forcibly removed from their home, it was strongly encouraged to vacate.

Most people agreed. As Tor'alan flew west, it stopped a handful of times near other cities, offering residents the chance to disembark. Two large temporary campsites were raised, far enough from the Rot and the battlefront near Gort'haal to be safe from conflict.

Zak opened the door to his room and jerked his head toward the hallway. Elpida rose from her bedding with a grunt and followed him up the spiral staircase to one of the upper balconies in the Dormitory.

The early morning gave them a clear view of the thick, unbroken blanket of snow covering the peaks and valleys of Darlangson below. Zak saw faint glittering to the north, like sun reflecting off glass.

"That must be Brenstel, Sorwin's home." He pointed to the distant light, and Elpida turned and raised her snout, sniffing the air.

*I would like to see another human city besides this one.*

"Yeah, maybe we can fly there together when this is all over." *If we survive*, he thought. But he kept it to himself.

Elpida rumbled her approval, claws scratching against the polished wood balcony.

"Don't let Inguma catch you doing that," Zak warned.

She immediately settled on her haunches and picked up her front legs. *That woman is the only person in Tor'alan worth fearing.*

"You may be right." Zak shivered, not just from the cold wind whipping over the railing, but at the memory of Inguma's cutting glares—especially when it came to his many laundry failures.

*What is the Year Festival?* Elpida asked.

Zak scratched the back of his head, wondering how Kal would explain it. "A celebration of the new year, mostly. But also of the beginning of the world."

*How did the world begin?*

Zak blew air between his lips. "Well, there's a day for each part of the story, but I'm not sure if it took more than five days or not." He cleared his throat. "The first day we fast and wear grey, to acknowledge the nothingness before the world existed. On the second day, Azubelux is honored for bringing light, and most people wear white or yellow. The third day is about Baltenebris creating darkness and demons—there's usually performances about that, and a lot of black clothes. The fourth day is about Cercvita creating the elements and people, so lots of green everywhere. Then the fifth day celebrates magic as the thread that binds the world together. And Tansil said that every century, the gods rotate the throne of power on the last day."

Elpida snuffled quietly, which Zak had come to recognize as her thinking tic. *It's strange that there are five days of celebration and only three gods honored.*

"You're right." He thought about Jolsu's memory from

the cave, where Karazul had stood next to the Three with a fifth mystery god beside him. "Maybe it was different, before."

Elpida hummed her agreement and settled into a comfortable silence beside him.

Zak sighed. He wanted to stay on that balcony, watch the sun completely rise and lean against Elpida's warm scales. But he couldn't delay any longer. "We should go, it's nearly time."

Elpida jumped over the railing, floating on bronze wings to the empty lawns below. Zak followed, his green wings disappearing as he touched down on the stone path.

The closer they drew to the entrance portal, the more crowded it became. Everyone remaining in Tor'alan—mostly soldiers and mages—had gathered near the raised dais and a temporary platform that had been built to extend it. Most of the council milled atop the structure in hushed conversations. A nervous buzz rippled over the crowd, further simmering Zak's acidic gut.

*We've done this before,* Jolsu said, trying to calm his nerves. *Remember how many battles you've already fought? This is just one more.*

Zak nodded to himself and knew Jolsu felt his gratitude for the comfort.

The crowd hushed and parted for Elpida as she padded to the platform, head held high. Zak had to admit she was an impressive sight—powerful muscles flexing under bright bronze scales, majestic wings tucked along her back. He overlooked the smug curl to her snout that exposed sharp fangs.

*A dragon's pride can be their downfall,* Jolsu warned. *But it can also be their boon in battle.*

*We'll take all the boon we can get.* Zak patted Elpida's flank as they stopped beside the council's platform.

Queen Alessa stepped forward and ran a finger up her throat. Her voice boomed over the assembly. "People of the League! You have fought long and hard. You have every reason to be tired, afraid, and defeated."

A restlessness washed over the crowd, but it did not deter Queen Alessa.

"You may very well feel that way, and that is the very reason why Zandorn should fear us."

The crowd stilled, caught in her weave of words.

"Though you may tire, you raise your swords and spells. Though you may be afraid, you face the oncoming enemy. Though you may feel defeated, you stand against the darkness, a beacon of light in these harsh times. For you are of Valecium, of the League of Kingdoms, and you shall give no quarter to evil!"

Scattered shouts sounded, building momentum with the queen's words.

"The Era of Dominion ended long ago, yet Zandorn would see us thrown to our knees in servitude to the gods once again. We stand against him not only for our lives and our families, but for all mortals in Valecium. We stand against unchecked power. We stand against unfettered control. We stand against the threat to our rights and freedoms."

The cries from the crowds rivaled Queen Alessa's enhanced voice, and she paused, letting the fervor overtake her people.

Behind her, the council clapped and cheered in various levels of excitement. The Archs—Sashina, Rinka, and now, Sorwin—wore broad, determined smiles. There hadn't been time for a ceremony for Sorwin's ascension to Archmagus. A formal Firepost had been sent to every member of the Elemental House, and for the time being, that would have to do. Even though Tansil's departure stung more than Zak thought it would, he was so proud of Sorwin. He had earned the position several times over.

The military representatives on the council stood still and stoic. General Lupa and Kaleb were absent—they'd already gone south to the front near Gort'haal to face the main body of the Consortium forces.

Euphemius and the other merchants appeared nonplussed. War was good for business, and it seemed that no matter the outcome of the day, their ledgers would suffer.

If that was what they truly cared most about, though, Zak had no sympathy for them.

Queen Alessa quieted the crowd with outstretched palms. "You know why you are here. Your job is to protect the *Nacusti* and Elpida, the first dragon in Valecium in over four hundred years."

Another surge of cheers erupted, and Zak, Olivia, and Elpida climbed the platform at Queen Alessa's beckoning.

The weight of the crowd's focus was stifling. Zak's throat thickened and his hairline itched. He didn't like the attention, but he understood it. The League had always needed symbols to rally behind, and for the last year, he had been one. But now, seeing Olivia and Elpida at his side, he smiled, because he wasn't alone.

*Before you say it, I already know,* he told Jolsu. *I was never alone.*

Jolsu rumbled his approval, warmth flooding their bond.

"Our new Archmagus will explain the finer points of our strategy." Queen Alessa stepped aside and Sorwin moved to the front of the platform. He made the same gesture along his throat with a single finger.

"As you've all heard by now, we successfully defeated the Rot for the first time." Ruckus cheering forced Sorwin to pause before continuing. "In Lindomer, Zakolor and Olivia cut through the Rot with their fire. During that time, we discovered that Elpida's dragon fire works on it too. Thus our plan is to have the three of them blaze a trail through the Rot right to the Consortium's gates."

Excitement and confusion murmured through the square, and Sorwin pounced upon both. "You may be wondering where you fit in. For too long, Zandorn has used the Rot as a shield, and more recently, as a spear. We now have the answer to his ultimate defense." He swept an arm out toward Zak, Olivia, and Elpida. "And when Zandorn realizes we're on the attack, he'll answer in kind. We don't know how he and the Consortium will respond, but we can guarantee they will do everything they can to stop the destruction of the Rot. You brave soldiers and mages will defend the *Nacusti* and the dragon Elpida while they focus their efforts on the Rot. You will shield them, fight for them, die for them if need be, for they hold the key to our victory."

Utter silence followed Sorwin's words. At first, Zak

thought he had quelled their fervor with brutal honesty. It was one thing to swear allegiance to the League, and quite another to die for it.

But a single sound—a boot stomped onto a cobblestone—rang across the gathering. It stomped again, and again.

Then another joined, and three more after that.

And within a minute, the entire platform shook as every soldier, mage, and council member stomped a foot in time together, giving voice to the cadence of their beating hearts.

One rhythm.

One people.

One purpose.

The pace quickened and soon the chorus grew cacophonous—spear butts sparking, fists punching, yells and chants piercing the air—Zak barely breathed as his heart threatened to burst through his chest. He grabbed Olivia's hand and placed the other on Elpida's shoulder.

It was up to them.

It was *all* up to them.

*Do not let their hope be a boulder upon your back, but the gust that lifts you to greater heights,* Vess said.

Zak and Olivia shared a wide-eyed look and nodded.

The Archs and generals took over from there, shouting orders to regiments and dividing the priests, summoners, and elementalists up for equal coverage between units.

Sorwin's strong hand squeezed Zak's shoulder. "Ready?"

"As I'll ever be. Thanks for leaving the part about the Three Fires out." Zak half expected him or Queen Alessa to mention the legendary magic as part of the rallying cry, but he was happy they didn't. It would have been motivational to hear the *Nacusti* and dragon had mastered the Three Fires.

It also would have been a lie.

Partially, at least. Elpida had no challenge using the Consuming fire. In fact, she'd nearly burned down court seven every day for a week straight while practicing. Olivia had struggled with the Curing fire at first, but just yesterday she had healed the wound on his arm, the one Zandorn had given him, the one not even Archlumen Sashina had been able to heal.

Zak looked down at the smooth skin, showing no trace of where the dagger had bitten through his flesh. He had tried—gods, had he tried—to discover the secret to the Creating fire. But no matter how hard he focused, how diligently he believed, he couldn't create the simplest of things.

He was the only one to fail.

"You are more than your magic, Zak." Sorwin offered his comforting smile—the one that slid sideways and revealed an elusive dimple. It usually appeared when Zak hadn't quite understood the lesson for the day, but Sorwin had faith he'd get there tomorrow.

"That goes for all of you." Sorwin nodded to Olivia and Elpida. "These people don't just believe in you because of your power. They believe in you because of who you are, how you treat them. They *know* you. They've spent the better part of a year battling beside you. That type of devotion and leadership cannot be bought, it must be earned. And you, Zak and Olivia, you have both earned it."

*Comforting.* Zak sighed, letting a little of the tension go between his shoulders. Sorwin always said the right thing.

Olivia spoke up. "Then how do you explain that?" She jabbed a thumb to the side.

Elpida had turned away from the conversation and sat on her haunches, preening in the glow of adoration from nearby soldiers. They ogled her scales, asked permission to touch her forelegs, and jumped and laughed nervously when Elpida playfully bared her fangs.

"That," Sorwin said, "is just natural. A *dragon*, in Valecium, for the first time in *four centuries*. Can you blame them?" Half a laugh crept from his throat, and it was clear Sorwin certainly couldn't.

After much coaxing, Zak dragged Elpida away from her new admirers and toward the entrance portal. Together with Olivia, the three of them had a moment before the plan swung into motion.

"Remember, we're the distraction," Zak said. "Don't burn through your magic too fast. Like Sorwin said, Zandorn will definitely come for us when he notices what we're doing."

"Think you can handle some restraint, oh Bronze One?" Olivia asked Elpida.

Her nostrils flared with a snort. *A dragon never wastes fire on mice.*

Olivia shrugged. "Good enough."

Jolsu's approval echoed through the bond. Over the last several weeks, Zak had conjured Jolsu's form and gave him and Elpida privacy for a few hours each day for what they had dubbed "dragon lessons." Zak could only guess at what else the two of them had covered in their time together.

"We can do this." Zak had to believe it. He hadn't mastered the Creating Fire, but the principle was simple enough. Believe a thing hard enough, give it the right amount of magic, and it could be true. Real.

He needed to believe that together, they could defeat Zandorn. The fate of the world depended on it.

And then he could finally bring Kalbick—his best friend, the closest thing to a brother he'd ever had—home.

# CHAPTER 19

# INFILTRATION

Karazul leaned on the railing of the quarterdeck, swaying with the choppy waves beneath the *Swift Star*. The ocean churned, a dark greyish blue. A storm approached.

Glancing ahead, the jagged cliffs of the Wastelands had finally come into view after weeks of sailing. He had spent most of that time retraining his recovered muscles and sharpening his blades to a deadly edge. Avoiding the loud and bothersome crew within the confines of the vessel tested even his mastery of stealth.

It had been a long few weeks.

Captain Swortizzle slapped Karazul's shoulder with a meaty hand. "Lookin' to be about time." The man always sounded cheerful, no matter the subject of conversation or time of day.

*Irritating.*

Karazul's black cloth shirt and leggings didn't make a sound as he descended to the main deck. Shira waited there, strategically avoiding the chaos of the crew scurrying about to bring the ship as close to the rocky shore as possible.

"You're sure you can get us over it?" Karazul flicked a hand at the cliffs, but he wasn't referring to scaling them.

Shira understood. She always did. "The Rot will start draining my magic the moment we're above it. I have a demon that should get us there before it kills me, but I wouldn't decline any help you could offer."

Karazul shrugged and said nothing. They both knew he had no idea how his powers worked. The Rot was connected to him somehow, but that didn't mean he could control it.

He stared at the grey and lifeless shores. Could that mass of death really be part of him? What could be so absent of life and magic? What was he the god of?

*Nothing good.* But he could have guessed as much on his own.

The *Swift Star* groaned beneath his feet as it struggled to turn port side against the crashing waves.

"This is as close as we can get!" Swortizzle yelled from the helm. He spun the wheel and caught it in an iron vise. "Whatever it is yer doin', now'd be the time!"

Shira had already been preparing. Her finger circled her *lapidaemas* before pointing at the deck. Out of the swirl of purple smoke, a tall winged figure appeared. He had the body of a man with rippling muscles beneath blue skin. Blue and green feathers ran from his forehead down his back, and his face appeared more akin to a bird with a sharp beak and round yellow eyes.

"A Nox demon?" Karazul grinned. "You should have told me you had this kind of power." A fourth level demon was no minor entity—even Renna could only manage a handful of them.

Shira returned his smirk with one of her own. "There's always a time and place to reveal one's hand, as you well know." She addressed the demon next. "Chidamee, we're going to Pywell Mountain, in the middle of the Rot. I'm sorry to ask this of you—but your speed is the only chance we have."

The bird man stood nearly double Karazul's height and scooped both him and Shira into his arms, careful to keep his sharp claws from cutting them. "It is no trouble. Together we will conquer this obstacle." Chidamee's voice was low and gravelly, befitting a creature of his stature.

The entire ship rocked when Chidamee crouched and launched himself into the air. Karazul heard the crew's shrieks turn into whoops of celebration as the demon soared up, circling and thrumming his enormous wings against the air. It didn't take long for him to rise above the cliff's edge.

"Hold on," Shira warned.

Karazul clutched Chidamee's arm, but it didn't make a difference.

The demon's wings glowed a bright blue, and with one thrust he surged forward.

*Such speed!*

The landscape blurred and the wind became heavy, like a horse stood upon Karazul's chest and threatened to crush him.

He laughed.

It was a giddy, exhilarating laugh.

Something about the pace, or flinging himself into certain peril, or maybe the sense that finding his heart would get him one step closer to finding his brother—Karazul wasn't sure what did it, but something deep within his core loosened just a little, enough for a genuine, real laugh. He didn't have a single memory of any mirth or joy.

It was short lived. To his left, in Chidamee's other arm, Shira looked nauseous and pale, and it had nothing to do with the incredible speed with which they flew.

The Rot already began extracting its heavy toll, draining her magic and life force.

Karazul scowled. There had to be *something* he could do.

Anti-magic wasn't an accurate moniker for his powers, but he never corrected the rumors or accusations. In truth, his ability closely resembled the Rotters' draining, and whenever he used it, the magic he drained flowed through him, he just didn't know where it went. That's why he never minded the nickname The Void—somehow it captured what he did to magic and how he felt.

Empty.

He couldn't feel Shira's magic draining, but Karazul gripped her hand and imagined the flow of magic, rushing from Shira to the swathe of death and emptiness beneath them. He couldn't reverse it, couldn't restore what had been taken, but he pictured the stream of magic stopping, freezing like a northern river in the depths of Winter.

Shira exhaled. "Whatever you're doing, don't stop."

He didn't. He focused on the magic, making it rigid and unmoving.

Chidamee never slowed. If anything, the wind whipped faster over Karazul as the demon raced ahead, desperate to reach the mountain. His wings stopped glowing and fanned out wide as he landed on the peak, setting Shira and Karazul down as careful as eggs he feared would crack.

Free of the Rot's influence, Shira dismissed Chidamee and fell to her knees. She caught her breath while Karazul scouted their surroundings. Hardly anyone ventured atop Pywell, so he wasn't surprised to find no evidence of recent visitors.

He climbed the old watchtower on the eastern face, leaping over cracked stonework and missing steps. Whenever the fortress had become too suffocating—or if Burvenin had grated his nerves to the point that Karazul swore he'd murder the man in his sleep—he would escape up here, getting lost in the whistling wind and endless sea of grey.

The nothingness always quieted his mind, and now he was beginning to understand why.

When he returned to Shira, she straddled half of a stone wall. A knitted towel and a tea kettle emitting a potent floral fragrance rested before her.

She held up a hammered copper cup. "Lavender. Always helps before a tense job."

Karazul took the offered tea and made the mistake of sniffing it, which dizzied him for a moment.

"Best enjoyed after a long steep, but we're in a bit of a rush." Shira winked.

He downed the drink in one gulp and handed the cup back, and the entire set disappeared as Shira conjured an iron staff and grunted as she stood.

"Keep your Nox demon handy," Karazul suggested.

She chuckled. "Oh trust me, I have a feeling you'll see much of my stable before the day is through." She faded from view as the Caries demon cloaked her in its mist, rendering her nearly invisible.

Karazul made his way down the weather-beaten path to the secluded entrance of Pywell Fortress, Shira's quiet footsteps padding close behind.

He had thought long and hard about where to look for his *cordeus* during the journey on the *Swift Star*. Most of the dwarven fortress had been open to him during his employ with the Consortium. It was roughly divided into three tiers: upper, middle, and lower.

The upper levels contained the old royal quarters, where Renna and Zandorn spent most of their time. The middle was home to the grand marketplace, with its wide stone platforms serving as mustering ground and portal crossroads. The old shops, workrooms, and homes had been converted into training rooms, barracks, and holding cells.

Karazul had spent much time on both tiers, attending meetings, giving reports, and planning assaults. While Karazul wouldn't claim to know all the secrets of those rooms, he didn't believe Zandorn would hide his *cordeus* right beneath his nose. It would've been a huge risk, and Zandorn didn't take those without sufficient calculation.

He was much more likely to hide it behind Karazul's back, out of sight yet reachable when Zandorn needed it. Somewhere that Karazul would never think to tread.

"We have to go to the bowels of the mountain," Karazul had said during one of the many planning conversations between him and Shira. "There's an old furnace buried deep within the mountain. The dwarves used the pit of fire to power everything, from forges to piped torches, to ovens and heated baths."

"Sounds marvelous," Shira had said with sincerity. "Why do you think your *cordeus* would be there?"

"Zandorn never rehabilitated the system, even though it would have made daily life much easier in Pywell. The core of the furnace was rumored to be home to a particularly nasty fire demon. That may be true, or..."

"It could be a deterrent. Clever."

"Yes. But knowing Zandorn, I'd wager there's something much worse than a demon guarding the *cordeus*."

Shira smiled. "Demons I can handle. I'll let you sort out the 'something worse,' if that's the case."

Karazul wouldn't admit to liking Shira—or anyone, for that matter—but he found her presence significantly more tolerable than any other person he had encountered.

Knowing where they had to go was only half the battle, though. The entrance from the top of Pywell was their best chance to get inside, but that also meant sneaking down the entire fortress to the very bottom.

Karazul led Shira through the upper tier halls, chiseled to perfection with inlaid gemstones and geometric designs. It was fortunate her invisibility demon cloaked her, otherwise Karazul may have left her atop the mountain. He didn't have time to slit every throat that crossed his path. Easier to stick to the shadows, dart around corners, and sneak beneath straying eyes. And he'd never found anyone that could keep up with him and remain stealthy.

He was about to round a corner when Shira held his shoulder back. Karazul glared in her direction when a pair of soldiers sauntered down the hall.

He'd almost been spotted.

"Handy thing, your Sight," he said after the patrol had passed.

"That's why I volunteered. That and the demons—makes me more versatile than the rest of our bunch of misfits."

"Anyone would have been better than the Hawk Mage." Karazul didn't disguise his loathing, and he thought he heard Shira stifle a laugh.

After the close brush with detection, Karazul refocused his attention on the infiltration.

Besides his near misstep, the upper tier didn't present much of a challenge to sneak through—most of the Consortium avoided the area because of Renna and Zandorn's lethal whims. But the middle tier presented a problem.

All tunnels ran through the former grand marketplace, making it a necessary hub between the tiers. There was no avoiding the populated area.

Shira could have danced right down the middle with her invisibility demon and no one would have been the wiser, but Karazul didn't have that option, and she stuck close to him anyway.

He crept behind stacked boxes filled with stolen supplies. They formed a convenient cover along the right wall that extended about halfway across the room. A wide open space stretched between his hiding spot and the archway leading to the lower tier.

*Watch and wait.* The simplest and most difficult parts of any stealth job. He'd fulfilled many contracts by sheer carelessness on the part of his targets. Inevitably, if he watched and waited, opportunity presented itself. They might stumble home alone after a long night at the tavern, almost begging him to slit their throats in a darkened alley. Or for the gluttonous, offering a free pastry laced with delayed poison had proven effective. Or if a storm rolled through, he could stage drowning or strangulation as succumbing to a natural disaster.

Patience had been crucial to his work for decades, even the ones he didn't remember, he suspected. Yet this close to his heart—to reclaiming part of his identity—had his knee bouncing and fingers itching to draw his blades and cut down anyone unlucky enough to step in his path.

Consortium soldiers and mages milled about the platforms, some approaching the stack of boxes Karazul hid behind and retrieving goods now and then. There didn't seem to be a clear patrol or regular movement in this area, though constant traffic flowed between the marketplace and the tunnels, like blood through arteries.

"I could lead them the opposite direction," Shira whispered to his left.

Karazul shook his head. "That would separate us, and we don't know what lies ahead. Our odds of success are better together."

"I didn't take you for a romantic, Karazul."

He grunted at the smile in her tone.

While they engaged in a hushed debate, something happened. The slow jaunts of soldiers quickened, some scurried from group to group or darted down hallways. A handful even jumped through portals to gods knew where. Voices raised, and the inane chatter turned into cutting orders and forming ranks.

The Consortium was preparing for battle.

"The *Nacusti*, they've done it," Shira said.

Karazul couldn't believe his luck. It had been part of the plan for them to draw the Consortium's attention while he and Shira searched for his *cordeus*, but he hadn't expected their timing to be so perfect.

"Gods-cursed Hawk Mage." The annoyingly brilliant man's plan was working, and the more Karazul witnessed of him, the more it made sense Sorwin had been the only mark Karazul had missed. His survival didn't appear to have been a fluke, at least.

"Now's your chance." Shira's voice came from ahead this time.

Karazul stepped out from behind the supply stores and kept his head down, using the pre-battle chaos to mask his haste to the lower tier. None of the soldiers paid him a passing glance, singular in their focus. He didn't slow when he reached the archway, but kept going as the tunnel pitched down and a rush of hot air assaulted him.

# CHAPTER 20

# RECLAMATION

A cold, forceful wind whipped through Merinthia's Pass. Zak, Olivia, and Elpida had walked the narrow path that cut between the Darlangson peaks, the only entrance into the Wastelands from the east without going over the mountains themselves. Flying over the ridge would have been impossible with the treacherous gusts and constant blizzards in the tail end of Winterfall.

Zak didn't feel the cold. The constant stream of fire—either from him, Olivia, or Elpida—coupled with the thick cloaks Sorwin insisted he and Olivia don, kept him warm. He paced behind Elpida, wrapped tight in wool as the dragon spat a funnel of bronze flames.

It had taken a few hours, but they'd made decent progress burning through the Rot. The path needed to be wide enough for Elpida to stand sideways, and any extra room would be welcomed by the nervous band of soldiers and mages following in their wake. They huddled together, squinting at the dark mass with hands twisting on weapon hilts and pulling cloaks tighter.

Zak couldn't blame them. The mountains shrank the further they encroached into the Rot, and his gut soured. It wasn't solely because any misstep meant certain death, but what he noticed when the Rot was gone.

Cold, lifeless ground. It was like hard-packed sand, the kind that stretched across Densba's beach during low tide. That sand had teemed with life—crabs and mussels and barnacles, even some fish in the tide pools left behind by the receding water.

But this sand was different. Grey and stagnant.

He had reached toward it with his magic, calling to the element of earth, searching for any remnant of its identity. But there was no response. Even when the Rot was gone, magic did not take hold.

Elpida cut her fire off, and Zak watched her ribs expand and contract as her scaly head dipped a little lower.

"Switch," Olivia commanded.

*I can do more,* Elpida argued.

Olivia strode to the dragon's side and crossed her arms. After a tense moment, Elpida snorted her displeasure and stalked back down the path as Olivia's amber fire appeared.

Zak bit his bottom lip but couldn't entirely hide his smile. "It's better to listen to her, she's usually right."

A small puff of smoke curled from Elpida's nostrils.

Something about seeing Olivia cow a dragon—adolescent as she was—through sheer force of will made his admiration for her grow all the more. *Olivia is a force of nature.*

That, at least, he knew for certain.

Movement from the squad drew his attention. Hushed

whispers passed between two captains, and a Firepost whizzed into the center of the clump of bodies. All was quiet and still for a breath, only the crackling of Olivia's fire in the background while the captains read the message. Then voices raised with orders, and half the squad trotted down the path through the Rot, back toward the pass.

Zak took a step toward the remaining captain to ask what had happened, but paused when Sorwin came into view, soaring overhead on golden brown wings.

"The Consortium is here," he said before his feet had touched the ground and his wings disappeared in a glitter of gold. "Half a dozen portals opened on the far side of Tor'alan. Looks like they'll attempt to flank us."

"Just as you predicted." Zak's optimism about Sorwin's plan didn't wipe away his apprehension, but for once, everything seemed to be going their way.

Olivia and Elpida approached when Sorwin had landed. "You're sure we should stay here?" Olivia asked.

*Let us take to the skies and hunt!* Elpida's wings twitched along her barbed spine.

Sorwin shook his head. "I know it's a lot to ask, but you three are the targets, so we'll draw the Consortium here. As much as I wish I could keep you from the battle entirely, it won't be long until it reaches us. Clear a little more of the Rot to give us some breathing room, and then conserve your energy."

He turned to the squad then, and Zak saw the leather pouch with Cerevita's *cordeus* clutched in Sorwin's grip.

Zak nodded to Olivia and Elpida, and the three set to

clearing a large circle in the Rot for the squad to fan out. Zak helped establish barriers around the perimeter and received a few shoulder pats of appreciation from the other mages. It seemed Sorwin was right that he had a knack for defensive magic as his sections were tighter knit than the rest.

Waiting was the hardest part. After half an hour, the ring of metal and grim shrieks of battle echoed through the narrow pass and filled the empty Wastelands.

Zak's fists shook at his sides. *How many could I save if I rushed in now?*

*A few, but many more would die should you fall,* Jolsu rumbled.

He grimaced, but agreed. Every soldier and mage on the field had volunteered, willingly throwing themselves between Zak and the Consortium. He knew they fought for more than him—for their families, loved ones, homes—for their very existence. Because if Zandorn won the day, the gods could return and put an end to free will once and for all.

But the very presence of the Consortium meant that Sorwin's plan was working, because they never expected to make it all the way to Pywell. They could if they had to, but burning through the Rot would take time and energy they didn't have.

For once, Zak was the distraction, and he had placed all his hope on one woman he adored and one man he detested.

Olivia wrapped her callused hand around his fist, and his nerves relaxed a little.

"Come on, Shira," he whispered to himself. "Wrangle that *stulmati* of a god."

Karazul sprinted, footfalls echoing through the bare tunnels of the lower tier. There was no reason to mask his presence any longer. The Consortium soldiers and mages didn't spend time here, only in passing to drag bodies of victims or failed converts to the mass graveyard outside the main entrance. The doors were rarely used since the Rot was impassable, and Zandorn's portal network turned the middle tier into a travel hub.

The laborer's tier was well-built but lacked the refinement and adornment of the middle and upper levels. He slowed when the tunnel opened into a cavernous room. The temperature had grown steadily warmer as he descended, but a wall of heat smacked into him then.

Shira padded in behind him, still invisible, but her panting gave away her location a step to his right.

"Definitely...a...fire...demon," she said.

Karazul frowned. "You're sure?"

"I can...sense it...below."

He peered over the edge of an enormous hollowed bowl that stretched at least a league deep into the earth—so far that the bottom was only a vague yellow light. A ring corkscrewed down around the outside. It may have been a service path at one point, and now it appeared to be the only way to the bottom of the furnace. Or the quickest, at least, and Karazul rolled his shoulders, feeling the pressure of time, wondering how much the *Nacusti* could buy him.

"Mind your step," he said, easing down the sloping path. "Wait until your breath slows and your knees aren't shaking. You're no good to me if you fall to your death."

Shira had the lung capacity for one barking laugh. "I'll be fine enough to handle a long walk and a fire demon. You just be ready for whatever else Zandorn brewed up."

*True enough.* While he walked, Karazul imagined all the devious defenses Zandorn could have constructed for something as valuable as a *cordeus*. It had to be unconventional, knowing Zandorn. But also nearly impenetrable because—presumably—Karazul was the only person who would come for the *cordeus*, if he had ever discovered the secrets of his identity or curse. And Karazul could undo even the most sophisticated barriers with a wave of his hand.

Well, most of them.

The *Nacusti* had stopped him once, but even that made sense now. The *Nacusti* had been created to fight the divine, and if Karazul were a god—or a former one—his anti-magic would struggle against them.

Zandorn wasn't a *Nacusti*, but he was a mad genius in possession of a *cordeus*. There was no telling what he'd be capable of making.

During the descent, Karazul passed a door set into the wall of the giant furnace every few minutes. He carefully opened each one, twisting the soot-covered handles and readying a sword in the other hand. Each time he was greeted with dusty furniture, rotting fabric, or rusting tools. Most of the rooms used to be workshops judging by the tables and equipment, though some had hearths and bunks piled high against the walls.

Karazul hadn't given much thought to the dwarves that built Pywell before, but now he wondered if he had anything to do with their demise. By all accounts, they withdrew from the world around the end of the Guardian War. Had he known any dwarves? Had he walked these halls before? Was the Rot the reason they left Pywell, or had any dwarves survived at all?

There was so much Karazul didn't know about himself, his past.

The further he went, the hotter it became. Sweat soaked his tunic, and he wiped his palms on his breeches, not wanting to slicken his blade pommels. He was close enough to the bottom to see a huge bed of coals in the basin with a bright yellow fire licking at the sides of a hammered metal pit.

He stepped off the path and onto the wide floor of the furnace, dirt and rock packed tight together. The air was so thick with heat that he could hardly breathe.

And there, in the center of the ring of coals, sat his *cordeus*.

"It's not even hidden," he said.

"He must not have felt the need." Shira had kept up well enough on the trek down, and now her footsteps echoed as she paced around the fire basin.

The *cordeus* looked bright in the yellow firelight, a grey storm swirling beneath a glassy sheen. It rested on a round platter, hovering above the coals.

Shira—still invisible—grunted with effort as she must have attempted casting some spell. "Telekinesis has no effect, and there seems to be a complex ward around the whole furnace."

"Many of them." Karazul watched the oscillating layers of defenses that never quite settled. The bullish approach would be to rip through them, but it wouldn't be easy. It would be like swatting cobwebs only to have a hundred more spring up in their place. Finesse would be even more difficult, like firing an arrow from a riverboat hoping to hit a button-sized target on a cantering horse.

With any other stakes, that sounded like a fun challenge, and he never strayed from those. But this time his heart was the wager, and he needed it to undo his curse and find his brother.

Zandorn had built these barriers specifically to delay his anti-magic abilities, that much was clear. He didn't know how long the Consortium would be distracted by the *Nacustis'* assault, either.

"Bullish approach it is. Shira, there's no telling what will happen once the first barriers are pierced. Be ready for anything."

"Naturally." The iron of her staff rang as she struck it against the hard-packed floor.

Karazul held a blade in his left hand and extended his right, peeling off the first barrier.

A wave of heat blasted him as a fiery form rose from the coals. The demon awoke, and Karazul sprang back, narrowly avoiding a swipe of a flaming hand.

"Shira!" he yelled. It was a caries demon, well within her capabilities to handle.

Purple smoke swirled near the edge of the coals, and a turtle-like creature launched itself through the air. The hot coals and flames didn't seem to bother its spiked shell or angular limbs. It clamped its jaw on the fire demon's arm and dragged it to the far side of the furnace. It appeared to be made of some sort of rock, but Karazul didn't have time to examine its structure.

He tore through three more barriers, each resisting more than the last. Not every barrier had an immediate effect upon dissolution. One transformed into a volley of spears, which Karazul deflected, and another created a gust of wind that blew him into the wall.

*Tedious.* He was so close. His *cordeus* glistened in the middle of the coals, entirely undisturbed by the chaos surrounding it. Zandorn was devious for knowing exactly how to slow him down and piss him off at the same time.

Karazul lost count of the barriers as they fell and he swatted through their sometimes not-so-meager attacks (one turned into a crude copy of himself, though its swordplay was no laughing matter). With a glance, he saw that Shira had dealt with the fire demon, nothing left of it but scorch marks where the rocky turtle had snuffed its flames.

"Of course it's you."

That voice.

"Renna." He didn't turn from his *cordeus* at first, but if he destroyed another barrier, she'd immediately attack. He let his arms hang at his sides.

"After everything we've done for you, this is how you repay us?"

"Done *to* me, you mean." He spun and glared at her. She stood near the bottom of the ramp, clad in dark leathers that looked more like shadows trapped in the shape of thin armor.

He'd given her too much thought since he woke from the *senligo*. Zandorn may have been the first one to ensnare him, to take advantage of his curse, but Renna was every bit his accomplice. She had lived and worked by her father's side for a century and had seen multiple manifestations of Karazul's service in that time. She had lied right to his face for years.

Renna smiled, that infuriating curl of her lips boiled his insides. "It's a shame you stumbled at the end of the race. You'd nearly finished, and we were going to give you every-thing you had wanted if you'd just hung on a little while longer."

"More lies!" His left hand twitched, and her eyes darted to the blade he gripped.

"Still too emotional. That's why you were never a match for Zandorn." She looked him up and down, appearing dis-appointed.

*Breathe.* The too-hot air of the furnace flooded his lungs. "You always feared me." He needed to reclaim his balance, find an advantage to press. Fighting Renna here and now was almost as bad as Zandorn himself.

Maybe worse. Desire and ego and insatiable curiosity drove Zandorn—all the tools of a mad genius determined to defy death itself. But Renna...Karazul had never discerned her goals, only witnessed her ruthless cruelty.

"Respected, not feared," she corrected.

He laughed. "My immunity to your Influence must be

infuriating."

A muscle along her jaw jumped. *Now we're getting some-where.*

She took a few slow, intentional steps along the rough wall. "I'm surprised, Karazul. You were never one for team-work."

*Shira.* Renna must have sensed her.

He squeezed the sword pommel tighter. "You left me with the League, to rot or die or simply to be out of your way. Seems some of their morality seeped into me."

"Oh, I wouldn't go that far, but you're right—your capture solved several problems."

"Apparently not." He held his blade and hand up, gesturing to his presence.

She shook her head. "Never short on confidence, are you? I've thought about this a lot, but I never wanted to fight you. Not because I had doubts—I *will* win—but because it is such a waste to lose a god to an entirely avoidable disagreement."

Karazul barely perceived her acknowledgement of his divinity before Renna's crimson magic lanced through the air.

CHAPTER 21

# DECIMATION

Karazul lined his blade with anti-magic and sliced a hole in the wall of crimson fire. Balanced on the lip of the furnace, inches away from the scalding bed of coals, he parried quick strikes from a demon with metallic claws and beady bug eyes. It squealed when he ran it through, a sickening crunch in the carapace, but he couldn't start pitying his victims now.

Renna was toying with him, sending lesser demons and widespread spells she knew he could easily dismantle. She inundated him, kept him busy and distracted, away from his *cordeus*.

*Is she stalling?* The only reason for her to do such a thing would be—

Zandorn.

He had to be on his way to the furnace, and though Karazul owed the man a thousand cuts for his lies, he was in no shape to fight both him and Renna. Not to mention Shira would be crushed in the midst of their clash. It was good she seemed to be hiding. She was a powerful mage, he couldn't deny that, but she'd never keep pace with monsters like Zandorn and Renna, or himself.

After all, he was still every bit the monster the Consortium had wanted him to be. Perhaps it was time he turned his skills on his former employers.

Karazul snatched a totem from his belt and whispered the command word. His Shadoweres appeared, dark coats blurring as they tackled the nearest demons, ripping into them with grizzled maws. He darted through the melee and thrust a hand against Renna's shield.

Her magic felt different from most. Since the first moment he'd met her, Karazul found her to be an enigma coated in riddles. But he'd never fought her before, and he found there was no better way to learn someone's deepest nature than to pit his life against theirs.

It was subtle, the difference—a little glimmer at the edge of a puddle, or a distant window reflecting the sun at just the right angle. But as he drained the magic fueling her shield, he felt the power, the unmistakable presence that he'd only encountered when fighting the *Nacusti*.

Divinity.

"Who are you?" His voice cracked against his will, and when her hungry smile flashed he swore at his faltering composure and stepped back.

"You're the first to notice." She didn't seem surprised, almost as if she expected it. "There's a better question to ask."

But she didn't let him.

Thorned vines erupted from the ground, and Karazul hacked at them as he retreated. One snuck behind and bit into his right ankle. He tripped and his sword clattered out of reach. Rolling over, the vines reared up like vegetal snakes rushing to skewer him.

A heavy wind rolled over Karazul, and the vines fell to the ground, slashed into hundreds of pieces.

Shira stood behind Chidamee.

"Master of the Winds," Shira had said about the Nox demon. And after that display, and flying with the creature, Karazul couldn't deny the title.

"Get to your *cordeus*," Shira called to him.

"You can't take her alone." Karazul grabbed his sword and found his feet again, running to Shira's side. Chidamee and the Shadoweres kept Renna busy for the moment, but that wouldn't last long.

"I don't need to." Shira was visible again, having dismissed the invisibility demon. "I just need to buy you enough time to get your heart, then the scales will tip in our favor."

"Maybe, but—"

She dropped a firm hand on his shoulder and stared up into his eyes. "Nothing else matters if we fail here. The plan hinges on you retrieving your *cordeus*."

Karazul grunted. "It's theoretical. I don't know if I can actually—"

Shira pulled him down as a fireball exploded overhead, then gave him a shove toward the furnace. "Go!"

There wasn't time for debate. He had agreed to Sorwin's foolhardy plan because he benefited from it, but after weeks of sailing with Shira and seeing the desperation in her furrowed brow, he didn't want to let her down.

*Caring for a mage? What is wrong with me?*

There also wasn't time for self-reflection.

He sheathed his blade and stumbled to the furnace, turning his back to Shira and Renna's duel.

Karazul held both hands out. Instead of ripping through the remaining barriers, he tried something different. He called to his heart, beckoning it to him.

The heat at the edge of the furnace forced sweat down his neck, and the explosions and shouting behind him fell away as he focused on the missing piece of him hovering just out of reach.

Karazul's knowledge of magic was limited to its undoing. He had labored under the belief that he had no magic and could not use it, that his gift was the destruction or abolishment of magic. But if he was a god, that was no longer true. In fact, it was quite the opposite.

He *was* magic.

*I'm doing this for you.* The ghost of his brother's hand pulled at his own, outstretched toward his heart. The grey stone shook and shuddered before soaring through the air, shattering the defensive barriers like glass as it flung into his waiting palm.

Power.

It surged through him. Overwhelming, unbridled, consuming.

It threatened to drown him, to flood his lungs and seep from his corpse after it ravaged him, leaving his empty husk behind. It would if he let it—somehow he sensed that—but it was his power, his divinity, and he grabbed hold of it and pulled like a rider taming a stallion.

He blinked and the floor fell away—no, that wasn't it—he *grew*. Gods were tall creatures, and his limbs stretched, changing his relationship with his surroundings. The furnace no longer felt hot or as wide. He barely had room to stand beside it, and a foot stepped on the coals and felt nothing. The truth he had struggled to believe became plain.

Karazul was a god.

And he was pissed.

He rounded on Renna, surprised at the anger in her eyes.

*No terror?* Yet she did back up a few steps. She always was smart.

But then, it wasn't preservation that moved her, not directly. Renna bent and tugged Shira by the collar of her robes to stand between them. Blood trickled down Shira's temple. Chidamee struggled on the other side of the room, bound to the wall with earthen restraints covering most of his body. The Shadoweres had long since dissipated into smoke.

"What an interesting turn of events," Renna said, expression still hard. Either she hadn't expected him to retrieve the *cordeus*, or hadn't predicted his divinity returning.

"*Let her go.*" He almost gasped at the booming voice. Could that really be his? He spoke, and it felt as if the world listened, vibrating with awareness.

Renna's lips tightened, and Shira's curled in a tired smile. A knife appeared in Renna's hand, and she pressed the metal against her captive's throat.

"Drop the heart and you can both walk away."

Karazul clutched his *cordeus* tight, encompassed by his

now much larger hand. The power—his power—was trapped in the stone. If he let it go, his divinity would withdraw, and then he'd be confronted with Renna and her mysterious power.

"Don't," Shira said, interrupting his internal debate.

Blood flowed over most of the left side of her face, and Karazul could tell she didn't have long if left untended.

Karazul glanced down at his altered body. The bullish approach would be to see what it could do, how his power manifested. Each god had a domain—light, dark, and life, with regards to the Three, and the minor ones had their specialties too—and he had suspicions of what his would be, if his anti-magic was any indication.

Finesse wouldn't be an option. This body may be his, but it was foreign, unfamiliar. He had trained for years to finely tune the movements of his mortal form, and he could not rush into the fray untested against someone like Renna.

She held every advantage, and she knew it.

"Leave, Karazul," Shira urged. "There is only one price we cannot pay this day."

He wanted to ask what she had Seen. That had to be the reason for her unerring focus, how in her ragged exhaustion she seemed somehow calm. Karazul had witnessed countless deaths—many by his own making—and most people were frantic at the end.

That wasn't necessarily fair, though. The deaths he was accustomed to were violent, poisoning or backstabbing or adrenaline-fueled contests that always ended with his blades slick and red.

He tried peering through the air of sagacity surrounding Shira, fumbling for her thoughts as if they were tangible things he could grasp.

"My how you have changed, and not just in appearance." Renna tutted and pressed the blade harder against Shira, puckering the sweat and soot-covered skin of her throat. "It wasn't long ago you would have sacrificed this mage to get at your target. What did the League do to you? Maybe you were telling the truth earlier, maybe that morality really did take root."

"*Nothing so grand as that.*" He looked at Shira, pleading, willing her to have a demon up her sleeve or a trick to escape. But each passing second she only looked more unsteady on her feet.

How could he have all this power and do nothing to save her?

He waved an arm—experimentally—to his right. The wall of the pit cracked and ruptured and a schism taller than a house formed.

Just as he thought.

"*I am Niltris, the God of Nothing. Release the mage, or your existence will cease.*" He stepped forward and the furnace groaned against the weight and the unstable fissure.

Renna retreated up the ramp, dragging a stumbling Shira. "Drop the *cordeus*, or she dies. Now!" She unraveled, fear finally piercing the thick veneer of swagger.

Karazul, emboldened, swiped at the air again, slicing at the stone just above Renna's head. She ducked as debris and dust fell, but she never lowered the blade at Shira's neck.

Yellow firelight flickered over Renna's dark hair, picking up the purple hues. Wordlessly, as a wildness danced in her raven-black eyes, she stared at Karazul as she drew a red line along Shira's throat.

She fell.

He screamed.

The walls shook and shattered, unable to withstand his pain.

Renna disappeared, walking backward into a portal with a venomous smirk.

He lunged forward, clumsily picking Shira up from the ground as the furnace crumbled around them. Chidamee was gone. Demons relied on their summoner's magic to sustain them, and that meant—

He carried her up the twisting ramp, squeezing his too-large body through the former front gates of the fortress.

A sliver of land existed between the Rot and the doors. Karazul laid Shira down on the crumbling steps, only vaguely aware of a pile of corpses a few paces away. The Consortium's other victims, tortured from interrogations or having failed the test to become one of their number. Zandorn's minions didn't even have the decency to put their remains fully in the Rot. At least then they would have been consumed, released from the world instead of decaying in a pile of flesh and bone and misery.

He wondered if he was meant to end up here with Shira. The first person he had cared about in years—centuries, probably, but he couldn't remember his other lives clearly—and she lay gasping for breath next to a mass grave. How unfair for one as pure as her.

How fitting for a monster as dark as him.

Shira bled, and Karazul searched his divinity for *anything*, an inkling, a notion, a hint of how to save her. But there was no spark, no salve, no last-minute miracle.

There was Nothing, because that was his domain.

She cupped his face with a trembling hand, and gods *damn* her because she smiled and pressed something into his palm.

Her *lapidaemas*. The stone swirled, and a bright light shot from it.

A tiny imp appeared at her side. Shira had conjured it dozens of times on the ship, it often sat upon her shoulder during their planning sessions, sneezing and pawing at its nose. What was its name?

"*Ubba.*"

The imp peered up at him, then back at Shira and whimpered. It burrowed into the crook of her arm, grasping at the folds of her robe, wings flitting frantically. It—he—knew. Of course he did. The bond between demon and summoner was unique, intimate on a level Karazul did not comprehend.

He wanted to turn away, as if that could obviate the pain. But he owed her a dignified death. That was all he could give her, in the end.

So he watched, and tears brimmed and fell, and Ubba wailed into her chest until it stopped rising and falling, and then the little imp disappeared back into the ether from whence he came.

Shira was gone.

He didn't know how long he sat there on his knees, staring at her vacant eyes, losing himself to the sharp stab in his chest.

He wondered at mortal fragility—something he thought himself prone to until recently. Would he ever die? It was possible, at the hands of a *Nacusti*. Maybe he'd let the little mage and his dragon exact their revenge. They'd been hungry enough for it before.

Thinking of the *Nacusti* reminded him of his promise, of the one thing he would attempt when he recovered his *cordeus*. It was the whole reason Shira had agreed to accompany him, after all. And now, well...

He gently guided her eyes closed and folded her hands across her middle. There would be time to do a proper ceremony later, one befitting a mage of her class.

The connection with the *cordeus* strained. Whatever curse plagued him, he could not maintain this divine form for much longer. Standing—and swaying slightly—he approached the edge of the Rot.

"*You should not exist,*" he told it. "*You are me, and we are Nothing, and there you shall return.*"

Arms spread wide, he stepped into the Rot.

Like a raging river flowing in reverse, the gray matter flooded into the *cordeus* clutched in his hands. He couldn't let go, couldn't move, as the Rot returned home to him, to his heart.

# CHAPTER 22

# ARROWS AND QUILLS

There were more of them than Zak had expected.

The Consortium snaked through Merinthia's pass, battled down the narrow slip of land free of the Rot, and assaulted the barrier where Zak, Olivia, Elpida, Sorwin, and a contingent of League mages stood their ground.

By the irregular reports Sorwin and the nearby captain received, the enemy focused on their small holdout in the Rot, only sparing enough forces to keep the League's main host occupied, which was spread thin covering the multiple portal openings.

A fireball burst on the barrier. Zak shielded his face and lobbed one back. It sizzled harmlessly against a hastily conjured wall of water.

"Is the plan working?" Zak shouted to Sorwin—who was only a pace away firing deadly lightning strikes into the enemy's ranks.

"Perfectly!" He grunted and reinforced the barrier against a deluge of stone shards. "Maybe too well. We still outnumber them, but the Consortium's guerilla tactics are more effective than anticipated."

Elpida lunged and clamped her jaw on a mage's neck, dragging him inside the barrier to tear into him with tooth and claw. Frenzied and bloodied, she looked every bit the terrifying predator.

*Let me fly!* Her wings twitched and she hopped with excitement.

*Stay down,* Jolsu instructed. *There isn't enough space to maneuver over the Rot.*

Smoke curled from her nostrils with a grunt.

Zak patted her flank, feeling the same frustration. Bazil was out there somewhere, deep in the fray. His heightened strength and speed and healing made him a target, and Zak worried for his friend's safety.

But Zak was the bait—one of three tantalizing lures for the Consortium—and couldn't abandon the plan now.

A crack of thunder, but it wasn't Sorwin's magic and no storm drifted overhead. Zak swiveled in time to see many hues of fire burn through a panel of the barrier.

Black and blue Consortium uniforms surged through the opening.

The red-clad League mages near the breach fell from the surprise attack.

Zak slowed his breathing—despite his pounding heart—and poured magic into his spell. "*Customateria.*"

Jolsu appeared fleshlike with defined green scales that

flashed in the chaos of spellwork. The domed barrier prevented him from reaching his full size, but he stood taller than a wyvern.

Zak ran behind the dragon as he swatted mages and soldiers aside like nuisances.

"Zakolor!" Sorwin recognized his intention before he'd crossed half the distance to the opening.

"Fix the barrier!" They had to if they had any hope of holding their position surrounded by the Rot, but it couldn't be done without a break in the assault.

Jolsu charged through the opening, all teeth and claws and fire. He twisted away from a lance and swiped his tail across three soldiers. They splayed into the Rot, and Zak couldn't look away as the color drained from their skin, their bodies atrophying decades in a matter of seconds. They crawled back toward the path, but it was too late. Their remains turned to dust and scattered on the wind.

An axe arced for Zak's head, and he parried with his bronze staff. He spun it around the haft and rapped the soldier on the head, knocking him out cold.

*Thank you*, he silently said to his father for the solid weapon.

Standing side by side, Zak and Jolsu pushed back the Consortium onslaught with a wave of green fire. They were careful not to burn more of the Rot and concentrated the flames in a narrow pillar that raced down the path.

Behind him, Olivia and Sorwin patched the barrier, the panels of swirling magic fusing back together while Elpida stalked back and forth, snarling curls of smoke.

They were going to make it. They could resume the defensive position.

He looked up at Jolsu's form—about to suggest their retreat—when an arrow flew through the dragon's neck. Jolsu roared from the pain and disappeared.

The echo of the shot pinched Zak's neck. It shouldn't have been possible—Jolsu had been made of magic, exhaustible but not easily dispelled.

Another arrow arced over the trail of fire. Zak held out his staff to stop it with telekinesis, but the arrow didn't slow. Panic rose right before the arrow sunk into his shoulder.

Bright, hot pain. He gasped and fell. Rolling over, he shakily found his feet, half jogging, half tripping back to the barrier.

The green flames along the path extinguished once the arrow hit him. Glancing over his shoulder, a new wave of soldiers charged.

With the staff in his left hand, he waved it toward them, intending to send a fireball into their ranks.

But nothing happened.

He winced and stumbled to a knee. Was the arrow poison? He couldn't think, mind muddied by confusion and pain and fear.

The soldiers brandished their weapons, mere paces away.

Zak closed his eyes.

A rush of water crashed, and Zak blinked.

Olivia stood over him, manipulating a veritable river, washing the soldiers back to the opening of Merinthia's Pass.

"Up we go." Sorwin carefully lifted him, guiding him

into the safety of the barrier.

A funny thing happened when Zak passed the magical defense. A portion of the wall of magic disintegrated when the arrow in his shoulder touched it.

Zak leaned against Elpida as she lowered him to the ground.

Sorwin knelt over Zak, hands hovering over the arrow and the wound.

"What is it?" Zak asked through clenched teeth.

"It's...anti-magic, somehow." Sorwin pulled a glove from his belt and grabbed below the black fletching. "We have to remove it or it'll keep draining your magic and prevent your casting."

Without further warning, Sorwin tugged and Zak yelped as the point left his flesh. A nearby priest rushed in with cloth bandages and a warm, peach-hued magic that began closing the wound.

Sorwin handed the arrow to the captain and muttered instructions that Zak couldn't hear.

*You were brave, Iparus.* Elpida nudged his cheek.

"Thank you. But I told you, I'm not your brother." He flinched as he raised a hand to pat her scaly snout.

*We share a nest, what else would you be?*

Zak laughed. "Fair enough."

Olivia crouched at his side, eyes roving over his wound and the rest of his tattered state. "You pushed too far."

"You're welcome," he said with a smile he didn't quite feel.

"I think those are my words," she countered, lips quirking.

The priest stopped most of the bleeding and wrapped his wound, telling him it would hurt for a few days. Zak couldn't think that far ahead with a new chorus of booms piercing the air as a fresh assault on the barrier began.

"How much longer can we do this?" Zak's voice was small and quiet.

Olivia sighed, exhaustion mingling with consideration. "An hour at most. We lost too many mages in the breach, and you're the best at barriers, but now you're injured. Why did you rush out like that? It should have been me."

"I thought Jolsu and I could—"

"Think better next time." A charged silence hung between them for a moment. "How is Jolsu?"

Zak reached for the bond. It felt weaker than it should have, drained somehow. The arrow, whatever it was, had injured him, and Zak hadn't known that was possible.

*I will be fine, Parignis. Rest will restore me.*

Zak relayed Jolsu's words and slowly stood, leaning against his staff. Elpida and Olivia were at each side, and the three of them watched the battle rage, a battle fought for them, over them, because of them.

It was hard not to feel responsible for each and every death the League suffered.

Olivia squeezed his good shoulder. "Look!"

Everything slowed, as if the battlefield had been submerged in a high tide. Were they moving? No, every soldier and mage stood still, but the ground around them flowed like grey water.

"The Rot," he whispered in disbelief. "It's disappearing."

It began lethargic, resisting at first. But the more it moved the quicker it flowed, and in moments the dark mass of death rose and fell, crashing like waves over the desolate landscape. It all moved toward Pywell Mountain.

"Shira and Karazul—they've done it!" Zak could hardly believe it.

Realization dawned on the rest of the League as cheers and whoops sounded. The further the Rot retreated, the louder they became.

Stunned Consortium forces began fleeing to the pass, probably back to their portals. Without the safety of the Rot, they were exposed, their fortress finally reachable by the League's greater numbers.

Zak looked between Elpida, Olivia, and Sorwin, mirroring their joy. At long last, the scales were finally tipping in their favor. The centuries-old scourge of Valecium had been eradicated, and that meant one thing.

Zandorn was next.

The doors of Zandorn's workshop flung open, banging against the walls and piles of abandoned furniture. Renna marched across the cobbles, footsteps sounding almost as irate as her thoughts. Gunther and Kalbick followed dutifully in her wake.

"We lost Karazul's heart," she said to Zandorn's back. "He has reclaimed his divinity." She could still scarcely believe she lost to the assassin. Skilled as he was, she should have overwhelmed him. That crafty little mage he brought kept her distracted for too long. At least Renna spilled her blood, small consolation that it was.

"Not yet he hasn't," Zandorn assured. His dark robe fluttered as he hunched over the table before him.

*He seems to know more about the assassin's curse.*

Troubling.

"Regardless, you don't have long. Your immortality relied on that heart. You'll need to perform the ritual immediately. And with the Rot gone, the League will be at our gates in a matter of hours."

"Good, because we'll be at theirs in a matter of minutes." He turned and held up a quill made from a single sleek dark feather.

"You've done it?" Renna took an involuntary step forward, restraining the urge to rip the quill from Zandorn's clutches.

"You had doubts?" His expression remained neutral, but Renna felt his examining stare, searching for information.

"Not about your success, it was eventual—but the timing with the Year Festival was always delicate." That was accurate, her honest belief. The best deception was always cloaked in truth.

Zandorn closed the distance between them and cupped her cheek. Renna stiffened. "Assuage your fear, dear daughter. By the end of this day, your mother will be returned to us."

She cleared her throat. "I look forward to my family finally being complete."

"Let us away." Zandorn approached the black caladrius, chirping and flapping in its cage. It looked sickly, plucked of most of its feathers for Zandorn's experiments. There was nowhere for it to escape, and it was too late anyway—it had served its purpose. Now, it only needed to remain alive and hidden. With a wave, Zandorn created a barrier around its cage, obscuring it from view behind a thick wall of dark magic.

"You go ahead, I'll join momentarily." Renna nodded to Gunther, and the giant lumbered behind Zandorn as they headed toward the portals in the middle tier.

Before joining them, Renna went to her chambers—with Kal drifting in her steps—and poured water into the porcelain bowl behind her desk. She swiped a dagger across her finger, and after her blood swirled into the liquid, she incanted, "*Nuntiumsanguis.*"

Despite the midday hour, the room darkened, appearing as it would on a moonless night.

"What news?" The water gurgled with a deep voice. He was louder, stronger, and Renna could hardly contain her excitement.

"Our time draws near, the ritual is about to commence."

"Good," he purred. "Was Zandorn successful?"

"Yes, he created a quill to channel the caladrius's power. We'll be able to use the bird for years to come."

"Excellent." Renna heard his satisfaction through the rippling water. "Go now, prepare. And together, we will end this Era of Freedom and usher in the next—*our* era."

The water stilled and the shadows retreated, and Renna

whispered, "Yes, Father."

Kal knew something important had happened. He frowned and stared at his boots—he couldn't seem to focus on much else.

Renna was everywhere, in his every thought, feeling, urge. He was aware enough to recognize her Influence, but unable to gather the will to push back against her.

She must have sensed his awareness too, because she paused halfway through her chamber doors and said, "Hesitation is weakness, Kalbick. Whatever you're struggling with will soon end. That much I can promise you."

Kal nodded and followed her through the fortress halls down to the portals. Torches and magelights flickered in the formerly grand marketplace, and Kal thought for a moment he spotted a green tinge at the edge of his vision.

# Chapter 23

# HEED

Bazil insisted on inspecting Zak's wound.

"It's *fine*, it's already been tended."

But Bazil could not be stopped, and so Zak relented.

A temporary healing camp had been set up near the entrance portal of Tor'alan so injured Leaguians didn't need to traipse all the way to the Center.

The council still congregated in the castle. Fireposts whipped back and forth from the tower to the camp with what Zak could only assume were orders and updates.

The Rot was gone—something no one had expected. Sorwin had postulated that if the Rot was an extension of Karazul, he could disable it at the very least. But eradicating or absorbing it or whatever he did had been unthinkable.

It had barely been an hour since it disappeared, and Zak bubbled with hope. With the path to Pywell clear, the war could finally be fought on equal footing.

"Ouch!" Zak flinched at Bazil's prodding.

"This is what sloppy healing gets you." A turquoise glow

surrounded his hands as they flashed over the wound with fresh bandages and herbs.

"They treated me in the middle of a battle, not exactly ideal circumstances."

"That is *exactly* when we're expected to perform at our best."

Zak didn't argue further, letting Bazil mutter his grievances as he worked. Instead, his attention drifted to the tents. Rows and rows of cots were laden with patients in ripped uniforms, and priests scurried between them with herbs and bandages.

So many injured already. How many more had been lost after one battle?

Sorwin appeared amongst the white tents and stepped gracefully between the hubbub. He looked alert, balanced on the tips of his toes and eyes a little too wide. True to form, he'd made it through the battle unscathed, and his lavender tunic had minimal soot and blood stains.

"Any word from Kaleb?" Zak asked as Sorwin approached. He didn't want to remind his magus of his absent partner, but figured he'd be on Sorwin's mind anyway.

"The latest Fireposts mention posturing and minor skirmishes between the two armies so far, though with the Rot gone I'd expect the Consortium to either retreat or launch an attack. It's hard to say what Zandorn will order, or what Queen Ymona will choose to do. She's made her own decisions in this war in the past."

Zak nodded. The former Queen of Evartia had proven unpredictable in previous encounters.

Finally finished with ministrations, Bazil stood and wiped his hands on a rag while Zak shrugged his uniform back on. "What happens next?" Bazil asked.

"We march on Pywell. The fortress defenses are most likely quite weak, so it's our best advantage to press. Scouts have already been sent ahead to provide an initial assessment."

Sorwin cleared his throat and continued. "You should know, Zakolor, that I sent a Firepost to Tansil. I'm not sure if it will reach him—I'm unaware of the enchantments in Nalawin. But I thought he should be informed of our impending confrontation with Zandorn."

"He knew where this would lead before he left," Zak said in a curt tone.

"He did."

"So what do you expect from him now?"

Sorwin sighed. "Nothing and everything." Zak only blinked at him, so he clarified. "Once he left, I planned for his uninvolvement, but that doesn't mean I'll stop reaching out. He's my magus, for one, and he himself said he was leaving Tor'alan but not the fight. I have to believe he's doing everything he can to support us from afar."

"I hope you're right." Zak didn't know what else to say, the wound from Tansil's departure more fresh than the one in his shoulder. He gestured to the black arrow sitting on the end of his cot. "Any idea what that is?"

Sorwin brightened at the prospect of edification. "Not for certain, but I have a theory." He drew near the arrow, curiosity stilting his movements. "What do you notice about the shaft?"

Zak peered at the thin cylinder. At first glance it seemed completely black, but as he looked closer, speckles of brown and grey dotted the length.

"I thought it was painted wood, but it's not, is it?"

Sorwin smiled. "Correct, it's a composite material. We recovered other arrows and weapons with this mysterious anti-magic property and have found they all contain a unique substance—a black powder."

It didn't take Zak long to put the pieces together. "The black caladrius."

"That was my assumption too, and perhaps why Zandorn waited so long to set his plan in motion. I think he wanted to harness the caladrius's power without sacrificing the bird. If I had to guess, he plucked most of the feathers from the poor creature and ground them down, made weapons, then distributed them amongst his forces to hamper our magic."

Bazil grunted. "Good timing for Zandorn after losing Karazul and the Rot."

"Indeed," Sorwin said. "Yet the effect seems to be limited to physical contact, so as long as we avoid touching the caladrius weapons, we can manage."

"What do you need me to do, Archmagus?" Zak asked.

Sorwin bristled a little. He'd never been fond of any titles, and the new one was no exception. "For now, rest. You, Olivia, and Elpida will hold back during the siege, but your magics can fell gods. The three of you remain our best hope of defeating Zandorn."

Sorwin returned to the other Archs and began planning

the assault on Pywell. Bazil checked Zak's bandages one more time then moved to a new patient down the row.

Zak couldn't sit still, otherwise his thoughts would drift—unhelpfully—to Zandorn and Renna and Kal, to their inevitable and quickly approaching clash.

He found Elpida preening at the edge of the healing tents, scales dazzling in patches of sunlight that pierced the overcast sky. At first she didn't want to leave the small group of admirers adorning her with compliments, but the mention of a meal and a bath were enough to convince her.

They went to the western stables, and besides a hissing contest with Burgo and two other wyvern, the reprieve remained uneventful. Elpida tore into deer and boar carcasses while Zak wiped down her bronze hide.

"What color do you think she'll be?" Zak asked Jolsu, wanting to distract himself and check on his Guardian. He'd been unusually quiet since the arrow pierced him.

*I hope red and purple, like Nelvowig.*

Young dragons were bright colors when they hatched—bronze, gold, or even white—and their scales darkened as they matured. Zak squinted as he ran a wet cloth over Elpida's scales. The pure bronze had become dappled the last few weeks with speckles of red, brown, blue, green, and yellow. It reminded Zak of Masdaan, of the beautiful glass mosaics and the hanging crystals that cast rainbows against earth-packed walls.

When Elpida finished eating, Zak wiped down her bloodstained snout and they made their way back toward the healing tents.

Olivia intercepted them and recruited Zak to help move supplies from the Temple's stores to the camp. She tried to coax Elpida to pull a cart, but the dragon spat a few profanities while declaring herself *far* above the menial work of horses—which, she reminded them, could be her food—and sat obstinately near the Archs as they strategized. The tirade caught Zak entirely by surprise and he had to hide a laugh beneath a cough when Olivia glared at him.

Zak lost count of how many boxes he carried. It felt good to move, to focus on the simple task. It was its own form of rest—maybe not the kind Sorwin had in mind, but the buzzing that ricocheted through his limbs quieted.

He heard snippets of conversations as he worked. Mages and soldiers expressing disbelief over the Rot's disappearance, and some—when they noticed him or Olivia—wore broad smiles and offered thanks and handshakes.

It was strange to receive the gratitude. They couldn't exactly explain that removing the Rot wasn't their deed, that a forgotten god had reclaimed his heart and rid the world of his curse. Nobody knew about Karazul yet outside their immediate circle besides Queen Alessa. Zak shrugged at Olivia and she rolled her eyes, a silent agreement to persevere through the awkward niceties.

Zak set down a box of tinctures and used the bottom of his tunic to wipe sweat from his brow. He rolled his shoulder, testing the wound. It had already closed and was healing nicely thanks to Bazil.

He was about to return to the Center for the next supplies when sudden movement caught his eye. He turned to the left.

Rauffe darted past the edge of the nearest tent.

Zak rounded the corner and watched as Rauffe went from walking to running and back again. He seemed...unstable. He had for months, ever since the battle over the black caladrius. Had something happened to him there? Rauffe had emerged unscathed for the most part, only minor bumps and bruises as far as he could remember.

*What do you think?* Zak asked Jolsu, wondering if he was being paranoid.

*Follow him, and either confirm or soothe your suspicions.*

Zak strode down the narrow alley between the tents, flaps snapping in the wind that rushed down the nearby Darlangson mountains and over Tor'alan. Rauffe continued his odd behavior, running between obstacles, pausing to look before rushing to the next. He reminded Zak of the children's game in Densba, where they were supposed to run and hide and wait to be found, except the youngest among them usually lost patience and flitted between hiding spots every minute or two.

Rauffe didn't appear impatient, but he stumbled over the edge of a cot, then ran into a passing priest.

Zak frowned. Rauffe was many things, but uncoordinated was not one. He was a fighter, an obnoxiously good one—Zak knew that first hand from sparring.

"Rauffe!" he called.

The man didn't turn, but kept blundering ahead.

"Rauffe, what are you doing?" Zak sped up, half jogging to close the distance.

The other man still didn't turn but must have felt Zak's closeness as he walked faster too.

Zak broke into a run, abandoning any pretense and caught Rauffe by the shoulder, spinning him around.

His eyes. They were completely black, like spilled inkwells. And his blank expression further indicated he was not wholly himself.

"Rauffe—" Zak gasped, and in the moment of shock, Rauffe shrugged off Zak's grip and ran.

"Wait!" Zak didn't know what was wrong, but he needed to help the man, or stop him before he did something.

Rauffe dashed left, and Zak's stomach dropped.

*The entrance portal!* Rauffe lumbered straight toward it.

*Stop him, Parignis!*

He couldn't get a clear path for a spell. Not with all the tents and injured soldiers and priests in the way.

Zak sprinted ahead, dodging past bodies and stacks of crates. "Stop him!" he shouted, pointing at Rauffe, but all he received were confused looks in return.

Rauffe reached the entrance portal and fell to his knees, smashing a hand into the dais. A surge of energy radiated outward, knocking Zak down and ripping through the nearest tents.

Zak sat up, heart pounding. There was a moment of impossible stillness where no one moved, spoke, breathed. Even Rauffe sat frozen next to the portal staring at his own fist.

Then the entrance portal shimmered, and a black and blue uniform stepped onto the dais.

Then another.

And another.

The Consortium had breached their defenses.

Tor'alan was under attack.

Sorwin heard the roar of flames before the screaming. Huddled over a map with Sashina and Rinka, he shared a wide-eyed look with the other Archs—their strategizing interrupted—before they all leaped into action.

Sashina's pink barriers covered the healing tents before the Consortium stepped off the dais. Sorwin knew she'd protect them with her life and evacuate anyone that couldn't fight to safety.

A squad of Rinka's demons charged ahead, all claws and wings and corded muscle. Mostly Caries—level three demons—but Sorwin spotted at least two Nox demons.

"Any chance there's a Malum in your ranks?" Sorwin asked.

Rinka scoffed. "Like I'd tell you, Archmagus. If there was, you wouldn't want me to summon it here."

True enough. Malums were unique and devastating creatures that stood atop the demonic hierarchy—fifth level demons that contained enough power to destroy a city in minutes. Despite Tor'alan's complex defenses, it was still a floating city that would likely not survive a Malum's attacks.

"Do what you can to slow them down. I'll join you momentarily."

Rinka hastened into the fray, and even though they'd never been on good terms before, Sorwin trusted her to defend the League with everything she had.

He wasted no time snatching a quill and parchment from a nearby desk and scribbling instructions. One Firepost whipped into the air, bound for the nearby League squadrons which had only just begun scouting the Wastelands, searching for a path to Pywell. Whatever forces Zandorn sent through the portal, they couldn't hope to match the numbers of the League.

In the middle of writing a second Firepost to the council, Zak ran up, breathless.

"It was Rauffe!" he said.

"Are you sure?" Zak and Rauffe had never been friendly, but Zak wouldn't throw accusations without good cause.

"His eyes...they were black. Then he touched...the dais." Zak bent over, hands on his knees.

"Possession? That's impossible, our wards should have detected it the moment he entered the city." How did Zandorn continue to outwit them at every turn?

"What do we do?"

"The entrance portal is the only way in or out of the city besides flying directly through the barriers. We need to shut the portal down. Destroy it if you have to. And Zak—" He caught his apprentice's arm before he dashed away. "Find Olivia and Elpida. You're all still targets, you'll be safer together."

Zak nodded and squeezed Sorwin's shoulder before turning and sprinting down the cobbled street.

Sorwin's quill raced across the parchment. When he finished, the Firepost blazed a bright orange and hurried to the council in the Center castle. Undoubtedly they were already aware of the ruckus, but they needed to know the severity of the situation. Hopefully Alessa already knew about the breach through her intelligence network, but it wouldn't change anything in the moment if she did.

Sorwin rubbed his shaking palm. Though he abhorred violence, there were—inevitably—situations when words became insufficient. Troubled times demanded action, asking scholars to become warriors. He drew the jeweled sword from his belt and marched into the fray, heeding the call.

# CHAPTER 24
# ACCEPTANCE

Tansil dug through the soil with a sharpened rock.

It had taken days to find the right location to plant the star seed. It required space to become the Arheim, but needed forests and waterways close enough for the elves to coax into *tredoms* and gardens. Though Tansil had grown accustomed to the human practice of clearing land and using lumber for construction, that would never do for the elves. In fact, such an act while creating their home would be the greatest dishonor.

The *Eldrimai* knelt across from Tansil, arms outstretched, communing with the earth, flora, fauna—life—around them. They'd leave pieces of themselves scattered about while the new Arheim sprouted, giving Tansil the chance to relocate all of the elves to the new settlement.

"You're still unsure," the *Eldrimai* stated, eyes closed.

Tansil struck the softened soil with the rock. "Of course I am." He had been banished for centuries, a lone elf in the world. And the moment he was summoned home, the future of his people had been thrust upon him—and no one except the *Eldrimai* seemed pleased. How could he not be unsure?

"This cannot be done in anger," the *Eldrimai* said.

"Then it may not be done at all!"

The *Eldrimai* paused the ceremony, resting ancient arms upon their knees as Tansil dropped the stone and adopted a similar position.

Annoyingly, the *Eldrimai* said nothing, waiting for him to confess what they already felt in his mind.

Tansil conceded. "I fought the pull. I thought each day that I held out it would weaken, shrivel like a sprout untended." He laughed at his own hubris. "But no, it only intensified. The star seed is irresistible, isn't it? There was never a choice to be made, only a demand to be met."

"It is a choice, though you have decided not to see it so."

"I was *forced* to accept this role."

"By whom?"

"By the star seed! By you! By the Arheim!" Tansil stood and paced around the future grove, which at the moment was mostly flat grassland with clumps of trees scattered at the edges.

The *Eldrimai* sighed and remained upon their knees. "There was another chosen before me."

That gave Tansil pause. "Another Tender?"

The *Eldrimai* nodded. "There were others before me, of course. We do not live forever. But there was also another chosen *instead* of me."

"What happened?"

"She did not see herself as *Eldrimai*. She preferred a simpler existence, and had a real knack with water lilies, if I recall. She refused the star seed, and it moved on to me."

"That's..." Tansil didn't think that was possible. Elves didn't have written records like humans. All of their knowledge was stored in the Arheim and the *Eldrimai*, shared verbally or telepathically, sometimes intentionally or accidentally through their intertwining connections. "Then why am I forced to accept this when others were not?"

"Resisting and refusing are not the same, Tansil. You are duty-bound—I believe that's why you were chosen in the first place—and you haven't outright refused the star seed. It will not move on until you do."

Tansil peered down at the glowing green seed, resting among a bed of leaves cut from the Arheim. He'd never considered it before, but in all his centuries of life, he'd never refused a request for help. Not directly. Maybe he didn't always fulfill it *exactly*, but he strived to help nevertheless.

That's what elves did, after all. They tended nature, and the *Eldrimai* tended them. Most elves chose a dedication, a specific plant or animal or landform or waterway and aided it throughout their lives.

"My dedication was gardens." He said it aloud, though he mostly spoke to himself, a reminder of a former life long past.

"An oddity amongst us. Gardens require planning and oversight, for the gardener to be a step removed, ready to shape and guide. These are not natural things for elves tied to the flow of nature."

"Perhaps." He recalled his small garden in Tor'alan, the

one reminder of home he had allowed himself. Then again, weren't all the mages in the Elemental House not his charges? Did they not make a garden of sorts?

Was that why he hadn't—couldn't—refuse the star seed? Was it asking him to return to his dedication, one that he now wasn't convinced he ever truly left?

"What was your dedication, *Eldrimai*?"

The *Eldrimai* smiled, a wistful thing. "Ah, I haven't thought about that in centuries. The world was different then, thousands of years ago. It was a time when gods, mortals, and others all lived in peace together. Humans refer to it as the Era of Mages."

Tansil nodded. "Before the Era of Dominion, when the gods forced their will upon us."

"Indeed. There were many more creatures of nature in those times, many that either left with the gods when the Contract was signed or have died out absent the divine. One such creature we called spirit. They embodied nature, a manifestation of its energy. There were many kinds—water, earth, air, but also curiosity and frustration and happiness and anger. My dedication was to spirits."

"A natural choice for *Eldrimai*, as you tended many parts of nature already."

"Perhaps," the *Eldrimai* conceded. "But I would not claim to fully understand the logic of the Arheim. You'll understand what I mean if you become *Eldrimai*."

Tansil picked up the star leaf seed and gazed into its light, unsure what he hoped to find. Questions, so many questions, echoed in his mind. He was old enough to realize he'd never have all the answers, yet young enough to cling to such a desire.

What would the elves think of him as *Eldrimai*? Upon his second return to Stjarunni he'd been met with more mixed feelings—some curious, some welcoming (no doubt thanks to the *Eldrimai's* influence), and many still cold and untrusting. He couldn't blame any of them for their feelings, they were all valid.

"Acceptance," the *Eldrimai* said, "is the basis of Tending. We do not guide to our whims, each branch and root knows its shape and only needs the occasional nudge to find it."

"How dare you make so much sense in my anguish," Tansil said, but there was no bite in his words, and the *Eldrimai* laughed warmly.

Tansil took a deep breath and approached the soil he had tilled. Bending, he reverently placed the glowing seed deep into the earth and pushed the rich soil over top of it.

"Can such a simple act be all that is required?" There had to be more to the ceremony than planting a seed, some kind of magical rite that solidified Tansil as the next *Eldrimai*. Then exhaustion washed over him as his energy drained into the seed. Not all of it, but at least half of his magical reserves.

The current *Eldrimai* stood and walked around the planted seed, placing a gentle hand upon his shoulder. "Nourishment is costly, but you are now connected with the next Arheim. The world is complicated enough, Tansil. Take the simple as it comes."

Tansil chuckled, and was about to thank the *Eldrimai* for

their words when a sudden shock in his chest doubled him over.

"Tor'alan...the wards..."

His city had been breached.

He leaped up, gazing east. Tor'alan would be near Merinthia's Pass if Sorwin's plan had worked, which it would have. No one in Valecium could compare to Sorwin's analytical prowess—not even Zandorn, so blinded by avarice.

There was no mistaking the Consortium's buzzing presence in the back of his mind. Tansil had woven most of Tor'alan's defenses himself, layering barriers and charms upon one another. The invaders couldn't have flown in from the sky without permission—there were simply too many protections to pierce.

They must have corrupted the entrance portal somehow.

"*Eldrimai*—" He turned, and the ancient elf wore a soft smile.

"I understand, Tansil. I am meant to remain and watch over the Arheim anyway. Go—you have unfinished business."

Tansil approached and held out his palms. The *Eldrimai* did the same, and they pressed palms and foreheads together, lingering in the embrace.

"Acceptance," Tansil said. It was suddenly so clear how permissive and supportive the *Eldrimai* had been, even when Tansil had lived among the humans.

"Ah, you're beginning to see." They pulled apart slowly, and the *Eldrimai* looked up at Tansil with misted eyes. "*Benevita*, Tansil."

"I'll return as soon as I can, *Eldrimai. Benevita.*"

He put some distance between himself and the Arheim's seed, then opened a portal and stepped through the shimmering blue door.

"Elpida!" Zak shouted.

He found the bronze dragon surrounded by a squad of Consortium mages. Luckily they didn't know how to fight a dragon. Their fire magic brushed harmlessly off her scales, and Elpida roared and raked the nearest mage with sharpened claws.

Zak whirled his staff and dropped one of the mages from behind with a strike to the head. He deflected a fireball with a well-timed barrier, then channeled his magic through the emerald at the tip of his staff.

"*Lapilectus!*" The cobbles underfoot leaped into the air and pelted the mage, burying them beneath the street.

*Finally the battle begins anew! I grew tired of waiting.* Elpida sauntered over, having dispatched the other two mages, tail lashing with excitement.

*You'll have your fill today, hatchling,* Jolsu warned.

"There will be plenty of fighting," Zak acknowledged. "We need to find Olivia and take down the portal—Sorwin's instructions."

Everything had moved so fast. The moment Zak saw the first Consortium soldiers emerge from the portal he had grabbed Rauffe by the collar and shoved him toward the healing tents. A moment later, Sashina's pink barrier had blazed into existence, and Zak dove behind the protection as swords and spells ricocheted off.

Bazil had looped an arm under his shoulder and helped him to his feet. "Let's get to Sorwin."

"No, I need you to take care of Rauffe. There's something wrong with him."

They had both looked to the other man as he crawled away on hands and knees. Zak couldn't see if his eyes had still been darkened.

"Evidently," Bazil relented. "Fine, I'm on Rauffe, you go to Sorwin."

With Sashina's barrier, the path to the Arch's tent had been clear of enemies, but a frenzy of priests moving patients to a safe location congested the area. Zak collided with three or four bodies each step he took, and after being tossed about, he finally sprang free of the tumult and found Sorwin bent over a desk penning a letter.

Breathless, he explained what had happened—as much as he was aware—and waited for Sorwin's brilliant mind to formulate a plan.

He hadn't waited long. And now that he'd found Elpida, all he needed to do was get Olivia and shut down the entrance portal.

"Let's head toward the Center," Zak told Elpida and Jolsu. "Olivia was probably on her way there to gather more supplies when the invasion began."

Zak ran down the wide road toward the Center, Elpida loping behind him. Skirmishes sprang up around them as

League and Consortium forces battled.

"Olivia!" He found her kneeling on a corner outside a bladesmith shop, hands pressed to the ground. A few paces away, a mage was trapped in a tangle of branches from her wood binding spell.

As Zak and Elpida neared her side, Olivia stood and dragged a sleeve across her forehead. "How did they get in?"

"Entrance portal. Sorwin needs us to disable it. Are you okay?" He didn't see any wounds, but the edges of her uniform were already tattered and soot-covered.

She waved a dismissive hand. "I'm fine, they just surprised me. Let's go. The sooner we shut down the portal, the sooner we can end this for good."

Zak, Olivia, and Elpida made their way back down the street toward the entrance portal, and Zak had the odd sensation that they were going against the current. More and more Consortium soldiers and mages crossed their path, and though they were quickly dispatched, something felt amiss.

"Over here," Zak called, waving Olivia and Elpida down a side street after the latest scuffle. He leaned against a garden wall enclosing a tidy yard.

"What is it?" Olivia asked.

"Look, what do you see?" He gestured to the main road.

Olivia and Elpida craned their necks to peer.

*Enemies. Many of them.* Elpida's wings rustled along her spine.

Zak rolled his eyes. "Yes, but what about their behavior?"

"Disorganized. Frantic." Olivia frowned. "They're not even really fighting all that much, not unless they have to.

They're pushing toward the Center and spreading out into the city."

Zak smiled. *I knew she'd see it too.*

*Focus, Parignis,* Jolsu chided privately before addressing all of them. *They search for something—we must stop them.*

"How? Unless we know what they're looking for, we can't beat them to it," Zak said.

"Zandorn has the Contract, the black caladrius, and Baltenebris's heart." Olivia counted the terrifying items on separate fingers as she spoke. "What more could they be after?"

Zak's mind whirred, thinking, pushing the shouts, metal clanging, and bursts of magic away. "The only thing he's lost recently is Karazul's heart, but that isn't in Tor'alan." At least, Zak didn't think the assassin and Shira had returned. That made him uneasy, and he hoped they'd made it out of Pywell and back to the *Swift Star* safely.

*We will not decipher their goal now.* Vess's high voice chimed, surprising Zak. She didn't often speak to anyone besides Olivia. *Stop the portal, then we may stop their pursuit.*

*She's right,* Jolsu agreed.

"Then let's copy their strategy. This way!" Zak led them away from the main road then turned right down a connecting alleyway. All the time he had spent running back and forth from Shira's apartment to the Center had paid off—he knew every inch of the Market district and navigated a path to the backside of the entrance portal, avoiding any Consortium forces along the way.

Zak crouched behind an abandoned fruit stand, gripping the edges of empty crates while observing the entrance portal.

A steady influx of Consortium members walked through the shimmering door every few seconds.

"Okay, here's what we'll—"

Kalbick.

Zak nearly choked at the sight of his old friend emerging from the portal. He had seen him in Pywell weeks ago as a spirit, had seen how much he'd changed, but it was different being only a stone's throw away.

He saw more now. The way his hands twitched with anticipation, the deep crease in his brow and shadows beneath his eyes. The way he shrunk from Renna as she appeared behind him. Kalbick made himself smaller, bowing his head, stepping out of the dangerous woman's path.

Zak gritted his teeth and snarled, much like Elpida had when he was late bringing her food. Yet all his anger froze when he saw the next figure emerge from the portal.

Zandorn.

# CHAPTER 25

# FORCE OF NATURE

"Zak!" Olivia lunged forward, but found only air as she missed grabbing his arm. He rushed across the square and threw a fireball directly at Zandorn.

It burst on a dark blue shield.

Olivia recognized that magic. "Kalbick."

She remembered him all too well from their fight a few months ago. She had lost, something that still made her cringe, but she had been under the *vitaligo* then, weakened from the binding.

She wasn't anymore, and this time it would be a fair fight.

She ran to Zak's side, Elpida following too, and the three of them stood facing Zandorn, Renna, and Kalbick.

"Would you look at this—two *Nacusti* and a dragon! I am shocked that those reports were true." Zandorn eyed Elpida hungrily, sending a tremor through Olivia.

"What are you searching for in Tor'alan?" Zak shouted. Rage radiated off his skin.

*We need to separate Zak from Zandorn,* Olivia told Vess. *He's too emotional for this fight, he isn't ready.*

Vess's calm presence washed over her. *Perhaps. Or perhaps he has mustered the necessary anger to overcome a force such as Zandorn.*

*Maybe.* But Olivia bit her lip as Zak's bronze staff rattled in his grip.

Zandorn laughed—actually *laughed*—at Zak. "Oh, young Zakolor. With your wealth of power, sharp observation and reasoning skills, no shortage of audacity. You have all the makings of a great mage. It's a shame you're so determined to oppose me."

"I am my magus's apprentice." Zak squared his shoulders and stood taller.

It was subtle, but something within Zak settled. Tightened. *He's finding his focus,* Olivia thought. Maybe Vess was right.

"And where is your magus now? I'd like to greet him." Zandorn spun, arms outstretched as he glanced around the square.

"You're dealing with me now." Zak stepped forward, and without a thought, so did Olivia and Elpida.

Zandorn shook his head, dark eyes ablaze with fervor. "You're not special anymore, Zakolor. There are two *Nacusti* now, and I only need one." He waved a hand at Renna, and she and Kalbick descended the dais and moved toward the Center.

"Stop!" Zak called. "Kal!"

Kalbick didn't stop or look back, but his step faltered for

a moment, falling out of sync with Renna. Her head snapped to Kalbick, and he quickly returned to her pace.

*Something is there.* Olivia could almost see it, a tiny rift between Renna and Kalbick.

The *sorgeus* was powerful, there was no doubt about that. If she had a chance to pry him from Renna's grip, she'd take it. Maybe she could get Zak and Kalbick together again, like they had been months ago, in the field fighting over Terasi...

"'You're dealing with me now.' Those were your words, correct?" Zandorn sauntered down the dais. Black lightning darted down his arms, and with a lazy flick of his wrist he shot a bolt straight at Zak.

Olivia barely had a chance to gasp. She couldn't protect him.

But Zak didn't need her to. He'd grown so skilled with shields in the past few months, they practically sprang up around him. A wall of pure emerald magic appeared—not just in front of him, but stretching over Olivia and Elpida too. The black lightning exploded, and thunder rumbled across the square. The shield held firm.

Zandorn wore an unsettling smile as more lightning raced across his shoulders and arms. But his confidence faltered as he stumbled. Olivia tracked his glance down to a thick vine curling up to his knee.

Then another vine burst between the cracks of the cobblestone, wrapping around his wrist. A third found his waist. A fourth, his neck. In a matter of seconds, Zandorn fought against a host of vines, twisting and pulling across his entire body.

Most surprisingly, a chilled wind swirled through the square as ice formed around Zandorn and the vines. It froze their movements, and in a breath he was completely encased in the clear crystal.

Tansil stepped out from behind a nearby tent, dark complexion unusually pallid.

"Archmagus!" Olivia said in her surprise.

"I am no longer," he said with a half-smile. He thrust a fist toward the dais, and the entrance portal crumbled.

Zak—mouth agape—recovered his composure. "Arch—er, Tansil, I thought you were with the elves?"

"I was, I am, and I will be. But for now, I am here too." He winced as he approached the trio. "This binding won't hold for long—"

Olivia blinked. "But that's a double fusion binding of wood and ice. It's one of the most powerful entrapment spells besides a *senligo*." She'd been working on her bindings for a few months in preparation for this battle and hadn't come across many spells stronger in her research.

Tansil nodded. "Yes, and our opponent is no ordinary mage. I arrived in time to see Renna and Kalbick make their way toward the Center. Pursue them—for no good can come of their meddling. Leave Zandorn to me."

*I do not like to abandon prey*, Elpida said.

"Are you sure? You seem exhausted already." Zak eyed Tansil, a softness in his voice. "I doubt Zandorn could stop all four of us together."

Olivia kept her attention on Zandorn while listening. The ice had already begun to melt, thick drips of water darkening the stone street. "We're running out of time."

"Exactly," Tansil said. "If you stay, we may defeat Zandorn together, but at what cost? Renna and Kalbick are up to something and must be stopped. We cannot focus on Zandorn alone."

*He speaks the truth, Parignis,* Jolsu rumbled. *You are already familiar with Zandorn's affinity for misdirection. Do not play into his plan.*

Zak grimaced but relented. "Fine. Olivia, Elpida—let's go." He paused, squeezing Tansil's shoulder. "I don't know what happened to you in Nalawin, but I'm glad you're here now, Tansil."

The elf—who had always been short but whose presence seemed so large—appeared small for the first time to Olivia. "As am I, Zakolor. Now, away."

Tansil watched the dragon and two *Nacusti* run past the rubble of the entrance portal and down the street toward the Center. It was the right decision to send them away, for many reasons.

Renna and Kalbick needed to be stopped—he'd caught a glimmer of anticipation in Renna's wild expression, and nothing good could come from that. Sorwin alone couldn't stand up to her. He and Tansil together had scarcely slowed her down in the battle for the black caladrius. This time, the *Nacusti* would have to get involved. Tansil could no longer shield them from the Consortium.

And selfishly, he needed to face Zandorn alone.

He folded his hands at his waist, gathering what energy remained in his bones. He'd given at least half of his stores to the Arheim during the ritual—much more than he'd thought.

The ice shattered with such a force that small shards sprayed across the empty square. A light blue shield appeared before Tansil, and the debris smashed against it with sharp crunches.

"Hello, Magus." Zandorn sloughed off the vines and stretched as if he'd woken from a restful slumber, dark eyes narrowing on Tansil. "Still a wily one—I didn't notice your presence until it was too late. Yet your spells don't quite pack the same power they used to."

Tansil swayed a fraction of an inch, shifting weight between his feet. "I should have confronted you a century ago, Zandorn. Not stopping you then is my biggest regret."

"Come now, you wound me, Magus." Zandorn—theatrical as ever—adopted a feigned pout. "I'm not convinced that is true. Surely whatever deed earned you banishment is a bigger regret?"

"You speak of things you know not of." Tansil barely kept his voice from tremoring, the scars of his past fresh after his recent return to Nalawin.

Zandorn smiled. "Indeed. You never confided in me what happened. Yet I never stopped wondering...what could be so terrible to force an elf from their homeland? And why would he teach magic to humans in Turrimare? That, of course, made me wonder about our relationship as magus and apprentice. Would things have been different if we'd been closer? Do you think you could have stopped me before I turned down this path if you'd been more present, more vigilant?"

"I—" Tansil had asked himself the same questions a thousand times over the decades, but he never once expected to hear them from his former apprentice.

Zandorn launched a dozen fiery arrows straight at Tansil's chest, catching him off guard. Almost a moment too late, Tansil's blue shield blocked them all, and Zandorn disappeared in a cloud of smoke.

"Tell me, Magus, did you divulge your secrets to Sorwin?" Zandorn's disembodied voice echoed around the square. "Or do you continue the mistakes of the past?"

Tansil closed his eyes, reaching out with his magic to find Zandorn's hiding spot. He spun and conjured a wave of water. It crashed against a wall of black fire. Both elements turned into steam, and Zandorn cackled in the murk.

"Ah, I've missed this, Magus! We've barely sparred in the last hundred years. Doesn't it feel good to stretch?"

"This may be a game to you, but it is life or death for me and the rest of Valecium."

Energy poured through Tansil. Icy blue spears jutted from the cobblestones, forcing Zandorn backward. A wall of earth broke from the street and stopped his progress. Branches sprang from it, tendrils reaching toward the man, but they burned to ash against dark flames.

The elf moved with fluid grace—arms weaving, legs twisting, head and torso in perfect alignment. Sorwin had told him once that there was no better Guide caster in the

League than him, and it was impossible to know if that were true, but he felt most alive in motion with magic.

He kept up the onslaught. A waterfall appeared overhead, washing the fire away. Zandorn bent under the force before thrusting an arm up and throwing the water aside.

A ring of lava erupted around Tansil's feet, melting through stone as it bubbled angrily inward. He leaped, wings appearing at his back to lift him skyward.

Wind. A powerful gust pushed him into a tiled roof at the edge of the square. Tansil gasped as air fled his lungs, but he couldn't stay down. He gripped the edge of a nearby chimney and found his footing, wings unfurling at his shoulders, chest heaving.

*Running out of time.* The number of spells and magnitude he was forced to use against Zandorn quickly took its toll. He had to end this fast, before it was too late.

Zandorn's pale visage sneered up at him from the middle of the square.

For a brief moment Tansil wished he'd had Cerevita's *cordeus* to channel his god's power. But he discarded the thought as soon as it appeared, knowing his pride would prevent him from relying on divine magic.

He had wanted to face Zandorn himself, and that meant *only* as himself. Not as a Devoted, an elf, or an Archmagus. Simply as a former teacher to a former student.

Heavy clouds condensed overhead, grey swirls curling with unnatural speed.

Lightning—hot and white—flashed in a strike. Zandorn had preemptively erected a shield, but he'd still been thrown bodily to the side under the pressure of the attack.

The clouds crackled again as Tansil reached toward them, Guiding the next strike. Zandorn hid beneath a dome of rock which was obliterated by the next bolt.

Saplings sprang from every nearby wooden structure—beams, market stalls, and tent poles all reclaiming past identities. Branches dug roots and sprouted trunks on their snaking course across the square toward Zandorn.

Next, Tansil pulled on the pool of lava from earlier, arcing it into a half circle opposite the encroaching forest.

Last, spikes of ice grew, making a field of daggers at Zandorn's feet and thunder rumbled overhead once again.

Zandorn's composure slipped as fear flickered in his eyes. He understood what Tansil was doing.

A skilled elemental mage could work two or three of the natural elements. The exceptional ones, like Olivia and Sorwin, could work fusions—advanced magic that combined elements to create something new. Water and air made ice, earth and fire made lava. But usually these exceptional mages could only master one fusion after years of study.

Zandorn had been beyond exceptional, commanding lava and lightning early into his studies.

Tansil, however, was an anomaly. He could control all four fusions.

Simultaneously.

From his rooftop perch, Tansil closed the forest and lava circle around Zandorn. The ice spikes continued to grow, limiting his movement, and thunder rumbled overhead, preparing the next strike.

Zandorn pulled a dagger from his belt. "You surprise me, Magus. You hid such abilities from me all these years?" he snarled. His veneer of confidence had cracked.

"I neglected many things in my time with you, Zandorn. Overlooked the signs that led you to this sorry state. But your hunger for power had always been apparent, something you were never able to hide. I knew if you found out about this, you'd never stop chasing this ability. And I was right to deny you—look how far you've gone to defy death itself."

"Then go on, Magus. Do what you must." He flung his arms wide, leaving his chest exposed.

The clouds lowered and the muscles in Tansil's entire body jumped with strain. *Almost there, a moment more.*

He could do it.

He had to do it.

He had to end this.

"Goodbye, Zandorn. I am sorry I failed you."

Lightning flashed, soundless as it raced down and tore through Zandorn's right shoulder. Branches and ice and lava all launched toward Zandorn too.

But something was wrong. Tansil had built up enough strength in the spell for a sustained bolt, lasting half a minute at least to pierce any defenses Zandorn would conjure up.

Instead, the lightning disappeared after barely a second. So did the rest of the elemental attacks.

Tansil fell to his knees, sliding to the edge of the tile roof.

Zandorn brandished the dagger overhead. The blade was black and smoking.

Like it had cut through lightning—and much more.

Zandorn's dark wings appeared at his back, and in three flaps he was on top of Tansil, thrusting the dagger into his heart.

Tansil laid back on the roof, chest exploding with pain. He had exhausted all of his magic in the last attack and couldn't stop the blade.

"How?" he wheezed. Tansil had mastered the four fusions, an impossible feat. No shield should have been able to stop them. Every escape should have been rendered unfeasible.

Zandorn's sour breath warmed Tansil's face as he laughed. He pulled the dagger from his chest and held the bloodied thing aloft. "An amazing creature, the black caladrius. I always thought it was a shame that its storied powers were a one-time use. But no one had thought to pluck its feathers and grind them into powder. No one had the ingenuity to channel the bird's anti-magic. No one except me."

Tansil's vision blurred, but he squinted at the dagger. Beneath his red blood the blade was entirely black and curved gracefully, like a feather.

The moment the blade pierced him, Tansil felt the connection to his magic close.

"That is...an abomination." He coughed, thick blood spurting over his lips.

"You will not suffer its existence much longer." Zandorn grinned. "Ah, Magus. How I've *longed* for this day! You, my first betrayer, finally undone." He wiped the dagger clean on Tansil's robes and paced to the edge of the roof, getting a better look at Tansil as he withered.

Darkness closed in. *It's over...not how I...thought.*

Death was a strange concept for elves. Such an elusive thing given their long lifespans, yet ever present in the tending of nature. It was, and would always be, part of the natural order. That was always why Tansil felt so responsible for Zandorn. He had been his magus, failed to guide him down the right path, and then failed to cull him when he threatened the rest of the garden.

*Some Eldrimai I would have been.*

A whisper of magic still clung to Tansil's fingertips. He couldn't reach his source, but he could use that last little bit for something.

His head swung to the right. With a twist of his fingers, the magic turned into a glittering blue bird and flitted off on a cold Winterfall breeze toward the Center.

Zandorn watched it with a furrowed brow. "Admirable, that you could still work a spell after being pierced by this dagger. But whatever you did doesn't matter. You'll be dead in moments, and I will enjoy every second of your passing."

Tansil's breath hitched. He closed his eyes, and smiled. "You will fail, Apprentice. My family...has what yours will never know."

"And what is that?" Zandorn's voice grew faint, and Tansil slipped down, down, down into the roots of the world.

"Love."

# CHAPTER 26

# BIRDS OF A FEATHER

Sorwin slashed with his sword, cutting down a Consortium soldier. Then he spun and waved an arm, toppling a wall onto a group of approaching enemies.

"They're converging," Rinka said to his right. "Whatever they were searching for in the city, they didn't find. Now they're coming to the Center."

Sorwin, Rinka, and a smattering of mages and soldiers had struck a defensive position outside the Center's gate. Consortium members had crept around the fortifications, seeking another way in, but the Center was impenetrable from all sides. The only way in or out was through the gate thanks to Tansil's thorough defensive charms.

"Sashina should have evacuated all of the injured by now." Sorwin parried a spear thrust, then pushed back the attacker with a blast of wind. "All we need to do is hold until she returns with reinforcements from below."

And, assuming Zak destroyed the entrance portal, hopefully Sashina could open a well-placed portal of her own upon the small dais.

Rinka spared him a knowing glance before her rust-colored flames blazed into a barrier and cut off half the intersection. "The entire council is in the castle behind us. We cannot fall, or else the League is finished."

"I know." *Too well*. His sister—his last blood relative—was among them. He couldn't lose her, not like his brother and parents. He was stronger this time, older, more experienced. He'd save Alessa and everyone else, no matter the cost.

Rinka marshalled the other mages and coordinated a barrier around the gate, giving them a temporary reprieve from the melee.

Sorwin sheathed his sword and took advantage of the moment, scanning the battleworn streets, evaluating the enemy's forces and their own, planning the next several moves and creating contingency plans. Tansil had always told him that his mind was his greatest weapon, more so than any spell or sword.

"Analysis fuels foresight," the elf had said. "You're exceptional at assessing a situation and determining the path to success. Strength alone does not make a victor or a leader."

Sorwin had always been more of a scholar than a soldier, that much he knew about himself. But hearing Tansil's frank summation of his abilities had altered his self-perception—it had given him the permission to lean into his intellectual side rather than force the martial, which was completely opposite of what his brother and father had wanted in his youth.

But they were gone, and he was not. Not yet, anyway.

Just then, something flew through the barrier. Sorwin instinctively readied a defense, but dropped it when he recognized Tansil's blue magic. He held out a hand, and the shimmering bird alighted on his palm and disappeared.

An image of Tansil—robes torn and bloodied—flashed before his eyes, and the elf's voice sounded in Sorwin's head. *I failed you, Sorwin. In so many ways. It's up to you now, Archmagus.*

A series of images followed his words. Zandorn standing over Tansil, gripping a black-bladed dagger covered in blood. Then Renna and Kalbick, running away from the entrance portal. Last, the Center castle, bright white stone with veins of purple and orange.

Tansil had pieced together that the Consortium were heading for the Center.

"He came back..." Sorwin clutched at his chest, pain lancing his heart.

*Tansil...*

He had fought Zandorn, gave his life for the League, for all Valecium. Sorwin had thought the elf would outlive them all. He'd never prepared for his Magus's death.

Foolish, perhaps, since their entire relationship had been built during a war. But Tansil was a force of nature, a constant in the world much like the gods themselves had been.

Tears spilled down his cheeks, hot and wholly untimely. He couldn't mourn now. He dragged a tattered sleeve across his eyes and shook his head. *Later. Hold it for later.*

Zak, Olivia, and Elpida sprinted toward him from a side

street. With a wave of his arm, the barriers parted and allowed them to pass through before sealing once again.

"Tansil is here!" Zak shouted, despite his gasping for air. "And he destroyed the entrance portal. The Consortium reinforcements are cut off."

"Good, that's good." Hearing the elf's name aloud stung after learning his fate.

"Sorwin, are you okay?" Olivia reached for him.

*They cannot know, not yet. They do not need this version of me.* He rolled his shoulders and gave a curt nod with a forced smile. "I'm fine, just thinking. We've confirmed the Consortium is coming for the Center, but we don't know why."

"For the council, maybe?" Zak asked.

"Possibly, but I doubt it. It seems they're after something or someone specific."

*Then we burn them all to ash,* Elpida suggested.

"Well, yes, that would be effective if we could. Defense is our best option, though." Sorwin mulled over the images Tansil had shown him. "Renna and Kalbick and Zandorn are all here."

"Yes, we saw them arrive," Olivia said.

Sorwin looked the three of them over. They wore only minor signs of combat, a smudge of soot on a cheek, tousled hair, drawn weapons.

"I'll need you three to stop Renna and Kalbick." Sorwin met each of their wide-eyed expressions. Each of them had been training for this day for months, and as much as Sorwin wanted to tuck them safely into a room until the danger had passed, the truth was he couldn't. The League needed their power if they hoped to survive, let alone win.

When none of them spoke, Sorwin prompted again. "Is that something you can do?" He looked directly at Zak this time, knowing he'd have the most difficulty fighting his friend.

Zak's jaw tightened. "We can do it. What about Zandorn? Tansil had him bound, but—"

"I'll handle him." Sorwin's hands balled into fists.

An explosion knocked them all to the ground. Sorwin's head rang and vision blurred as he leaned on an elbow. The barriers had disappeared and left them vulnerable. *How?*

Kalbick ran by, ignoring them all as he ducked through the Center gate. Renna flashed a venomous smile as she followed in his wake.

"Godsforsaken *sorgeus*," Sorwin cursed. He helped Zak and Olivia up as Elpida bristled and shook, bronze scales glinting in the setting sunlight.

Zak clasped Sorwin's hand with his own, then his shoulder in a strong grip. "Magus."

The back of Sorwin's throat burned as he mirrored the embrace. "Apprentice."

Olivia gave him a sideways smirk, then the two *Nacusti* and dragon pursued Kalbick and Renna into the Center.

"Touching."

Sorwin whirled. Zandorn perched on a nearby balcony, black wings furled along his back. He didn't move, simply watched and waited. Smiling. Expectant.

*We both know what happens next.*

"Rinka, reassemble the defense of the gate," Sorwin said.

The Archalium followed his gaze to Zandorn and reached for the *lapidaemas* at her neck. "Sorwin, I will assist—"

"No." He whispered harshly. "One of us needs to lead our people, and I have a better chance at defeating him." He patted the leather pouch at his waist holding Cerevita's *cordeus*.

She gave him a solemn frown but didn't argue further, and instead turned away and shouted orders to pull the mages and soldiers back together after the explosion had scattered their formation.

Wings with brown and gold feathers appeared at Sorwin's back, practically glowing in the orange and purple rays of late afternoon. He soared to a flat rooftop opposite Zandorn.

Zandorn studied him in silence for a moment. "You already know about Tansil, don't you?"

"I do." Sorwin fought against opposite urges—one to fall down and cry, another to launch himself at Zandorn and tear into him like a feral beast. Neither would keep him alive, let alone protect the League, and so he restrained his grief and attempted to keep his composure.

Nothing less than perfection would work against Zandorn.

"Hmph. An annoyance to the very end, our magus. That makes us brothers in a way, doesn't it? Siblings in magic, as it were."

"No. We happened to share a magus, that is all."

Zandorn's lips curled in a fiendish smile. "Come now, you're smarter than that. Everyone says you are, anyway. You would deny our similarities? Both with powerful magic, genius-level intelligence, and both finding Tansil in our youth after familial trauma. A recipe for greatness, if there ever was one."

Sorwin had heard the stories of Zandorn's origins from Tansil, of course. About his abusive mother and her unsolved murder. How he had lived on the streets performing magic tricks for entertainment to earn coin. That was how Tansil had discovered him and his vast potential beneath his illusions.

Despite the similarities in their paths, Sorwin was certain of one thing. "I can't stress this enough, Zandorn—we are *nothing* alike. But it is curious you seem so desperate to forge a connection. Have you asked yourself why that is?"

Zandorn's smile twisted into scowl.

*Good.* Agitated opponents made mistakes. And he had one more barb to use.

"I heard your moniker was the Raven Mage when you became a magerus. Fitting, given your dark wings and the bodies you leave behind."

"My thoughts exactly," Zandorn preened.

"Ah, but did you know that in the wild, hawks hunt ravens?" Sorwin extended his wings and gave Zandorn a broad, mocking grin.

And that proved too much for the man to handle.

Black lightning surged toward Sorwin, but he'd been ready. He teleported to the next rooftop in a flash of orange lightning.

Zandorn arced another bolt toward him, and Sorwin disappeared further down the street. Snarling, Zandorn leaped into the air, black wings spread wide, and hurled half a dozen bolts as Sorwin ran and blinked between rooftops.

Sorwin had considered thousands of strategies over the weeks leading up to this confrontation. He hadn't known for certain if he would fight Zandorn, but when Tansil had left the city to be with the elves, it seemed inevitable.

And once Zandorn had appeared outside the Center moments ago, Sorwin had spent each second piecing together a plan.

Accounting for each variable at play, he identified exactly four steps to defeating Zandorn.

First, Sorwin needed to lead him away from the others. He couldn't have the council or the defenders outside the Center get caught in the crossfire of their battle.

A black bolt exploded on the shingles to his right, and Sorwin dove to the left in a flash of orange.

*Part one is going well.*

The next part, however, would be much trickier.

Sorwin pivoted and thrust both arms toward Zandorn, blasting him with air. Zandorn curled his wings in and dropped, landing hard on a roof but keeping his footing.

"This seems as good a spot as any," Sorwin said. He'd lured them to the avenue between the Market and Crock districts.

Zandorn seemed to be done with talking as he launched into another attack. He stomped a foot, and hundreds of roof tiles rose into the air and sharpened themselves into points. They flew toward Sorwin like angry hornets of stone and clay.

Sorwin didn't move.

The daggers exploded on a barrier mere inches away, but Sorwin kept his back straight, staring at Zandorn through the onslaught.

Zandorn's eyes narrowed. "Leveraging the city's defenses? Are you afraid to fight me with your own magic?"

"Quite the contrary—this *is* my magic. Tansil and I laid these barriers around each district together. No hostile magic may cross their borders." Getting them to this specific spot had been part two of the plan.

"Very well." Zandorn lifted a sleeve of his robe and pressed fingers to a leatherbound stone on his wrist. Even from a distance, the swirls of color within the smooth surface were unmistakable.

*A lapidaemas—he's summoning demons!*

A cloud of phasmas appeared, ranging in size and color. There had to be at least twenty or thirty of them. It would have been a beautiful sight on any other occasion, but not when each of those gaseous entities floated toward him with the intent to kill.

Still, they were only level two demons, and ones with a very specific weakness.

Sorwin jumped back and conjured a giant ball of fire. It hovered in the air, his hands darting around its edges to keep it contained. Smaller orbs of fire launched from it as each phasma passed through the barrier between districts. In a matter of seconds, each phasma burned and hissed out of existence, back to the ether from whence they came.

As Sorwin let the fireball dissipate, Zandorn appeared at his side in a black cloud. He lunged, stretching toward Sorwin's ribs with a dagger.

In his final act, Tansil had shown Sorwin how the dagger cut through magic like Karazul. It was the only reason Zandorn had beat Tansil, who had been much stronger than both of them.

Sorwin couldn't hope to win while Zandorn wielded the dangerous weapon. He couldn't so much as sustain a scratch from the wicked blade, or else his magic would be neutralized.

Which led him to part three of the plan.

Sorwin leaned right and struck Zandorn's wrist, deflecting the attack.

With his other hand, Zandorn spouted black flames.

Sorwin spun and water swirled, enclosing him in a protective sphere. The flames hissed against the barrier as he put distance between them.

Zandorn—dots of sweat darkening his temples—didn't pursue immediately.

*Finally.* The sequential battles were catching up with him. Which made it no surprise when he opted to speak again, buying himself time.

"You're smarter than Tansil, that much I already knew." Zandorn sounded breathier than before. "Still, it's impressive how you conserve magic. You don't waste any movements. The only flaw in your strategy is constant defense. You'll never win that way."

"Who said I wasn't attacking?"

A figure dropped from the eaves of a neighboring building and swung a sword at Zandorn's head, forcing the man to defend with the dagger. The shock was apparent on his face when the figure looked exactly like Sorwin, yet he parried the ensuing blows.

"An illusion?" Zandorn sent a gust of wind toward the original Sorwin, which would have wiped away a fragile, intangible illusion.

The breeze rustled Sorwin's brown curls.

"I'm afraid we're both quite real."

Copy Sorwin launched a complex flurry of sword strikes at Zandorn. Metal clanged as he blocked the first two, then dodged a third, but he was sorely outmatched in hand-to-hand combat.

He'd been inspired by Zak and Jolsu after seeing the dragon manifest in physical form, and Sorwin wondered why he couldn't do something similar. Of course, the *Nacusti* version was much more powerful given Zak and Jolsu cast it together. But Sorwin had developed a rudimentary version of it, creating a copy of himself purely from magic.

Real Sorwin gestured, and the roof beneath Zandorn shook violently just as Copy Sorwin thrust. Caught off balance, the silver sword pierced Zandorn's shoulder and he instinctively released the dagger, which clattered to the street below.

Without hesitation, Real Sorwin gripped Cerevita's *cordeus* with one hand as the other glowed a bright green. He ran to the pinned Zandorn and placed his palm upon his forehead.

"Part three and four, complete." Sorwin had defeated Zandorn.

For the first time all day, he sighed and allowed himself a smidge of relief.

"Separating him from the dagger then placing a binding? Well played," Copy Sorwin said, sheathing his sword at his belt.

Real Sorwin stood and clapped him on the shoulder. "Indeed, beautiful swordplay, if I do say so myself."

"I think that's the only option, given the circumstances." He wiggled a finger between their identical selves.

"Right, well, before this gets any weirder." Real Sorwin waved a hand, and Copy Sorwin faded with a laugh.

"What...have you done?" Zandorn croaked.

Sorwin peered down at the man. "A *senligo*—fueled by Cerevita's heart."

Zandorn's brow twitched, as if to frown, but most of his body was now immobilized. "Yet I am awake, aware, able to speak."

"Mostly, yes," Sorwin said. Zandorn's speech was rather slurred but intelligible. "A normal binding wouldn't work on you. Each binding has a way to undo the knot, and you could either force your way out or decipher the loophole in most, given time. So this binding isn't tied by power or trickery."

"And I assume you won't tell me what it is tied by, then?"

"Oh yes, I'd be happy to tell you if you'd like."

Zandorn paused, his rattled breath the only sound while he puzzled through his predicament. "You would give away the key to this prison?"

"Yes, because even if you know what it is, you'll never be able to use it."

"Test your theory then, Prince," Zandorn spat.

A firmness settled over Sorwin. "It's love. The moment you feel real, authentic love, you'll be free."

Tansil's final moments, delivered to Sorwin through his magus's last spell, played in his mind's eye. "Tansil told you your weakness, and then he told me. And he was right, you'll never feel real love."

"I've felt it for over a hundred years! Why do you think I started this war? I'm fighting for my wife, to make my family whole again."

"Then by all means, stand up."

Zandorn's face flushed, straining with effort. But he didn't move an inch.

Sorwin shook his head. "You're fighting for power, for control over death itself. She was just your excuse to pursue forbidden magic. You mistake ego for love."

"I'll undo this binding without your ridiculous emotions."

"Perhaps, but not for a good long while. And in the meantime, there's something you need to see."

"What?"

"The *Nacusti* defeating your progeny."

# CHAPTER 27

# VESSEL

The Center was empty except for a small contingent of guards battling Renna and Kal near the castle doors.

Zak sprinted across the lawns, but the guards fell too fast for him to help. He slowed and signaled Olivia and Elpida to do the same.

Renna and Kal didn't have a scratch on them after dispatching thirty guards. Kal prowled back and forth like a caged animal waiting to be released, and Renna folded her arms across her chest, smiling. Staring. Taunting.

Zak returned her stare, but spoke to Olivia and Elpida. "If you two stall Renna, I can get to Kal. I can get him on our side again."

"Are you sure?" Olivia asked.

Zak heard the underlying questions.

*Are you sure you can save him?*

*Are you sure there is someone in there to be saved?*

*Are you sure you can fight your best friend?*

"I have to be," he said. It was the only answer he had.

Cold fingers interlaced his own, and he looked down

at Olivia's hand in his, wondering how a simple gesture could mean so much. He met her gaze then—framed by wild auburn curls—and he had the urge to say so many things, but it wasn't the right time or place.

"Survive," he said instead. His voice cracked, and he cleared his throat to try again. "You better survive."

She squeezed his hand. "That should be my request of you, *Nacusti*. You still haven't bested me in sparring."

"True." He looked at Elpida, smoke curling from her flaring nostrils, and took that as a sign of readiness.

*Jolsu?* Zak asked of his Guardian.

*I am with you, Parignis. Always.*

"Let's go."

Zak ran to the right and hurled a fireball at Kal.

He leaned out of the way, letting the attack explode against the castle wall.

"You've been training," Zak shouted to his friend. "Let's see what you've got."

Renna nodded her permission, and Kal charged toward Zak.

Kal brandished no weapon, but when he swung, Zak blocked Kal's fist with his staff, and it rang loud like metal on metal. In the barrage of blows, flashes of dark blue magic covered Kal, hardening his limbs.

Zak raised his staff to block the next attack, but Kal grabbed the shaft instead and ripped it away, tossing it to the side.

"*Dracomanus.*" Zak's arms glittered with emerald scales and dark claws protruded from his fingertips. He swiped at

Kal. He blocked, but the dragon claws pierced his magic shell, drawing thick lines of blood on his forearm.

Jolsu's confidence bubbled in Zak's chest. *We dragons are not so easily deflected, hatchling.*

Kal's eyes widened, surprised at hearing Jolsu for the first time.

Zak smiled and lunged, pressing an open palm to Kal's chest. He pushed a burst of magic into his friend, and he flew backward with the hit.

More importantly, Zak felt him absorb the magic.

Kal gritted his teeth and shook his head.

*It's already working.* Zak had packed as much magic into that blow as he could. If Kal kept feeding on his magic, it would loosen Renna's grip on his mind like last time. Then Zak could speak to the real Kal, reason with him, and get his friend back once and for all.

*Ready yourself, Parignis. He's recovered.*

Dark blue flames roared through the air. Zak's green shield materialized, deflecting the fire. A volley of fire spears arced at him from all sides, but they burst harmlessly against his defense.

*He's keeping his distance,* Jolsu observed. *You need to get close again or use magic he cannot defend. Force him to absorb it.*

"Right." Zak couldn't keep pace with Kal in hand-to-hand combat, that much he'd already learned. Big magic was the better option.

"*Parperignis.*" He stomped the ground, and green fire raced across the manicured lawns. It looped behind Kal, who dodged out of the way, but Zak wasn't trying to hit him.

He was trying to trap him.

And it worked.

A wall of fire completely encircled Zak and Kal. Unfortunately that meant Zak couldn't keep an eye on Olivia and Elpida as they fought Renna, but he had to trust his friends to handle themselves.

Kal looked at the fire, then at Zak with a quizzical expression. "Why are you doing this?"

"You attacked us, remember? You and Renna broke into Tor'alan and the Center and slaughtered those guards."

"No, I meant—" Kal's brow furrowed. "I know what you're doing. You're trying to get in my head, like *her*. Why?"

"You have to ask?" The fact that he'd even wonder why stung more than Zak expected.

Kal shook his head. "I've done terrible things, Zakolor. I've killed people...I almost took Olivia from you, even when I knew you loved her."

The muscles in Zak's entire body tightened, remembering the moment he found Olivia on the floor of the throne room. "That wasn't you, that was Renna controlling you. That's why I'm fighting—why I've been fighting this entire time. I'm going to save you, Kal." He stepped toward his friend, but Kal took a step back.

"I'm not worth it," Kal said.

"Kal..." He took another step forward. Kal's back was to the wall of green fire and he couldn't retreat further. "You saved me that night from Burvenin. He was sent there to take me, but you protected me, like you always did when we were kids." Another step. "It's my fault you were captured."

Kal clutched at his head, hands running through his strawlike hair. "There's too many voices, so many orders."

"I know what it's like to hear others in your head."

That caught his attention, and he looked at Zak with misty eyes. "You do?"

Zak nodded. Another step. "Yes. When I first started training, I thought I was losing my mind. I heard whispers on the wind, around corners. I didn't know it at the time, but it was Jolsu, my Guardian. He was buried, and I was grasping at him in the dark."

*We can help you*, Jolsu said to Kal. *Take our fire.*

Zak had closed the distance between them and held out a small green flame toward his friend.

Kal inhaled sharply, his hand hovering over the flame. His eyes darted to Zak's, and he nodded reassuringly. Softly, Kal held Zak's hand, absorbing the fire, the magic.

Immediately, Zak was taken back to all those months ago, standing in the middle of a battlefield with Kal, inextricably linked. But this time was different, less forceful, more gentle. They both knew what was happening this time—Zak could feel the edges of Kal's thoughts drift past their connection as well as a deeper, darker presence lurking behind his friend.

Renna.

The wall of green fire surrounding them shrunk and hissed as if snuffed by a giant blowing out a candle. Zak kept hold of Kal's hand, but turned to see Elpida trapped in a cage of crimson fire, and Olivia held at knifepoint.

"Clever, clever *Nacusti*," Renna said. "You really need to

stop messing with my toys, or else I'll break yours."

"People are not toys," Zak said.

"No? Then why are they *so* entertaining?" She pushed the knife against Olivia's throat, drawing blood, and Zak instinctively lunged forward, but Kal held him back.

Renna laughed. "You see? Entertaining."

Zak's mind raced. He had to do something. "What do you want, Renna? Why are you here?"

"A simple ritual. There's something here I need, and I also require the assistance of a *Nacusti*. Which of you will it be?"

"Neither of us."

"Tsk, tsk. You're in no position to negotiate. Shall I kill your pet dragon to show you I'm serious?" The crimson cage shrunk, and Elpida roared with pain as the fire pressed in.

"Stop! Just—stop." Zak sighed. "Let them live, and you can take me for the ritual."

Renna's lips spread in a blade-thin smile.

Jolsu sent *fear-anger-attack* through their bond. Fire alone wouldn't kill Elpida, but even a dragon could be crushed to death.

*She has Olivia too*, Zak reminded Jolsu. *We cannot attack haphazardly.*

"No, Zak!" Olivia shouted. "I failed, let me pay the price."

"My, how sweet," Renna said. "But alas, Zakolor and I have history—an understanding. I'd prefer to use him anyway." She pushed Olivia to the side, and a second crimson cage appeared around her.

Kal guided Zak toward Renna. "It's easier if you listen to

her," he said.

"You can fight this—fight *her*," Zak pleaded. He felt the magics warring within his friend, each thrashing for dominance. "Find your way back to me."

Kal let go of him when they reached Renna and conjured a large blue barrier, encircling the three of them. Crimson shackles appeared around Zak's wrists and ankles. He pushed against them with his magic, but it had no effect.

"Consent is a powerful thing, Zakolor," Renna said. "A magic of its own, in a way. I wouldn't have been able to place these chains on you without it. But, it makes this next part all the easier."

Zak held his breath, fighting against the fear tightening every inch of his body as Renna began her ritual. He didn't bother asking what would happen—she wouldn't tell him. Or she would, especially if knowing what was coming would make him feel worse.

She faced the castle, raised her arms, and the ground shook.

*An earthquake?* No—not on a floating island. Tor'alan was only subject to gales.

*She conjures something*, Jolsu said. *Something beneath the castle.*

Zak felt it too—the pull of Renna's magic. It was large, whatever it was. He jumped when the white and purple stone walls began cracking and shifting.

If she kept going, the entire castle would fall.

Sorwin landed hard outside the Center gate, wings disappearing in a glitter of gold. Zandorn's extra weight had made flying more difficult, but it had been the quickest way to return to the castle.

Rinka still commanded the defense, though fewer and fewer attacks seemed to be mounted. She approached, wide-eyed at the sight of Zandorn's arm slung across his shoulder.

"You...you did it? You did it!"

Sorwin wanted to laugh—he would have any other day. The stoic, almost bitter, Rinka reverting to childlike excitement was a strange sight.

"He is but part of the problem. His daughter still remains."

"Do not belittle this achievement, Sorwin. You succeeded where no one else could in the last century. Not even Tansil."

"I—" Her heartfelt praise was most unexpected. "Thank you, Archalium."

She nodded once, her usual gravity settling back in. "The council has been evacuated as well, through the castle tunnels. They're all below the city in a new headquarters camp."

"Excellent." He didn't have to worry about Alessa, then. At least for now.

"What will you do with him?" She pointed at Zandorn.

"There's something he has to see. Are the *Nacusti* in there?" He nodded toward the gate leading into the Center.

"Yes, I did as you asked. No one else has entered since you left."

"Good. Once the Consortium is handled out here, get yourself and anyone else that remains safely out of the city."

Rinka's eyes narrowed for a moment. It was the expression she adopted whenever she was about to argue with him. But it cleared as quick as it came. "Very well, you've earned that much and more today."

Sorwin squeezed her shoulder with his free hand. "Thank you, Rinka. For everything."

With that, he dragged Zandorn's limp body through the gate.

A mess of corpses dotted the lawns, and Sorwin spotted a large blue shield and two smaller red constructs near the castle doors. He propped Zandorn against the Temple wall on the right, angling him toward the magic. He'd been telling the truth before—he wanted Zandorn to witness his complete failure.

"You're too late," Zandorn said. "The ritual has already begun."

The ground tremored, and Sorwin braced himself against the wall to keep from falling.

"What is she conjuring?" Renna's magic, and the intention behind it, screamed through the air.

"Watch and see, you cannot stop them anyway."

"As my dear Shira would say, 'Shut it, *stulmati*.'"

Sorwin took a few steps away from Zandorn. "*Visus accipiter.*" His eyesight sharpened to that of a hawk, allowing him to observe the battlefield.

Elpida and Olivia were caught in crimson cages. Powerful ones. Nearly unbreakable. Renna's work—he recognized the evil red magic.

The blue shield was Kalbick's. He stood within, next to Zak and Renna. But wait, was that—Zak wore mage's shackles? Those required consent, he had to *agree* to be chained.

Why would he do such a thing?

A glance back at Elpida and Olivia gave him the answer.

*Oh, Zakolor.*

He'd collected enough information. Sorwin pulled the *cordeus* from his belt and channeled pure magic through it and aimed carefully—blasting the blue shield. It rippled with the force, but otherwise remained intact.

"Impossible!" He'd fired divine-infused magic at the barrier. Nothing could withstand that, only—

"Divine magic, he wields it," Zandorn said, making a gurgling sound that may have been a laugh.

Kalbick looked in Sorwin's direction, but made no attempt to stop him.

"He's a *sorgeus*. Kalbick absorbed divine energy, but from where?" He'd had Zakolor's magic in his system before—it's possible he absorbed more if they fought earlier. Still, probably not enough for a sustained barrier such as that. He'd burn through those stores in moments.

*Think*, Sorwin berated himself. He had little time to solve this puzzle.

The castle walls exploded, and Sorwin ducked as an orange dome appeared over him and Zandorn. Thick slabs of stone burst on the shield. When the dust cleared, a single object sat amongst the rubble of the castle.

A throne.

A large, dark, twisted throne.

"Baltenebris." Sorwin's breath caught. "That's your plan? Summon the architect of the Guardian War? That's mad even for you, Zandorn."

Zandorn gasped. "N-no, it was meant to be Azubelux. He's the next sitting god, the deity of order and justice. *He* would return my wife to me. Renna, what are you doing?"

Sorwin fell to his knees, helpless to stop the coming darkness.

Zak coughed as the crumbled castle settled, revealing Baltenebris's throne. He recognized it instantly. It had sat beside Cerevita's living throne of brown and green—so opposite in its murky darkness, like frozen smoke, sharp and curled.

Renna pulled a parchment from the folds of her slender leathers. She unrolled it upon a small table she conjured. "It is time. I can unlock the door, but you—dear *Nacusti*—will open it." A long black quill appeared in her hand, and she stabbed it into Zak's wrist, covering the tip with his blood.

Zak winced and looked at the parchment, which was no ordinary thing. "The Contract!" This is what he'd feared most when they had lost the magical document. "You're summoning Baltenebris?"

"Clever boy." Renna—rather unceremoniously—used the quill to draw a red line through Baltenebris's name at the bottom of the Contract. Next, she stabbed the quill into the tip of her own finger and drew another red line with her blood, so that the two formed an X over the god's name.

"Once bound, now free. By divine and *Nacusti*, so mote it be."

Renna dropped the quill on the table and pulled a dark stone from her pocket—a *cordeus*. It was Baltenebris's. Zak recognized it as the one stolen from Vermig months ago.

Renna walked behind Zak and pressed the stone between his shoulderblades.

The hairs on his neck stood on end. "Don't do this, Renna. Don't summon him! He's the reason for the Era of Dominion, he's the one that pushed for it! Jolsu told me, he showed me how bad it was, how hard the *Nacusti* and other gods fought against him. Please, Renna!"

She laughed. A cold, piercing sound. "That's exactly *why* I'm summoning him."

Magic shot through Zak—violent and torrential. The force took his breath away, or maybe it was the screaming. His lungs and throat burned as he cried out. He thought he heard someone calling his name, maybe Olivia or Kal, but he couldn't focus on anything but the pain.

He forced his eyes open, he had to see what happened. Renna's magic collided with the throne and burst into white and blue light.

A portal.

It swirled lazily in the air, seconds stretching into hours as the magic funneling through Zak died out. He panted, drained from serving as the vessel for Renna's ritual.

A tall figure stepped out from the portal. Pale skin, almost luminescent, with dark hair and eyes. A small quirk tipped his lips into a smile.

"It's him." Zak said. He recognized the god from Jolsu's memory.

*Yes*, Jolsu strained, also weakened from the ritual. *Baltenebris*.

"*Well done, Daughter,*" Baltenebris said.

"Thank you, Father," Renna replied.

# CHAPTER 28

# SHADOWS AND DESPAIR

"Renna is..." Zak fell to his knees, red chains clanking against the hard stone pathway.

"A demigod, child of Baltenebris," Renna stated smugly.

*Impossible!* Jolsu said. *The Contract—we made it impregnable.*

"*You did, nearly,*" Baltenebris said. His voice shook the ground, as powerful as Cerevita's. "*Except your precious Na-custi never expected a mortal to willingly accept my gift. A flaw I had always intended to exploit.*" He glided soundlessly across the courtyard and loomed over Zak. "*Spawn of Adrastus, what shall I do with you?*"

Zak stared at what he thought was the hem of the god's robes, but a black fog clouded his feet. Facing Baltenebris, an untethered god, Zak shook uncontrollably.

Yet, he placed one foot beneath himself, then the other. He raised his chin, and met the god's gaze.

Baltenebris smiled. "*Defiant, like your ancestor. I think*

*I'll take my time breaking your spirit."*

"You will fail," Zak said.

Pure magic blasted into Baltenebris's shoulder, forcing him back a step. His demeanor shifted instantly as shadows flared around him, darkening the entire Center.

Zak turned toward the attacker. "Sorwin!"

His magus held Cerevita's *cordeus*, hurling spell after spell at the God of Darkness.

After the third volley, Baltenebris had had enough. Shadows leaped from behind statues and trees, wrapping Sorwin's entire body in ghostly clutches.

*"Come closer, all of you."*

With the order, everyone in the Center drifted through the air toward the god. Sorwin, within his shadowy binds, Olivia and Elpida in crimson cages, and—to Zak's surprise—Zandorn, whose body appeared rigid. His eyes alighted on Renna as she and Kal walked calmly around the prisoners to stand by Baltenebris.

"The whole time?" Zandorn asked. "Did you ever plan to resurrect your mother?"

Renna's lips twisted. "No. Why would I bring her back when my true father is a god?"

"I knew," Zandorn said, and Renna frowned. "Of course I knew—I sensed the divinity in you the moment I held you as an infant. But I didn't care. Deirdre and I wanted a family, and I knew you'd be powerful enough to change the world someday."

Renna spread her arms wide. "At least you were right about one thing."

"How is it possible that you're his child?" Sorwin asked. "The Contract prohibits—"

"*It prohibits Dominion*," Baltenebris said. "*And keeps us barred from the physical plane. But we may bestow gifts upon mortals if accepted. I was the sitting god before Cerevita, and Deirdre one of my attendants. She was a Devoted and craved a closer connection to me. I simply gave her what she wanted.*"

"So Renna became your loophole in the Contract." Olivia's voice was low and hard, fists balled at her sides, and Zak wanted to reach out and hold her.

"*Yes. Though I applaud her use of Zandorn, he was always a tool for my purpose, never the one in control.*"

Renna preened under the praise, back straightening and chin lifting higher. The pale skin, dark hair, cruel countenance—Zak saw the resemblance. Renna was Baltenebris's unmistakable progeny.

"*Now, I am unbound from the Contract. The sole god upon this plane. I alone will be your new religion, your reason for existence. My Dominion will reign unfettered. Forever.*"

It may have been an illusion, but Baltenebris seemed to grow larger with each proclamation. Shadows crept up what remained of the destroyed castle walls, stretching unnaturally far, blotting out most of the setting sun.

*Despair.* Zak recalled Baltenebris's formal title. *God of Shadows and Despair.*

*It takes but a small ember to light a glorious fire, Parignis.* Jolsu sent hope through their bond. *Vess and I fought Baltenebris before and survived. We can do so again, together.*

Zak cradled the small bubble of hope, letting it warm his

lungs and heart. The reprieve from the darkness cleared his mind and he remembered something important.

"You're not the only god in Valecium," he said.

"Of course he is," Renna spat. "Hold your lies, *Nacusti,* or else—"

"*Silence!*" Baltenebris growled, and Renna bowed her head in deference—something that Zak never thought he'd see. Shadows curled like slow-moving smoke as Baltenebris leaned his too-large face before Zak. "*Speak, Guardian-born. What do you know?*"

He glanced to the side, but the others didn't offer him any inclination if his plan was a good one or not. Sorwin wilted beneath the crushing shadows, and Olivia sat unmoving in her cage.

"There's another—one who escaped the Contract."

"*Name them.*"

"Let us go, and I shall."

Baltenebris laughed, a high-pitched, grating sound that made Zak cover his ears with his shackled hands. "*You amuse me,* Nacusti. *I like you far better than Adrastus. Almost enough to acquiesce. However.*" He turned to Renna. "*Which one does he love most?*"

Renna's hungry smile returned, and Zak's stomach lurched. She pointed a finger at Olivia.

"No!" Zak shouted.

The crimson cage disappeared and Olivia floated into Baltenebris's bony grip. With his other hand, he pointed a long black fingernail at her throat. "*Mortals are so fragile. I asked Cerevita why she made you this way. She claimed there was beauty in the delicate, and I'm inclined to agree, but not for the same reasons. She enjoys nurturing. I enjoy crushing.*"

Baltenebris's finger twitched, and a red line appeared at Olivia's throat. Her eyes widened, and she choked and coughed, grasping at her neck as the god dropped her to the ground.

"Olivia!" Zak ran toward her, but Kal caught him halfway. They both fell to their knees, Zak wailing through wet tears, and Kal silently holding him.

"*Name the other god, or we will do this again.*" Baltenebris gestured, and Sorwin floated into his deathly grip.

"Malu!" Zak cried. His throat burned, but it was nothing compared to the pain in his heart. "Malu is the other god—he's in Haramil!"

Baltenebris smiled. "*Of course, that snake.*" He looked from Sorwin to Zakolor, evaluating them. "*Obedience is a difficult lesson, Nacusti. A final one your magus can teach.*"

The god readied to slit Sorwin's throat, but before Zak could beg for mercy, he was thrown backward, skidding across the lawn. He sat up. The chains around his wrists had disappeared, and magic pulsed through his body once again.

He searched the courtyard, desperate to see if Sorwin lived.

*There! To the left!* Jolsu said.

Sorwin laid on the ground by the Center's gate and shook his head as he recovered. Elpida approached and nudged his side, her crimson cage having disappeared as well.

But what had pushed them from Baltenebris's clutches?

Zak looked toward the dark god and gasped.

Karazul stood before him, nearly eye-to-eye with Baltenebris.

"*Hello, brother,*" Karazul said to the god.

"He found his heart!" Zak cheered. He and Shira had successfully infiltrated Pywell, and that meant they had a god to fight a god.

Hope surged within him once again. They could actually win this.

Baltenebris sneered. "*You remember me? How? With the Contract—*"

"*You shouldn't be here with the Contract. Yet...*" Karazul gestured to his brother. "*I don't remember everything, but pieces of a shattered past have begun returning since reclaiming my heart. You cursed me to this existence, an eternity of meaningless lives.*"

"*A fitting sentence for the God of Nothing, don't you think?*"

"*And what was the charge for such a fate?*" Karazul countered.

"*Betrayal.*" Baltenebris's dark eyes flashed with fury. "*You swore neutrality in the Guardian War. You weren't meant to fight, yet when our precious brother begged, you cast your oath aside.*"

"*Filecae.*" Karazul stared daggers at Baltenebris. "*I remember his name now. Filecae, God of Magic. You banished him from Valecium, didn't you? I remember that too. Where did you send him?*"

"*He deserved his fate just as much as you. This reunion has gone on long enough.*" Baltenebris held out his hand, and

Renna rushed to his side, dropping something in his oversized palm.

His *cordeus*.

Baltenebris tipped his head back as the stone melted into him. He absorbed the heart, a part of his power that had been separated from him centuries prior. When he straightened, he stared hungrily at Karazul.

*"Last time we fought, you lost. Let us see how you fare this time."*

The gods moved too fast for Zak to follow. Flashes of grey and black clashed together around the Center.

*Collect everyone. We need a plan, Parignis,* Jolsu advised.

Kal was behind Zak, groaning as he rolled over and held a hand to his head. Zak saw no blood or sign of a wound. He reached for his friend, but Kal swatted his hand away.

"Go, I will not fight you, but I do not deserve your help," Kal said.

"Kal—"

"No, Zak. There's no coming back, no redemption for me. Why don't you see that yet?" He met Zak's gaze, blinking tears back. "It may as well have been me that slit Olivia's throat."

Zak shook his head. Though watching her die had been overwhelmingly painful, there was one important fact he held in his thoughts. "You've never met a phoenix, have you?"

Kal frowned, and Zak almost wanted to laugh at the absurdity of it all—of debating with his oldest friend in the middle of a battle, of being on opposite sides in the war they fantasized about winning together for years.

Instead, he turned and held out an arm. "*Terramotus!*"

The ground beneath Olivia's body rippled and rose, speeding her across the courtyard to Zak's side. He beckoned Sorwin and Elpida over—Zandorn slung across the dragon's back—and erected a large green dome around them all, Kal included.

Zak knelt at Olivia's side, waiting. The others stood by, quiet.

*Any minute.* He didn't know exactly how long it would take, but he didn't care. He would wait as long as he had to for Olivia. He always would.

"Zakolor!"

Bazil sprinted to the edge of his barrier. Zak opened a door in the green magic, and his friend passed through before resealing it.

"Bazil—what are you doing here?"

"There are *gods* here—you thought I wouldn't notice?" He half-smiled, half stared at the flashes and booms as the divine battle raged overhead. Then he crouched and held two fingers to Olivia's wrist. "How long has she been out?"

"A few minutes."

Bazil stood again and put his hands on Zak's back. A coolness spread through his shoulders and down his arms.

"What are you—"

"Giving you a little energy. You've been fighting most of the day, Zak."

"I...thank you." Something in Zak's chest twisted, but not in a bad way. It tightened from feeling unusually lucky to have the friends that he did, and he'd never let himself take them for granted.

Yellow fire sparked at Olivia's feet.

"It's starting!" Zak slid back, giving her more room.

The fire worked its way up her body, and soon it was so bright that Zak had to turn away. When the crackling died down and the immense heat receded, a pile of ash rested where Olivia had been.

He waited.

The ash pile shifted, and a pale hand burst forth, followed by a mess of auburn hair. Olivia shook the ash from herself and coughed. "I'm sorry, Vess. I've already burned through two of your lives in as many months."

*War is cruel, dear one. Our fire is not so easily extinguished,* Vess said.

Zak smiled and moved in, tentatively resting a palm on her shoulder. "You're back." There was no trace of the slash at her throat.

"So it seems." She leaned into his touch, then looked up—the thunderous battle catching her attention. "What are we going to do about that?"

"Sorwin?" Zak turned so he, Olivia, Bazil, and Elpida formed a small circle with Sorwin.

"Well, in a perfect world, Karazul defeats Baltenebris and we force him to sign the Contract again."

"Since when do we plan for the best-case scenario?" Bazil quipped.

Sorwin sighed. "Certainly not now. We aren't aware of the conditions of Karazul's curse, either. There's a real possibility he isn't fully a god yet. His powers may be temporary, or lesser than they appear." He studied the surrounding area. "Renna seems content to wait. Zandorn is neutralized. What about…?" Sorwin jutted a thumb toward Kal, sitting just inside the edge of the barrier, cradling his head in his hands.

A mixture of pity and anger and sorrow swirled in Zak as he watched Kal struggle with the magics inside him. "He won't interfere." He said as much, and Zak believed him.

Sorwin nodded, accepting Zak's word. "Then our original plan—slightly altered—is still our best chance. If Karazul fails, the three of you," Sorwin's eyebrows arched at Zak, Olivia, and Elpida in turn, "will need to fight Baltenebris. Your magics are the only ones that can stand against him."

"What about Renna?" Olivia asked.

"Bazil and I will slow her down if she engages, but I fear we won't be able to stop her either. She's every bit as cunning as Zandorn, and much more powerful. At least now we know why."

"Right." Zak took a deep breath. "So, we'll defeat a god, then defeat his daughter. Sounds simple."

*Finally, a direct hunt,* Elpida purred.

"You confuse straightforward with simple, but yes, that's more or less the gist," Sorwin said. He hesitated, mulling over his next words. "I wish I could be of more help, but I've already channeled Cerevita's *cordeus* too much today, and—"

Zak put a hand on his magus's shoulder. "You've done more than your share, Sorwin. You bested Zandorn, you got us here in one piece. Let us do the rest."

Something dark flickered in Sorwin's face, and it almost spurred him to say something further. But he closed his eyes and nodded instead.

The Temple exploded, bright stone shooting across the Center.

Karazul laid in the center of the rubble, much smaller than he had been before.

He was no longer a god.

Sorwin's guess had been right—his divinity seemed temporary. Or was he even still alive?

Baltenebris floated to the ground, and the nearby shadows collected around him, dark pools swirling in the fading sunlight. "*You may have reclaimed your heart, brother, but your curse remains. That will entertain me for centuries.*"

The god turned from the rubble and smiled wickedly at Zak, then raised his eyebrows at the sight of Olivia, alive. "*And you—I grow tired of the* Nacusti *rebellion. I will have my vengeance on Adrastus and Temaway by eliminating their lines once and for all.*"

CHAPTER 29

# FIRE AND CLAW

Baltenebris's dark magic blasted against Zak's shield.

"So...strong." The force of the god's magic was incredible. With both arms raised, Zak grunted and bolstered the defense. He couldn't let go. His shield was all that protected himself and his friends from certain death.

Movement to the left. Renna strode confidently around the courtyard. *What is she planning?*

"Bazil, let's go," Sorwin said. He nodded at Zak before departing safely through the rear of the green wall of magic with the priest in tow.

Elpida clawed at the ground. *Let us hunt!*

"Hold, we need a plan," Olivia said.

"Plan fast!" Zak barely kept his knees from buckling beneath the sustained attack while Baltenebris's unnaturally loud cackle shook the ground around him.

"The Three Fires, they're our best chance," Olivia said. "We all have the Consuming, I have the Curing, and—"

"And none of us have the Creating," Zak grunted.

They'd trained hard, practiced for days and days, but to no avail. The complexity of the belief-fueled fire had been beyond what they were able to achieve in such a short amount of time.

*We may not need it,* Jolsu said. *Our Consuming fire is effective against gods.*

"I have a feeling a simple flame—even a powerful one—won't be enough to defeat *him*."

Baltenebris finally relented, cutting off the stream of dark magic. "*Your resistance is wonderful,* Nacusti. *I've waited centuries for this. Do not die too quickly.*"

Zak was already breathless, and sweat soaked into his uniform. His shield held, but for how much longer?

Shadows gathered around Baltenebris as the god extended both hands. It'd be an even more powerful attack this time.

"Here it comes!" Zak shouted. He reinforced the emerald dome around them, pouring more magic into it, hoping it would be enough.

"I'm sorry." It was a whisper, barely audible above the chaos of battle, but Kal's voice brushed Zak's ear as he sprinted by, leaping in front of the shield, intercepting Baltenebris's dark magic.

"No!" Zak froze, helpless as his friend blocked the god's attack with widespread arms.

"Zak, now! We have to attack *now!*" Olivia pulled him to the right. His shield faltered and disappeared, and Olivia, Elpida and Zak gathered in one spot.

*Together,* Elpida said. She opened her jaws, fire crackling up her throat. Olivia's hands were covered in amber flames.

"Kal..." Zak was numb. *How? Why?* He watched his friend's body shake, wracked with the destructive power, and flicker from view amongst the sea of shadows.

Olivia grabbed his shoulder. "We need you, Zakolor. I know this isn't fair, but we need you *now*. Please!"

The pleading in her eyes, the desperation, pulled him back to his senses. Kal had given them an opening, one chance to win this battle.

And they had to take it.

"*Ignitempesta!*" Green fire poured from Zak and swirled around Baltenebris. A storm of fire surrounded the god.

He immediately tried to turn and direct his attack at Zak, but he couldn't. Baltenebris grimaced as he pulled again on his arms, but something held him back.

Kal clung to the stream of magic like a rope, keeping them linked together.

*The sorgeus is clever*, Vess said. *He's controlling the absorption—Baltenebris is defenseless!*

Elpida's bronze and Olivia's amber fires both joined Zak's green. Together, the three fires roared around the god. The shadows retreated, falling to the bright flames that ate their way up until all of Baltenebris burned.

"*MORTALS?!*" he bellowed in disbelief.

Then an explosion sent Zak flying back, crashing hard against a half-crumbled wall. He shook the dizziness away and when he looked up, no god was in sight, and thousands of shadow-tinged embers drifted through the air.

Baltenebris was dead.

They'd killed a god.

"Kalbick," Zak breathed.

He ran to his friend's side. Kal lay motionless on the battle-marred lawn. He wasn't breathing.

Zak tenderly brushed his straw-colored hair from his face. It had grown long over the months they'd been apart. Tears fell, splotching the ash on Kal's cheeks. Zak wiped them away as he trembled, then rested his head on Kal's chest and sobbed.

A moment later, Olivia gently stroked the back of his head.

Then Elpida's scaly snout grazed his ribs.

*I'm sorry, Parignis. He was brave, and immensely power-ful to defy Renna's Influence.* Jolsu sent love-sorrow-comfort through their bond.

Zak had no words, but he sat upright and sniffed, wiping a sleeve across his face.

"Impossible," Renna hissed. She held up a hand, letting one of the dark embers fall into her palm.

Sorwin leaned against what remained of the Temple's outer wall, and Bazil crouched on one knee nearby. Both of them looked exhausted and made no move to resume the fight that Renna had abandoned.

She turned and spotted Zak huddled over Kal. Ren-na trembled, and crimson fire erupted around her. "YOU!" She leveled an accusing finger at Zak. "You took EVERY-THING!"

Zak's shield appeared just in time to stop a wave of crim-son fire. The clash of magic roared, throwing flames into the air.

"*Daemateria!*" Renna cried. Red smoke churned around her, and when it cleared, a tall figure appeared. It had a humanoid body but was covered in black fur, had pointed ears, and a sharp muzzle.

*No—not him,* Vess said.

"Who is that?" Olivia asked.

*Raum. He's*—Vess faltered, her fear riling Zak's—*Baltenebris may have created demons, but Raum is considered their king. He's a malum, the most powerful kind, and uniquely cruel.*

Zak watched the demon through his shimmering green barrier. His yellow eyes darted around the courtyard and long ears twitched when Renna spoke, though Zak couldn't hear what she said.

*Zakolor,* Jolsu said. *Summon me. You cannot fight this demon.*

Zak nodded. "We can do it together." He began gathering his magic, the spell on the tip of his tongue—

*No, not the usual way,* Jolsu said. *There is another spell you can use.*

Zak frowned. "What do you mean?"

*Do you remember when Temaway fought Karazul, and he summoned Vess? Do you remember how it felt?*

He did. He'd never forget the pure surge of power when Vess had appeared. Her form had been more than magic, like she had really been there. Corporeal.

*That is the spell you must cast. We can do it now, our bond is strong enough. It will allow me to use my full power.*

"Why didn't you say so before? Of course I'll do it, tell

me the words."

*There is a risk,* Vess said.

*Vess, not now—*

*He must know, Jolsu. Do not be selfish.*

"What risk?" Zak asked.

Jolsu sighed. *This spell...temporarily grants me my body. And with that, I am mortal. I can be killed.*

"What?" Zak couldn't believe that Jolsu would suggest such a risky idea. "Then no, we'll find another way."

"Watch out!" Olivia said.

They'd been distracted with their conversation, and Raum had noticed. He moved so fast that Zak swore he had teleported, but no—he crossed the courtyard in a flash and punched straight through Zak's barrier.

Zak had just enough time to cross his arms over his chest, covering them in green scales. Still, the demon's attack sent him crashing backward.

"I will take it ALL!" Renna screamed.

Thunder rumbled overhead. Bolts of lightning struck the courtyard, the castle, the Dormitory.

Zak winced and sat up. Olivia ran toward him and slid along the ground, pulling a wave of rock and soil behind her. Two lightning bolts struck the earthen barrier as soon as she reached his side.

"Focus, Zak," she said. She grabbed his wrists, and the bruises that had bloomed from Raum's strike disappeared in the warmth of her Curing fire.

*Parignis,* Jolsu said.

"Fine...I know." Zak couldn't argue with Jolsu and

Olivia, not now. "I'll cast the spell."

"Elpida and I will distract Raum. If you take Renna down, he'll disappear," Olivia said.

"What do I do?" Zak asked Jolsu.

*Open your heart and mind, listen to our bond. This is what we've worked toward, the incantation will come.*

Zak took a deep breath and closed his eyes. Olivia's barrier held against the lightning strikes, and he tried to ignore the other sounds—fire raging, buildings crashing, rock cracking. Renna must be destroying all of Tor'alan—

*Listen, Parignis.*

He let the distractions go. Let stillness and quiet dampen everyone and everything around him.

When he opened his eyes, Jolsu sat before him, slightly greyed, yet still a dazzling shade of emerald.

He'd made it to their *inriloc*.

*Well done, Parignis.* The dragon's maw curled up at the edges.

Zak smiled too. "You're brilliant, you know that? I'd be dead a few times over without you. I should have said it more often, but—"

*I feel what you feel, Parignis. We do not need many words between us.*

"Right."

*Yet some are important. Do you have the ones we seek?*

"Y-yes." Somehow, the incantation had snuck into his thoughts, and he knew exactly how to cast the spell.

*Then let us save our friends, family, and all Valecium.*

Zak's eyes snapped open. A ball of green fire formed in

his cupped hands, and he tossed it into the air. "*Custocorpus!*"

The ball of fire exploded, and a leathery *crack* sounded as enormous wings unfolded. Jolsu—the *real* Jolsu—soared across the sky and swung his tail into the unsuspecting Raum. The demon crashed through the wall of the Center straight into the neighboring Farm district.

Jolsu roared, a sound that shook the ground, and angled his flight toward Renna. Elpida howled at the sight.

"Be safe, Zakolor," Olivia said.

"You too," he answered.

She smiled, then ran toward the wall that Raum had crashed through, Elpida cantoring at her side.

Zak passed Sorwin and Bazil on his sprint to Jolsu. His friends were whole, at least, and he spared them a nod as they huddled near the remains of the training courts.

Raven-like wings appeared on Renna's back as she launched into the sky.

Jolsu immediately pursued, corded muscles rippling beneath emerald scales as he flew.

"*Pennilma!*" Zak's green wings formed, and he chased his Guardian and their enemy into the sky.

Clouds covered all of Tor'alan in shadows as the storm raged. More thunder boomed as lightning struck at the city below. Renna seemed intent on destroying the floating island.

Jolsu, bigger and faster than Renna, quickly caught up. He flew above, breathing green fire down in her path. She swerved away, narrowly avoiding the deadly spout.

Renna shot up and rolled, then fired a blast of dark magic toward Jolsu. He tucked his wings and dropped out of the way.

Zak tracked the magic, which hit a tall wooden house below. It disintegrated upon contact.

"Jolsu!" he cried. "Don't let that spell hit you!"

The dragon snaked through the air, looping up and around so that he flew next to Zak. His large yellow eyes peered at the destroyed building below. *She wields death magic. That will eat through anything—even our shields. Well-spotted, Parignis.*

"There's two of us. We can win this, together."

Jolsu's chest hummed, and Zak smiled as he realized the dragon was *laughing*.

*You* have *been listening.*

"It's hard not to, when a dragon lives in my head." Zak laughed too, despite their predicament.

*Together,* Jolsu said.

"With fire and claw," Zak finished.

They surged through the air, two green blurs, hunting. Renna wasn't hard to find—she did not hide. She cast spell after spell upon the empty city, destroying everything in reach.

Zak threw fire at her, but a crimson shield blocked it. She twisted and fired back, and his green shield stopped the flames.

Shockingly, as he drew close to her, tears covered Renna's cheeks.

She screamed and hurled a dark blast of death magic.

Zak dipped to the right, dodging. As he circled around, Jolsu launched fiery attacks at Renna, but she deflected them all.

*One clear shot,* Zak thought. *We defeated Baltenebris with Consuming fire, we only need one clear shot to fell Renna.*

Yet as they traded blows with the demigod, Zak realized this would be more difficult. She may not be a god, but Renna had almost a century of battle experience. She was every bit as vicious as Baltenebris, as clever as Zandorn, and now enraged by the loss of her real father, her power soared.

But Zak had every bit the motivation he needed to keep fighting. He and Jolsu alone stood between Renna and their friends.

No, not alone.

Together.

Zak channeled a river of fire through the air, crashing against Renna's shield and capturing her attention.

"Now!" he yelled.

Jolsu darted from the cover of a cloud overhead and spun, whacking Renna's shield with his tail. She hadn't been prepared for a physical attack—let alone one from a full-grown dragon—and she plummeted to the ground.

Zak followed, landed, wings disappearing as his arms grew scales and claws. He slashed at Renna, but she moved fast, dodging and ducking his strikes. Blood covered her dark leather armor, and a bruise darkened on her forehead, yet still she moved with unnatural speed.

She caught him by the wrist and twisted.

"Agh!" Zak fell to a knee.

Renna raised her other hand, dark magic clouding around it. Death magic.

"Goodbye, *Nacusti*," she sneered.

Her arm swung down, and with a loud *snap* it disappeared.

Renna and Zak blinked at each other, both confused at what had happened.

Jolsu stood next to them and spit out the limb. He had bitten her arm off.

Renna's eyes widened. She screamed and she let go of Zak's wrist with her remaining hand.

Zak thrust a claw-tipped fist into her chest, piercing her heart.

She coughed, blood dripping down her pale chin and dropped to her knees.

"You stupid *child*," she cursed, gasping for air. "You have no idea what you've done."

"I know *exactly* what I've done." Zak pulled his fist back, and Renna fell. Her eyes were frozen open, and her chest stilled.

Zak turned to Jolsu. "You saved me. We did it!" he cheered.

Jolsu stumbled and fell on his side, coughing. Smoke poured from his mouth.

"Jolsu!" *What happened?*

*I'm sorry, Parignis. I could not...let you...have all the glory.* He coughed again, and his emerald scales began flaking into tiny ashes.

"Jolsu..." Zak crouched at the dragon's head, stroking his rough cheek, staring into his large yellow eye.

The death magic. He'd touched Renna's spell when he

took her arm.

"Jolsu, you shouldn't have. You should have struck her, or covered us in fire. Dragons can't burn, remember?" His words became slurred with sobs. Each second that passed, there was less and less of Jolsu for him to hold.

*Watch over Elpida for me, Parignis.*

As the last ashes of his Guardian drifted away on the wind, Zak sat alone in the battle-torn courtyard.

# CHAPTER 30

# BALANCED LEDGERS

Olivia ducked under a slice of the jackal demon's claws, rolled away, and thrust her palm toward him. A jet of water crashed into his chest, pushing him back a few paces.

Elpida swooped in from the left, diving and spitting fire. Raum sidestepped and put more distance between them.

Olivia's brow knit together.

"Why aren't you fighting us for real?"

Raum smirked. "You could tell I'm holding back? Observant." He folded his dark-furred arms across his lithe frame. "What do you know of demons?"

Olivia kept her muscles tense, coiled and ready. "That you live in the ether—have your own plane of existence."

Raum nodded. "And who created us?"

"Baltenebris."

"And you killed him. So," Raum's smooth voice lilted as he waved a hand through the air. "That leaves me in a curious position, summoned by his daughter."

*Raum never liked Baltenebris, but he respected his power as his creator,* Vess whispered.

*You've dealt with him before?* Olivia asked through their connection.

*Minimally. Most of what I know is through secondhand stories. He is wily and fearsome.*

"Why?" Olivia asked aloud. "Isn't the agreement between demon and summoner straightforward?" She wasn't a summoner herself, but she'd picked up some knowledge around Shira and the other summoners in the Center.

"There are two ways a demon enters into a pact with a summoner. Either the mage overpowers the demon and forces them into servitude, or there's a mutual bargain struck."

"I'm assuming yours was the latter." Judging by his phrasing and casual stance, he had no real interest in this fight.

"Indeed. Promises were made by the child of a god, and now that god is dead. Which leaves me wondering who will provide the reward for my services."

Elpida landed next to Olivia, kicking up soil from the torn-up crop field. *Why do you speak to this creature? We are supposed to be fighting!*

"No, we're supposed to be *distracting*," Olivia reminded the young dragon.

Raum's long ears twitched. "And you're doing a *wonderful* job of it."

*Three Fires,* Olivia cursed. "What promises did Renna make you?" Perhaps, if she knew the details of the agreement, Olivia could offer the demon something else instead.

Raum's sharp nose snapped to the side and lifted, as if he smelled something on the wind. The demon's pointed teeth shone through his wicked smile. "That's an excellent question. You should ask me again sometime." Then he waved and disappeared in a cloud of smoke.

The only way Raum would disappear was if Renna was defeated, and that meant—

"Zakolor!"

Olivia sprinted across the empty field and through the hole in the Center's wall. Elpida had taken to the air, gliding overhead.

She found Zak hunched on his knees in the destroyed courtyard. "Zak!" she said, rushing to his side. Crouching next to him, he didn't move. He sat, frozen, covered in ash.

"Zak?" Sorwin approached from behind with Bazil, both of their faces grim.

"What happened?" Olivia asked.

Sorwin shook his head. "Zak, is Jolsu...is he...?"

"Gone," Zak's voice cracked. "Kal too." He stared at his hands resting in his lap.

Elpida—still airborne—roared and darted toward the Darlangson mountains in the west.

Olivia wanted to call out to her, but it wouldn't make a difference. She'd just lost the only family she'd ever known, and Olivia knew exactly how that felt. The dragon needed time to mourn.

So did Zak.

She pulled him into a rough hug, pressing his cheek against her chest.

*Vess?* She asked. *Is Jolsu really gone? Can you sense him?* Jolsu had sensed Vess before, through their strange Guardian connection. Maybe he was still there, still within Zak.

Sadness emanated from Vess—their bond was still developing, and Olivia had only just started sensing her emotions.

*He is gone,* Vess said.

Olivia squeezed Zak tighter.

A fissure appeared along the castle's front as it began sinking below the courtyard.

"We have to go—Renna destroyed Tor'alan. The charms holding the island afloat won't last much longer," Sorwin said.

Olivia glanced at Renna's body, resting no more than three paces away. One of her arms was missing, and her wide-eyed expression made Olivia want to vomit.

She gently slung one of Zak's arms over her shoulders and stood. He didn't resist, but he remained vacant, overwhelmed with shock.

Sorwin opened a portal, and Bazil picked Zandorn's limp body up.

"Leave me here," Zandorn said.

"But, the island, it's—" Bazil started.

"I will not live a half-life. Leave me beside my daughter."

Bazil looked to Sorwin, who shrugged and nodded. The priest kicked a few rocks out of the way and laid Zandorn down on the lawn of the courtyard, positioning his head to be next to Renna's.

It was a cruel fate, even for someone as evil as Zandorn and Renna. Olivia almost felt sorry for them.

Almost.

The island shook and shuddered, and Olivia wasted no time in pulling Zak through the blue shimmering portal.

A moment later, Olivia stepped out of the portal, which had dropped them *right below* Tor'alan.

"Sorwin!?" Olivia spat, confused and annoyed. "We're trying to *escape* the crumbling island!"

"Look around!" he shouted. "Everyone else is here!"

Olivia spun and saw the council, the rest of the armed forces, and everyone that had been evacuated from the medical tents. They'd all taken the entrance portal before it was destroyed, which left them directly below Tor'alan.

The island that now fell from the sky.

"Cerevita's grace," she cursed. "Open more portals!"

"Working on it." Sorwin waved an arm, and two blue doors appeared. He moved through the masses, directing them toward the portals. People started pouring through, but Sorwin was clearly exhausted. He couldn't open more portals, and the magic was so new to the League that Olivia didn't know if any other mages had mastered it yet. Maybe one of the other Archs. Still, it would take any number of minutes to get everyone to safety.

And as small stones began pelting the ground like hail, it was time they didn't have.

Olivia lifted Zak's arm from around her shoulder and guided him to Bazil. "Take him through the portal, and stay with him."

Bazil accepted Zak without resistance, a frown deepening his concern for his friend. "What will you do?"

"Help," she said.

Amber barriers appeared overhead as more and bigger rocks fell. They crashed against her shields, and the crowd jumped and gasped with each thud. Yet they were mostly soldiers and mages, trained for war. They kept to orderly lines, keenly aware of the need to remain calm in the face of their predicament.

A loud boom sounded, and to the north, it looked like half of the Lion district fell to the earth, shaking the ground beneath Olivia's feet.

The island's enchantments were failing too fast.

Olivia pushed through the crowd, wanting to hurry any stragglers along toward the portals. Near the back of the group, Euphemius—the merchant's fine suit covered in a thick layer of dust—pulled an ironbound traveling trunk that was almost as large as him.

It didn't budge an inch.

"Your greed will kill you," Olivia said, watching his struggle. Undoubtedly, he had gold and treasures hidden in the trunk.

Euphemius paused, glaring at her. Half of a house dropped to the ground nearby, and he yelped in surprise.

"Help me," he ordered.

Olivia felt the pull of the magical contract between them. She must obey his direct orders, so she grabbed him—but not the trunk—and began dragging him away.

"No!" He yelled, breaking from her grip. He ran back to the trunk and grabbed its handle, pointing to the other one. He opened his mouth to speak again when a loud *crack* from above interrupted him.

A huge boulder had dislodged from the island and was plummeting straight for him.

Olivia ran to his side and covered them with a barrier. The boulder exploded into a thousand pieces and scattered about the clearing.

When the dust settled, Olivia released the barrier and brushed the front of her uniform.

Euphemius fixed the tall hat upon his head, pale but undeterred. "Carry this trunk."

Olivia didn't move.

Euphemius scowled. "Carry this trunk. That's an *order*."

"No," Olivia said. There was no pull, no power in his words.

Flustered and mumbling to himself, Euphemius pulled a parchment from the inner pocket of his jacket. Unrolling it, his eyes darted across the inky lines.

Olivia already knew what he'd find there. "I'm free, aren't I?"

"How?" Euphemius stared at the parchment, appearing genuinely confused.

"I saved your life, of my own free will. Apparently, that's a service worth something. More than my remaining debt owed, anyway. I suggest you make your way to the evacuation portals before you're crushed to death. Good day, Mr. Van Ilia."

With that, Olivia turned on her heel and strode back to the group, ushering refugees toward the portals.

Despite the horrible day, and horrible circumstances, she

couldn't hold back a wide, toothy grin.

She was finally free.

Sorwin sipped at a warm cup of black currant tea, savoring the rich, fruity flavor while a fire crackled in the hearth. He was in his old chambers in Brenstel, in the castle he had once called home—though not for many, many years.

Kaleb draped a thick woven blanket over Sorwin, tucking it between his legs and the plush armchair.

"It's not that cold," Sorwin said with a smirk.

"It is, and it's only been a week since your fight with Zandorn. You're still recovering from significant exertion. This is the time when the body is *most* likely to get sick." Kaleb brushed the back of his hand along Sorwin's forehead and tutted softly.

"Of course, darling." Sorwin knew better than to argue with his overprotective soldier.

A knock at the door drew Kaleb to the far end of the chamber. There was a moment of discussion before he stepped aside. "Queen Alessa is here," he announced. "I'm heading to the kitchens—I had them prepare a soup for you for lunch."

When Kaleb left and closed the door behind him, Alessa strode over to the fire. She sat in the opposite armchair and raised her eyebrows at Sorwin in silent question.

Sorwin rolled his eyes. "Not a word," he warned.

"I didn't say anything." Amusement danced in Alessa's

eyes.

"It makes him feel better, the fluttering and fussing."

"I suppose it would. There's not much any of us can offer to the man that defeated Zandorn."

"That's not an entirely accurate accounting." Sorwin shifted in his seat, careful not to undo the tucked blanket. Kaleb would only reset it when he returned, with no shortage of scolding. "I'm just happy Kaleb wasn't harmed in the battles to the south. I read the reports—they grew quite vicious." The last stand of the Consortium had been bloody. The army hadn't heard of Zandorn's fate and the fighting lasted another day before Fireposts arrived at the front.

"Queen Ymona proved herself a competent general. She also eluded capture, for now." Alessa's attention drifted around the room. "I haven't been in here since the day you left."

Sorwin nodded. "For Tor'alan, to study with Tansil. But now the city is gone—crashed back into the mountains from which it sprung—and so is Tansil." Sorwin closed the book in his lap, worrying the gilded edge with a thumb.

"You'll be happy to know that Brenstel's inns are full of refugees, and temporary camps have been set up just outside the city's gates for overflow. I directed the League's soldiers to keep them organized, fed, and to facilitate finding new homes for everyone."

"That is good news." Resettling an entire city's population was no small feat, but Alessa seemed to manage the crisis with ease. "What happens next, with the League?"

"The council met yesterday and voted to dissolve the

League of Kingdoms. Without Zandorn and Renna, the Consortium has collapsed. The Rot is gone, too, so the existential and literal threats to Valecium have been dealt with. There's no reason for the League to remain. I expect it to take several months for each nation to untangle from the decades-long agreement."

"I'm sorry I asked you to lead this sinking ship. I never expected you to oversee the League's downfall."

Alessa was quiet, tapping her knee with a single finger. "I'm not sorry. Seeing it from within, I think we were all lucky the League lasted as long as it did, and now its time has passed. Darlangson will be fine. The other nations, however, are in upheaval. Only time will tell if—without the League—Valecium's politics will be more or less stable."

"True enough." As Sorwin reflected on the other nations—Regadensia still sifting through its nobles for a new monarch, Aghoomi in civil war, Evartia continuing to establish its democracy—he wondered how long it would take for the next international conflict to emerge, especially without a longstanding common enemy.

"How is Zakolor?" Alessa asked.

Sorwin tensed. "He hasn't left his room all week. I have visited each day, but he doesn't eat much, or speak. Olivia and Bazil are keeping an eye on him too." Seeing Zak curled into a ball in bed reminded Sorwin of just how young he was, or had been. Despite being seventeen, with what Zak had lived through, he was certainly no longer a boy.

"And his Guardian, Jolsu. Is the dragon really gone?"

"It seems so, according to Vess and Olivia. He gave everything to save all of us—again."

Alessa gave a solemn nod, then squared her shoulders. "Well, we have some information Zakolor will be interested in hearing. It's about his friend Kalbick."

# Chapter 31

# After Everything

"Kal is alive?"

Zak's voice sounded strange to his own ears. Rough from neglect. Ever since losing Jolsu, he'd felt a step behind, like his spirit hovered just behind his hollow body. Without the dragon, everything was wrong, for what was the sea without the sky?

It had taken every bit of his strength to get out of bed when Sorwin summoned him—and no small amount of encouragement from Bazil and pushing from Olivia. Yet he had dressed and shuffled through Brenstel's castle to his magus' chambers.

Sorwin's expression lit with a scholarly fervor. "He is! A recovery team combing through Tor'alan's wreckage heard a sudden explosion and saw a bright light. Then when a figure appeared, one of the witnesses—a priest—recognized Kalbick from his time in the Temple's healing wards."

"But...how?" Zak had held Kal's body. The stillness, the lack of breath, had been so loud.

"Well, he's a *sorgeus*. He'd absorbed Renna's magic for nearly a year, and then in one big rush, much of Baltenebris's. Two divine sources. My hypothesis is that Kalbick is now a god."

"*What?*" Zak exclaimed.

"Light me," Bazil said at the same time. He and Olivia stood just behind Zak's armchair.

"Where is he now?" Olivia asked.

"He flew off to the west. We've sent scouts to track his path."

Zak leaned back, arms flopping on the tufted cushion. *He's alive.* Which was good, obviously. But why did Kal flee? Why hadn't he sought Zak out? With Tor'alan gone, maybe he hadn't known where to look. Or maybe he didn't want to see Zak.

He sat up straight again. "I need to see him, to speak to him."

Sorwin nodded, as if he expected the words. "The moment he's located, I'll tell you."

"I'd check Pywell," a voice said.

Zak and his friends all turned toward the window. Karazul crouched on the sill, playing with a dagger.

"I could check for you," the assassin continued. "Though my work isn't free or cheap."

"Where have you been?" Sorwin asked. "You didn't show up for our appointment. I'm meant to gather your account of what happened in Pywell."

"I told you the only thing of note." The muscles along Karazul's jaw twitched, but he otherwise remained still.

Sorwin put his hand to his heart.

*Shira,* Zak thought. They'd all heard of her fate a few days ago from Sorwin. How long was the list of friends he had failed to protect now?

*Vermig, Temaway, Terasi, Shira, Tansil, Jolsu.*

And all of Tor'alan—the island, if not the people.

*Too long.*

Bazil took a step forward. "A-aren't you a god now? Why do you need to work?"

Karazul scoffed. "As you can see, I am *not* a god. Not completely." He gestured to his very mortal-sized stature. "And there's a specific form of payment I will accept. I will track down Kalbick in exchange for the Contract."

Olivia folded her arms across her chest. "That'll never happen."

"Even if we wanted to, the Contract isn't ours to bargain away," Sorwin said, then frowned. "Actually, with the League dissolving, I'm not sure who would take custody of it."

"Perhaps one of its victims," Karazul said, venom lacing his words. "Baltenebris said enough in our brief reunion for me to believe my curse is wrapped up in the Contract. I need to inspect it and learn what I can, then you can have it back."

"And *we* need to inspect it to make sure Renna's ritual won't unleash any other gods upon Valecium," Sorwin countered.

"Then let us work together," Karazul suggested with a sigh.

"Offering cooperation? That sounded like it hurt," Olivia said.

"More than you know," Karazul conceded.

"I'm going with you." Zak stood abruptly.

Sorwin looked at him, clearly concerned. "Zak, after everything—"

"Yes, Magus. After everything. That's why I need to go. If there's even a chance Kal's still himself, I need to find him. I can't lose one more person I love."

Olivia pressed against his side, squeezing the back of his neck with cold fingers. Relief washed through him at her touch. "I'll go with you too."

"You're not leaving me behind again," Bazil said.

Sorwin removed the blanket covering his legs and stood with them. "Very well. We can retrieve Shira too. Give her the proper rites that she more than deserves." A heavy silence settled over them all as they shared tentative glances.

"I think I'd rather go alone if it's going to be like this," Karazul said.

"Shut it, *stulmati*!" Zak, Bazil and Olivia all said in unison.

The flight from Brenstel to Pywell took half a day, though it didn't seem long at all to Zak. Stretching his wings after a week in bed was the good kind of pain, but the sight of them—the green scaled edges—made his heart hurt with the bad kind.

*Jolsu...*

He angled toward the ground when they reached the mountain and stumbled on landing.

Olivia caught his arm. She hadn't left his side since they arrived in Brenstel, and he was happy for it. Her presence, the coolness of her touch, made the pain recede, even just a little.

"Thanks," Zak said. "How was your first flight?"

Her yellow wings fluttered, and the specks of purple and red and orange winked in the midday light. "Good. I see why you enjoy it so much. There's a freedom in flying, somehow exhilarating and calming at the same time."

"Jolsu said thinking and hunting are best done with the wind." He looked down, fingers curling into fists as he squeezed his eyes shut.

Olivia looped an arm around his, guiding him toward the others. She didn't offer distractions or try to cheer him up. She simply existed beside him through the pain, and that was enough.

Bazil and Karazul dismounted Burgo the wyvern. Sorwin conjured a mound of meat for the beast, and he happily feasted while the group approached Pywell.

The large front doors were flung open, and though it appeared to have been a grand entrance many years ago, it was marred by piles of bones and rotting flesh.

"What is this?" Zak asked.

"A mass grave," Bazil said.

"Another of Zandorn's atrocities." Sorwin walked up the steps, picking his way around the carnage. He crouched just outside the door.

Zak followed, peering over Sorwin's shoulder. "Shira."

She laid with her arms bent at the elbow, draped across her midriff. She looked peaceful, like she could have been sleeping if it wasn't such an absurd place to rest.

"I didn't want to leave her here, but options were limited at the time," Karazul said.

"It's okay, we're here now." Sorwin's hand hovered over her cheek, but he pulled back at the last second. He stood and opened a portal with a wave. "I'll take her to Brenstel and then return to aid in the search for Kal."

"I'll help," Karazul said.

Sorwin nodded. "Perhaps you can tell me about your time on the *Swift Star*. For the records, of course."

Zak watched the odd pair—the assassin that had tried to kill him, and the magus that had saved him—carefully move Shira to a flat stone slab Sorwin had conjured. With a tap, the slab rose into the air, and Sorwin, Karazul, and Shira disappeared through the portal.

After a deep breath, Zak turned back to the mountain. "Let's go."

He led Bazil and Olivia through the cavernous entrance and up the stairs. Karazul had told them about the layout of the fortress, and based on his account, Kal wouldn't have gone to the furnace below. If any part of his old friend lingered within the new god, he would have gone somewhere familiar.

The winding steps and twisting halls opened into a huge chamber with wide platforms. Zak recognized it immediately—he'd been there before as a spirit, when he spied on Renna. Last time it had bustled with activity, with bodies in motion, Consortium agents ferrying supplies and prisoners between portals and piles and cages.

Now it was silent. Still. Abandoned.

"I know where Kal is," he said.

He ran across the platform and down a narrow corridor. Bazil and Olivia followed close behind, all of their footsteps echoing through the empty halls. Zak found the right chamber, the one where Kal had been training while Renna watched. His heart thudded in his chest as he slowly opened the door.

Kal crouched on his knees in the middle of the room, back to the door. Folded up as he was, Zak could tell he had grown much taller. His tattered sleeves ended near his elbows, and his pale, exposed skin had a dull glow. There was no denying the truth of what he saw.

Kal was a god.

Zak asked Olivia and Bazil to wait by the door. They did, though both looked anxious about it.

He approached his friend like he would a wild animal, slow and steady, giving a wide berth as he circled around to his front. Zak knelt too, mirroring Kal's posture.

"Hi Kal," Zak said. He kept his voice low and soft, but in the empty room it broke the silence like a shout.

Kal didn't move.

"I'm glad you're alive, that you're okay."

"*Okay?*" Kal's voice boomed, shaking the walls of the circular chamber.

Zak winced. "Yeah. I don't know what you're going through right now, but you're *here*. You're with us. All I've wanted since Burvenin took you was to get you back, to see you safe and whole."

Kal stared at his open palms resting on his thighs. "*You think I'm safe? You think* any *of you are safe?*" He waved an arm to the side and black magic erupted, destroying three neighboring chambers in the blink of an eye.

Bazil whistled from the doorway, and Olivia elbowed him in the gut.

Zak kept his focus on Kal. "Actually, I *do* know what you're going through. One day I was your magicless best friend, and the next I was the last *Nacusti*. You went from a mind-controlled *sorgeus* to a new god. So what? Are you going to let fear isolate you?"

"*Stop, Zak—*"

"No, Kal—you stop. Look at what you've survived! You were abducted, then you lived with Renna and Zandorn for a year. I don't know the half of what you dealt with, but it had to be dark and painful and lonely. And you're feeling all of that right now, I know. But guess what? They're gone. They're *all* gone. And you're here, with me. With us."

Zak waved Olivia and Bazil over. They took the same circuitous route Zak did, coming to stand just behind him.

Kal looked all three of them over, and Zak held in a gasp. His strawlike hair was the same, dangling nearly to his chin. But his eyes. They had always been a blue that had reminded Zak of the shallow water near the beach. The kind that shimmered in the sun.

Now they were dark, a deep black.

Like a shadow.

*"How can you want me, after everything I've done?"* Tears ran down his face as he stared down at his hands once again.

Zak crept forward and tentatively reached for Kal's hands. His friend didn't pull away, didn't move. Zak gripped them lightly at first, but then firmer. Kal met his gaze, and Zak smiled. There was so much pain in his eyes, yes, but wonder too, and curiosity. Zak saw a sliver of his old friend for the first time in months.

"You have the power to right any wrong you may have committed. Tenfold. Don't you want to see what you can do? How you can make this world better for those yet to come?"

More tears streamed from both of them, and Kal pulled Zak into a vigorous hug.

"Careful!" Zak wheezed. Kal wasn't quite as large as Baltenebris had been, but incredible strength coursed through his long limbs.

*"Sorry,"* Kal said, easing back from the embrace. *"This body will take some getting used to."*

"I, um," Bazil stuttered then coughed. "I could help, if you'd like. I had to learn how to control exponential speed and strength when opening the inner gates."

"Azubelux better watch his back, he might lose one of his *most* devoted," Olivia teased.

But Bazil didn't react. He couldn't tear his eyes away from Kal.

*"I'd be grateful,"* Kal said.

Zak convinced Kal to follow them outside. He didn't want to spend any more time within Pywell than he had to, but he also didn't want to return to Brenstel. It was a fine city, beautiful even, but Zak's grief tainted every stone in the castle. Instead, he gathered pieces of broken chairs and other wooden furniture on their descent and built a fire a little ways from the main gate.

"It'll be like home," Zak said to Kal. "A night under the stars." They'd spent countless hours together in their youth, talking late into the night about joining the League, Kal's blossoming magic, and when Zak would manifest his, as if it were a certainty and not almost impossible. Often while laying on their backs, gazing up at the tapestry of constellations, dreaming of the tomorrows they'd live.

How blissfully unaware they had been of what awaited them.

Kal gave him half a smirk, and Zak considered that a monumental success, considering how he'd found him.

Sorwin and Karazul returned not long after the campfire had been built. Zak could tell both of them wanted to question Kal—Karazul probably to see if he could do anything about his half-god status, and Sorwin undoubtedly had infinite scholarly curiosities. Yet they both restrained themselves and opted for an investigation of Pywell.

"I need to see what else Zandorn was working on, in case anything needs to be dealt with," Sorwin said.

"And I need to find out if Zandorn held any more information on my curse," Karazul said.

Before leaving, Sorwin conjured loaves of rosemary bread, seasoned chicken, and buttered potatoes. "Courtesy of Kaleb," he said. "He made me promise you'd all eat well. It was the only thing that kept him from following me through that portal himself."

Zak, Olivia, and Bazil dug into the hearty meal with thanks. Zak noticed Kal hesitantly watching each of them.

"Are you hungry?" he asked.

"*I don't think I need to eat anymore,*" Kal said.

Zak shrugged. "Maybe you don't need to, but you can if you want to."

Kal thought for a moment, then picked up a potato in his oversized hand and nibbled at it.

After dinner they sat around the fire, trading stories. Zak prompted Kal with memories a few times, since most of his stories were from their shared past, and he was determined to help his friend remember who he was, regardless of who he'd become. With each story, Zak reclined further and further until he lay flat on the ground, and the last thing he remembered was Bazil's warm tone vibrating in his ears as he drifted off to sleep.

The first *good* sleep he'd had since Jolsu.

Yet it wasn't uninterrupted.

Zak dreamed of the tree. The dreams hadn't stopped, but had been different than when he dreamed of the black caladrius. Not as insistent or urgent, but present.

He approached the tree, still a sapling, and brushed its tender branches. It pulsed with energy, almost like it had a heartbeat.

It called to him. It had been patient, waiting, and now it was time.

And Zak was ready.

# CHAPTER 32
# CREATION

When Zak awoke, most of the camp was quiet. Everyone slept except Sorwin, who hunched over a thick book. Kal was nowhere to be seen, but Zak didn't panic. He sensed his friend nearby. If gods didn't need to eat, they probably didn't need to sleep, either.

He wiped the sleep from his eyes, drank deeply from a waterskin, and stretched.

"It's strange, seeing so much nothing," he said.

Sorwin looked up from his book, following Zak's gaze to the empty expanse. "The Rot is gone, but the Wastelands remain empty. Perhaps forever—there's no telling if life and magic can take hold here again."

"Maybe," Zak said. The ashen land didn't suggest it would recover, but the pull in his chest, the pulse from his dream, said otherwise.

"I found the black caladrius," Sorwin said.

Zak turned toward his magus. "Really? Alive?"

"Alive, though worse for the wear. Zandorn had plucked the creature of most of its feathers. I brought the poor thing to Brenstel last night. Croi is keeping an eye on him while we locate a rare beast expert."

"Another survivor," Zak whispered. At least his failure to save the bird before hadn't meant its doom.

Bazil stirred, and a small dust cloud rose with his movements. "So hungry," he murmured.

Sorwin smiled. "Ah, I can help with that." With a flourish, Sorwin conjured a bowl of eggs, butter, raw strips of meat, and another loaf of rosemary bread.

Bazil blinked at the spread. "But this isn't cooked."

"Correct," Sorwin said, staring blankly back at the priest.

Bazil groaned and snatched the iron pan that had also appeared, smacking it onto the bed of coals from last night's fire before stomping toward Pywell's gate to collect more furniture for firewood.

Zak shook his head and laughed. "You're mischievous, Magus."

Sorwin shrugged. "Bazil likes it, deep down."

"Very, very deep down," Zak joked.

Olivia and Karazul rose when Bazil had almost finished searing the meat and frying the eggs, and Kal had wandered back from wherever he'd gone off to.

Zak took a big bite of bread and looked at each face hovering around the campfire. They were a motley crew—an Archmagus, an assassin, a priest, a god, and two *Nacusti*. Together, they'd done what no one in a century had been able to. They defeated Zandorn, Renna, the Rot, and even Baltenebris—the architect of all the mayhem.

Yet, there were so many faces missing. So many lost to the

cause.

And, despite all the sacrifice and the victory, Zak's work wasn't done.

He felt her at the edges of his mind before he spotted a gold speck in the sky, sun glinting off amber scales. Elpida glided down to the camp. She didn't appear any bigger than when Zak had last seen her over a week ago, yet she had changed.

Without a thought, Zak ran to her, throwing his arms around her broad shoulders. "I missed you."

*Iparus*, she said, resting a scaly cheek against his fleshy one. *I needed time, after...*

"I know," he said. "Me too."

*I do not return alone.*

They pulled apart, and Elpida craned her neck to the east.

Pordu the Druid ran across the barren land, a cloud of dust rising where she stepped. Zak hadn't seen her in months, not since his time with Temaway.

"*Nacusti,*" she said when she approached, only moderately breathless, though she must have sprinted all day to cross the Wastelands. There wasn't even a glisten of sweat on her dark green skin. Her sleek antlers moved as she spoke. "Do you feel it?"

Zak clutched at his chest.

"*Benevita,* Pordu," Olivia said. "You don't waste any time, do you?"

Pordu nodded slowly at Zak, ignoring Olivia. "You do. I do too. It's not far—follow me." The Druid reminded Zak of a lone plant that survived a wildfire, vibrant green against the ashy ground.

"Zak? What's happening?" Bazil asked.

He drifted behind Pordu, waving a hand for his friends to follow. He couldn't put words to the pull in his chest, the *knowing* that there was a task unfinished, a wrong to right.

Olivia sighed. "Come on, it's best we follow."

Pordu led them around the western side of the mountain along a narrow strip of rocky terrain that had been untouched by the Rot. Beautiful veins of red and blue striped the brown, and Zak tripped more than once while distracted by the patterns.

"Here," Pordu said.

They hadn't gone far, and Zak nearly fell to his knees when Pordu stepped aside.

The tree. The one from his dreams.

It stood—little more than a sapling—a few paces from the base of the mountain.

"How?" Zak asked. Green grass and stems and multicolored flowers sprung beneath its boughs, defying the lifeless earth surrounding it.

"ter-Terasi," Pordu said, gesturing to the tree.

Zak, mouth agape, stared at the Druid. "Terasi is the tree?"

"Of course. When our lives are spent, our final reincarnation sprouts, and we return to nature." Pordu said it flatly, as if it were an obvious fact.

"Fascinating," Sorwin breathed.

Zak glanced at the group—everyone had followed him

and Pordu—before turning back to the tree. He frowned and stepped toward it, reached out a hand—hesitated—then brushed a velvety leaf with his fingertips.

"Why have I dreamed of you?" he whispered.

A lower branch nudged his knee, and Zak looked down. It was shorter than the others, and curved, like it waited to hold something. And the leaves—they were different, too. Instead of thin, papery webbing, the kind that ripped so easily, these leaves had thick, round scales. Green ones, like a dragon.

Like Jolsu.

Zak crouched to get a closer look, and there was no mistake. He thumbed over the rough edges, and it felt exactly like the scales that sprouted on his body when he used Jolsu's magic.

He stood abruptly, an idea taking hold. "I need everyone to produce a flame."

Bazil and Olivia did almost instantly. Zak took their flames—turquoise and amber—and held them in his palm.

"Zak, what are you—" Sorwin began.

"I can't explain, Magus." Which was true—he couldn't. "It will be clear in a moment—I promise."

That seemed sufficient, as Sorwin smiled and produced an orange flame, which Zak took and added to his palm next to the others.

Elpida breathed a small bronze flame into his hand, and Pordu placed a deep mossy green one next to it.

Zak stood before Karazul, waiting.

"You forget who I am?" Karazul asked.

"The opposite, actually. We all remember you now. You

were one of the Five, one of the first gods. You were there when fire was created."

"Presence has no bearing on skill. I have some divine magic, but I cannot produce a flame."

"I think you'll find you can," Zak said.

Karazul huffed in annoyance and held out a hand. Zak felt the surge of magic, and Karazul's eyebrows leaped up his forehead when a grey flame appeared.

"Not a word," Karazul said.

Zak bit his lip to keep silent and took the flame, then moved to the last amongst them.

"*I shouldn't be part of whatever this is,*" Kal said.

"Guilt is a heavy thing to carry, Kal." Zak had to look up to meet his friend's eyes, which was strange. They'd always been similar heights, ever since they were little. "I should know, I've carried the guilt for what happened to you every single day since you were taken. I thought it kept me going. I thought it helped me, lit a fire in my belly when I needed it. But I was wrong.

"It weighed me down, and every failure added another stone to the pile. But repentance, redemption, making up for our mistakes, not because of guilt but out of a desire to help others...that lifts us from the mire of guilt. Every time I helped someone during this last year, I felt lighter. Happier. More myself than I ever did wallowing."

Kal listened, and no one else moved as the flames flickered in Zak's hand.

"*Whoever heard of a repentant god?*"

Amusement lilted Kal's tone, and Zak shrugged. "You

have to be the god of *something*, don't you?"

"*Perhaps*," he said, then held out a small flame in his large hand. His magic had been a dark blue before—and it still was, mostly. Yet streaks of black sparked through the flame.

Zak took it and held it with the others and returned to the tree. One by one he added the flames to the little space between the scaly leaves.

Turquoise. Amber. Orange. Moss green. Bronze. Grey. Blue and black. Zak added his emerald flame too, and when they all danced together, dancing in a fiery rhythm, he stepped back.

The leaves didn't burn. The fires didn't extinguish. Somehow, this tree had grown a natural brazier, as if it had a plan. An intention.

And it did.

It started slow, but Zak and the others gasped when the ashy ground turned brown. They stepped carefully as the dust turned into rich soil. Then came the green grass and clover. Flowers were next, colorful petals popping up all around them. With a pulse and a brisk wind, the green raced to the horizon, further than any of them could see.

The Wastelands were gone. The scar of the Rot had been healed.

Pordu whooped at the return of nature, and Bazil laughed, and Elpida frolicked in the new meadow, and Sorwin uttered a dozen *Oh mys*, and Kal wiped a tear from his cheek while Karazul nodded approvingly, and Olivia wrapped her cold hand around Zak's.

"Still full of surprises, aren't you?" she said soft and quiet, just for him.

"Maybe a few." He reached for her other hand and looked into her eyes. Waiting. Wanting.

A wry grin tilted her lips. "Go on, then."

Zak pulled her into him, lips crashing like waves upon the sand, salty and sweet. And when they finally parted, he wanted to dive back in and swim in her tide forever.

He wrapped his arms around her instead, and she melted into his chest, squeezing back just as tight. And in the euphoric haze, something stirred in his mind.

"We revived the land," he said.

"How did you know to do such a thing?" Olivia asked.

"I didn't, I just—Terasi must have told me somehow. But, everything was gone, and now it lives again."

Olivia looked up at him, brow scrunched. "That *is* how reincarnation works."

Zak shook his head and broke away from their embrace, pacing. "No, reincarnation brings the dead back to life. When you died, Vess's magic regenerated your body. This magic was different—the Rot had *erased* all magic and life. There was nothing to revive. This...this was creation."

"What are you saying?"

Zak ran a hand through his hair, bewildered by his own ritual. "I have an idea."

"Will it work?" Zak asked.

Sorwin and Olivia traded a look—one that they'd perfected over the last week. One that said, *We want to help you, Zak, we want to believe in you, but—*

"Will it work?" Zak asked again.

"Plausibly," Sorwin said. "But—"

"Olivia?" Zak interrupted. "Is there anything else in the journal?"

She gestured over the weathered pages of Temaway's journal, laid bare upon the table. "Vess and I have read it cover-to-cover, many times. I've shared all of Temaway's research that is relevant."

"Vess?" Zak's voice ebbed, like a candle before wind, fighting to stay lit.

*I cannot say if it will work or not, but the ritual has merit,* the phoenix said.

Zak strode back and forth, wearing a groove in the grass. He glanced nervously at Terasi's tree. He hadn't left its vicinity since they had healed the Wastelands. He hadn't wanted to—not once his idea took hold. It seemed fueled by the tree, by the life they had created. Plus, Kal and Elpida didn't want to return to Brenstel, and he needed them both close.

He came to an abrupt stop and spun on his heel to face Sorwin. "Summon them."

Sorwin drummed his fingers on the polished table he had conjured a week ago when Zak first announced his idea. It looked ridiculous at first, the fine craftsmanship sitting in the middle of the rejuvenated meadow. But little by little, Sorwin conjured more pieces until a makeshift camp had grown outside the gates of Pywell. That suited Zak just fine. He, Sorwin, and Olivia needed a place to research, debate, and theorize how this would work.

"Of course," Sorwin said. He stood, rounded the table, and squeezed Zak's shoulder. "Just—promise me, if this doesn't work, that you'll be okay."

Zak caught the plea in his magus's tone, in the subtle arch to his brow.

"It will work if we believe it—isn't that what you taught me?" A ghost of a smile flitted across his face, but the tumult of feelings in his gut kept it from staying.

Within an hour, Sorwin had tracked down the rest of their motley group. Bazil had been helping refugees in Brenstel's healing tents. Pordu had returned to her grove. And Karazul had been in the royal libraries, researching his curse.

"A week ago, before we parted, I told you of my intention," Zak said. He held each of their gazes in turn. "The magic we worked was nothing short of miraculous. Together, we used the Creating fire."

The revelation had come quickly after the ritual. Somehow, with Terasi's guidance, they had poured themselves into the fire, and when offered to the tree, it made the land anew.

"I would ask your help once more, for there is one that made all of this possible. Without them, none of us would be here. All of Valecium owes them a debt, and it must be repaid."

Silence settled over the new grove by Terasi's tree, and each of Zak's friends stood, unflinching. They knew what was coming, had arrived with the expectation of the request.

"With the Creating fire, Jolsu may live again. Will you help me?"

Bazil nodded. "There is no one more deserving."

Pordu's antlers gleamed in the afternoon sun as she inclined her head. "It would be an honor."

Karazul crossed his arms. "Fine, but you'll owe me, and I intend to collect."

Kal hunched, trying—and failing—to shrink his godly stature. "*May this be the next step of my atonement.*"

Sorwin smiled, a weary but warm thing. "We've come so far, Apprentice. Let us walk further, together."

Olivia bumped her shoulder into his. "I wouldn't let you do this without me."

Elpida's wings rustled. *Bring him home to us, Iparus.*

Zak blinked away the burning at the corners of his eyes and busied himself with preparations. The ritual wasn't complicated—that was never the challenge, based on what they learned from Temaway's research. The elf had explored restoring Vess's body after the Guardian War, but the power needed had been deemed nearly unattainable.

Nearly, but not completely.

"You are of his blood. One of your scales will provide the foundation for his new body." Zak waited as Elpida plucked a bronze scale from her foreleg, then he placed it on the ground, arranging them all in a circle around it.

"Produce your flames," Zak said.

Colors appeared in palms—and in maw, in Elpida's case—and at his gesture, they each laid their magic upon the scale.

When Zak set his emerald flame down, he straightened and took a step back. There was only one more ingredient to add. And he hesitated, unsure if he was ready to risk his only chance at this.

But since when was he *ever* ready for *anything* that occurred in his life?

"I only have enough of Jolsu's magic left to try this once." He inhaled deep, letting the air fill his lungs and expand his ribs until they hurt before breathing out some of the nerves.

He'd hoarded that small piece of Jolsu still lingering within him, keeping it safe and sheltered. He'd tried to grow the magic, hoping that if he did, Jolsu would return. But it wasn't a living thing—it was a remnant, a piece of the whole, but not the dragon himself.

Now, he realized, it was a key. A key to the door that could bring his Guardian back.

Zak pulled on Jolsu's magic. A jolt ran through him as it raced down his extended arms and out toward the scale. It collided with the many-hued flames and the scale, and a bright flash covered the young grove.

He held up an arm, blocking the blinding light. He dug through his essence, searching for more of Jolsu's magic to give, but it was gone. He'd thrown all that had remained in one shot.

The white light turned green, then flickered and faded.

Zak blinked, clearing the dancing spots from his vision.

And there, in the middle of the circle, sat a large green dragon.

*Parignis*, Jolsu said. His voice trembled. *How? Why?*

Zak smiled, looking up into the dragon's astonished golden eyes before rushing ahead and throwing his arms around a giant green leg.

"What is the ocean without the sky?"

# EPILOGUE

Karazul dropped a scroll on the reading table before him. It nestled among the dozens of others, lost in the sea of brown parchment and black ink. He dragged a calloused hand across his face, wishing he could wipe more than sweat away.

He paced to a window and stared out of the clear glass. It was a beautiful view from Turrimare's royal record room. The city's curved streets made it appear to swirl like the waves cresting on the nearby beach. People scurried about in clumps, bouncing from shop to shop, no doubt preparing for the impending Year Festival.

"What a mockery," he spat.

"It isn't their fault."

Karazul startled. Lost in his self pity, he hadn't heard her approach, but he recognized the voice at once.

"Ymona." He turned and greeted the former queen with a tilt of his head. "How unlike you, defending the rabble."

She flashed him a sharp smile, her lavender dress shimmering as she crossed to the reading table. "Not defending, simply stating. They don't remember you or your brother.

They don't remember that before the Three, there was the Five."

Karazul crossed his arms. "And I'm to believe that *you* do?"

Ymona shrugged, somehow making the movement graceful as she lifted the edge of an abandoned scroll. "You seem to be running out of history to sift through."

Unfortunately, Ymona was right. Karazul had spent the better part of a year traveling across Valecium, hunting through dusty shelves and moldy parchment for a single mention of his brother or himself. Anything that spoke of them as gods. Anything that would put him on the path to finding his lost sibling. He'd even stooped so low as to ask Sorwin for help gaining admittance to Turrimare's record room. It was a wonder what doors the Hawk Mage's signature could open.

But Sorwin was still a twat.

And Karazul had found nothing for his efforts.

"Why are you here?" he asked Ymona. He circled the room toward the hearth, resting an arm on the mantel. The flames wicked away the cold that had set in from the window.

"We have similar pursuits. You seek a lost brother, and I seek to restore what mine lost." Her hand drifted to the jewel hanging around her neck. "Perhaps we could be of assistance to one another."

Karazul's eyes narrowed. "You know something." It wasn't a question. Ymona was intelligent, perhaps as brilliant a strategist as Sorwin. She wouldn't approach Karazul unless she believed he could help and had something to offer, something he wanted.

She nodded once and stared, eyes earnest. All pretense had fallen away. Ymona appeared as desperate as Karazul felt. He'd run into wall after wall in his hunt, and she must have too.

"Tell me," he demanded, stepping toward her.

Ymona flinched but recovered immediately. "Not until I have assurances of your help."

Karazul scoffed. "I am not Zandorn. I cannot create a body for your brother to inhabit." He glanced at the jewel on Ymona's necklace. "How much longer can you keep him trapped in there?"

"Not long. And it won't be you to restore Yuri. It will be your brother, the god of magic."

Karazul's heart pounded. "Tell me what you know," he hissed.

"I know his name, and I know where both of your curses are held."

Before Karazul knew what he was doing, he had pinned Ymona against the wall with a blade at her throat. "Tell me."

"Not...before...you agree." She struggled to speak against the blade, but still found the audacity to smile despite the fear that wracked her limbs.

Karazul grunted and withdrew the dagger, letting Ymona collapse to her knees. He sheathed the blade and put a few paces between them. "Fine. I will plead your case with Filecae *if* we find him and *if* he is whole and *if* he is a god or made such once again."

"I could not refuse such a generous offer," Ymona said.

She stood, brushed at the folds of her dress, and regained most of her composure, though her cheeks flushed. "Zandorn showed me your true name, Niltris. Filecae's was beside it. You had both signed the Contract."

"That's impossible." Karazul had inspected the document himself after it was recovered from the rubble of Tor'alan. "Only the *Nacusti* and the Three signed the document."

"There's a hidden layer, a contract beneath the one that ended the Guardian War. I don't know how or why, but you and your brother willingly signed the terms that enacted your curses."

Karazul remained frozen for a time, staring at the flickering flames. It didn't make sense. *None* of what Ymona said made sense. And yet, what else did he have to go on? No other leads had emerged in almost a year.

He couldn't trust Ymona completely, but she had too much to lose to risk coming to him without something of value. He could feel the weak pulse of Yuri's life force within the necklace, confident he could snuff her brother out with a single touch. Ymona would know that, too.

Plus, she knew his godly name. And if Zandorn had been good for anything, it was keeping secrets from Karazul. It was plausible he reveled in telling everyone the truth of his curse *except* Karazul.

That left only one choice to make, one path to walk.

Karazul stalked over to a writing desk, snatched a quill and fresh parchment, and wrote with such ferocity he almost tore a hole in the letter. When he finished, he folded it, sealed it with wax, and addressed the front.

"Here." He held the letter out to Ymona. "You have some magic, don't you? Send this Firepost, then we'll be on our way."

She took the letter and read the address. Her eyebrows arched. "Are you sure?"

"Unfortunately," Karazul sighed. He had to ask Sorwin for yet another favor.

But there were no lengths he would not go to if it meant finding his brother.

Zak stretched, aching muscles in his back begging for relief. They'd receive none yet, though it had been well over an hour, and a stack of letters rested on the bench beside him in the garden. But he hadn't finished his work.

He breathed in the crisp, metallic taste of Winterfall, then hunched over the next parchment, aided by the dappled afternoon sun.

*Sorwin Darlangson*
*Kingdom of Darlangson*
*Accipia*
*Cabin by the Lake*

*Dear Magus,*
*I enjoyed the novel you loaned me. I didn't realize elementals had such vivid adventures, or devious humours. You may*

*make a reader of me yet.*

*Anyway, to the purpose of writing: You are cordially invited to mine and Olivia's for the Year Festival next week. I know you're here often enough what with portals connecting our homes and my weekly lessons continuing, but Olivia encouraged a formal invitation. I think she worries that Kaleb doesn't appreciate my unannounced visits.*

*And I don't know if that's true or not, but, well, I'm sure he knew we were a bit of a packaged deal. But if there is a problem, I hope you'd tell me.*

*You may get a reprieve soon, for a while. I've been thinking more about the elves' invitation to study in the Eyewood. It's an opportunity few humans have had, and maybe I'll finally learn to control my Sight, or at least focus it more.*

*I know Shira would've wanted me to go.*

*Plus, remember how close Tansil's Arheim was to the forest? We were only allowed to visit that one time, but I bet I could see him more often if I were in the Eyewood, even though he's not exactly himself. He's different, not alive in the same way, but still caring for the lives of those around him. So, I guess he's still more or less the same, even as a tree.*

*(Isn't it strange how many of our friends have become trees? Temaway, Tansil, Terasi...is that a common fate for elves? Pordu said Druids return to nature, but is it always as a tree?)*

*If I do go, I'll need your help with Olivia. She wouldn't want me telling you, but she's much further in her plans for the school than she's let on. A whole room in our home has been swallowed by blueprints and curriculum plans and towers of tomes. I think she wants you to be involved, but she doesn't want to burden you.*

*I've told her a hundred times that asking you to help build a magic school for kids that are overlooked—like she was—would be one of the best gifts she could give you. But you know how stubborn she can be. She's more likely to hear the truth of the words from your tongue.*

*I've written to Bazil to ask for his help too, but I'm less confident he'll be available. It's been a few weeks since I've heard from him, but last I did, he was traveling between Kal's temple and Aghoomi, liaising between the Disciples and Regadensia. Apparently, it's still quite a mess with Regadensia wanting to restore the Woolbins. Plus, Azubelux is the sitting god now, of course, and Bazil finds his way to his temples whenever he can.*

*Well, would you look at that? It seems I learned to ramble almost as effectively as you, Magus. That's a lesson I didn't intend to absorb, yet here we are.*

*I'll see you tomorrow—and I'm very much looking forward to finally starting water magic.*

*-Zak*

He folded the parchment into a tiny rectangle, sealed it with the tap of his finger, and gathered the rest of the letters from the bench before heading inside.

A thick stew bubbled over the crackling fire. Zak set the letters down on the table and filled two bowls, the scent of thyme and bay tickling his nose. He set one bowl before Olivia—on top of a pile of papers—and sat across the table from her.

"Careful!" she said, lifting the bowl. "You'll stain my notes."

"Then maybe your notes can retreat, at least during dinner." He smirked, never once imagining that *he* would be the tidier one of the two. If only Inguma could see him now. His mother had been beside herself on the first few visits, with nothing to clean or cook or tend.

Olivia rolled her eyes but gathered most of the ink-covered pages into somewhat precarious stacks, clearing enough of the table for her to set the bowl down on the polished wood surface.

"Did you finish the invitations?" Olivia asked. She sipped at the stew, a hum of delight escaping her throat.

"Every last one. Except for Kal's, but I'm seeing him tomorrow."

"You haven't visited him in a while." She said it as an observation, almost a question.

"He hasn't needed me as much. He has his own followers now, a temple. Redimere has grown from a cluster of houses to a bustling town."

"And how do you feel about that?" Olivia asked.

It was a good thing that Kal was finding his way—as a god, as a person. The sudden power would have corrupted most, and terrified others. But Zak found confidence in their last conversation.

*"Being in darkness is a choice,"* Kal had said. *"It is not inherently bad or evil. Quite the opposite, I'm finding. There is safety in the dark. It can be a blanket that covers the lost and the weak and the scared and the furious.*

*"And there are also many secrets lurking in the shadows, ones that can fester and puncture and torture. Redemption isn't about forgetting our wrongs, but being ready to face them. Hear them, feel them, atone for them, and then let them go. The shadows are where we live until—if—we are ready for the brutality of the light."*

Zak shrugged and swirled a spoon through his stew, watching the steam curl. "I'm happy he's alive. I'm happy he's my friend."

Olivia reached across the table and squeezed his warm hand with her cold one.

"Speaking of gods," Zak said, changing the subject. "Any word from our not-quite friend?"

Olivia sighed and leaned back in her chair. "Karazul wants to come here and study the Contract. He says he's exhausted all other avenues of research on his curse and his brother."

"Do you believe him?"

It was Olivia's turn to shrug, and Zak found the jostle of her shoulders adorable. "I'm inclined to—it's been a year, which admittedly isn't that long for an immortal being, but it's not nothing."

Zak glanced at the far wall where the Contract hung. A jagged scar seethed toward the bottom where Renna had struck Baltenebris's name from the document. They kept it in plain view, though it was buried behind layers and layers of protective charms—the most powerful ones that Zak, Olivia, and Sorwin could construct. Theoretically, Karazul could storm in and steal the document with his anti-magic, but it wouldn't be easy by any stretch.

"What does Vess say about the matter?" Zak asked.

"She says knowledge can be a boon or a bane, an antidote or a poison."

"Still fond of riddles, then?"

"Endlessly."

Zak laughed, and Olivia smiled. She stood and cleared the dishes and wiped down the table and counters. Watching her—them—go about a normal life astounded Zak. The odds had been so thoroughly stacked against them when facing Zandorn and the Rot. Yet here they were, talking and making dinner for one another, planning for the future. *Their* future.

He'd never take a moment of it for granted.

He moved behind her, slid his arms around her waist and kissed her neck, just once, very soft, the way she liked it. Then he rested his chin on her shoulder and stared out the window, admiring Terasi's tree in the distance.

Olivia conjured water and scrubbed the bowls in the washbasin. "What do you think Jolsu would say, about Karazul?"

"Hmmm." Warmth spread in his chest. Olivia knew he liked to think about his Guardian. "He'd tell you to let him study the Contract if you keep a claw at his throat."

"Sound advice," she said.

"I thought so."

After his revival, Jolsu and Elpida had stayed with Zak and Olivia for a few months as they built their home. They flew together during the day and talked late into the night, and though Zak and Jolsu were separate now, no longer *Na-*

*custi* and Guardian, they had never been closer.

But for the first time in centuries, Jolsu was truly free, and he had many unanswered questions. Nelvowig had perished centuries ago, and the rest of his flight had left Valecium for another place, another home. A continent to the southwest.

And when Elpida had grown large enough to make the journey, when her bronze scales turned deep blue, they said their tearful goodbyes.

*I will return, Parignis,* Jolsu had said. *You're not rid of me yet.*

Zak had hugged him then, hoping that was true.

Olivia set down the bowls to dry and wiped her hands on a towel, then turned toward him. "And what do *you* think?"

He pulled her closer. "I'm not a *Nacusti* anymore, it isn't my place to decide what happens to the Contract."

Olivia stared at him with a flat expression. "You saved all of Valecium, Zakolor, and your ancestor co-authored the Contract. If you don't have a right to share your opinion on the matter, no one does."

"Oh *fine,*" he sighed, faking exasperation. "I'd agree with Jolsu. Let Karazul study it, but with oversight. I believe his intentions are noble—he wants information on his curse and to find his brother. But we can't let him damage the Contract in his pursuit."

"There, was that so difficult?" A sly grin puckered her lips.

Zak wrapped a strand of her auburn hair around his finger. "Nothing is, with you."

He kissed her, and she kissed him back, and Zak had never

been happier.

THE END

# GLOSSARY AND PRONUNCIATIONS


## CHARACTERS

**Ageric Keldin** (uh-jare-ick): Zakolor's father

**Alessa Darlangson** (uh-less-uh): Queen of Darlangson, Sorwin's sister

**Baltenebris** (behl-tuh-neh-briss): God of Shadows and Despair

**Bazil Ben** (bas-ill): priest and Zakolor's friend

**Bill Solura** (bihl): Kalbick's father

**Burgo** (burr-goh): wyvern

**Burvenin** (burr-venn-in): Magerus, general of the Consortium

**Cerevita** (suh-reh–vih-tah): Goddes of Life

**Chidamee** (chee-duh-mee): Shira's Nox demon

**Clairise Keldin** (clare-eese): Zakolor's mother

**Croi** (kroy): hawk, Sorwin's familiar

**Eldrimai** (ell-drih-mahy): the leader of an elven settlement, bonded with the Arheim. The title translates to "The Tender"

**Elpida** (ell-pih-duh): bronze lizard, Terasi's companion

**Euphemius Van Ilia** (you-fem-ee-us): merchant, member of the League's council, Olivia's sponsor

**Fanum Ket** (fah-numb keht): Eelikuh of Weslinton

**Lord Gideon Woolbin** (gidd-ee-in): Baron of Masdaan

**Gunther** (gun-thur): Renna's servant

**King Gyrnavo** (gear-nah-voh): King of Weslinton

**Hildewyn** (hill-duh-win): Steward of Regadensia

**Inguma Foucher** (in-goo-mah): Magus in the House of Elements, director of the Dormitory

**Minister Jeppida Qor** (jep-id-uh core): Prime Minister of the Republic of Evartia

**Jolsu** (jole-soo): dragon, Zakolor's guardian

**Joryl** (jore-ill): Densba council leader

**Kalbick Solura** (kal-bihk): Zakolor's best friend

**Major Kaleb Deidaku** (kay-lub day-dah-koo): member of League's army

**Karazul** (care-uh-zool): assassin working for Zandorn

**Limba Dar** (limb-buh): advisor to High King Marius

**General Lupa** (loop-uh): leader of the League's army

**High King Marius Fern** (mare-ee-us): leader of the League's council, King of Regadensia

**Malu** (mah-loo): notorious trickster and owner of Zindost, a pet and familiar shop

**Marralee Solura** (mare-uh-lee): Kalbick's mother

**Nathan Greyson** (nay-thin): merchant, friend of Euphemius

**Olivia Pratinos** (oh-liv-ee-uh): elementalist, Euphemius' ward, and Zakolor's friend

**Pordu** (poor-dew): Druid, friend of Temaway

**Rauffe Werbeggen** (rawf): adept in the League, rival of Zakolor

**Raum** (rahm): a dangerous Malum widely considered to be the king of demons

**Renna** (wren-uh): Zandorn's daughter

**Rinka** (reen-kah): newly elected Archalium

**Sashina** (sosh-in-uh): Archlumen, leader of the Temple of Light

**Shira Motchit** (sheer-uh): summoner, Sorwin's friend

**Sorwin Darlangson** (soar-win): Prince of Darlangson, Magerus, Zakolor's magus

**Tansil Windover** (tan-zill): Archmagus, Magerus, leader of the House of Elements, elven

**Temaway Galeria** (tehm-uh-way): one of the six original Nacusti that fought in the Guardian War and co-authored the Contract

**Terasi** (teh-rah-see): Druid

**Archivist Tinora** (tin-ohr-uh): works in the Archives

**Ubba** (ub-uh): Shira's imp

**Vermig** (vir-miig): Archalium, leader of the Den of Darkness

**Vess** (vehs): Temaway's Guardian, a phoenix

**Queen Ymona** (ee-mohn-uh): former Queen of Evartia

**King Yuri** (yuhr-ee): former King of Evartia

**Zakolor Keldin** (zak-oh-lore): Nacusti

**Zandorn** (zan-doorn): Magerus, leader of the Consortium

## PLACES

**Accipia**: a village near Sorwin's castle that was a hideaway in his youth.

**Aghoomi**: one of the oldest nations in Valecium, renamed Weslinton after the Woolbins took over.

**Bernadooth**: largest port city in the Southern Isles, on the northern tip of Carshandyn.

**Brenstel**: Darlangson's capital, where Sorwin is from.

**Carshandyn**: the largest of the Southern Isles, where Densba and Bernadooth are located.

**Darlangson**: western kingdom and member of the League. Home to Sorwin.

**Densba**: small village on the southern side of Carshandyn, where Zak is from.

**Dunes of Ajax**: section of Aghoomi's desert where the god of war hosted battles and bloodsports.

**Republic of Evartia**: eastern country and member of the League. Recently underwent a rebellion, overthrowing its previous twin monarchs and establishing a democratic republic. Led by Minister Jeppida Qor.

**Eyewood**: forest in the south of Nalawin, rumored to be the birthplace of Sight magic.

**Florinshire**: a village on the plains of Darlangson, reportedly where Zak's true parents were hiding when he was born and they were killed by the Consortium.

**Gort'haal**: southwestern country and land of the dwarves. They were furious with the destruction of the Guardian War and soon after buried themselves in their mountain home. No dwarf has been seen since.

**Haramil**: capital of Aghoomi / Weslinton. Translate to "jewel of the sand."

**Janlaka**: city on the northern bank of the Karanadee, known for its famous hardwood and carpentry.

**Kapana**: the glass dream, a famous monument housing one of the largest markets in Valecium.

**Karanadee River**: waterway that serves as the border between Evartia and Weslinton.

**Lark's Jewel**: a lavish and mysterious tavern in Tor'alan.

**Lindomer**: port city on the southern tip of Regadensia.

**Masdaan**: city on the southern bank of the Karanadee, known for its spices and glass works.

**Merinthia's Pass**: a narrow passage through the mountains connecting Darlangson to the Wastelands.

**Nalawin**: northern country and land of the elves. While a few stray elves interact with the outside world, the country closed its borders centuries ago, isolating itself from the rest of Valecium.

**Pywell Mountains**: hiding place of the Consortium, where Zandorn has found a way to survive in the Rot and extend lifespans beyond the mortal coil.

**Regadensia**: central kingdom and member of the League. Led by High King Marius Fern.

**Stjarunni**: elven settlement where Tansil is from.

**Tor'alan**: capital of the League. The floating city usually resides near the middle of Regadensia.

**Turrimare**: capital of Regadensia

**Wastelands**: formerly a country, the land was devastated as a result of the Guardian War.

**Weslinton**: eastern kingdom and member of the League. Led by King Gyrnavo.

**Zindost**: Malu's pet and familiar shop.

## MAGIC

**Anima mea telum**: appear, weapon of my soul

**Aquatelum**: water spear

**Bracteaveru**: leaf dart

**Custocorpus**: incarnate, Guardian

**Customateria**: appear, Guardian

**Daemateria**: appear, demon

**Dormiligo**: sleep binding

**Dormio**: sleep

**Dracomanus**: dragon arm

**Fumus**: smoke

**Igniligo**: fire binding

**Ignis**: fire

**Ignisaveru**: fire dart

**Ignitelum**: fire spear

**Ignitempesta**: fire storm

**Invepati**: find the path

**Lapilectus**: stone throw

**Magus expurgo**: cleanse of magic

**Nuntiumignis**: fire message

**Nuntiumsanguis**: blood message

**Parperignis**: wall of fire

**Pennilma**: wing of air

**Relentesco**: slow

**Senligo**: thought binding

**Sylvaligo**: wood binding

**Tegofortis**: strong shield

**Tegoperignis**: fire shield

**Tempraes memoria**: memory from time

**Terramotus**: earth move

**Visus accipiter**: sight of the hawk

**Vitaligo**: life binding

## OTHER

**Archalium**: leader of the Den of Darkness, carries Baltenebris' cordeus.

**Archlumen**: leader of the Temple of Light, carries Azubelux's cordeus.

**Archmagus**: leader of the House of Elements, carries Cerevita's cordeus.

**Arheim**: the tree that serves as the center of elven settlements

**Benevita**: blessed life, an old-fashioned but still used greeting and parting phrase.

**Black Caladrius**: bird of immense power thought to be a myth. Its feathers have the ability to negate anything in existence.

**Caladrius**: bird with powers to heal most wounds and illnesses, as well as foretell death.

**Calinus**: dark one, term for destroyers of nature.

**Clarignis**: bright one, term for esteemed mages.

**Cordeus**: heart of a god, a powerful magic artifact.

**Devoted**: mortals that pledge themselves to a god.

**The Disciples**: a radical religious group seeking to destroy the Contract.

**Eelikuh**: leader of mages in Weslinton.

**Familiar**: an animal that bonds with a mage. They generally require a high degree of skill and self-awareness of any mage seeking their companionship.

**Far Sight**: a type of Sight magic that peers into the more distant future.

**Firepost**: a means of long-distance communication where letters are delivered in a blaze of fire.

**Fire Post**: iron posts that create a network for Fireposts to travel between.

**Indagomius**: a pair of charmed gems used for tracking magic.

**Inriloc**: a mental space for mages to meditate, also serves as an important meeting place for Nacusti and Guardians.

**Iparus**: draconic term meaning "wing sibling."

**Is shalri**: elven term meaning "a knife"

**Jyrnen**: draconic term meaning "thunder, family, flight"

**-Ko**: suffix denoting royal dragons

**Lapidaemas**: demon stone

**Magtrophitis**: a degenerative disease that atrophies a mage's magic and life force.

**Nacusti**: Guardian-born

**Near Sight**: a type of Sight magic that peers into the more immediate future.

**Parignis**: Little Fire

**Rotters**: amorphous creatures that are highly resistant to magic.

**Silvefni**: a magic-imbued silk produced by tree worms.

**Skinaru bush**: round shrubbery with bright glowing flowers.

**Sorgeus**: a rare mage that can absorb magic, either to their benefit or detriment.

**Star leaf**: the species of tree of the Arheim.

**Stulmati**: Evartian slang for idiot.

**Temp sin-is snerta**: elven phrase meaning "How long has it
    been since your last touch?"

**ter-**: prefix meaning "sibling," often used among Druids.

**ter-amis**: earth friends

**Tredom**: elven dwellings hollowed out by tree worms.

**Tree worm**: creatures attracted to the Arheim. They eat parts
    of the surrounding trees, creating dwellings for elves and
    process the wood into silvefni.

## MAGICAL HOUSES

**Magical Houses** are both physical structures and orders of mages organized by the primary form of magic they study and use. Each of the three houses has a patron god and is led by one of the Archs.

**Temple of Light**: Governing body for priests and any mages studying physical magic. In the Era of Dominion, the structure held monuments and altars for the entire pantheon and was dubbed the Temple of Light, as all mortals needed the gods to guide them, much like a lantern in the dark. The name stuck in the Era of Freedom as Azubelux remained the patron god for the order. Led by the Archlumen.

**Den of Darkness**: Governing body for summoners and any mages contracting demons. Originally an acronym, the Demonic Entropy Nexus (D.E.N.) was shortened to Den for its likeness to a cozy dark room often found in larger abodes. Baltenebris is the patron god. Led by the Archalium.

**House of Elements**: Governing body for traditional mages and any mage studying elemental magic. Elemental magic was the first to be used in Valecium and is often thought of as the "original" magic. The first magic colleges were Elemental, and the tradition of collecting and housing apprentices during their studies sustained through the eras. Hence, the Dormitory is under the direction of the House of Elements, despite its semi-regular incineration due to the reckless use of fire magic. Cerevita is the patron god. Led by the Archmagus.

**THREE FIRES**

Fire magic holds a special place of power in Valecium as it is useable by all mages with relatively little study. While there are varying forms it may take, the pinnacle of excellence is in pursuing the mastery of the Three Fires. Few have achieved it, even among the gods. The most famous user of the Three Fires is the phoenix.

**Consuming Fire**: a fire so strong that it destroys anything it touches, leaving not even ash behind.

**Curing Fire**: a fire so pure it heals almost any wound and burns many types of diseases.

**Creating Fire**: a fire so wild it pushes the boundaries of life and imagination, manifesting the caster's true desires.

**ERAS OF VALECIUM**

**Era of Mages**: the first age in Valecium, when elves, dwarves, and humans openly studied magic and built the great nations.

**Era of Dominion**: the second age in Valecium, when the gods forced mortals to become Devoted and restricted their magical studies.

**Era of Freedom**: the third age in Valecium, when mortals fought the Guardian War and created the Contract to free themselves from the gods.

**CALENDAR**

The Valecium calendar has four seasons, each lasting three months. Each month has six weeks, and each week has five days. The Year Festival is both the end of one year and the beginning of the next, lasting for a full five days to transition. Each nation and people celebrate a little differently, though many involve feasts and revelry.

Year festival (one week)
Springrise
Spring
Springfall
Summerrise
Summer
Summerfall
Autumnrise
Autumn
Autumnfall
Winterrise
Winter
Winterfall

Weeks are five days, each day is numbered:
Onesday
Twosday
Threesday
Foursday
Fivesday

# ACKNOWLEDGEMENTS

Certainty is a dangerous thing. After *The Black Caladrius* poured out of me in a matter of months, I thought I'd figured something out in the writing process—and that this book would follow a similarly smooth path.

It did not. The outline alone took several months, and the drafting and editing nearly a year. But I *did* learn plenty along the way, namely, that the process of writing is fluid. Everchanging. It isn't building a structure piece by piece, one block at a time. It's planting seeds, watering the soil, growing and harvesting and—most importantly—resting.

Writing means tending our creative land, and now that I'm aware of that, I can say with certainty that no book I produce will ever follow a predetermined path. And *that* is a wonderful and exhausting fact.

And luckily, I'll never walk this path alone.

Kourtney, you wonderful editor. I handed you a manuscript I believed was a heap of scraps held together by worn thread and desperate hope. Somehow, you saw a tapestry in its tattered folds. Your deep devotion to each character and the care with which you guide stories never ceases to amaze. Plus, your margin comments always make me laugh, even when you're mad at me for ending certain characters in certain ways (anger well-earned, in my estimation).

Jane, thank you for beta-reading. You were the first set of eyes on this book, and your feedback made me realize it might not be *quite* as disastrous as it felt.

Kelly, you once again triumphed in creating a cover from nothing but my rambling concepts.

Thank you, Mama, for proofreading and your unending support and interest in my pursuits, and to Papa for the big hugs, delicious Sunday meals, and for always asking how my writing is going.

Kenz, Paul, Calvin, and Sylvie, thank you for being real, for tethering me to the ground, and for living and loving in all the effortless ways.

Thank you to all the friends who asked questions along the way or picked up the book when it was finished. Your support means the world to me.

Alfredo, you've been my best friend and my "person" for years. You listen, support, and bring so much light into everyday moments, big and small. I'm so grateful we chose to walk side-by-side. Te amo mucho.

Lastly, thank you, Reader, for spending time with Zak and friends. While his main adventure has come to an end, there will be more tales in the world of Valecium and beyond. *Benevita!*

# About the Author

J. R. Douglas began writing as a teenager when daydreams introduced recurring characters. While he keeps busy working in adult education and trying to stay healthy with some yoga, he plans to continue sharing the worlds he discovers. J. R. lives with his partner, Alfredo, and their sweet dog, Samson.

www.jrdwrites.com
www.jrdwrites.substack.com
Instagram: j_r_douglas